Louis Bayard

Louis Bayard is a writer and book reviewer whose work has appeared in the *New York Times* and *Washington Post*. His first novel, *Mr. Timothy*, was published by John Murray in 2004. He lives in Washington, DC.

The
Pale Blue Eye

A Novel

Louis Bayard

John Murray

© Louis Bayard 2006

First published in Great Britain in 2006 by John Murray (Publishers)
A division of Hodder Headline

Paperback edition 2006

A CIP catalogue record for this title is available from the British Library

ISBN-13 978-0-7195-6704-9
ISBN-10 0-7195-6704-1

Printed and bound in Great Britain by Clays Ltd, St Ives plc.

Hodder Headline policy is to use papers that are natural, renewable and recyclable
products and made from wood grown in sustainable forests. The logging and
manufacturing processes are expected to conform to the environmental regulations of
the country of origin.

John Murray (Publishers)
338 Euston Road
London NW1 3BH

For A. J.

The sorrow for the dead is the only sorrow from which we refuse to be divorced.

Washington Irving
"Rural Funerals"

The
Pale Blue Eye

'Mid the groves of Circassian splendor,
    In a brook darkly dappled with sky,
    In a moon-shattered brook raked with sky,
Athene's lissome maidens did render
    Obeisances lisping and shy.
There I found Leonore, lorn and tender
    In the clutch of a cloud-rending cry.
Harrowed hard, I could aught but surrender
    To the maid with the pale blue eye
    To the ghoul with the pale blue eye.

Last Testament of Gus Landor

April 19th, 1831

In two or three hours . . . well, it's hard to tell . . . in three hours, surely, or at the very outside, four hours . . . within four hours, let us say, I'll be dead.

I mention it because it puts things in a certain perspective. My fingers, for instance, have become interesting to me of late. Also the lowermost slat in the Venetian blinds, a bit askew. And outside the window, a wisteria shoot, snapped off the main stem, waggling like a gallows. I never noticed that before. Something else, too: at this moment, the past comes on with all the force of the present. All the people who've peopled me, don't they come thronging round? What keeps them from bumping heads, I wonder? There's a Hudson Park alderman by the hearth; next to him, my wife, in her apron, ladling ashes into the can, and who's watching her but my old Newfoundland retriever? Down the hall: my mother—who never set foot in this house, died before I reached the age of twelve—she's ironing my Sunday suit.

Curious thing about my visitors: none of them says a word to the others. Very strict etiquette in place, I can't work out the rules of it.

Not everyone, I should say, minds the rules. For the past hour, I've been having my ear bent—torn, nearly—by a man named Claudius Foot. I arrested him fifteen years ago for robbing the Rochester mail. A vast injustice: he had three witnesses who swore he was robbing the Baltimore mail at the time. He flew into a fine rage about it, skipped town on bail, came back six months later, crazy with cholera, and threw himself in front of a hackney cab. Talked all the way to death's door. Still talking now.

Oh, it's a crowd, I can tell you. Depending on my mood, depending on the angle of the sun through the parlor window, I can attend to it or not. There are times, I admit, when I wish I had more traffic with the living, but they are harder to come by these days. Patsy never stops round anymore ... Professor Pawpaw is off measuring heads in Havana ... and as for *him*, well, what is there to call him back? I can only summon him in my mind, and the moment I do, all the old talks play out again. That evening, for instance, we spent discussing the soul. I wasn't persuaded I had one; he was. It might have been amusing to hear him go on if he hadn't been in such terrible earnest. But then, no one had ever pressed me so strongly on this point, not even my own father (traveling Presbyterian, too busy with the souls of his flock to plant much of a boot on mine). Again and again, I said, "Well, well, you may be right." It just made him hotter. He'd tell me I was just putting off the question, pending empirical confirmation. And I would ask, "In the absence of such confirmation, what more can I say than 'You may be right'?" Round and round we went, until one day, he said, "Mr. Landor, there will come a time when your soul turns round and fronts you in the most empirical fashion possible—at the very moment it quits you. You will clutch for it, ah, in vain! See it now, sprouting eagle wings, bound for the Asiatic eyries."

Well, he was fanciful that way. Gaudy, if you must know. Myself, I've always preferred facts to metaphysics. Good hard homely facts, a full day's pottage. It is facts and inferences that will form the spine of this tale. As they've formed the spine of my life.

One night, a full year into my retirement, my daughter heard me talking in my sleep—came in to find me questioning a suspect twenty years dead. *The corner won't square*, I kept saying. *You do see that, Mr. Pierce.* This particular fellow had cut up his wife's body and fed the pieces to a pack of watchdogs at a Battery warehouse. In my dream, his eyes were pink with shame; he was very sorry for taking up my time. I remember telling him, *If it hadn't been you, it would have been someone else.*

Well, it was *that* dream that made me see: a career won't be left behind. You may slip away into the Hudson Highlands, you may screen yourself behind books and cyphers and walking sticks ... your job will come and find you.

I might have run. A little farther into the wilderness, I might have done that. How I let myself be coaxed back I can't honestly say, though sometimes I believe it happened—all of it—so that we should find each other, he and I.

But there's no point in speculating. I have a story to tell, lives to account for. And since those lives were, on many sides, closed to me, I've made way where needed for other speakers, my young friend especially. He's the true spirit behind this history, and whenever I try to imagine who'll be the first to read it, he's the one who presents himself. *His* fingers tracing the rows and columns, *his* eyes picking out my scratches.

Oh, I know: we can't choose who will read us. Nothing left, then, but to take comfort in the thought of the stranger—still unborn, for all I know—who will find these lines. To you, my Reader, I dedicate this narrative.

And so I become my own reader. For the last time. Another log in the fire, would you please, Alderman Hunt?

And so it begins again.

Narrative of Gus Landor

1

My professional involvement in the West Point affair dates from the morning of October the twenty-sixth, 1830. On that day, I was taking my usual walk—though a little later than usual—in the hills surrounding Buttermilk Falls. I recall the weather as being Indian summer. The leaves gave off an actual heat, even the dead ones, and this heat rose through my soles and gilded the mist that banded the farmhouses. I walked alone, threading along the ribbons of hills . . . the only noises were the scraping of my boots and the bark of Dolph van Corlaer's dog and, I suppose, my own breathing, for I climbed quite high that day. I was making for the granite promontory that the locals call Shadrach's Heel, and I had just curled my arm round a poplar, preparing for the final assault, when I was met by the note of a French horn, sounding miles to the north.

A sound I'd heard before—hard to live near the Academy and *not* hear it—but that morning, it made a strange buzz in my ear. For the first time, I began to wonder about it. How could a French horn throw its sound so far?

This isn't the sort of matter that occupies me, as a rule. I wouldn't even bother you with it, but it goes some way to showing my state of mind. On a normal day, you see, I wouldn't have been thinking about horns. I wouldn't have turned back before reaching the summit, and I wouldn't have been so slow to grasp the wheel traces.

Two ruts, each three inches deep, and a foot long. I saw them as I was wending home, but they were thrown in with everything else: an aster, a chevron of geese. The compartments leaked, as it were, one into the other, so that I only half regarded these wheel ruts, and I never (this is unlike me) followed the chain of causes and effects. Hence my surprise, yes, to breast the brow of the hill and find, in the piazza in front of my house, a phaeton with a black bay harnessed to it.

On top was a young artilleryman, but my eye, trained in the stations of rank, had already been drawn to the man leaning against the coach. In full uniform, he was—preening as if for a portrait. Braided from head to toe in gold: gilt buttons and a gilt cord on his shako, a gilded brass handle on his sword. Outsunning the sun, that was how he appeared to me, and such was the cast of my mind that I briefly wondered if he had been *made* by the French horn. There was the music, after all. There was the man. A part of me, even then—I can see this—was *relaxing,* in the way that a fist slackens into its parts: fingers, a palm.

I at least had this advantage: the officer had no idea I was there. Some measure of the day's laziness had worked its way into his nerves. He leaned against the horse, he toyed with the reins, flicking them back and forth in an echo of the bay's own switching tail. Eyes half shut, head nodding on its stem. . . .

We might have gone on like this for some time—me watching, him being watched—had we not been interrupted by a third party. A cow. Big blowzy lashy. Coming out of a copse of sycamores, licking away a smear of clover. This cow began at once to circle the phaeton—with rare tact—she seemed to presume the young officer must have good reason for intruding. This same officer took a step backward as though to brace for a charge, and his hand, jittered, went straight to his sword handle. I suppose it was the possibility of slaughter (whose?) that finally jarred me into motion—down the hill in a long waggish stride, calling as I went.

"Her name is Hagar!"

Too well trained to whirl, this officer. He depended his head toward me in brief segments, the rest of him following in due course.

"At least, she answers to that," I said. "She got here a few days after I did. Never told me her name, so I had to give her one."

He managed something like a smile. He said, "She's a fine animal, sir."

"A republican cow. Comes as she pleases, goes the same. No obligations on either side."

"Well. There you . . . it occurs to me if . . ."

"If only *all* females were that way, I know."

This young man was not so young as I had thought. A couple of years on the good side of forty, that was my best guess: only a decade younger than me, and still running errands. But this errand was his one sure thing. It squared him from toe to shoulder.

"You are Augustus Landor, sir?" he asked.

"I am."

"Lieutenant Meadows, at your service."

"Pleasure."

Cleared his throat—twice, he did that. "Sir, I am here to inform you that Superintendent Thayer requests an audience with you."

"What would be the nature of this audience?" I asked.

"I'm not at liberty to say, sir."

"No, of course not. Is it of a professional order?"

"I'm not at—"

"Then might I ask when this audience is to take place?"

"At once, sir. If you're so inclined."

I confess it. The beauty of the day was never so lucid to me as at that moment. The peculiar smokiness of the air, so rare for late October. The *mist*, lying in drifts across the forelands. There was a woodpecker hammering out a code on a paperbark maple. *Stay.*

With my walking stick, I pointed in the direction of my door. "You're sure I can't fix you up with some coffee, Lieutenant?"

"No thank you, sir."

"I've got some ham for frying, if you—"

"No, I've eaten. Thank you."

I turned away. Took a step toward the house.

"I came here for my health, Lieutenant."

"I'm sorry?"

"My physician told me it was my one chance of living to a ripe old age: I had to go *up*. To the Highlands. Leave the city behind, he said."

"Mmm."

Those flat brown eyes of his. That flat white nose.

"And here I am now," I went on. "The picture of health."

He nodded.

"I wonder if you agree with me, Lieutenant, that health is rated too highly?"

"I couldn't say. You may be right, sir."

"Are you a graduate of the Academy, Lieutenant?"

"No, sir."

"Oh, so you came up the hard way. Through the ranks, did you?"

"Yes indeed."

"I never went to college myself," I said. "Seeing as how I had no particular call for the ministry, what was the point of more schooling? That's what my father thought—that's how fathers thought in those days."

"I see."

It is good to know this: the rules of interrogation don't apply to normal conversations. In a normal conversation, the one speaking is *weaker* than the one who's not. But I wasn't strong enough just then to follow another course. So I gave the wheel of the phaeton a kick.

"Such a fancy conveyance," I said, "for bringing back one man."

"It was the only one available, sir. And we didn't know if you had your own horse."

"And what if I should decide not to come, Lieutenant?"

"Come or not, Mr. Landor, it's your own concern. Why, you're a private citizen, and this is a free country."

A free country, that's what he said.

Here was my country. Hagar, a few steps to my right. The door of my cottage, still ajar from when I'd left it. Inside: a set of cyphers, fresh from the post office, and a tin of cold coffee, and a bereaved-looking set of Venetian blinds and a string of dried peaches and, hanging in the chimney corner, an ostrich egg given me years earlier by a 4th Ward spice merchant. And in the back: my horse, an oldish roan, tied to a paling, walled round with hay. Name of Horse.

"It's a fine day for a ride," I said.

"Yes, sir."

"And a man may have his fill of leisure, that's a fact." I looked at him. "And Colonel Thayer waits, that's another fact. Does Colonel Thayer qualify as a fact, Lieutenant?"

"You might take your own horse," he said, a bit desperately. "If you'd rather."

"No."

The word hung in the silence. We stood there, enclosing it. Hagar kept circling the phaeton.

"No," I repeated at last. "I'd be just as glad to go with you, Lieutenant." I looked at my feet to be sure. "Truth be told," I said, "I'm grateful for the company."

It was what he'd been waiting to hear. Why, didn't he drag a little ladder from the vehicle's interior? Didn't he prop it against the carriage, even offer me an arm up the rungs? An arm for old Mr. Landor! I set my foot on the lowermost rung, I tried to hoist myself up, but the morning walk had wrung me hard, and my leg gave out, and I fell against the ladder, fell hard, and had to be pushed and tipped into the phaeton. I lowered myself onto the hard wooden bench, and he climbed in after me, and I said, falling back on *my* one sure thing, "Lieutenant, you might think of taking the post road on the way back. The lane by Farmer Hoesman's is a bit rough on the wheels this time of year."

It was just what I was hoping for. He stopped. Tilted his head to one side.

"I'm sorry," I said. "I should have explained. You may have noticed there were three very large sunflower petals trapped in your horse's harness. Of course, no one's got bigger sunflowers than Hoesman—they practically attack you as you pass. And that slash of yellow on the side panels? The very shade of Hoesman's Indian corn. I'm told he uses a particular type of fertilizer—chicken bones and forsythia blossoms, that's the native gossip, but a Dutchman never tells, does he? By the way, Lieutenant, do your people still live in Wheeling?"

He never looked at me. I only knew I'd hit the mark by the slump of his shoulders and the fierce rapping he made on the roof. The horse lurched up the hill, my body tipped back, and it occurred to me then that if there were no wall behind to catch me, I could just keep tipping . . . back, back . . . I saw it all very clearly in my mind. We reached the crest of the hill, and the phaeton turned northward, and through the side window, I caught a glimpse of my piazza and the gracious figure of Hagar, no longer waiting for an explanation, already leaving. Never to return.

Narrative of Gus Landor

2

Tum. Tuh tuh tuh tum. Tum. Tuh tuh tuh tum.

We'd been traveling for some ninety minutes and were about a half mile from the reservation when the drums came. Just a trouble in the air at first, and then a *pulse*, in every precipice. When I next looked down, there were my own feet moving to the drums' rhythm, and not a word from me. I thought: *This is how they make you obey. They get in your blood.*

It had certainly turned the trick with my escort. Lieutenant Meadows kept his eyes forward, and to the few queries I put to him, he made but token replies, and he never changed his position, not even when the phaeton, riding up on a boulder, came within inches of toppling over. Through it all, he kept the bearing of an executioner, and there were times, it's true, when that carriage became—because I was still not in my waking mind—a tumbrel, and ahead lay the mob . . . the guillotine. . . .

And then we came to the end of a long ascent, and the ground to our east fell away, and there was the Hudson. Glassy, opal-gray, crumpling into a million billows. The morning vapor already a butter-haze, and the outlines of the far shore cutting straight for the sky, and every mountain melting into a blue shadow.

"Nearly there, sir," offered Lieutenant Meadows.

Well, this is what the Hudson does for you: it clears you. And so, by the time we had taken the last push up to the West Point bluff, by the time the Academy came peeping out of its mantle of woods—well, I felt equal again to what would come, and I was able to take in the views the way a tourist might. There! the gray-stone bulk of Mr. Cozzens' hotel, belted by a verandah. And to the west, and rising above, the ruins of Fort Putnam. And rising still higher, the brown muscles of hill, bristled with trees, and above that, nothing but sky.

It wanted ten minutes to three when we reached the guard post.

"Halt!" came the call. "Who's there?"

"Lieutenant Meadows," answered the coachman, "escorting Mr. Landor."

"Advance and be recognized."

The sentinel came at us from the side, and when I peered out, I was startled to see a boy staring back. The boy saluted the lieutenant and then caught sight of me, and his hand itched its way to a half salute before my civilian status could make itself felt. Down it came, still trembling by his flank.

"Was that a cadet or a private, Lieutenant?"

"A private."

"But the cadets walk guard, too, don't they?"

"When they're not studying, yes."

"At night, then?"

He looked at me. For the first time since we'd left the cottage.

"At night, yes."

We passed now into the Academy grounds. I was going to say we *entered*, but you don't really enter because you don't exactly *leave* anything. There are buildings, yes—wood and stone and stucco—but each one seems to rise on Nature's sufferance and to be always on the brink of being drawn back. We came at length to a place that is *not* Nature's: the parade ground. Forty acres of pitted ground and patched grass, light green and gold, punched with craters, running northward to the point where, still hidden behind trees, the Hudson makes its dart to the west.

"The Plain," announced the good lieutenant.

But of course, I already knew its name, and being a neighbor, I knew its purpose. This was the windswept pitch where West Point cadets became soldiers.

But where *were* the soldiers? I couldn't see anything but a pair of dismounted guns and a flagpole and a white obelisk and a narrow fringe of shadow that the midday sun hadn't quite pushed away. And as the phaeton passed down the hard-packed dirt road, there was no one abroad to remark on our coming. Even the drumming had stopped. West Point was folded in on itself.

"Where are all the cadets, Lieutenant?"

"In afternoon recital, sir."

"The officers?"

A slight pause before he informed me that many of them were instructors and were to be found in the section rooms.

"And the rest?" I asked.

"Not for me to say, Mr. Landor."

"Oh, I was just wondering if we had ourselves an alarum going on."

"I'm not at liberty to say. . . ."

"Then maybe you can tell me, am I to have a private audience with the superintendent?"

"I believe Captain Hitchcock will be present as well."

"And Captain Hitchcock is . . . ?"

"The Academy commandant, sir. Second in authority to Colonel Thayer."

And that was all he would tell me. He meant to stick to his one sure thing, and he did: delivered me straight to the superintendent's quarters and led me into the parlor, where Thayer's manservant was waiting for me. Name of Patrick Murphy, a soldier himself once, now (I would later discover) Thayer's chief spy, and like most spies, the soul of good cheer.

"Mr. Landor! I trust your journey was as beautiful as the day. Please, won't you follow me?"

He showed you all his teeth but never gave you his eyes. Guided you down the stairs and opened the door to the superintendent's office and called out my name like a footman, and by the time you'd turned to thank him, he was gone.

It was a point of pride, I later learned, for Sylvanus Thayer to carry out his affairs in the basement—a bit of Common Man stagecraft. All I will say is the place was damnably dark. The windows were shrouded by bushes, and the candles seemed to be illuminating only themselves. And so my first official meeting with Superintendent Thayer was conducted under cover of blackness.

But I've leapt ahead of myself. The first man to present himself was Commandant Ethan Allen Hitchcock, Thayer's second in command. He's the fellow, Reader, who does the dirty work of watching over the cadet corps, day after day. Thayer proposes, it's said, and Hitchcock disposes. And anyone who intends to truck with the Academy must first truck with Hitchcock, who stands like a dyke against the onrushing waters of humanity—leaving Thayer high and dry, pure as the sun.

Hitchcock, in short, is a man used to being in shadow. And that was how he first showed himself to me: a hand bathed in light, the rest of him conjecture. Only when he drew nearer did I see what a striking man he was (in appearance, I'm told, not unlike his famed grandfather). The sort of man who earns his uniform. Hard-middled, flat in the chest, with lips that look always to be compressing around a hard object: a pebble, a watermelon seed. Brown eyes streaked with melancholy. He gripped my hand in his and spoke in a surprisingly mild voice, his tone that of a sickbed visitor: "I trust your retirement agrees with you, Mr. Landor."

"It agrees with my lungs, thank you."

"May I please introduce you to the superintendent?"

A patch of suety light: a head bowed over a fruitwood desk. Chestnut-haired, round-chinned, cheekbones high and hard. Not a head or a body made for love's uses. No, the man sitting at that desk was fashioning himself for posterity's cold eye, and it was hard work, for look how slender he was, even in his blue coat and gold epaulets and gold trousers, even with that quillback blade resting quietly at his side.

But all this was the stuff of later impressions. In that dark room, with my chair pitched low and the desk pitched high, the only thing I saw, in truth, was this *head*, steady and clear, and the skin of his face just starting to pull away, like a mask about to be peeled off. This head looked down at me from its perch, and it spoke, it said:

"The pleasure is all mine, Mr. Landor."

No, my mistake, it said, "Shall I send for coffee?" That's right. And what I said in reply was, "Some *beer* would do nicely."

There was a quiet. An umbrage, maybe. *Does Colonel Thayer abstain?* I wondered. But then Hitchcock called for Patrick, and Patrick fetched

Molly, and Molly made straight for the cellar, and all it took was just the merest flexing of the fingers of Sylvanus Thayer's right hand.

"I believe we have met once before," he said.

"Yes, at Mr. Kemble's. In Cold Spring."

"Just so. Mr. Kemble speaks of you very highly."

"Oh, that's kind of him," I said, smiling. "I was lucky enough to be of some use to his brother, that's all. Many years ago."

"He did mention that," said Hitchcock. "Something to do with land speculators."

"Yes, it beats all creation, doesn't it? All the people in Manhattan who'll sell you land they don't have? I wonder if they still do that."

Hitchcock pulled his chair a little closer, and rested his candle on Thayer's desk, next to a red leather document box. "Mr. Kemble," he said, "suggests you were something of a legend among New York City constables."

"What kind of legend?"

"An honest man, to start with. That's enough, I expect, to make anyone legendary among the New York police."

I could see Thayer's eyelashes lowering themselves like shades: *Well done, Hitchcock.*

"Oh, there's nothing too honest about legends," I said, very easy. "Although I guess if anyone's famous for honesty, it would be you and Colonel Thayer."

Hitchcock's eyes narrowed. He was asking himself, maybe, whether this was flattery all the way through.

"Among your other accomplishments," Thayer went on, "you were instrumental in apprehending the leaders of the Daybreak Boys. Scourges of upstanding merchants everywhere."

"I suppose they were."

"You also had a hand in breaking up the Shirt Tails gang."

"For a time. They came back."

"And if I recall correctly," said Thayer, "you were credited with solving a particularly grisly murder which everyone else had pretty well given up on. A young prostitute in the Elysian Fields. Not quite your jurisdiction, Mr. Landor?"

"The victim was. The killer, too, it turned out."

"I've also been told you're a minister's son, Mr. Landor. Hailing from Pittsburgh?"

"Among other places."

"Came to New York while still in your teens. Put in your oar with Tammany Hall, do I have that right? No stomach for faction, I gather. Not a *political* animal."

To the justice of this, I bowed. In fact, I was just getting a better fix on Thayer's eyes.

"Talents include code breaking," he was saying. "Riot control. Fence-building with Catholic constituencies. And the—the gloveless interrogation."

There it was: a tiny sweep of the eye. Something he no more could have felt than I could have seen, had I not been looking for just that.

"May I ask, Colonel Thayer?"

"Yes?"

"Is it a pigeonhole? Is that where you've got your notes hidden?"

"I don't follow you, Mr. Landor."

"Oh, please, no, it was *me* not following. Why, I was feeling like one of your cadets. They come in here—already a bit cowed, I can believe that—and you sit there and tell them their exact class ranking, I'll bet, how many demerits they've got piled up, and oh, with just a bit more concentrating, you can even tell them just how far in debt they are. Why, they must leave here thinking you're next to God."

I leaned forward and pressed my hands into the mahogany plane of his desk. "Please," I said. "What else does your little pigeonhole say, Colonel? About *me*, I mean. It probably says I'm a widower. Well, that should be obvious enough, I don't have a particle of clothing that's less than five years old. And I haven't darkened the door of church in a long time. And oh, does it mention I had a daughter? Ran off a while back? Lonely evenings, but I do have a very nice cow—does it know about the *cow*, Colonel?"

Just then the door opened, revealing the manservant, bearing a tray with my beer. Good fizzy near-black. Stored deep in the cellar, I guessed, for the first sip sent a thrill of cold through me.

Over me spilled the soothing voices of Thayer and Hitchcock.

"Very sorry, Mr. Landor. . . ."

"Got off on the wrong foot. . . ."

"No desire to offend. . . ."

"All due respect. . . ."

I held up my hand. "No, gentlemen," I said. "I'm the one ought to apologize." I pressed the cold glass to my temple. "Which I do. Please carry on."

"You're quite sure, Mr. Landor?"

"I'm afraid you've found me a bit done in today, but I'm happy . . . I mean, please state your business, and I'll do my best to—"

"You wouldn't prefer a . . ."

"No, thank you."

Hitchcock stood now. It was his meeting once again.

"From here on we must tread very carefully, Mr. Landor. I hope we may count on your discretion."

"Of course."

"Let me first explain that our sole purpose in reviewing your career was to ascertain whether you were the right man for our purposes."

"Then maybe I should ask what your purposes are."

"We are looking for someone—a private citizen of well-documented industry and tact—who might carry out certain inquiries of a sensitive nature. In the Academy's behalf."

Nothing in his manner had changed, but *something* was different. Maybe it was just the realization, coming on as sudden as that first blast of beer, that they were seeking help from a civilian—from *me*.

"Well," I said, inching my way along, "it would depend, wouldn't it? On the nature of those inquiries. On my—my capacity to . . ."

"We have no concern about your capacities," said Hitchcock. "The inquiries are what concern us. They are of a highly complex, I should add, a highly *delicate* nature. And so before we go a step further, I must once again be assured that nothing said here will be breathed anywhere outside the Point."

"Captain," I said, "you know the life I lead. There is no one for me to tell but Horse, and he's the soul of discretion, I promise you."

He seemed to take this as a solemn assurance, for he resumed his seat and, after a conference with his knees, raised his face toward mine and said:

"It concerns one of our cadets."

"So I figured."

"A second-year man from Kentucky, by the name of Fry."

"*Leroy* Fry," added Thayer. That level gaze again. As though he had *three* pigeonholes full of notes on Fry.

Hitchcock wrenched himself once more from his chair and passed in and out of the light. My eyes found him at last pressed into the wall behind Thayer's desk.

"Well," said Hitchcock, "there's no point in dancing around it. Leroy Fry hanged himself last night."

I felt in that moment as though I had stepped in at the very end or the very beginning of a large joke, and the safer course would be to play it out.

"I'm very sorry to hear it," I said. "Indeed I am."

"Your sympathies are—"

"A dreadful business."

"For all concerned," Hitchcock said, advancing a step. "For the young man himself. For his *family.* . . ."

"I've had the pleasure," said Sylvanus Thayer, "of meeting young Fry's parents. I don't mind telling you, Mr. Landor, sending them word of their son's death is one of the saddest duties with which I have ever been tasked."

"Naturally," I said.

"We hardly need add," Hitchcock resumed—and here I felt something rising to a head—"we hardly need add this is a dreadful business for the Academy."

"You see, nothing of this kind has ever happened here before," Thayer said.

"It most certainly has not," answered Hitchcock. "Nor will it again, if we have anything to say about it."

"Well, gentlemen," I said. "With all due respect, it's not for any of us to have a say in, is it? I mean, who can know what goes through a boy's mind from day to day? Now, *tomorrow* . . ." I scratched my head. "Tomorrow, the poor devil might not have done it. Tomorrow he might be alive. Today, he's . . . well, he's *dead,* isn't he?"

Hitchcock came forward now, leaned against the spindle back of his Windsor chair.

"You must understand our position, Mr. Landor. We have been specifically charged with the care of these young men. We stand in loco parentis, as it were. It is our duty to make them gentlemen and soldiers, and toward that end, we drive them. I make no apologies for that: we *drive* them, Mr. Landor. But we like to think we know when to *stop* driving."

"We like to think," said Sylvanus Thayer, "that any of our cadets may approach us—whether myself or Captain Hitchcock, an instructor, a cadet officer—come to us, I mean, *whenever* he is troubled in mind or body."

"I take that to mean you had no warning."

"None at all."

"Well, never mind," I said. (Too breezy, I could tell that.) "I'm sure you did the best you could. No one can ask anything more."

They both brooded over this a bit.

"Gentlemen," I said, "I'm guessing—and now I may be wrong, but I'm *guessing* this is the part where you tell me what I'm wanted for. Because I still can't make sense of it. A boy hangs himself, that's a matter for the coroner, surely? Not a retired constable with—a weak lung and poor circulation."

I saw Hitchcock's torso rise and fall.

"Unfortunately," he said, "that's not the end of it, Mr. Landor."

And this was followed by another long silence, even warier than the last. I looked back and forth between the two men, waiting for one of them to venture further. And then Hitchcock drew another long breath and said:

"During the night—between two-thirty and three o'clock A.M.—the body of Cadet Fry was removed."

I should have recognized it then: the *beat*. The sound not of any drum but my own heart.

"'Removed,' you say?"

"There was—there was apparently some confusion about the protocol," Hitchcock conceded. "The sergeant detailed to watch the body left his post, under the impression that he was needed elsewhere. By the time his mistake was discovered—that is to say, when he returned to his original post—the body had vanished."

I set my glass down on the floor, with great care. My eyes closed of their own accord and then startled open at a peculiar noise, which, I soon found, was my hands rubbing against each other.

"Who did the removing?" I asked.

For the first time, Captain Hitchcock's warm brown voice betrayed a note of harshness. "If we knew that," he snapped, "we would have had no need to summon you, Mr. Landor."

"Can you tell me, then, whether the body has been found?"

"Yes."

Back to the wall went our Hitchcock, on a guard duty of his own making. There followed another length of silence.

"Somewhere on the reservation?" I prompted.

"By the icehouse," Hitchcock said.

"And has it been returned?"

"Yes."

He was going to say more but stopped himself.

"Well," I said, "the Academy has its share of pranksters, I don't doubt. And there's nothing so very unusual about young men playing with bodies. Count yourselves blessed they're not digging up graves."

"This goes far beyond a prank, Mr. Landor."

He leaned into the lip of Thayer's desk and then this highly seasoned officer began stammering into the air.

"Whichever person—whichever *persons*—removed Cadet Fry's body, I should say they perpetrated a unique, I'll call it a uniquely *terrible* desecration. Of a sort that—that one can't . . ."

Poor man, he might have gone on like that forever, tiptoeing round the thing. Leave it to Sylvanus Thayer to make straight for the center. Erect in his seat, one hand resting on the document box, the other closing round a chess rook, he tilted his head and brought out the news as if he were reading the class standings. He said:

"Cadet Fry's heart was carved from his body."

Narrative of Gus Landor

3

When I was a boy, you never set foot in a hospital unless you were planning to die or unless you were so poor you didn't care if you died. My father would have sooner turned himself into a Baptist, but maybe he would have changed his tune if he'd seen the West Point hospital. It was barely six months old the day I first entered it, its walls freshly whitewashed, its floors and woodwork hard-scoured, every bed and chair bathed in sulphur and oxymuriatic gas, and a current of moss-air twining through the halls.

On a normal day, there might have been a pair of scrubbed matrons ready to greet us, maybe show us the ventilation system or the operating theater. Not today. One matron had been sent home after fainting dead away, and the second matron was too harassed to say anything at all when we came. Looked *through* and beyond us, as though there might be a regiment trailing after, and finding none, she shook her head and led us up the stairs to Ward B-3. Walked us round an open fireplace and over to a blacksmith bed. Paused a bit. Then pulled the linen sheet off Leroy Fry's body. "If you'll excuse me," she said. And closed the door behind her, like a hostess leaving the male guests to their chew.

I could live a hundred years, Reader, spend a million words, and not tell you what a sight it was.

I will come at it in small steps.

Leroy Fry, cold as a wagon tire, lay on a feather mattress girded by iron hoops.

One hand rested on his groin; the other was curled into a ball.

His eyes were half ajar, as though the drums had just beat reveille.

His mouth was twisted askew. Two yellowish front teeth protruded from his upper lip.

His neck was red and purple, with black streaks.

His chest . . .

What remained of his chest, this was red. A number of different reds, depending on where it had been torn and where it had simply been *opened*. My first thought was that he had been worked on by some large concussive force. A pine tree had toppled—no, too small; a *meteor* had dropped from a cloud. . . .

He hadn't been hollowed through, though. It might have been better if he had. You wouldn't have had to see the hairless scrolled-back flaps of his chest-skin, the shivered ends of his bones, and, deeper inside, the gummy something that lay folded and still secret. I could see the shriveled lungs, the band of his diaphragm, the rich warm brown plumpness of his liver. I could see . . . *everything*. Everything but the organ that wasn't there, which was the thing you saw clearest of all somehow, that *missing* piece.

I'm embarrassed to say I was taken, in this moment, with a speculation— of the sort I wouldn't normally trouble you with, Reader. It seemed to me that the only thing left of Leroy Fry was a *question*. A single question, posed by the rictus in his limbs, by the flush of green in his pale, hairless skin. . . .

Who?

And by the throbbing inside me, I knew it was a question I had to answer. No matter the danger to *me*, I had to know who'd taken Leroy Fry's heart.

And so I fronted this question the way I always do. By *posing* questions. Not to the air, no, but to the man who stood three feet away: Dr. Daniel Marquis, West Point surgeon. He had followed us into the room, and he was gazing at me with shy avid blood-lined eyes, eager, I think, to be consulted.

"Dr. Marquis, how does a person go about"— I pointed to the body on the bed—"doing *this*?"

The doctor dragged a hand down his face. I mistook it for weariness; in fact, he was hiding his excitement.

"Making the first incision," he said, "that's not so hard. A scalpel, any good sharp knife could do it."

Warming to his subject now, he stood over Leroy Fry's body, plying the air with an invisible blade.

"It's getting to the heart, that's the tricky part. You have to get the ribs and sternum out of your way, and those bones, well, they're not so dense as the spine, but they're plenty tough. You wouldn't want to pound them," he said, "or *crack* them, else you'd risk damaging the heart." He stared into the open crater of Leroy Fry's chest. "Now, the only remaining question is, where do you cut? Your first option is to go straight down the sternum. . . ." *Whish*, went Dr. Marquis' blade, bisecting the air. "Ah, but then you'd still have to pry away the ribs, and even with a crowbar, that's a fair bit of labor. No, what you do—what was *done*—is a circular cut. Through the rib cage, and then two cuts across the sternum." He took a step back and surveyed the results. "From the looks of things," he said, "I'd say he went at it with a saw."

"A saw."

"Such as a surgeon might use to amputate a limb. I've got one in the pharmacy. Lacking that, he might have made do with a hacksaw. Hard work, though. You'd have to keep the blade moving and keep it out of the chest cavity at the same time. Why, just have a look over here, at the lungs. See those gashes? About an inch long? More gashes in the liver. Collateral ruptures, is my guess. Comes from angling the blade *outward* to save the heart."

"Oh, this is awfully helpful, Doctor," I said. "Can you tell us what happens next? After the rib cage and the sternum are cut away?"

"Well, from there it's a fairly simple business. You cut away the pericardium. That's the membrane around the epicardium, helps anchor the heart."

"Yes. . . ."

"Then you'd sever, oh, the aorta. The pulmonary artery. You've got the vena cavae to get through, but that's just a matter of minutes. Any decent knife would serve your purpose."

"Would there be a spurting of blood, Doctor?"

"Not in somebody who'd been dead a few hours. Depending on how quickly he went, there might have been some small quantity of blood still in there. I suspect, though, that by the time he got hold of it, that heart"—he said this with a certain note of satisfaction—"that heart was played out."

"What's next?"

"Ooh, you're pretty much done now," said the surgeon. "The whole bundle comes up pretty clean, I expect. Very light, too, most people don't know that. Just a bit larger than your fist, and no more than ten ounces. Comes from being hollow," he said, rapping his chest for emphasis.

"So, Doctor—you don't mind my putting all these questions to you, I hope?"

"Not at all."

"Maybe you can tell us more about the fellow who did this. What would he require besides tools?"

A slight bafflement as his eyes drew away from the body. "Well, let me think on that. He'd—he'd have to be *strong*, for the reasons I mentioned."

"Not a woman, then?"

He snorted. "No woman as I've ever had the pleasure of meeting, no."

"What else would he need?"

"A goodly amount of light. Carrying out such an operation as that in pitch darkness, he'd need *light*. Wouldn't surprise me if we found a deal of candle wax in the cavity."

His eyes, hungry, returned to the body on the table. It took some pressure on his sleeve to tug him away.

"What about his medical pedigree, Doctor? Would he need to be"—I smiled right into him—"as well educated and surpassingly well trained as yourself?"

"Oh, not necessarily," he said, newly bashful. "He'd need to know ... what to *look* for, yes, what to expect. Where to cut. Some small knowledge of anatomy, yes, but he wouldn't have to be a doctor. Or a surgeon."

"A madman!"

This was Hitchcock breaking in. Startling me, I confess. I'd come to feel that Dr. Marquis (and Leroy Fry) and I were the only ones in the room.

"Who else but a madman?" Hitchcock asked. "And still out there, for all we know, ready for some new outrage. Am I ... is no one else *galled* to think of him? Still *out* there?"

He was a sensitive man, our Hitchcock. For all his hardness, he could bleed. And be comforted, too. It took only the slightest pat from Colonel

Thayer on the back of his shoulders, and all the tightness went out of him.

"There, Ethan," said Thayer.

That was the first and not the last time I would think of their alliance as a sort of a marriage. I mean nothing by it except to suggest that these two bachelors had a pact of sorts, ever fluid and grounded in things unspoken. Once, and once only (I later came to learn), they had divorced: three years earlier, over the issue of whether West Point's courts of inquiry violated the Articles of War. Never mind. A year later, Thayer was calling Hitchcock back. The rupture was healed over. And all this was conveyed in a pat. This, too: Thayer was in command. Always.

"I'm sure we all feel as Captain Hitchcock does," he said. "Don't we, gentlemen?"

"And it does the captain great credit for putting it in words," I said.

"Surely the point of all this," the superintendent added, "is to leave ourselves better positioned to find the perpetrator. Is that not so, Mr. Landor?"

"Of course, Colonel."

Not mollified, not really, Hitchcock sat himself down on one of the spare beds, stared out through a north-facing window. We all gave him a moment. I remember tolling off the seconds. *One, two* . . .

"Doctor," I said, smiling. "Maybe you could tell us how long it would take someone to perform this kind of operation."

"Hard to say, Mr. Landor. It's been years, you know, since I've dissected any kind of body, and never quite to this—this *extent*. If I had to guess, given the difficult conditions, I'd say upward of an hour. An hour and a half, maybe."

"Most of it in the sawing."

"Yes."

"And what if there were two men?"

"Well, then, each man could take one side, and they'd be done in half the time. Now, *three* men, that'd be a crowd. A third man wouldn't add much, unless he was carrying a lantern."

A lantern, yes. That was the unaccountable thing about looking at Leroy Fry: I had the feeling that someone was holding a light to him. I would attribute this to the fact that his eyes were, in fact, angled toward mine, *looking* at me through their drooping lids, if looking you could call it. For the pupils had scrambled up like blinds, and there was only a sliver of whiteness left.

I drew closer to the bed and, with the tips of my thumbs, pulled the lids down. They paused there for the barest second before springing back up. I scarcely noticed, for now I was tracing the lacerations on Leroy Fry's neck. They didn't form a single band, as I had first thought, but a *weave*, a pattern of worry. Long before the noose had closed off this cadet's windpipe, the rope had been gouging and chafing—a full pound of flesh by the time it was finished.

"Captain Hitchcock," I said. "I know your men have mounted a search, but what exactly have they been looking for? A man? Or a heart?"

"All I can tell you is that we've canvassed the surrounding grounds and found nothing."

"I see."

He had strawberry-blond hair, this Leroy Fry. Long white eyelashes. Musket calluses on his right hand and bright blisters on the tips of his fingers. And a mole between two of his toes. The day before, he'd been alive.

"Would someone please remind me?" I said. "Where was the body found? After the heart was taken?"

"By the icehouse."

"Now, Dr. Marquis, I'm afraid I must call on your expertise one more time. If you were—if you were to go about *preserving* a heart, how would you do it?"

"Well, I'd probably find a container of some kind. Wouldn't need to be too big."

"Yes?"

"Then I'd wrap the heart in something. Muslin, maybe. Newspaper, if I was hard up."

"Go on."

"And then I'd—I'd surround it with—" He stopped. His fingers climbed to his throat. "*Ice*," he said.

Hitchcock raised himself from the bed.

"So it's come to this," he said. "The madman has not simply taken Leroy Fry's heart. He is actually keeping it on ice."

I shrugged. Showed him my palms. "It's possible, that's all."

"For what ungodly purpose?"

"Oh, well, that I couldn't tell you, Captain. I only just got here."

By now the poor matron had come back, chaffed with duty, eager for Dr. Marquis to attend to something, I have no memory of what. I only remember the look of regret on Dr. Marquis' face: he didn't want to go.

So that left just me and Thayer and Hitchcock. And Leroy Fry. And then came the drum, for now the cadets were being called to evening parade.

"Well, gentlemen," I said, "there's no getting round it. You've got yourselves a poser." My hands again, planing each other down. "I'm a bit stumped myself. One thing in particular I can't make out. Why haven't you called in the military authorities?"

A long silence then.

"Surely this is a matter for *their* attention," I said, "not mine."

"Mr. Landor," said Sylvanus Thayer, "I wonder if you wouldn't mind walking with me?"

We didn't go far. Just down the hallway and back. Repeat. Repeat again. It had the feeling of a military maneuver. Thayer was shorter than me by four inches, but straighter, too, with more conviction in his carriage.

"You find us in a delicate position, Mr. Landor."

"I don't doubt it."

"This Academy," he began. But the key was too high; he lowered it a step or two. "This Academy, as you may know, has been in existence for less than thirty years. I have been superintendent for nearly half that time. I think it's safe to say that neither the Academy nor I have earned the distinction of permanence."

"Only a matter of time, I'd guess."

"Well, like any young institution, we have acquired some estimable friends. And some formidable detractors."

Looking at the floor, I ventured, "President Jackson falls in the second camp, does he?"

A quick sidelong glance from Thayer. "I don't pretend to know who falls out in which camp," he said. "I know only that we have been placed under a unique burden here. No matter how many officers we turn out, no matter how much honor we do our country, we are always, I fear, in the position of defending ourselves."

"Against what, Colonel Thayer?"

"Oh." He scanned the ceiling. "Elitism, that's a common theme. Our critics say we favor the scions of rich families. If they only knew how many of our cadets came from *farms,* how many are the sons of mechanics, manufacturers. This is America writ small, Mr. Landor."

It rang nicely in that hallway. *America writ small.*

"What else do your critics say, Colonel?"

"That we spend too much time making engineers and not enough time making soldiers. That our cadets take up the Army commissions that should go to men in the ranks."

Lieutenant Meadows, I thought.

Thayer kept advancing, matching his step to the drumbeat outside. "And I don't need to tell you," he said, "about our last group of critics. The ones who want no standing army of any kind in this country."

"What would they put in its place, I wonder?"

"The militias of old, apparently. Ragtag boys on the village common. Make-believe soldiers," he said, with no trace of bitterness.

"It wasn't militias won us our last war," I said. "It was men like—General Jackson."

"How nice to know we're in agreement, Mr. Landor. The fact remains there are still a goodly number of Americans who recoil at the sight of a man in uniform."

"That's why we don't wear any," I said, softly.

"'We'?"

"I'm sorry, *constables.* Look where you like, you won't find a constable—come to think of it, *any* New York City law officer—wearing something to announce himself. Uniforms do put folks off, don't they?"

Funny, I hadn't planned on volunteering that, but it did touch off a fraternal spark between us. Which is not to say I saw Sylvanus Thayer smile—I've never in my life seen him do *that*—but his edges could be honed down.

"I'd be remiss, Mr. Landor, if I didn't tell you that I myself have come in for the lion's share of attacks. I've been called a tyrant. A despot. *Barbarian,* that's a favored term."

With this, he stopped. Let the word settle over him.

"Well, now, it's a bad fix, isn't it, Colonel?" I said. "Looking at it from your side, I mean. If word got out cadets were actually breaking down under this—this brutal regime of yours, going so far as to take their own lives. . . ."

"The word about Leroy Fry *has* got out," he said, icy as a star. (Gone was the fellow feeling.) "I can't prevent that, nor can I prevent people from construing it how they may. My only concern at present is to keep this investigation out of the hands of certain parties."

I looked at him.

"Certain parties in *Washington,*" I offered.

"Just so," he replied.

"Parties who might be hostile to the Academy's very existence. Looking for a reason to raze it to the ground."

"Just so."

"But if you could show them you had things in hand—somebody on the job—then maybe you could hold off the hounds awhile longer."

"A *little* while, yes," he said.

"And what if I find nothing, Colonel?"

"Then I shall make my report to the chief of engineers, who will in turn consult with General Eaton. We shall then await their collective judgment."

We had stopped now by the door to Ward B-3. From downstairs, we could hear the fretting sound of the matron and the slow sliding sound of the surgeon. From outside, the piercing lines of a fife. And from inside Ward B-3, nothing at all.

"Who would have guessed?" I said. "One man's death could leave so much in the balance. Your career, even."

"If I can persuade you of nothing else, Mr. Landor, let me persuade you of this. My career is nothing. If I could be sure the Academy would survive, I would leave here tomorrow and never look back."

Giving me his most genial nod, he added, "You have a gift for inspiring confidences, Mr. Landor. I don't doubt it comes in handy."

"Well, that depends, Colonel. Tell me now. Do you honestly think I'm your man?"

"We wouldn't be speaking if I didn't."

"And you're bound to follow this out? To the very end?"

"And beyond," said Sylvanus Thayer, "if need be."

I smiled and looked down the hall, to the oculus window, where the light was calling up a floating chain of dust.

Thayer's eyes narrowed. "May I interpret your silence as a yes or a no, Mr. Landor?"

"Neither, Colonel."

"If it's a question of money . . ."

"I have enough money."

"Some other concern, perhaps."

"None you can help me with," I said, as kindly as I could.

Thayer cleared his throat—a small rasping, was all, but I had the clear impression of something stacked in him.

"Mr. Landor, for a cadet to die so young, and by his own hand, that is a hard thing to bear. But that he should have such an offense committed against his defenseless body is beyond sufferance. It is a crime against nature, and I consider it also a strike at the heart—" He stopped himself, but the word was already out. "—at the *heart* of this institution. If it is the work of some passing fanatic, so be it, that is in God's hands. If it is the work of one of our *own*, I will not *rest* until the offender has been bodily removed from the Point. In leg irons or walking free, it makes no difference, he must be sent away on the next steam packet. For the good of the Academy."

Having rid himself of this, he exhaled softly and bowed his head.

"That is your charge, Mr. Landor, if you accept it. To discover the person who did this. And to help us ensure it never happens again."

I watched him a good while longer. Then I drew my watch from my pocket and tapped once on its glass casing. "Ten minutes to five," I said. "What would you say to meeting back here at six? Would that inconvenience you too much?"

"Not at all."

"Good. I promise you'll have my answer then."

*   *   *

I had some idea in mind of strolling off on my own—it was my usual way—but the Academy could not countenance such a plan. No, I would have an escort, if you please. And for this work, Lieutenant Meadows was once again detailed. If the prospect had made his face fall, someone must have rearranged it for him: he was brighter in spirits than during our last go-round. I took this to mean he had not been granted a sight of Leroy Fry.

"Where do you wish to go, Mr. Landor?"

I swept my hand in the direction of the river. "East," I said. "East would do nicely."

To get there, of course, we had to cross round the Plain, which was no longer empty, no, not at all. The evening parade had come. The cadets of the United States Military Academy were fanned out in companies—four seething formations. The band, led by a man with a tasseled cane and a red pudding-bag hanging from his head, was playing the final strains, and the evening gun was firing, and the Stars and Stripes was fluttering to the ground like a pretty girl's handkerchief.

"*Sent harms!*" cried the adjutant. At once came the clash of two hundred guns, and in less than a second, each cadet was staring into his gun barrel. The officer in charge drew his blade and slammed his heels together and cried, "*Cree hump!*" Followed by (or so it sounded to me) "*Charge peanuts!*" At the conclusion of which, every cadet was turned half to the right, ready to stave off the enemy.

Oh, it was quite a show: the divots kicking up from the pale green turf, the last rays of the sun snagged on the bayonets. And the young men in their tight collars and tapering uniforms, plumes sprouting mighty from their heads.

"*Cree hump! . . . Der hump!*"

The news about Leroy Fry—part fact, part rumor—had by now become common currency among these cadets. And it was a measure of Thayer's system that it could bear such a blow with no sign of strain. The space normally occupied by Leroy Fry was now taken by another—the gap had been bridged—and anyone looking on would never have known there was one fewer in the ranks. Oh, a more trained watcher might have picked out the lost step here, the half shuffle there. A stumble, even. But that could easily be put down to the twenty or so plebes who filled each company. Boy-men only a few months free of their ploughs, still finding their rhythm . . . and all the same, swept up in the larger music.

"Front your section, mister!"

Yes, a fascinating sight, Reader, in the last hours of an October day, with the sun dropping, and the hills somehow twinning the blue and gray of the uniforms, and somewhere a mockingbird grouching . . . a fellow could do worse. There were others, too, passing time in much the same way. A raftload of tourists, down by the quartermaster's office. Ladies in leg-of-mutton sleeves and men in blue frock coats and beige waistcoats . . . a holiday lightness about them. They'd come up that morning from Manhattan, probably, on the day boat, or maybe they were Britishers working their way through the Northern Tour. As much a part of the spectacle as anything else.

"Snied States Milita' 'Cademy, 'S Point, 'en York, 'tober twe'six, 'and thirty! 'Shal 'lorders 'umber TWO!!!"

And who should be in the midst of the onlookers but Sylvanus Thayer? Not about to let a dead body keep him from his rounds. Indeed, he looked as if he'd never been anywhere but *here* the whole day long. Marvelous balance. He talked when he had to, stayed silent when that suited, bent an ear to any gentleman's question, pointed out the stray detail to the ladies, never once bore down. I could almost *hear* him, you know:

"Mrs. Brevoort, I don't know if you've noticed a certain esprit d'Europe to this particular maneuver. It was created by Frederick the Great, later elaborated upon by Napoleon during his Nile campaign. . . . Oh, and perhaps you spotted the young man at the head of Company B? That's Henry Clay, Junior. Yes, yes, son of the great man himself. Lost the headship of his class to a Vermont farmer's boy. America writ small, Mrs. Brevoort. . . ."

And now the cadet companies were being marched off in double time by the orderly sergeants, and the band was disappearing over a hill, and the spectators were falling back, and Lieutenant Meadows was asking me if I wanted to stay or keep walking, and I said walk, and so we did, all the way to Love Rock.

And there was the river, waiting a hundred feet below. *Rolling* with boats. Freight boats bound for the Erie Canal and packet boats bound for the great city. Skiffs and canoes and dugouts, all burning with geranium light. I could hear, not so far off, the ring of cannon on the proving grounds: a fat boom and then a trail of echoes, climbing the hillsides. To the west was river, to the east more river, and river to the south. I stood there at the crux of it, and if I'd been of a more historic cast, I might have communed with the Indians or with Benedict Arnold, who'd once stood on this very point, or with the men who dragged the great chain across the Hudson to stop the British navy from penetrating north. . . .

Or if I'd been a deeper soul, I might have given some thought to Fate or God, for Sylvanus Thayer had just asked me to save the honor of the U.S. Military Academy by once more taking up the work I had sworn off for good, and surely there was a larger pattern at work—I won't call it divine—but an *intervention*, yes.

Well, my mind doesn't sound that deep. Here's what I was thinking about: Hagar the cow. To be honest with you, I was wondering where she'd gone now. Toward the river? The highlands? Was there some cavern out there, back of a waterfall? Some private place only she knew about?

So yes, I thought about where she might have gone and if anything would bring her back.

At precisely ten minutes to six, I turned away from the river and found Lieutenant Meadows exactly where I had left him. Hands clasped behind his back, eyes locked, all other cares blacked away.

"I'm through, Lieutenant."

Five minutes later, I was back in Ward B-3. Leroy Fry's body was still there, draped in that nubby linen sheet. Thayer and Hitchcock were standing at something like parade rest, and I was just inside the door, and I was about to say, "Gentlemen, I'm your man."

But I said something else. Before I even understood I was speaking.

"Do you want me to find who took Leroy Fry's heart?" I asked. "Or do you want me to find who hanged him in the first place?"

Narrative of Gus Landor

4

October 27th

It was a locust tree. A hundred yards up from the South Landing. A *black* locust, slender and monkish-looking, with deep furrows and long mahogany pods. No different from most of the locust trees that cluster in the Highlands. No different, that is, except for the vine straggling from its bough.

Well, I *thought* it was a vine, more fool me. In my own defense, more than thirty-two hours had passed since the event in question, and the rope had already begun the slow work of bleeding into its surroundings. I suppose I expected someone to have taken it down by now. But they'd followed the swifter course: on finding the body, they'd severed the rope just above the dead man's head and left the rest dangling, and there it remained, lean-muscled, morning-dappled. And there was Captain Hitchcock, wrapping his hands round it. A testing tug and then a *pull*, as though there were a church bell on the other end. His weight sank into it, and his knees sagged a fraction, and I realized then how very tired he was.

No wonder. Up on his feet for a night and a day and then a six-thirty breakfast summons to Sylvanus Thayer's quarters. Me, I was just a hair fresher, having spent the evening at Mr. Cozzens' hotel.

The hotel, like so many things at the Point, had been Thayer's idea. If day-boat passengers were to see the Academy in all its glory, they would need somewhere to rest their heads at night. And so the United States government, in all its wisdom, decided to put up a fine hotel right on the

Academy grounds. Every day in the high season, tourists from all ends of the world would lay themselves down on Mr. Cozzens' newly plumped feather mattresses, hushed with wonder at Thayer's mountain kingdom.

Me, I was no tourist, but my own house was too far from the Academy for easy coming and going. So, for a term indefinite, I was given a room overlooking Constitution Island. The shutters kept out nearly all the starlight and moonlight—sleeping was a dive into a pit, and the sound of reveille seemed to come from a distant star. I lay there, watching the red light steal through the bottom of the shutters. The darkness felt delicious. I wondered if maybe I'd missed my true career.

But then I did the unsoldierly thing of lying abed another ten minutes, and I dressed at my leisure, and instead of dashing out for the morning roll call, I wrapped a blanket round me and strolled down to the boat landing, and by the time I got to Thayer's quarters, the superintendent had bathed and dressed and squeezed the tidings out of four newspapers and was poised over a plate of beefsteak, waiting for me and Hitchcock to do it the justice it demanded.

We ate in silence, the three of us, and drank Molly's excellent coffee, and when the plates had been pushed back and we had slouched back in their chairs—well, it was then I laid out my conditions.

"First off," I said, "if it's all the same to you gentlemen, I'd like my own horse about me. Seeing as how I'll be staying in your hotel for some time."

"Not too long, we hope," put in Hitchcock.

"No, not too long, but it'd be good to have Horse around in any event."

They promised to fetch him and make a place for him in the stables. And when I told them I'd like leave to go back to my cottage every Sunday, they said that as a private citizen, I could leave the post whenever I wanted, so long as I told them where I was going.

"And finally this," I said. "I'd like free rein while I'm here."

"How are we to take that term, Mr. Landor?"

"No armed guard. No Lieutenant Meadows, God bless him. No one walking me to the backhouse every three hours, no one kissing me good night. It won't do, gentlemen. I'm a solitary sort, I get chaffed by too many elbows."

Well, they told me this was impossible. They said that West Point, like any other military reservation, had to be closely patrolled. They had a congressionally mandated Responsibility to ensure the safety of every visitor and avoid Compromising Operations and on and on. . . .

We found a middle path. I would be permitted to walk the outer perimeter on my own—the Hudson was all mine—and they would give me the paroles and countersigns to satisfy the sentinels who'd be stopping me at intervals. But I was not to enter the core grounds without escort, nor was I to speak to any cadet unless there was a representative of the Academy present.

All in all, I would have called it a first-rate chat . . . until they started sliding in conditions of their own. This I should have expected, but have I mentioned yet? That I was still a shade off my best?

Mr. Landor, you may not breathe a word of this investigation to anyone inside or outside the Academy.

So far . . .

Mr. Landor, you must report to Captain Hitchcock on a daily basis.

. . . so good. . . .

Mr. Landor, you must prepare a detailed weekly report that outlines all your findings and conclusions, and you must be ready to recount your investigations to any Army official whenever so called upon.

Delighted, I said.

And then Ethan Allen Hitchcock gave his mouth a brutal swipe and cleared his throat and nodded sternly at the table.

"There is one final condition, Mr. Landor."

He looked distinctly uncomfortable. I felt sorry for him until I heard what it was, and then I never felt sorry for him again.

"We'd like to ask that there be no drinking—"

"No *untoward* drinking," said Thayer, working in a quieter key.

"—during the course of your investigations."

And with that, the whole affair expanded before my eyes—it took on a dimension of time. For if they knew about *that*, it meant they'd been making inquiries—buttonholing neighbors and colleagues, the boys at Benny Havens'—and that was more than a morning's work, that was days of husbanding. The only conclusion was this: Sylvanus Thayer had long ago cast his eye on me. Before he knew he had a use for me, he'd sent his scouts out to learn everything that could be learned about me. And here I sat now, eating his food, swallowing his terms. At his mercy.

If I'd been in a fighting mood, I might have denied it. I might have told them no drop of liquor had touched my lips in three days—it was the Lord's truth—but then I remembered that was the very thing I used to hear from the micks who slept out by the Garnet Saloon. "Three days," they always said, "*three* days since I touched a drop." As fast a turnabout as dead Jesus, to hear them tell it. How I used to smile.

"Gentlemen," I said, "you'll find me, in all our dealings, as dry as a Methodist."

They didn't press the point too hard. Thinking back on it, I wonder if they weren't more alarmed by the example I might set for the cadets, who were, of course, denied the pleasures of the bottle. The pleasures of the bed, the card table. Chess, tobacco. Music, novels. It hurt my head sometimes, thinking of all the things they couldn't do.

"But we haven't yet spoken of your fee," said Captain Hitchcock.

"We needn't."

"Surely . . . some compensation . . ."

"Only to be expected," said Thayer. "I'm sure in your previous capacity . . ."

Yes, yes, as a constable, you work on commission. Either you get paid by someone—the city, the family—or you stay out of it. But now and then you forget the rule. It's happened to me once or twice, to my sometime regret.

"Gentlemen," I said, drawing the napkin from my shirt, "I hope you won't take it wrong, you seem like grand fellows, but once this business is done, I'd be most grateful if you'd leave me alone. Except for a note now and again to let me know how you are."

I smiled to show I bore them no ill will, and they smiled, too, to show they'd saved a sum of money, and they called me a fine American and I forget what else, though I know the word *principle* got used. *Paragon,* too. And then Thayer went about his business, and Hitchcock and I went to our locust tree, and here now was the weary captain, leaning into that severed length of rope.

One of Hitchcock's own cadets was standing not ten feet off. Epaphras

Huntoon. Third-year man, a tailor's apprentice from Georgia. Tall and ox-shouldered and still in awe of his own bulk, I thought, for he seemed all the time to be appeasing it, with a dreamy brow and a wheedling tenor. It was this cadet's fate to have found Leroy Fry's body.

"Mr. Huntoon," I said, "please accept my sympathies. It must have been an awful shock."

He jerked his head in a nettled way, as though I were calling him away from a private talk. And then he smiled and started to speak and found he couldn't.

"Please," I said. "If you'd take me through what happened. You were on guard duty Wednesday night?"

That turned the trick: coming at it in pieces. "Yes, sir," he said. "I went on post at nine-thirty. Got relieved at midnight by Mr. Ury."

"What happened then?"

"I made my way back to the guardroom."

"And where is that?"

"North Barracks."

"And . . . where was your post?"

"Number four, sir. Over by Fort Clinton."

"So . . ." I smiled, looked around. "I'll admit I'm not very familiar with the grounds, Mr. Huntoon, but it seems to me this patch we're standing on right now isn't on the way from Fort Clinton to North Barracks."

"No, sir."

"What took you off course, then?"

He stole a look then at Captain Hitchcock, who gazed back a moment before saying, in a dull tone, "You needn't fear, Mr. Huntoon. You won't be reported."

Relieved of this care, the young man gave his big shoulders a shake and looked at me with a half grin.

"Well, sir. Thing is sometimes . . . when I'm on guard duty . . . I like to get me a feel of the river."

"A feel?"

"Put in a hand or a toe. Helps me sleep, sir, I can't explain it."

"No need to explain, Mr. Huntoon. Tell me, though, how you got your-self down to the river."

"I just took the path to the South Landing, sir. Five minutes down, ten minutes up."

"And what happened when you reached the river?"

"Oh, I didn't get there, sir."

"Why not?"

"I heard me something."

Here Captain Hitchcock shook himself and, in a voice that belied his weariness, asked: "What did you hear?"

It was a *sound,* that was all he could say. Might have been a branch creaking or a flaw of wind; might have been nothing at all. Whenever he was moved to say what it was, it showed itself as *other.*

"Young sir," I said, laying my hand on his shoulder. "I beg of you, don't start kicking in the spurs. It's no surprise you can't get at it . . . all the excitement, all the running about, it tends to rattle a fellow's brain. Maybe I should ask what made you *follow* this sound?"

That seemed to calm him. He got very still for a stretch.

"I reckoned it might be an animal, sir."

"What sort?"

"I don't rightly know, I . . . maybe it got itself caught in a trap . . . I'm terrible partial to animals, sir. Hounds, 'specially."

"So you did what any Christian man should do, Mr. Huntoon. You went to the aid of one of God's creatures."

"I reckon that's what I done. I was just fixing to go up the hill a piece, it being pretty steep and all, and I was all ready to turn back—"

He stopped.

"But then you saw . . . ?"

"No, sir." Back he came with a rush of air. "I didn't see anything."

"And not seeing anything, you . . ."

"Well, I just had me this feeling somebody was by. Some*thing.* So I said, 'Who goes there?' As I'm charged to do, you see. And there weren't any answer, so what I did, I brought my musket to 'charge,' and I said, 'Advance and give the countersign.'"

"Still no answer."

"That's correct, sir."

"And what did you do then?"

"Well, I kept going a few paces. But I never once seen him, sir."

"Who?"

"Cadet Fry, sir."

"Well, then, how did you find him?"

He waited a few seconds to steady his voice.

"I brushed him."

"Ah." I cleared my throat, gently. "That must have been a surprise, Mr. Huntoon."

"Not at first, sir, 'cause I didn't know. But once I *knew,* why, yes—yes, it was."

I've often thought since that if Epaphras Huntoon had passed a yard to the north or a yard to the south, he might never have found Leroy Fry. For it had been almighty dark that night, cloudy with a bitty thumbnail of a moon and just the lantern in Huntoon's hand to show the way. Yes, a yard in either direction, and he might have passed right by Leroy Fry and been none the wiser.

"What then, Mr. Huntoon?"

"Well, I jumped back, is what I did."

"Perfectly natural."

"And the lantern fell. Out of my hand."

"It fell? Or maybe you dropped it?"

"Um . . . dropped it, that may be. Can't say, sir."

"And what next?"

He fell silent again. At least his voice box did. The rest of him was talking at a mad pace. Teeth dancing, toes sliding. One hand playing with his tunic, the other with the buttons that ran down the side of his trousers.

"Mr. Huntoon?"

"I didn't rightly know what to do, sir. See, I weren't at my post, so I weren't sure anyone'd hear me if I called. So I run, I expect."

His eyes were cast down now, and that was all it took to press the picture into my mind's eye: Epaphras Huntoon dashing half blind through the forest, clawing the branches out of his face, brass and steel rattling under his cloak, cartridge boxes shivering. . . .

"I run straight back to North Barracks," he said, quietly.

"And who did you report this to?"

"Cadet officer of the guard, sir, and he went and got Lieutenant Kinsley, sir, who was army officer of the day. And they had me go and fetch Captain Hitchcock, and we all of us run back and . . ."

He looked at Hitchcock now with an unmistakable plea. *Tell him, captain.*

"Mr. Huntoon," I said. "I think we might take a step back, if you don't object. Back to when you *first* found the body. Do you think you could face that again?"

Fierce-browed, vise-jawed, he nodded. "Yes, sir."

"There's a good man. Now, let me ask you, did you hear anything else at the time?"

"Nothin' you wouldn't hear in the normal way. An owl or two, sir. And . . . a bullfrog, maybe. . . ."

"And was there anyone else about?"

"No, sir. But then I wasn't looking for no one."

"And I would guess—after that first contact, you didn't touch the body again?"

He twitched his head back to the tree. "I couldn't," he said. "Once I seen what it was."

"Very sensible, Mr. Huntoon. Now maybe you could tell me—" I paused to scan his face. "Maybe you could tell me just how Leroy Fry looked."

"Not well, sir."

And that was the first time I heard Captain Hitchcock laugh. A *squoosh* of merriment, gouged out of his middle. Surprised even him, I think. And it had this other virtue: it saved me from doing the same.

"I don't doubt it," I said, as softly as I could. "Which of us would have looked our best in such a setting? I was thinking . . . more the position of the body, if you recall that."

He turned now and faced the tree head on—for the first time, maybe? Letting the memory work through him.

"His head," he said, slowly. "The head was twisted to one side."

"Yes?"

"And the rest of him was . . . he looked knocked *back,* sir."

"How so?" I asked.

"Well." He fluttered his lids, chewed his lip. "He wasn't hanging straight.

His *backside*, sir, it was . . . like maybe he was getting ready to set. In a chair or hammock or some such."

"Did he look that way because you'd knocked into him?"

"No, sir." He was quite definite on that point, I remember. "No, sir, I only grazed him, word of honor. He never budged."

"Go on, then. What else do you remember?"

"The legs." He extended one of his own. "They were split wide, I think. And they were—they were ahead."

"Not following you, Mr. Huntoon. You say his legs were *ahead* of him?"

"On account of they were on the ground, sir."

I walked to the tree then. I stood under that dangling length of rope, feeling its tickle against my collarbone.

"Captain Hitchcock," I said. "Do you have any notion of how tall Leroy Fry was?"

"Oh, average or above—maybe an inch or two shorter than yourself, Mr. Landor."

Epaphras Huntoon's eyes were still closed when I came back to him. "Well, sir," I told him, "this is very interesting. You mean to say his feet . . . his *heels*, maybe—"

"Yes, sir."

"—were resting on the ground, do I have that right?"

"Yes, sir."

"I can verify that," said Hitchcock. "He was in the same position when I saw him."

"And how much time passed, Mr. Huntoon, between your first sighting of the body and your second?"

"No more 'n twenty minutes, I reckon. Half an hour."

"And did the body's position change at all during that time?"

"No, sir. Not so's I noticed. It was terrible dark."

"I've got just one more question, Mr. Huntoon, and then I'll trouble you no longer. Did you know it was Leroy Fry when you saw him?"

"Yes, sir."

"How?"

A flush of red sprang to his cheeks. His mouth skewed right.

"Well, sir, when I first run into him, I swung the lantern out. Like this. And there he was."

"And you recognized him right off?"

"Yes, sir." That pickled grin again. "When I was a plebe once, Cadet Fry shaved off half my scalp. Right before dinner formation. Lord, did I catch it."

Narrative of Gus Landor

5

Lazarus began stinking after a few days—why should Leroy Fry have been any different? And as no one was planning to raise *him* from the dead anytime soon, and as his parents weren't expected for another three weeks, the Academy administrators had a problem on their hands. They could bury the boy right away and brave the ire of the Fry family, or they could keep him above ground and risk the decay of his hard-used body. After some talk, they chose the latter course, but ice was still in demand, and Dr. Marquis was forced to fall back on a practice he'd witnessed many years back as a medical student at Edinburgh University. Which is to say, he submerged Leroy Fry in an alcohol bath.

And that was how we found him, Captain Hitchcock and I. Naked, in an oak box filled with ethyl alcohol. To close his mouth, a stick had been wedged between his breastbone and jaw, and to keep him from rising, a load of charcoal had been dumped inside his chest cavity, but his nose kept breaking the surface, and his eyelids still refused to close. And there he floated, looking more alive than ever, as though he were being carried back to us on the next wave.

The box had been caulked but not tightly enough, for we could hear a dripping on the trestle. All round us rose cool snarly fumes of alcohol, and I figured this was as close to drunk as I would get for some time.

"Captain," I said. "Maybe you've been to the ocean?"

Hitchcock answered that he had, on several occasions.

"Me, I've only been once," I said. "I remember seeing a young girl there—eight, maybe—making a cathedral in the sand. Remarkable thing, abbeys and bell towers . . . I couldn't even tell you all the details she piled on. She'd planned for everything—except the tide. The faster she worked, the faster it came on. Before another hour was out, that beautiful thing of hers was just a set of humps in the sand."

I made a leveling motion with my hand.

"Wise girl," I said. "Never shed a tear. I think about her sometimes when I try to pile things on top of these simple facts. You can make something beautiful, and then a wave comes along, and all that's left is the humps. Your foundations. Shame on anyone who forgets them."

"So what are our foundations?" asked Hitchcock.

"Well," I said, "let's look and see. We have this idea that Leroy Fry wanted to die, which seems like a damned good foundation, Captain. Why else would a young man hang himself from a tree? He was beaten down, it's an old story. So what would a beaten man do? Why, he'd leave a note, that's what. Tell his friends and family why he was doing such a thing. Get the hearing he never got when he was alive. So . . ." I held out my palms. "Where's his note, Captain?"

"We've found none."

"Humm. Well, no matter, not every suicide leaves a note. Lord knows I've seen more than a few just take a leap off a bridge. Very well, Leroy Fry hies himself straight to the nearest bluff—oh, no, stop a minute, he decides to hang himself. Not—not where anyone can *find* him easy, but maybe he doesn't want to be any trouble. . . ."

I stopped, then started again.

"Very well, he finds himself a good strong tree, loops the rope around the branch . . . oh, but he's too distracted to—to *test* the rope's length, so . . ." I extended one leg, then the other. "He finds this little gallows of his won't even lift him off the ground. All right, he ties the rope all over again . . . no, no, he doesn't do that. No, Leroy Fry wants to die so badly he just . . . keeps kicking."

I gave my leg a good shake.

"Till the rope finishes its work." I frowned at the floor. "Well, yes, it's certainly a *longer* business, going about it that way. And if his neck isn't broken, it takes even longer. . . ."

Hitchcock was rising to the challenge now. "You said yourself he wasn't in his right mind. Why should we expect him to behave rationally?"

"Oh, well. In my experience, Captain, there's nothing so rational as a man bent on killing himself. He knows just how he means to do it. I once—I once saw a *woman* take her life. She had a very fine picture of it in her head. When she finally got round to it, you'd have sworn she was *recollecting* the thing. Because she'd already seen it happen, over and over."

And Captain Hitchcock said, "This woman you mention, was she . . . ?"

No. No, he didn't say that. He said nothing for a short while. Just sketched a path around Leroy Fry's coffin, scuffing up the wax with his boots.

"Perhaps," he said, "it was a trial run of sorts that got out of hand."

"If we're to credit our witness, Captain, there's no way it could have got out of hand. Feet on the ground, upper limb within reach: if Leroy Fry had wanted to call the whole thing off, he very easily might've."

Still Hitchcock kept scuffing the floor. "The rope," he said. "The rope might have given way after he hanged himself. Or perhaps Cadet Huntoon jostled him harder than he knew. There could be any number . . ."

He was fighting hard, it was his nature. I should have admired him for it, but he was starting to make my eyes hurt.

"Look here," I said.

Whipping off my baize jacket, I rolled up my shirt sleeves and plunged my hand into the alcohol bath. A shock of cold, then a phantom shock of hot. And this, too: the queer feeling that my skin was melting and hardening at the same time. But my hand stayed true, hauled Leroy Fry's head toward the surface. And with the head came the rest of the body, as hard and straight as the trestle on which it lay. I had to lace my other hand beneath him just to keep him from sinking down again.

"The *neck*," I said. "That's what first struck me. Do you see? Not a clean cinch at all. The rope *grabbed* at him. Ran up and down the neck, looking for a purchase."

"As though . . ."

"As though he was fighting. And look, if you would. The fingers."

I gestured with my chin, and Captain Hitchcock, after a brief pause, rolled up *his* sleeves and bowed over the body.

"You see?" I said. "On the *right* hand. Very tips of the fingers."

"Blisters."

"Just so. *Fresh* blisters, by the look of them. I'm thinking he was . . . *clutching* at the rope, trying to peel the thing off him."

We stared down at Leroy Fry's sealed mouth, stared *hard,* as though by doing so we might unseal it. And by some strange accident, the room did fill with a voice—not mine, not Hitchcock's—ringing with such force that our hands pulled away, and Leroy Fry sank back with a hiss and a gargle.

"May I ask what is going on here?"

We must have been quite a sight to Dr. Marquis. Bent over the coffin in our shirt sleeves. Daylight grave robbers, by the looks of us.

"Doctor!" I cried. "I'm delighted you could join us. We're in dire need of a medical authority."

"Gentlemen," he sputtered. "This is somewhat irregular."

"It certainly is. I was wondering if you wouldn't mind feeling round the back of Mr. Fry's head?"

He wrestled with the propriety of it, or at least he gave propriety a few more seconds of his time, and then he followed our lead. And by the time he had secured the back of the skull, the wince of effort on his face had been planed into something like peace. A man at home.

"Anything, Doctor?"

"Not yet, I'm . . . Mm. Mm, yes. A contusion of some sort."

"A lump, you mean?"

"Yes."

"Maybe you could describe it for us."

"Parietal region, best I can make out . . . perhaps three inches in circumference."

"How thick, roughly speaking?"

"Rising . . . oh, a quarter inch or so above the skull."

"Now, what might have made such a lump as that, Doctor?"

"Same thing causes any lump, I expect: something hard comes in contact with the head. Can't tell you any more without looking at it."

"Might the bruise have been inflicted after death?"

"Not very likely. A bruise comes from extravasated blood—blood escaping from its vessels. If there's no blood circulating—no *heart,* in plain truth—" He had the good sense to stop his laugh in midcourse. "There can be no bruise."

It was slow, almost bashful work, making ourselves civilized again—rolling our sleeves down and putting our jackets back on.

"So then, gentlemen," I said, cracking my knuckles. "What exactly do we *know?*"

Getting no reply, I was forced to answer my own question.

"We have here a young fellow who tells no one he wishes to die. Leaves no note. Dies, it would seem, with his feet still on the ground. On the back of his head we find a—a *contusion,* as Dr. Marquis will have it. Blisters on his fingers, rope burns up and down his neck. I ask you now, does all of this suggest a man going willingly to his Maker?"

Hitchcock, I remember, was stroking the two bars on his blue coatee, as though to remind himself of his rank.

"What do *you* believe happened?" he asked.

"Oh, I have a theory, that's all. Leroy Fry quits his barracks room sometime between the hours of ten o'clock and, say, eleven-thirty. He knows, of course, that in doing so, he runs a—I'm sorry, what risk is he running, Mr. Hitchcock?"

"Leaving the barracks after hours? That's ten demerits."

"Ten, is it? Well, then, he does run a risk, doesn't he? Why? Is he longing to see the Hudson, like the charming Mr. Huntoon? Maybe so. Maybe your cadet corps harbors a secret squad of nature lovers. But in the case of Mr. Fry, I have to believe he has a special errand in mind. Only because someone is waiting for him."

"And this someone . . . ?" said Dr. Marquis, leaving the question unsaid.

"For now, let's assume it's the someone who swatted him in the back of the head. Threw that noose round his neck. Drew it *tight.*"

I took a step away and smiled at the wall and then back at them and said, "Of course, it's only a theory, gentlemen."

"I think you are being a bit coy with us," said Captain Hitchcock, the heat rising in his voice. "I can't believe you would proffer a theory if you didn't place some credence in it."

"Ah yes," I answered, "but tomorrow the ocean will sweep over it and . . . *whoosh.*"

A silence then, broken only by the drip drip on the coffin trestle and the slow scuffing of Hitchcock's boots . . . and at last Hitchcock's own voice, sounding tauter with each word.

"In the meantime, Mr. Landor, you have left us with two mysteries where previously we had just one. According to you, we must find both Leroy Fry's desecrator and Leroy Fry's killer."

"Unless," said Dr. Marquis, tossing timid glances at us both, "it is the *same* mystery."

Odd that he should have been the one to suggest it, but suggest it he did, and the silence that followed had a new quality. We were, all of us, I think, venturing up different roads, but feeling the same change in altitude.

"Well, Doctor," I said, "the only fellow who can tell us is that poor boy right there."

Leroy Fry was rocking ever so slightly in his bath—his eyes still ajar, his body still rigid. Soon, I knew, the rigor mortis would end, the joints would thaw . . . and maybe *then,* I thought, this body of his might yield up something.

That was when I noticed—noticed *again,* I should say—the balled-up fist of his left hand.

"Excuse me," I said. "If you don't mind."

I think those were my words, but I was no more conscious of what I was saying than of what I was doing. I knew only that I had to get to Leroy Fry's hand.

And because dragging it to the light would have meant hauling up the whole body, I contented myself with working just below the surface. The other two had no idea what I was up to until they heard the crack of Leroy Fry's thumb being pried from his palm. Even traveling through alcohol, it was a savage sound, like a chicken getting its neck broken.

"Mr. Landor!"

"What on earth?"

The other fingers broke faster. Or maybe I just knew now how much force was needed.

Snap. Snap. Snap. Snap.

The claw lay open, and there in Leroy Fry's hand was the tiniest of bundles, yellow and sodden and torn. A scrap of paper.

By the time I had lifted it to the light, Hitchcock and Marquis were on either side of me, and we read it together, our three sets of lips silently sounding, in the manner of students watching a line of Latin being chalked across a blackboard.

NG

HEIR A

T BE L

ME S

"Well, it may be nothing," I said, folding it back into its original shape and dropping it in my shirt pocket. I let out a long whistle and then, gazing into the faces of my companions, I said:

"Shall I put the fingers back the way I found them?"

I wasn't a complete prisoner during my stay at the Academy. There would be times, over the span of the next several weeks, when my escort would step away for a brief while or let me veer a few yards off course. And for a minute, or two minutes, even, the tether would fall slack, and I would be standing alone in the heart of West Point, and my body would show itself to me again: the fringe of hair on my head, the rasp in my left lung, the twinge in my hip . . . and, coursing through it all, that *beat beat beat*, the cadence I'd felt in Thayer's office. I took every symptom as a cause for rejoicing, for it meant there were parts of me that still lay apart from the Academy, and how many of the cadets, how many even of the officers, could say that?

So then let me take you back, Reader, to the moment when Captain Hitchcock and I (having left Dr. Marquis to mend the insults to Leroy Fry's person) were stopped en route to the superintendent's quarters by a certain Professor Church. The professor had himself a complaint, meant specially for Hitchcock's ears. The two men drew themselves apart, and I sidled away a bit until I was standing in the superintendent's garden. A pleasant little space: rhododendrons, asters, an oak tree spidered with rose vines. I closed my eyes and felt myself sinking into a copper beech. Alone.

Except I was not. From behind me stole a voice, speaking under great compression.

"Pardon."

And that was when I turned and found him. Half hidden behind a Saint Michael's pear tree. As unreal to me then as a leprechaun, for hadn't I already watched (or heard) the cadets of the Academy being marched to breakfast, dinner, supper? Marched to class, parade, barracks? Marched to sleep, marched awake? I had come to think of these boys in the passive voice, and the idea that one of them could split from the ranks and pursue a mission of his own (more urgent than dipping a toe in the Hudson) was as likely to me as a rock sprouting feet.

"Pardon me, sir," he said. "Are you Augustus Landor?"

"Yes."

"Cadet Fourth Classman Poe, at your service."

Start with this: he was too old. At least when set next to the other members of his class. *Those* boys still had garlands of pimple on their jaws, they had big hands and receding chests, and they startled easy, as if the schoolmaster's switch were still singing in their ears. *This* plebe was different: the pimples had scarred over, and the bearing was erect, like that of an officer on convalescence.

"How do you do, Mr. Poe?"

Two strands of lank black hair hung down from the absurd leather cap, making a cameo of his eyes, which were hazel-gray and much too large for his face. His teeth, by contrast, were tiny and exquisite, the sort you might find on the necklace of a cannibal chieftain. *Delicate* teeth, as fitted his frame, for he was thin as straw, *slight*—except for that forehead, which even the hat could not contain. A pale and hulking thing, it bulged through its envelope, in the way an anaconda's meal makes a knot of protest in its neck.

"Sir," he said. "Unless I mistake, you have been tasked with solving the mystery surrounding Leroy Fry."

"That's so."

The news had not yet been made official, but there seemed no point denying it. And in fact, the young man was under no illusion I would, though he did hesitate, long enough that I felt obliged to ask:

"What might I do for you, Mr. Poe?"

"Mr. Landor, I believe it incumbent upon me and the honor of this institution to divulge some of the conclusions which I have reached."

"Conclusions. . . ."

"Regarding *l'affaire* Fry."

He threw back his head as he said it. I remember thinking that anyone who used a phrase like "*l'affaire* Fry" should probably throw back his head. Exactly like that.

"I'd be most interested to hear them, Mr. Poe."

He made as if to speak, then stopped himself and cut his eyes both ways—assuring himself, I suppose, that no one could see—or, more likely, that I would pay him the greatest possible notice. Stepping at last from behind the tree, he stood in full view for the first time . . . and then leaned toward me (a hint of apology in this movement) and whispered in my ear:

"The man you're looking for is a poet."

And with that he touched his hat, took a deep bow, and marched away. When I next saw him, he had merged with no apparent effort into the stream of cadets proceeding to mess.

Lost in a cloud, most of our meetings. Only when someone becomes vital do we try to give that first encounter the importance it would later have . . . although, if we are to be honest, that man, that woman, was just a face or a circumstance. In *this* case, however, I have to believe my first impressions were every bit as full as the later ones. For the simple reason that nothing about him was quite right. Or would ever be.

Narrative of Gus Landor

6

October 28th

The very next day, I broke my vow of abstinence. It began, like all great falls, with the best of intentions. I was on my way home to gather some belongings when what should come my way but the steps leading to Benny Havens' tavern? I could conclude only that Fate had brought me here. For wasn't my mouth dry as bone? Wasn't there a fine stack of hay in back for Horse? Weren't there *civilians* inside?

And even when I passed through the doors of Benny's Red House, I had no idea of taking a drink. One of Mrs. Havens' buckwheat cakes, maybe. A glass of lemon juice and iced water. But Benny had made his famous flip—the hot iron had just been plunged into its eggs-and-ale bath—and the air crackled with caramel, and a fire shivered in the hearth, and before I knew it, I was sitting at the counter, and the missus was slicing up her roast turkey, and Benny was pouring the flip into a pewter flagon, and I was home again.

Here, on my right: Jasper Magoon, a former assistant editor at the *New York Evening Post*. Left the city (like me) for his health and was now, a scant five years later, half deaf and all blind, reduced to begging people to read the latest news into his left ear. *Fair at Masonic Hall . . . Weekly Report of Deaths . . . Compound Syrup of Sarsaparilla. . . .*

In that corner: Asher Lippard, an Episcopalian rector who nearly fell into the sea off Malta and, in a fit of reform, became one of the founders of the American Society for the Promotion of Temperance . . . before being taken by another fit of reform. He was now as devout a drinker as you could know. Took his drinking as seriously as a priest takes unction.

Next table over: Jack de Windt, in the midst of a lengthy lawsuit over claims he had invented the steamboat before Fulton. A local legend for two reasons: he paid for everything in Russian kopecks, and he backed only doomed candidates. Porter in '17, Young in '24, Rochester in '26—if a ship was sinking somewhere, they said, de Windt would find it. But he was buoyant as a cork and would be pleased to tell you how, once the Fulton folk had given him his due, he would find the Northwest Passage—he was even now looking for dogs.

And here was Benny himself, tender of these sheared sheep. A short man, well into his thirties, with an old man's mouth and a young man's eyes and a thatch of black hair tousled by sweat. A prideful man: he might be serving bargemen and idlers, but you'd never find him in anything but a boiled shirt and bow tie. And though by most accounts Benny had lived his whole life in the Hudson Valley, you could often hear a brogue nagging at his vowels.

"Now did I ever tell you, Landor, about Jim Donegan's daddy? The village sexton he was. Dressed up the corpses for funerals, put on their best clothes and such, tied their neckties for 'em. Well, whenever my pal Jim needed help getting his tie on, his daddy said, 'Now, Jim, I'll have you lie down on this here bed, there's a boy. And close your eyes, would you? And yes, put your arms crost your chest just so.' I'm telling you, it was the only way he could dress his sons. Man had to lay down just to dress himself. And never gave a thought to how he looked from behind, for who ever sees a dead man's ass?"

At Benny Havens', you won't find any of the cocktails served in Manhattan's finer saloons. It's raw whiskey and bourbon, thank you, it's rum and it's beer, and if someone is a bit out of his senses, perhaps a root beer passed off as bourbon. But do not think, Reader, our Benny is as common as his surroundings. He and his wife (as they themselves will be the first to tell you, voices tottery with pride) are the *only* U.S. citizens enjoined by law from setting foot on West Point. On account of their being caught a few years back running whiskey onto the reservation.

"You ask me now, the Congress should've given us a medal," is what
Benny Havens says. "Soldiers need drink same as they need grapeshot."

The cadets have been inclined to see it Benny's way, and when they
are parched enough, they take their chances and run it to the Havens establishment. And if by chance they can't, there is always Benny's barmaid,
Patsy, to ferry a load right onto the reservation under cover of darkness.
This is the way preferred by many cadets, for Patsy is never too proud, they
say, to add herself to the bill of sale. It's possible (and don't think we haven't
placed bets) that at least two dozen cadets have been led into the female
mystery by our Patsy. And yet who can be sure? Patsy talks about everything but the act itself, and it may well be that she's only squeezing herself
into the idea that people have of barmaids. Playing a type, as it were, and
also contemplating this type from a great remove. In truth, I can vouch for
her giving herself to only one man, and he's not likely to brag to anyone.

Here she came now: in passage from the scullery, all black eyes and
batiste drawers. Bonnet too small, hips a touch wide (for some tastes). "My
angel," I cried, not insincerely.

"Gus," she said.

Her voice was as flat as a table, but it didn't stop Jack de Windt. "Ohh,"
he moaned. "I'm a famished man, Miss Patsy."

"Mm," she said. "Hum." And passed her hands across her eyes and
disappeared into the kitchen.

"What's grieving her?" I asked.

"Oh." Blind Jasper shook his head darkly. "You'll have to excuse her,
Landor. She lost one of her boys."

"That so?"

"You must have heard," said Benny. "Fellow name of Fry. Once gave me
a Macintosh blanket for two shots of whiskey. Not his own blanket, goes
without saying. Well, the poor devil hanged himself the other night. . . ."
Casting his eyes left and right, he leaned into me and, in the loudest possible whisper, added, "What *I* heard? Pack of wolves tore the liver right out
of his body." He straightened again, wiped a tankard with great care. "Ah,
but why'm I telling *you*, Landor? You've been up at the Point yourself."

"Where'd you hear that, Benny?"

"The whippoorwill, I think."

The smaller the town, the faster word gets around. And Buttermilk Falls is nothing but small. Even its citizens are a mite smaller than the mean. Except for a gigantic tinplate peddler who blows in twice a year, I may well be the tallest man about.

"Whippoorwills are chatty beasts," said Blind Jasper, nodding sullenly.

"Listen, Benny," I said. "You ever talk to Fry yourself?"

"Once or twice, is all. Poor lad needed help with his conic sections."

"Oh," said Jack, "I don't think it was *his* conic sections he wanted help with."

He might have said more in the same line, but Patsy was coming out again, with a plate of bannocks. Shamed us into silence. Only when she passed within a foot of me did I dare to touch her hem.

"I'm sorry, Patsy. I didn't know this Fry fellow was . . ."

"He wasn't," she said. "Not in that way. But he *wanted* to be, and that has to count for something, don't you think?"

"Tell us," said Jasper, half panting. "What kept him out of your favor, Patsy?"

"Nothing he could help. But Lord, you know I like a darker coloring in a man. Red hair is all well on top, but it won't do below. It's one of my principles." She set down the plate and frowned at the floor. "I can't understand what would possess a boy to do such a thing to himself. When he's too young even to do it proper."

"What do you mean, 'proper'?" I asked.

"Why, Gus, he couldn't even measure the rope right. They say it took him three hours to die."

"'*They*,' Patsy? Who is this 'they'?"

She thought about it for some moments before lowering her original estimate. "*Him*," is what she said, nudging her head toward the far corner.

This was the corner farthest from Benny's fire, occupied on this particular evening by a young cadet. His musket rested against the wall behind him. His leather cap lay at the very edge of the table. His black hair was smeared with sweat, and his pale swollen head bobbed in the half shadows.

Hard to say how many rules he'd broken by coming here. Leaving the West Point reservation without authorization . . . visiting a place where

spirituous liquors were sold . . . visiting said place for the purpose of drinking said liquors. Many another cadet, of course, had broken these same
rules, but almost always at night, when the watchdogs were abed. This was
the first time I'd seen Benny's broached in daylight.

He never saw me coming, Cadet Fourth Classman Poe. Whether it was
reverie or stupor, I can't say, but I stood there a good half minute, waiting
for him to lift his head, and I had about given up on him when I heard
faint sounds coming from somewhere in his neighborhood: words, maybe,
or spells.

"Afternoon," I said.

His head snapped back; his enormous gray eyes swiveled. "Oh, it's you!"
he cried.

Half tipping his chair over, he rose and seized my hand and began
pumping it.

"Dear me. Sit. Yes, sit down, won't you please? Mr. Havens! Another
drink for my friend here."

"And who would be paying?" I heard Benny mutter, but the young
cadet must not have heard, for he beckoned me toward him and, under his
breath, said, "Mr. Havens, there . . ."

"What's he saying about me, Landor?"

Laughing, Poe cupped his hands round his mouth. "Mr. Havens is the
only congenial man in this whole godforsaken desert!"

"And it's touched I am to hear it."

There was, I should make this clear, a doubleness to everything Benny
said. You had to be a long-timer to catch it: the thing said and the comment on the thing said, both happening at the same moment. Poe was not
a long-timer, and so his impulse was to say his piece again—louder.

"In this whole *benighted, godforsaken* . . . den of . . . rapacious *philistines*.
The only *one*, may God strike me down if I'm a liar!"

"You'll make me weep, you go on, Mr. Poe."

"And his lovely wife," said the young man. "And Patsy. The blessed . . .
the Hebe of the Highlands!" Pleased with this coinage, he raised his glass
to the woman who had inspired it.

"How many drinks would this be?" I asked, sounding uncomfortably
like Sylvanus Thayer to my own ears.

"I don't recall," he said.

In fact, four empty glasses lay in formation alongside his right elbow. He caught me in the act of counting them.

"Not *mine*, Mr. Landor, I assure you. It appears Patsy isn't keeping the place as neat as she might. Owing to grief."

"You do seem a bit . . . liquid, Mr. Poe."

"You're referring, probably, to my fearfully delicate constitution. It takes but one drink to rob me of my senses. Two, and I'm staggering like a pugilist. It's a medical condition, corroborated by several eminent physicians."

"Most unfortunate, Mr. Poe."

With the curtest of nods, he accepted my sympathy.

"Now, maybe," I said, "before you start staggering, you can tell me something."

"I would be honored."

"How did you come to learn about the position of Leroy Fry's body?"

The question affected him as an insult. "Why, from Huntoon, of course. He's been spouting the news like a town crier. Perhaps someone will hang *him* before long."

"'*Hang* him,'" I repeated. "I assume you don't mean to imply that someone hanged Mr. Fry?"

"I don't mean to imply anything."

"Tell me, then. Why do you think the man who took Leroy Fry's heart was a poet?"

This was a different sort of inquiry, for he was all business now. Pushing away his glass. Correcting the sleeves of his coatee.

"Mr. Landor," he said, "the heart is symbol, or it is nothing. Take away the symbol, and what do you have? A fistful of muscle, of no more aesthetic interest than a bladder. To remove a man's heart is to traffic in symbol. Who better equipped for such labor than a poet?"

"An awfully literal-minded poet, it seems to me."

"Oh, you cannot tell me, Mr. Landor, you cannot *pretend* that this act of savagery did not startle literary resonances from the very crevices of your mind. Shall I delineate my own train of association? I thought in the first moment of Childe Harold: 'The heart will break, yet brokenly live on.' My next thought was for Lord Suckling's charming song: 'I prithee send me back my heart / Since I cannot have thine.' The surprise, given how little use I have for religious orthodoxy, is how often I am thrown back on the Bible: 'Create in me a clean heart, O God.' . . . 'A broken and contrite heart, O God, thou wilt not despise.'"

"Then we might just as easily be seeking a religious maniac, Mr. Poe."

"Ah!" He brought his fist down on the table. "A statement of creed, is that what you're saying? Go back to the original Latin, then: the verb *credere* is derived from the noun *cardia*, meaning—meaning 'heart,' yes? In English, of course, *heart* has no predicative form. Hence we translate *credo* as 'I believe,' when literally it means 'I set my heart' or 'I *place* my heart.' A matter not of denying the body, in other words, nor of transcending it, but rather of *expropriating* it. A trajectory of secular faith." Smiling grimly, he leaned back in his chair. "In other words, poetry."

Maybe he saw the corners of my mouth shrink, for he seemed all at once to be questioning himself . . . and then just as suddenly, he laughed and rapped himself on the temple.

"I neglected to tell you, Mr. Landor! I am a poet myself. Hence inclined to think as one. I cannot help myself, you see."

"Another medical condition, Mr. Poe?"

"Yes," he said, unblinking. "I shall have to donate my body to science."

It was the first time I figured him for being good at cards. For he was able to carry a bluff as far as it could go.

"I'm afraid I don't get round to poetry much," I said.

"Why should you?" he replied. "You're an American."

"And you, Mr. Poe?"

"An artist. That is to say, without country."

He liked the sound of this, too. Let it revolve in the air, like a doubloon.

"Well, now," I said, standing to go. "I do thank you, Mr. Poe. You've been a great help."

"Oh!" He grabbed my arm and drew me back down. (Great force in those slender fingers.) "You'll want a second look at a cadet named Loughborough."

"Why is that, Mr. Poe?"

"At evening parade last night, I happened to notice his steps were amiss.

He repeatedly confused 'left face' with 'about face.' This indicated to me a mind laboring under distraction. In addition, his demeanor at mess this morning was altered."

"And what would that tell us?"

"Well, if you were acquainted with him, you would know that he jabbers more than Cassandra, and to similar effect. No one listens, you see, not even his best friends. Today, he desired no listeners."

As though to dramatize the scene, he draped his face with an invisible veil and sat there, as wrapped in thought as Loughborough himself. There was this difference, though: Poe brightened in a flash, as though someone had tossed a match into him.

"I don't think I mentioned," he said. "Loughborough was, in former days, Leroy Fry's roommate. Until they had a falling out, the nature of which remains uncertain."

"Strange you should know of this, Mr. Poe."

A lazy shrug. "Someone must have told me," he said, "for how else would I know? People *do* tend to confide in me, Mr. Landor. I hail from a long line of Frankish chieftains. From the dawn of civilization, great trusts have been placed in us; these trusts have never been *mis*placed."

Once again, the head was thrown back in that accent of defiance—the gesture I remembered from the superintendent's garden. He would brave any scorn.

"Mr. Poe," I said, "you'll pardon me. I'm still getting a fix on the Academy's comings and goings, but it seems to me more than likely you're expected somewhere."

He gave me the wildest look just then, as if I'd jostled him from a fever dream. Shoved his glass away and sprang to his feet.

"What time is it?" he gasped.

"Ohhh, let's see," I said, drawing the watch from my pocket. "Twenty . . . twenty-*two* minutes past three."

No reply.

"P.M.," I added.

Behind those gray eyes, something began to kindle.

"Mr. Havens," he announced, "I shall have to make good next time."

"Oh, there's always next time, Mr. Poe."

As calmly as he could, he put the leather pot back on his head, rebuckled the yellow-brass bullet buttons, grasped his musket. Easily done: five months of cadet routine had left their stamp on him. Walking, though, this was another thing. He crossed the floor with great care, as though he were stepping over a creek bed, and upon reaching the door, he steadied himself against the lintel and, smiling, said:

"Ladies. Gentlemen. I bid you good day."

Then he flung himself through the open door.

I don't know what drove me after him. I would like to think I had some concern for his welfare, but more likely, he was a story that had not ended. And so I followed . . . hard on his heels . . . and as we passed up the stone steps, I heard a measured tramp of boots, echoing from the south and fast converging on us.

Poe was already running toward the sound. And when he reached the topmost step, he turned and gave me a fractured smile and put a finger to his lips before twining his head round the trunk of an elm tree to see what was coming up the butt road.

There came the familiar rattle of the drum and then, through the frames of the trees, the silhouettes of bodies. It was a double rank of cadets, mounting a long hill and already, by the looks of things, halfway through a day march. Slowly they came, bodies tipped forward, shoulders slumping beneath knapsacks. So exhausted they gave us not a sidelong glance as they passed, but simply threaded by, and only when they were nearly out of sight did Poe set off in pursuit, gradually shrinking the distance between him and them. Fifteen feet . . . ten . . . and at last he was abreast, marching into the very back of the column—tucking himself in as safely as an acorn—and then off he went, over the crest of the hill and into a shower of russet leaves, nothing to separate him from his fellows but his carriage, slightly stiffened, and this, too: a brief farewell flutter of his hand as he disappeared from view.

I watched a few moments longer, not quite willing to break the memory of him. Then I turned back to the tavern, where I arrived just in time to hear the Reverend Lippard say, "I'd have joined the Army myself if I'd known you could drink so regular."

Narrative of Gus Landor

7

October 29th

The next order of business was to interview Leroy Fry's intimates. Lined up, they were, outside the officers' dining rooms—grim young men with lips greased by dinner. As they came in, Hitchcock returned their salutes and said, "Stand at ease," and they clasped their hands behind their backs and pushed out their jaws and if that is "at ease," Reader, you can have it. It took them a minute or two to understand that I would be the one questioning them, and still they kept their eyes fixed on the commandant, and when the interview was finished, they asked, still looking at Hitchcock, "Will that be all, sir?" Yes, the commandant said, and they saluted and stalked out, and in this way, a dozen or so cadets passed in and out of our care in under an hour. After the last of them left, Hitchcock turned to me and said, "I'm afraid we've wasted your time."

"Why is that, Captain?"

"No one knows anything of Fry's last hours. No one saw him leaving barracks. We're right where we began."

"Hm. Would someone mind fetching Mr. Stoddard again?"

Back came Stoddard, wriggling like an alewife. A second classman from South Carolina. Son of a sorghum planter. He had a purple-black mole on his cheek, and he had a record, poor soul: some 120 demerits to his name, and two months still left in the year. He was ripe for dismissal.

"Captain Hitchcock," I said, "if a cadet could give us some insight into

Leroy Fry's last hours, maybe we'd consider, oh, passing over any offenses he *might* have committed?"

After some hesitation, it was so ordered.

"And now, Mr. Stoddard," I said. "I'm wondering if you've told us quite all you can."

No, he hadn't. Seems on the night of October twenty-fifth, this Stoddard had been coming back late from a friend's room. It was a good hour or so after tattoo when he crept up the stairs of North Barracks, only to hear the sound of descending feet. It was Sergeant Locke, he thought, on one of his nighttime rounds. He pressed himself as far into the wall as he could go and listened as the steps drew closer. . . .

He needn't have worried. It was only Leroy Fry.

"And how did you know who it was?" I asked.

Stoddard hadn't, at first. But Fry, as he descended, grazed his elbow against Stoddard's shoulder and then cried, in a sharp voice:

Who's there?

It's me, Leroy.

Julius? Any officers about?

No, all clear.

Fry continued down the steps, and Stoddard, not knowing this was the last time he would see his friend, went straight to bed and slept till reveille.

"Oh, this is most helpful, Mr. Stoddard. And now I wonder what else you might tell us. How did Mr. Fry look, for instance?"

Ah, it had been so very dark in that stairwell he couldn't trust himself to say much on that account.

"Did you see anything else on his person, Mr. Stoddard? A length of rope, something along those lines?"

None that he could see. It'd been dark . . . considerable dark. . . .

No, stop a bit, he said. There *was* something. As Fry was leaving, Stoddard had called after him:

Where are you off to at such an hour?

And this was what Leroy Fry had said:

Necessary business.

A bit of a joke, you see. When cadets have to relieve themselves at night—don't care to leave it in the chamber pot—they hie themselves to the outdoor privies, and if met by an officer, they have only to say, "Necessary business, sir," and they are suffered to pass (though expected back soon). But what stuck with Stoddard in this instance was the weight Fry had laid on the *first* word.

Necessary. Necessary business.

"And what did you take that to mean, Mr. Stoddard?"

He didn't know. Fry was half whispering, so it had all come out a little gaspy.

"He sounded urgent, then?"

Maybe he was urgent. Maybe he was just having a lark.

"So he seemed cheerful to you?"

Cheerful enough, yes. Not like a man who was ready to snuff his own taper. But then you never can say, can you? Stoddard had once had an uncle who one minute was lathering up his face and whistling "Hey, Betty Martin" and next minute was drawing the razor across his throat. Never even finished shaving.

Well, that was all Cadet Julius Stoddard had to tell us. He left us that afternoon with a tinge of regret . . . and a bashful sort of pride, too. I had seen it in the other cadets as well. They were all glad to claim their connection with Leroy Fry. Not because he was great or good, but because he was dead.

Hitchcock watched him go and, without taking his eyes off the door, asked the question that was foremost on his mind.

"How did you know, Mr. Landor?"

"About Stoddard, you mean? His shoulders, I think. I'm sure you've noticed, Captain, when cadets are interviewed in the presence of officers, a certain tension creeps into their bodies. Beyond the normal, I mean."

"I know it well. We call it the examination hunch."

"Well, of course, once the ordeal is over, the shoulders naturally go back to their starting point. Not so with Mr. Stoddard. He left the room just as he entered."

Hitchcock's handsome brown eyes regarded me for a short while. The possibility of a smile played along his lips. Then he said, with almost too much gravity:

"Are there any other cadets to be called back, Mr. Landor?"

"Not *back,* no. But I would enjoy a talk with Cadet Loughborough, if you please."

This took a little more doing. Dinner was done, and Loughborough was in his natural and experimental philosophy section—standing before the blackboard, when the call came like a reprieve from above. It stopped being a reprieve, probably, when he came into that room and saw the commandant, arms folded on the table, and me ... what did he make of *me,* I wonder? He was a short-limbed fellow from Delaware, with dumplings for cheeks and shiny obsidian eyes that looked *in* rather than out.

"Mr. Loughborough," I said. "You were Mr. Fry's roommate, I believe."

"Yes, sir. When we were plebes."

"And you later had a falling out?"

"Oh. Well, as to that, sir, I wouldn't perhaps call it a falling out. More a matter of diverging paths, sir. I think that's closer to the fact of it."

"And what was it made you diverge?"

A crease formed in his brow. "Oh, nothing so ... matter of course, I'd say."

He winced as Captain Hitchcock's voice rang out.

"Mr. Loughborough. If you know of anything pertaining to Mr. Fry, you're bound to disclose it. At once."

I felt for the boy, I admit. If he really was a prattler, as Poe had said, it must have pained him to be at a loss for words.

"It's like this, sir," he said. "Ever since I heard about Cadet Fry, I've been reviewing a certain incident in my mind."

"When did this incident take place?" I asked.

"A long time ago, sir. Two years."

"Not so long. Please go on."

And then he said: "I won't tell, goddamn you."

No, what he said was: "It was an evening in May."

"May of eighteen twenty-eight?"

"Yes, sir. I remember because my sister had just written to tell me she was marrying Gabriel Guild, and the letter got here just a week before the wedding, and I had to reply in care of my uncle down in Dover, for I knew my sister would be stopping there the week *after* her wedding, which was the first week in June—"

"Thank you, Mr. Loughborough." (He had found his wellspring.) "Let's move on to the incident itself, may we? Can you tell us—in brief—what happened on that particular evening?"

He had his task now. His brows bore down on it. "Leroy ran it," he said.

"Where did he go?"

"I don't know, sir. He just told me to cover for him best I could."

"And he came back the next morning?"

"Yes, sir. Though he got hived for missing the reveille roll call."

"And he never told you where he'd gone?"

"No, sir." He glanced briefly at Hitchcock. "But it seemed to me he was a bit on the troubled side afterward."

"Troubled?"

"And I only say *that*, sir, because even though he could be shy on first meeting, it wasn't so hard to get him talking once you got to know him, and *now* he didn't wish to talk at all, which I didn't take too hard except he had trouble even *looking* at me. I kept asking if I'd offended him somehow, but he said no, it wasn't me. I asked him—seeing how we were best pals of a sort—who it *was*."

"He wouldn't tell you."

"That's the long and short of it, sir. But one night, this was sometime in July, he allowed as how . . . he said he'd fallen in with a bad bunch."

Out of the corner of my eye, I saw Hitchcock lean forward in his seat, just the merest inch.

"Bad *bunch*?" I repeated. "Those were the words he used?"

"Yes, sir."

"He didn't tell you the—the *nature* of this bunch."

"No, sir. I told him, of course, if there was anything of an illegal nature going on, he was bound to report it." The second classman smiled at Hitchcock, waiting for a sign of approval, which never came.

"By 'bunch,' did he mean other cadets, Mr. Loughborough?"

"He never said. I guess I assumed it was cadets because who else does a fellow see here? Unless, of course, Leroy got mixed up with some bombardiers, sir."

I'd been at the Point long enough to know that the "bombardiers" were members of the artillery regiment that shares space with the cadet corps. They're regarded by the cadets the way a farmer's pretty daughter regards an old mule: necessary but lacking in glamor. As for the bombardiers, they think the cadets as coddled as any egg.

"So, Mr. Loughborough. Despite all your best efforts, your friend would give you no more on the subject. And over time, the two of you . . . I think *diverged* was the word you used."

"I suppose so, sir. He never wanted to loiter about the room anymore or go for a swim. Even the cadet hops, he stayed away. And then he went and joined the prayer squad for a piece."

Hitchcock's hands were sliding apart: farther, farther.

"Well, that's curious," I said. "He found religion, did he?"

"I wouldn't . . . I mean, I never knew he'd lost it, sir. I don't think he stuck with it too long, though. He was always one to complain about chapel. But by that time, he'd fallen in with a new crowd, and I suppose I was still the old crowd, and that's—that's how it flies, sir."

"And this new crowd? Would you know any of their names?"

Five names, that was as many as he could conjure, and they were all in the group we had just interviewed. And still Loughborough kept throwing out the same names, over and over again, slathering them with lore . . . until Hitchcock raised his hand and asked:

"Why didn't you come forward earlier?"

Caught in midphrase, the young man's lips flapped open. "Well, there it is, sir. I wasn't—I didn't quite see that it had any bearing. Happening so long ago."

"All the same," I said, "we're most obliged, Mr. Loughborough. And if you think of anything else that might be helpful, please don't hesitate."

The second classman nodded to me and saluted to Hitchcock and went to the door. There he stopped.

"Is there anything else?" Hitchcock asked.

We were back to *this* Loughborough, the one who'd first walked into the room. "Sir," he said. "There's a—there's a particular concern, you might say, I've been grappling with. Pertaining to ethics."

"Yes?"

"If a fellow knows his friend is bothered over something, and this friend goes and does something . . . untoward . . . well, then, my dilemma revolves around, should the original fellow feel accountability? Thinking maybe if he'd been a better friend, then the friend in question might still be here, and everything would be, on the whole, better?"

Hitchcock gave his ear a pinch. "I think, Mr. Loughborough, in the hypothetical case you propose, the fellow could enjoy a clear conscience. He did his very best."

"Thank you, sir."

"Is there anything else?"

"No, sir."

Loughborough was almost out the door when Hitchcock's voice went charging after him.

"The next time you present yourself before an officer, Mr. Loughborough, you will take care to button your coatee all the way down. One demerit."

My gentleman's contract with the Academy demanded that I have regular meetings with Hitchcock. On this occasion, Thayer asked if he could also be present.

We gathered in his parlor. Molly brought us johnny cakes and beef dodgers; Thayer poured the tea; the grandfather clock in the hallway ticked away the intervals; the burgundy curtains held the sun off. Horror, Reader.

A full twenty minutes passed before anyone dared to bring up business, and even then it was nothing more than general queries as to my progress. But at precisely thirteen minutes to five, Superintendent Thayer laid his teacup on the table, laced his fingers together in his lap.

"Mr. Landor," he said. "Is it still your belief that Leroy Fry was murdered?"

"It is."

"And are we any closer to knowing the murderer's identity?"

"I'll only know when I'm there."

He gave this some thought. Then, after nibbling a dime-sized hole in a johnny cake, he asked:

"Is it still your belief that the two crimes are linked? The murder and the desecration?"

"Well, as to that, all I'll say is, you can't take out a fellow's heart before he's ready to give it up."

"And that means?"

"Colonel, how likely is it that two different people, on the very same night in October, should have had evil designs on Leroy Fry?"

It was not a question, I could see, that Thayer hadn't already asked himself. But hearing it still had its effect. The grooves round his mouth cut deeper into his skin.

"So," he said, more quietly. "You are acting on the assumption that one man is behind both crimes."

"One man and an accomplice, maybe. But for now, let's just say one. That seems a good place to start."

"And it was merely Mr. Huntoon's intervention that kept this man from removing Leroy Fry's heart on the spot?"

"For now, let's suppose that."

"Having been diverted from his task—please correct me if I go too far—the man thereupon seized his chance to abduct Mr. Fry's body from the hospital, and then proceeded to carry out his original intention?"

"Let's suppose that, too."

"And the man in question. Is he one of us?"

Hitchcock stood abruptly and faced me head on, as if he were making to block my escape.

"What Colonel Thayer and I would like to know," he said, "is whether any others of our cadets may be in danger from this madman."

"And that's the one thing I can't tell you. I'm very sorry."

They took it as well as they could. I had the feeling they almost pitied me for being so ignorant. They poured themselves more tea and busied themselves with questions of a narrower nature. Wanted to know, for instance, what I made of the scrap of paper I'd pried from Leroy Fry's palm. (I told them I was still working it over.) Wanted to know if I'd care to interview faculty members. (Yes, I said, anyone who'd ever taught Leroy Fry.) If I'd be interviewing other cadets. (Yes, anyone who'd ever known Leroy Fry.)

It was a sedate deadly time there in Colonel Thayer's parlor, with the clock puttering along in the background. We were all quiet before long, all except for me, for my heart had begun to shake from its very root. *Thumpeta. Thumpeta.*

"Are you feeling poorly, Mr. Landor?"

I brushed a ring of sweat from my temple. I said:

"Gentlemen, if it's all right, I'd like to beg a favor from you."

"Name it."

They were expecting me, probably, to ask for a cool towel or a draft of air. This was what they heard instead: "I'd like to engage one of your cadets as my assistant."

I knew, as I said it, I was trespassing. Thayer and Hitchcock had been careful, from the start of our relationship, to hold the line between military and civilian. Yet here was I, ready to undo their work, and oh, it roused them. Down went the teacups, up snapped the heads, out came all their calm, good, *reasoned* reasons. . . . I had to clap my hands over my ears to make them stop.

"Please! You don't follow me, gentlemen. There's nothing statutory about this position. I'm looking for someone to be my eyes and ears within the cadet corps. My *agent,* if you like. As far as I'm concerned, the fewer people know about it, the better."

Hitchcock's eyes flared a little as he looked at me. In that gentle voice of his, he asked:

"You're looking for someone to spy on his fellow cadets?"

"To be *our* spy, yes. That won't do too much violence to the Army's honor, will it?"

And still they resisted. Hitchcock gave the utmost attention to his teacup. Thayer kept brushing the same speck of lint from his blue sleeve.

I got up from my seat and strode to the far side of the room.

"Gentlemen," I said, "you've tied my hands. I may not go freely among your cadets, I may not speak to them without your leave, I may not do this and this. Even if I *could,*" I said, raising my hand to Thayer's objection, "even if I *could,* where would it get me? If young men can do nothing else, they can keep secrets. With all due respect, Colonel Thayer, your system *forces* them to keep secrets. Which will only be revealed to one of their own."

Did I really believe that? I don't know. I've found that saying you be-lieve something can, on occasion, pass for the real thing. At the very least, it silenced Thayer and Hitchcock.

And then—slowly—they came round. I don't recall who budged first, but one of them did, just a fraction. I assured them their precious cadet could still go to his recitals and drills, meet all his duties, keep his class standing. I told them he would get grand experience in intelligence gath-ering, which in turn would bode well for his career prospects. Medals, ribbons . . . a whole glorious future. . . .

Yes, they came round. Which is not to say they truly warmed to the idea, but before too long, they were bunting names at each other like cro-quet balls. What of Clay, Junior? What of Du Pont? Kibby was the soul of discretion, Ridgely had a quiet resourcefulness. . . .

In my seat now, with a corncake in my palm, smiling milkily, I leaned toward them.

"And what would you say to Cadet Poe?" I asked.

Their silence I took at first to mean they did not recognize the name. I was wrong.

"Poe?"

The objections were almost too many to consider. Start with this: Poe was a fourth classman who had not yet sat for examinations. Add this: in his short time at the Academy, he had already become a disciplinary prob-lem. (There was a shock.) He had been marked down for missing evening parade, class parade, and guard mounting. He had betrayed, in several in-stances, a spirit of mild insolence. Last month, his name had shown up on a list of top cadet offenders. His current ranking was. . . .

"Seventy-first," said Thayer, promptly. "Among eighty in his class."

That a mere plebe, checkered, untried, should be given preferment over cadets who were his superiors in class, rank, and deportment would set a terrible example . . . a . . . a precedent without precedent. . . .

I heard them out—being military, they rather insisted on that—and then, once they were done, I said, "Gentlemen, let me remind you. This job, by its very nature, cannot go to anyone in the upper ranks. The cadet officers—well, it's widely known they report to *you,* is it not? If *I* had something to hide, believe me, I wouldn't take it to a cadet officer. I'd take it to a—a Poe."

Thayer did a strange thing just then: he plied the corners of his eyes—stretched out the skin to reveal the red membrane beneath.

"Mr. Landor," he said. "This is highly irregular."

"This whole business is a bit irregular, isn't it?" With a touch of roughness, I added, "It was Poe put me onto this Loughborough fellow. He has powers of observation. Which, I allow, are buried in a load of cockalorum. But I'm a good sifter, gentlemen."

To my right, I heard Hitchcock's voice, hushed with amazement. "Do you honestly believe Poe is suited to this?"

"Well, I don't know. But he does show signs of it, yes." Seeing Thayer shake his head, I said: "And if he fails to suit, then I'll take one of your Clays or Du Ponts and call it a bargain."

Hitchcock's hands were tented over his mouth, so that his words, as they came forth, sounded as if they were already being taken back. "Regarded strictly on academic grounds," he said, "Poe *is* rather strong. Even Bérard can't deny he has intellect."

"Nor can Ross," said Thayer, dismal.

"One might also argue that, relative to some of the other plebes, he's not completely immature. His prior service, perhaps, gives him a certain poise."

And so, for the first time that afternoon, I learned something.

"Poe's been in the Army?" I asked.

"He was an enlisted man for three years, I believe, before coming here."

"Well, that takes me aback, gentlemen. He told me he was a poet."

"Oh, he *is*," said Hitchcock, smiling sadly. "I am the beneficiary of two of his volumes."

"Do they have any merit?"

"Some merit, yes. Very little *sense,* or at least none that my poor faculties can make out. I believe he drank too much Shelley at a young age."

"Would that were all he drank," murmured Thayer.

You'll excuse me, Reader, if I paled at this last remark. It was less than twenty-four hours since I'd watched Cadet Poe totter away from Benny

Havens', and it would not have shocked me to learn that Thayer had posted eyeballs on every trunk and vine.

"Well," I said, talking faster, "I'm relieved to know the poet business pans out. He strikes me as the sort who likes making up stories. Just so he may be at the center of something."

"Intriguing stories, too," Hitchcock said. "He has told no fewer than three people that he is the grandson of Benedict Arnold."

I suppose it was the madness of it that caught me in the midsection, sent a laugh spinning through that cool airless sleepy parlor. To make such a claim at West Point—the very place that General Arnold had plotted to hand over to King George—the place he *would* have handed over if Major André hadn't gotten himself arrested—oh, that was beyond gumption.

It was certainly not a claim to endear yourself to Sylvanus Thayer. His lips, I noticed, were unusually thin, and his eyes had gone almost blue with cold as he turned to Hitchcock and said, "You've forgotten Poe's *most* intriguing story. He claims to be a murderer."

There was a rather long pause after that one. I could see Hitchcock shaking his head and grimacing at the floor.

"Well," I said, "you can't believe a tale like that. The young man I met wouldn't—wouldn't take a human—"

"If I believed it," Thayer snapped, "he would no longer be a cadet at the U.S. Military Academy. Of that you may be sure." He picked up his teacup again, drained away the last bitter remnants. "The question, Mr. Landor, is whether *you* believe it." The cup wobbled on his knee and slipped, but Thayer's hand was already sliding forward to catch it. "I suppose," he said, half yawning, "if you're so very keen on using this Poe fellow, you might want to ask him yourself."

Narrative of Gus Landor

8

October 30th

Once all the dust had cleared, the only question left was how best to broach this Poe fellow. Hitchcock liked the idea of dragging him into some cockloft for a clandestine encounter. Me, I inclined toward approaching him in plain view, the better to hide what we were doing. Which was why, on Wednesday morning, Hitchcock and I went as unannounced visitors to Poe's morning sectional, headed by one Claudius Bérard.

Monsieur Bérard was a native Frenchman with a history of evasion. As a young man in the days of Napoleon, he had avoided army duty by the civilized means of hiring a substitute. This had worked out very well until the substitute thoughtlessly took a cannonball in Spain, leaving M. Bérard once again in line for duty. No fool, he picked up and fled overseas, where he made himself into a roving French instructor, first at Dickinson College and then, yes, the United States Military Academy. No matter how far you fly, the army *will* have you. And if that be the case, M. Bérard must have thought, how much nicer to serve out your time in the Hudson Highlands, listening to American youths grind the French language into meal. And yet had this not proved to be a torment as deep as any he had risked back home? M. Bérard had reason, in short, to question himself, and this skeptical note never left him, it formed a moving black speck in the center of his eye even as he remained utterly still.

Now, though, at the sight of his commandant, he jumped straight to his feet, and the cadets likewise rose from their backless benches. Hitchcock waved them back down and motioned me to a pair of seats just inside the door.

Sinking back into his chair, M. Bérard gazed with blue-veined lids at the fourth classman who stood unguarded in the center of the room, squinting into a red-leather quarto.

"Continue, Mr. Plunkett," said the Frenchman.

This unfortunate cadet once more clawed his way through the overbrush of prose: *"He arrived to an inn and put away his horse. He then ate . . . a hearty dinner on bread and . . . poison."*

"Ah, Mr. Plunkett," said the instructor. "That would not be a very palatable meal, even to a cadet. *Poisson* translates as 'fish'."

So corrected, the cadet made ready to resume until he was stopped by M. Bérard's plump white hand.

"Enough. You may be seated. The next time, I entreat you to take greater care with your prepositions. One-point-three is your grade."

Three more cadets broke themselves on the same book, coming away with grades of 2.5, 1.9, and 2.1, respectively. Another pair labored away at the blackboard, conjugating verbs to similar effect. No one spoke a word of French. Their whole end in learning the tongue was to translate military texts, and many a lad must have asked himself why he was wasting his time with bread and poison when he might instead be taking down Jomini's theories on terrain. It was left to M. Bérard to make the case for Voltaire and Lesage, and he was too weary. Only once, ten minutes before the end of the recital, did he see fit to rouse himself. Which is to say, he pressed his hands together and inflected his voice ever so slightly upward.

"Mr. Poe, please."

From the far side of the room, a head jerked to attention; a body sprang forth.

"Mr. Poe. Would you please translate the following passage from Chapter Two of *Histoire de Gil Blas*?"

Three paces brought the cadet to the center of the room. Fronted by Bérard, flanked by his peers, watched by the commandant: he was on the spot, and he knew it. Opening the book, he cleared his throat—twice—and began.

"*While they were preparing my eggs, I joined in conversation with the land-lady, whom I had never seen before. She struck me as pretty enough. . . .*"

Two things were clear right away. First, he knew more French than the others. And second, he wanted to make *this* rendition of *Gil Blas* linger for generations unborn.

"*He came up to me with a friendly air: 'I have just heard that you are'* . . . oh, shall we say, '*the* eminent *Gil Blas of Santillane, the ornament of Oviedo and the torch*'—sorry, '*the leading light of philosophy*'."

I was so caught up in the performance—the jab of the jaw, the slicing motion of the hands—that I was slow to notice the change in Bérard's face. He was smiling, yes, but his eyes had a feline hardness that made me think a trap had been sprung. And soon I had all the confirmation I needed, as the first titters came leaking from the seated cadets.

" '*Is it indeed possible that you*'—by which he means the other people in the room, I expect—'*that* all *of you behold this* genius, *this master wit whose reputation is so great throughout the land? Don't you know,*' he went on, addressing himself to the landlord and landlady, '*don't you know what you* possess *here?*'"

The titters grew in volume. The looks grew bolder.

"'*Why, your house harbors a veritable* treasure!'"

One cadet elbowed his neighbor. Another jammed his forearm into his mouth.

"'*You behold in this gentleman the eighth wonder of the world!*'"

Gasps and chortles, and still Poe bore on, his voice rising to match the voices around him.

"*Then, turning himself toward me and throwing his arms about me: 'Pardon these transports,' added he; 'I can never hope to master the*'—"

And at last he did pause, but only to hurl himself full bore on those final words:

"—'*the absolute joy your presence causes me!*'"

Bérard sat there softly smiling as the cadets squealed and howled. They might have torn the Academy's roof right off had they not been stopped by the clearing of Captain Hitchcock's throat. One unit of sound, barely loud enough to reach my ears, and the room went quiet.

"Thank you, Mr. Poe," said Bérard. "As usual, you have gone beyond the demands of literal translation. I suggest in the future you leave the embellishments to Mr. Smollett. However, you have nicely captured the sense of the passage. Two-point-seven is your grade."

Poe said nothing. Didn't move. Just stood there, in the center of the room, with his eyes flaming and his jaw angled out.

"You may be seated, Mr. Poe."

Only then did he return to his seat—slowly, stiffly—without looking at another soul.

A minute later, the drums were beating assembly for dinner formation. Up stood the cadets, pushing away their slates and clapping on their shakos. Hitchcock waited until they were filing through the open doorway before calling out:

"Mr. Poe, if you would."

Poe stopped so quickly that the cadet behind him had to spin clear to avoid colliding with him.

"Sir?" He squinted us into his sights. His hands, glazed with chalk, danced across his leather visor.

"If we might speak to you, please."

He set his mouth in a tight line and came toward us, wheeling his head just as the last of his classmates marched out.

"You may sit, Mr. Poe."

Hitchcock's voice, I noticed, was even softer than usual as he motioned the cadet to his bench. You can't be too rough, I guess, on someone who's given you two editions of his poetry.

"Mr. Landor here would like a few minutes of your time," said the commandant. "We have already excused you from dinner formation, so you may come to mess when you're ready. Do you require anything else, Mr. Landor?"

"No, thank you."

"Then, gentlemen, I will bid you good day."

This I hadn't expected: Hitchcock taking himself out of the picture, and Bérard following him, leaving just the two of us in this small, sawdusty room. Sitting on our benches and staring staight ahead, like Quakers at meeting.

"That was a brave performance," I said at last.

"Brave?" he answered. "I was merely doing as Monsieur Bérard requested."

"I'd bet good money that you've read *Gil Blas* before."

It was only from the corner of one eye, but I could see his mouth slowly lengthening.

"You're amused, Mr. Poe."

"I'm only thinking of my father."

"The senior Poe?"

"The senior *Allan*," he said. "A purely mercantile beast. He came upon me—oh, it was some years ago—reading *Gil Blas* in his parlor. Demanded to know why I would waste my time on such rubbish. And here we are. . . ." He extended his arm to take in the whole room. "In the land of engineers, where Gil Blas is king." Smiling briefly, he rattled his thin fingers. "Of course, Smollett's translation has its charms, but he does gild the lily, doesn't he? If I have time this winter, I shall write up my own version. The first copy will go to Mr. Allan."

I pulled out a quid of tobacco and popped it in my mouth. The sweet spicy juice burst off the lining of my cheeks, sent a tingle through my back teeth.

"If any of your classmates asks you," I said, "you'll kindly tell them this was a routine interview. We did nothing more than discuss your acquaintance with Leroy Fry."

"There was no acquaintance," he said. "I never knew him."

"Then I was sadly misled. We had a fine laugh over it and parted on good terms."

"If this is not an interview, what is it?"

"An offer. Of employment."

He looked me square in the face. Said nothing.

"Before I go on," I said, "I'm to inform you—let me see—that 'this position is contingent on the satisfactory execution of your duties as a cadet.' Oh, and 'should you fail or waver in these duties at any time, the position will cease to be yours.'" I glanced over at him before adding, "That is what Colonel Thayer and Captain Hitchcock would have you know."

The names had their intended effect. I would guess that most plebes—

even this one, with his large claims on the world—think themselves beneath the notice of their superiors. The moment they learn otherwise is the moment they begin striving to be worthy of that notice.

"There's no pay," I went on. "You'll need to know that. You won't be able to boast about it. None of your classmates may ever know what you're doing until long after you're done with it. And if they do find out, they're likely to curse your name."

He gave me a lazy smile. His gray eyes glistened. "An irresistible offer, Mr. Landor. Please tell me more."

"Mr. Poe, when I was a constable in New York City, not so long ago, I relied more than I care to say on *news*. Not the kind that comes from newspapers, but the kind that comes from people. Now, the people who brought this news were almost never what you'd call well bred. You wouldn't have them over to dinner or go to concerts with them, or indeed be seen *anywhere* in public with them. Out-and-out criminals, mostly—thieves, fences, scratchers. For two bits, they'd auction off their children and sell their mothers—invent mothers they didn't have. And I don't know of a single policeman who could have done his job without them."

Poe's head was bowed over his hands as the import of this worked its way through. Then, sounding each syllable very slowly, as though he were waiting for its echo, he said:

"You wish me to be an informer."

"An *observer*, Mr. Poe. In other words, I wish you to be what you already are."

"And what is it I am to observe?"

"I can't tell you."

"Why not?"

"Because I don't yet know myself," I said.

I jumped up then—made straight for the blackboard.

"Would you mind, Mr. Poe, if I told you a story? When I was a boy, my father took me to a midnight camp meeting in Indiana. He was gathering some news of his own. We saw these beautiful young women sobbing and groaning, shrieking themselves blue in the face. What a noise! The preacher—fine upstanding gentleman—got them so worked up that after a while they fainted dead on their feet. One after another, like dead trees.

I remember thinking how lucky they had people ready to catch them, because they never looked to see where they were falling. All except one: *she* was different. Her head ... *turned* a little just before she dropped. She wanted to be sure, you see, who would catch her. And who was the lucky fellow? Why, the preacher himself! Welcoming her into the kingdom of God."

I passed my hand along the blackboard, felt its rasp against my palm.

"Six months later," I said, "the preacher ran off with her. After first taking care to kill his wife. He didn't want to be a bigamist, you see. They were caught just a few miles south of the Canadian border. No one had any inkling they were lovers. No one but *me*, I suppose, and even I didn't ... I didn't *know* it, I only saw it. Before I knew what I was seeing."

I turned back and found him studying me with the driest of smiles.

"And in that moment," said Poe, "a vocation was born."

It was a curious fact. Other cadets, when I spoke to them in private, would hold me in roughly the same awe as they did the commandant. Poe never did. There was, from the start of our relations, something ... I won't call it familiar—*familial*, maybe.

"Let me ask you," I said. "When you marched back into the ranks the other day ..."

"Yes?"

"That gentleman at the very end of the column, marching alone. He's your friend—your roommate, maybe?"

A longish pause.

"He is my roommate," said Poe, guardedly.

"I thought as much. He *turned* his head, you see, as you came into line. But he never flinched. I took this to mean he was expecting you. Is he a friend, Mr. Poe? Or a debtor?"

Poe tilted his head back and gazed at the ceiling.

"He is both," he answered, sighing. "I write his letters for him."

"His letters?"

"Jared has an inamorata, back in the wastes of North Carolina. They are engaged to be married upon his graduation. Her very existence is enough to earn him dismissal."

"Why do you write his letters, then?"

"Oh, he's half literate at best. Wouldn't know an indirect object if it crawled up his nose. What he does have, Mr. Landor, is a neat hand. I merely hash out some *billets-doux*, and he transcribes them."

"And she thinks they're his?"

"I'm always careful to throw in the—the awkward phrase—the rustic misspelling. I consider it an adventure in style."

I sat myself down on the bench directly across from him.

"Well, there you are, Mr. Poe. I've learned something very interesting today. And all because I happened to catch a fellow turning his head. Just as *you* caught Cadet Loughborough missing his steps in parade."

He snorted, stared at his boots. Said, half to himself, "Set a cadet to catch a cadet."

"Well, now, we don't yet know it *is* a cadet. But it would be a great help to have someone on the inside. And I can't just now think of anyone better than you. Or anyone who would more enjoy the *challenge* of it."

"And that would be the extent of my mission? Observing?"

"Well, as we go on, we'll know better what we're looking for, and you can train your eyes accordingly. In the meantime, I've got something for you to look at. It's a fragment of a larger note. I'd like you to try your hand at deciphering it. Naturally," I added, "you'll have to work as secretly as you can. And be as precise as you can. You can never be too precise."

"I see."

"Precision is all."

"I see."

"And *now*, Mr. Poe. This is the part of our talk where you say yes or no."

He rose, for the first time since our conversation began. Went to the window and stood looking out. I won't presume to say what feelings vied inside him, but I will say this: he knew that the longer he stayed there, the more intense the effect would be.

"It will be yes," he said finally.

There was a lopsided smile on his face when he turned back to me.

"I would be perversely honored, Mr. Landor, to be your spy."

"And being your spy*master*," I said. "No less an honor, I'm sure."

By mutual consent, we shook hands. It was as formal as we would ever again be with each other. We jerked our hands away as though we had already breached some code.

"Well," I said, "I suppose you'll be off to dinner now. Why don't we plan on meeting Sunday after chapel? Do you think you could find your way to Mr. Cozzens' hotel without anyone seeing you?"

He nodded, twice, and then, without another word, made ready to go. Shook the starch back into his coatee. Put the leather pot on his head. Marched toward the door.

"May I ask you something, Mr. Poe?"

He took a step back. "Of course."

"Is it true you're a murderer?"

His face erupted then into the gaudiest smile I think I have ever seen. Imagine, Reader, a chorus line of lovely jewel-teeth, all dancing in their sockets.

"You'll have to be much more *precise* than that, Mr. Landor."

Letter from Gus Landor to
Henry Kirke Reid

October 30th, 1830

c/o Reid Inquiries, Ltd.
712 Gracie Street
New York, New York

Dear Henry,

It's been forever since you've heard from me. I am sorry. Ever since we came to Buttermilk Falls, I've been meaning to get back for a visit, but days pass, boats come and go, Landor stays. Some other time, maybe.

In the meantime, I have a job for you. Don't worry, I mean to pay you well, and as time is of the essence, I mean to pay you a little better than well.

Should you be willing, your task is to learn all you can about one Edgar A. Poe. Late of Richmond. He is at present a fourth classman at the U.S. Military Academy. Prior to that, he served in the Army. He has also published two volumes of poetry, not that anyone knew. Beyond that, I have only the sketchiest notions of him. I wish you to find out—everything— family history, upbringing, past employments, present entanglements. If he's made a dent anywhere in the world, I'd have you find it.

I need also to know if he has ever been charged with a crime. Murder, for example.

As I said, this is pressing business. If you can forward me all your findings by the close of four weeks, I will be your eternal servant and will vouch for you at the gates of Heaven. (No use vouching for me.)

As always, bill me for any expenses.

And remember me to Rachel! Also, when you write back, tell me all about this omnibus creature that is now menacing the city streets. I have heard only bits and pieces, but I understand it is the end of cabs and civilization. Please reassure me. I could do without civilization but never cabs.

Yours,
    Gus Landor

Letter to Gus Landor

October 30th, 1830

Dear Mr. Landor,

　　I am leaving this letter for you at your hotel in advance of our next meeting.

　　Your insistence on precision—in all things!—has inspired me to resurrect a sonnet of mine which you may find to the point. (Never forgetting, of course, that you do not "get round" to poetry—yes, I do remember.)

> Science! true daughter of Old Time thou art!
> 　　Who alterest all things with thy peering eyes.
> Why preyest thou thus upon the poet's heart,
> 　　Vulture, whose wings are dull realities?
> How should he love thee? or how deem thee wise?
> 　　Who wouldst not leave him in his wandering
> To seek for treasure in the jeweled skies,
> 　　Albeit he soared with an undaunted wing?
> Hast thou not dragged Diana from her car?
> 　　And driven the Hamadryad from the wood
> To seek a shelter in some happier star?
> 　　Hast thou not torn the Naiad from her flood,
> The Elfin from the green grass, and from me
> The summer dream beneath the tamarind tree?

I often have recourse to recall these lines when I am being suffocated by spherical geometry and La Croix' algebra. (Had I it to do over again, I might substitute a past participial adjective for the green *of the penultimate line.* Gor'd? Gull'd?)

A word of warning, Mr. Landor: I have a new composition to show you—as yet unfinished. I think you will "get round" it and will deem it of no small relevance to our investigations.

Your faithful servant,
E.P.

Letter to Edgar A. Poe, Cadet Fourth Classman

October 31st, 1830

Mr. Poe:

I read your poem with the greatest enjoyment and—I hope you'll excuse me—bewilderment. I'm afraid all that Naiad and Hamadryad business is far beyond my ken. How I wish my daughter were here to translate for me, as she was herself a thoroughgoing Romantic and knew Milton backwards and every which way.

I hope my dimness will not discourage you from sending along more verse, whether or not it pertains to the matters at hand. I suspect I want improvement as much as the next fellow and don't really bother about who is doing the improving.

And as for Science, I pray you won't confuse anything I do with Science.

Yours,

G.L.

p.s. A friendly reminder: we're to meet at my hotel on Sunday afternoon, following chapel. I am in Room 12.

From the "Items" Column
Poughkeepsie Journal

October 31st, 1830

School for Young Ladies.—Mrs. E. H. Putnam continues her school at 20 White Street from the 30th of August. The number of pupils in English Studies is limited to 30, who are wholly under Mrs. P.'s own instruction. Lessons in French, Music, Drawing, and Penmanship, by Teachers of first respectability.

Horrid Affair.—A cow and a sheep belonging to Mr. Elias Humphreys, of Haverstraw, were discovered Friday in a terrible condition. The animals had been dispatched by means of a slash across the throat. Mr. Humphreys also reports that the animals had been most cruelly carved open, and from each, the heart removed. No trace of those organs remained. The villain responsible for these assaults cannot be identified. Word has reached this journal of similar reports pertaining to a cow in the possession of Mr. Joseph L. Roy, a neighbor of Mr. Humphreys. These reports could not be corroborated.

Canal Tolls.—The tolls collected on the state canals up to the 1st of September amount to $514,000; being about $100,000 more than were collected . . .

Narrative of Gus Landor

9

October 31st

"Cattle and sheep!" cried Captain Hitchcock, brandishing the newspaper like a cutlass. "*Livestock* are now being sacrificed. Can we consider any of God's creatures immune from this madman?"

"Well," I said. "Better cows than cadets."

I could see his nostrils flaring like a bull's—I knew again what it was to be a cadet.

"I beg you, Captain, please don't get yourself in a stew. We don't yet know this is the same man."

"It would be an extraordinary coincidence if it were not."

"Well, then," I said, "we can at least take comfort knowing he's moved his attentions away from the Point."

Frowning, Hitchcock ran his finger along the quill of his dress sword. "Haverstraw is not so very far from here," he said. "A cadet might reach it in upwards of an hour—a good deal less, if he managed to wangle a horse."

"You're right," I said. "A cadet could certainly cover the distance." And maybe I really *did* mean to provoke this good soldier and fine American, for why else would I have thought to add, "Or an officer?"

All I got for my pains was a steely look and a shake of the head. Followed by a brisk interrogation. Had I inspected the icehouse? Yes, I had. What had I found there? A great deal of ice. What else? No heart, no clues of any sort.

Very well, then, had I spoken with the Academy instructors? Yes, I had. What had they told me? They'd apprised me of Leroy Fry's grades in mineralogy and mensuration, and they had wished me to know he was fond of hickory chips. And they could have filled caverns with all their theories. Lieutenant Kinsley had advised me to look into the position of the stars. Professor Church had wondered if I'd heard about some of the extreme Druidical practices. Captain Aeneas MacKay, the quartermaster, had assured me that heart stealing was a coming-of-age ritual in certain Seminole tribes (such as still existed).

Hitchcock drew it all in through his hard-pursed lips, then blew it out in a slow hiss.

"I don't mind telling you, Mr. Landor, I am more uneasy than ever before. A young man, and a pair of dumb beasts. There must be a connection between them, and yet I can find none. I can't, for the life of me, see what one man could want with all these—"

"All these *hearts*," I said. "You're right, it's a curious thing. Now, my friend Poe there, he thinks it's the work of a poet."

"Then perhaps," said Hitchcock, giving his coat sleeves a hard brush, "we should heed the counsel of Plato and banish all poets from our society. Starting with your Mr. Poe."

That particular Sunday was cool and boundless. I remember I was sitting alone in my hotel room; the sash was up, and if I tipped my head, I could see all the way up to Newburgh and, farther still, the Shawangunk Mountains. The clouds were frayed like collars, and the sun had laid down an aisle of glitter along the Hudson, and flaws of wind shuddered down from the gullies, stamping pinwheels on the water's belly.

And there! Right on time: the North River steamer, the *Palisado*, four hours out of New York City and just drawing in to the West Point landing. Round every deck the passengers crowded, more intimate than lovers, leaning over balustrades and crouching under awnings. Pink hats and robin's-egg-blue parasols and ostrich feathers of the deepest purple—God himself couldn't have matched it for color.

A whistle sounded, and the steam blew up in a shroud as the roustabouts took their places along the gangplanks, and I could see, fluttering like an aspen leaf, a tiny skiff—weighed down by bodies and luggage—being lowered to the water. More tourists bent on swarming into Sylvanus Thayer's kingdom. I leaned toward them, trying to fix them in my sights . . .

Only to find them peering back at *me*.

Their faces were tilted upward, yes, their opera glasses and binoculars were trained on *my* window. I rose from my chair and stepped back . . . back . . . until they had nearly dropped from view, and still I could feel them chasing me into the room, and I was all set to slam down the sash and close the shutters after it when I caught sight of a hand—a single human hand—clawing its way onto the lintel.

I didn't cry out. It's doubtful I even budged. The only feeling I recall is a bare curiosity, of the sort I suppose an infantryman must feel as he contemplates the cannonball that is about to meet his head. I stood there in the center of the room and watched as another hand—the twin of the first—seized the lintel. I heard a small deep molish grunt, and I waited, scarcely breathing, as an upside-down leather pot, slightly askew, pushed its way into the window frame. Followed by a damp fringe of black hair and two large gray eyes, staring and straining, and two nostrils dilated with effort. And oh, yes, two lovely rows of teeth, gritting hard.

Cadet Fourth Classman Poe, at my service.

Without a word, he hauled his torso through the open window . . . paused there a bit to catch his breath . . . and then dragged his legs after him, crawling forward on his arms until he landed in a heap on the floor. At once, he sprang to his feet, lifted his hat to give his hair a swipe, and once again proffered me that European bow.

"My apologies for being late," he said, panting. "I hope I haven't kept you too long."

I stared at him.

"Our meeting," he said. "Directly after chapel, as you suggested."

I went to the window and looked down. It was a three-story drop—followed by a hundred-foot incline—ending in rocks and river.

"You fool," I said. "You damned fool."

"It was you who insisted I come in daylight hours, Mr. Landor. How else was I to escape notice?"

"Escape notice?" I slammed the sash down. "You don't think every last soul on that steamer noticed you? Crawling up a *hotel*? I wouldn't be surprised if an Army guard's already been dispatched."

I strode to the door and actually *waited* there, as though at any second the bombardiers must come storming through. And when they didn't, I could feel (with some disappointment) my anger falling away in tatters. The best I could do was mutter:

"You might have been killed."

"Oh, the drop's not so bad as all that," he said, all business now. "And at the risk of exalting myself, Mr. Landor, I must tell you that I'm an excellent swimmer. When I was fifteen, I swam seven miles and a half in the James River, under a hot June sun and against a tide of three miles per hour. Next to that, Byron's little paddle across the Hellespont was child's play."

Wiping his brow, he sank into the spindle-backed rocking chair by the window and sat there yanking on his fingers, one by one, until the knuckles cracked—not unlike the sound Leroy Fry's digits made when I broke them.

"Please tell me," I said, lowering myself onto the end of the bed. "How did you know which room was mine?"

"I saw you from below. Needless to say, I tried to catch your eye, but you were too engrossed. At any rate, I am pleased to report that I have successfully decoded your message."

Reaching inside his coat, he drew out the scrap of paper, still stiff from its alcohol bath. Carefully unfolding it, he spread it across the bed and, kneeling on his haunches, ran his index finger along the rows of letters.

NG

HEIR A

T BE L

ME S

"Shall I begin by limning the stages of my deductive labors for you, Mr. Landor?" He didn't wait for a yes. "We begin with the note itself. What may we say of it? Being handwritten, it is patently of a personal nature. Leroy Fry had it with him at the time of his death; from that we may presume this note was sufficient to draw him from his barracks on the night in question. Given that the rest of the message was torn from his hand, we may presume that the note in some way *identified* its sender. The use of rather primitive block capitals would also indicate that the sender wished to disguise his identity. What are we to infer from these points? Might this note have been an invitation of sorts? Or might we more accurately call it a trap?"

He paused just a bit before that last word. Enough to make it obvious how much he was enjoying this.

"With that in mind," he continued, "we concentrate our labors on the *third* line of our mysterious fragment. We are rewarded here with the one word that we know, for a fact, is complete: *be*. The English lexicography harbors few simpler or more declarative words, Mr. Landor. *Be*. This immediately places us, I conceive, in the terrain of imperatives. The sender would bid Leroy Fry *be* something. 'Be' what? Something that begins with an *l*. 'Little?' 'Lucky?' 'Lascivious?' None of these gibes with the nature of an invitation. 'Be *lost*?' Too ungainly a construction. Surely one *gets* lost, one loses one's *way*. No, if in fact Leroy Fry's attendance was desired at a particular time and place, there is but one word that can suffice: *late*."

He held out his hand, as though the letters were resting in his palm.

"Two words, then, Mr. Landor: *be late*. A bizarre request to affix to any invitation. *Late* was the last thing our sender should have wished Leroy Fry to be. Ergo, as we scan this third line, we can only conclude that we are in the midst of a negative construction. And with that, the identity of that first word becomes almost insultingly simple to deduce: *don't*. *Don't be late*."

He stood now and began pacing round the bed.

"Time, in short, is of the essence. And what better way to make that clear than with the fourth and, as far as we know, final line? A reinforcement of that earlier message. Begin with this enigmatic *me*. Is it a word unto itself, in the manner of the aforementioned *be*? Or is it, as I believe its position indicates, the latter portion of a larger word? Assuming the second case, we need not journey far to find a suitable candidate. Leroy Fry might be *going* to this predetermined location, but to the sender, Fry was—do you anticipate me, Mr. Landor?—he was *coming*." He extended his hand in a beckoning motion. "*Come*, Mr. Fry. With that in place, it is the height of simplicity to deduce the next word. Can it be any other than *soon*? We insert the word, *et voilà!* Our little message reveals itself at last: *Don't be late, come soon*. Or even, depending on the degree of urgency, *come soonest*."

He clapped his hands together and bowed his head. "And there you have it, Mr. Landor. The solution to our *petit énigme*. Respectfully submitted."

He was expecting something—applause, maybe. A gratuity? a blast of cannon? All I did was pick up the scrap of paper and smile.

"Oh, this is first-rate work, Mr. Poe. Absolutely first-rate. I do thank you."

"And I thank *you*," he said, "for offering me such a pleasing diversion." Easing himself back into the rocker, he planted one of his boots on the windowsill. "However short-lived," he added.

"No, it was *my* pleasure. *Truly*, it was my . . . oh, there's just one thing, Mr. Poe."

"Yes?"

"Did you have any luck with the *first* two lines?"

He gave me a wave of his hand. "No getting anywhere with those," he said. "The first line contains but two letters. As for the second, the only possible choice is *their*. A word begging for an antecedent, which sadly is lost to us. I was forced to declare the first two lines a loss, Mr. Landor."

"Hmm." I went to the bedside table and pulled out a stack of cream-colored paper and a pen. "I wonder, Mr. Poe, are you a good speller?"

He raised himself up a little. "I was judged a flawless speller by no less an authority than the Reverend John Bransby of Stoke Newington."

You see? No simple yeses or nos with him. Everything had to be freighted down with allusions, appeals to authority . . . and what authority was this? John Bransby? Stoke Newington?

"So I take it you've never done what so many of us do," I said.

"And that is . . . ?"

"Confuse the spelling of similar-sounding words. By which I mean, for example, *their*," I said, writing out the word so he could see it. "And *they're* . . . oh, and *there*."

He bent his face over the paper, then shrugged.

"An abysmally common solecism, Mr. Landor. My roommate commits it ten times a day—or *would* if he wrote his own letters."

"Well, then, what if our note-writer were, say, more like your roommate and less like *you*? What might we have then?" I crossed out *their* and circled *there*. "An invitation indeed, eh, Mr. Poe? Meet me *there*. Oh, but we run up against another word, don't we? Beginning with an *a*."

Squinting down again, he ran the letter along his lips. A few more seconds before he said, in a tone of wonder:

"*At*."

"*At*, of course! Why, I wouldn't be surprised if there had been a time following hard on: *Meet me there at eleven P.M.*, something of that sort, That would be direct enough, wouldn't it? But, now if our sender did set a specific time, I'm not sure he'd be asking Fry in that fourth line to *come soon*. Bit of a contradiction, isn't it? Maybe *Come see me* would be closer to the mark."

Poe gazed dully at the paper. Quiet he was.

"There's only one problem," I said. "We still don't know *where* they were to meet, do we? And all we have to go on is those two letters, *n* and *g*. Now the curious thing about that letter combination—as I'm sure you've noticed, Mr. Poe—is that it turns up quite often at the *ends* of words. I wonder, can you think of any place on the Academy grounds that might have an *ng* trailing behind?"

He looked out the window, as though the answer might be framed there—and found that it was.

"The *landing*," he answered.

"The landing! Now that, Mr. Poe, is an excellent choice. *I'll meet you at the landing*. Oh, but there are two landings, aren't there? Both guarded by the Second Artillery, as I understand it. Not much in the way of privacy, eh?"

He gave that some thought. Looked at me once or twice before venturing to speak again.

"There's a cove," he said at last. "Not too far from the North Landing. It's where Mr. Havens brings his wares."

"Where—where *Patsy* brings them, you mean. Ah, then it must be a rather secluded sort of place. Would it be known to your fellow cadets?"

He shrugged. "Anyone who's ever smuggled in beer or whiskey knows about it."

"Well, then, we have—for now—a solution to our little puzzle. *I'll be at the cove by the landing. Meet me there at eleven P.M. Don't be late. Come see me.* Yes, that'll do quite nicely for the time being. Leroy Fry receives this invitation. He finds himself obliged to accept. And if we're to believe Mr. Stoddard's testimony, he accepts it with a light heart. We might even believe he was *glad* to accept this invitation. 'Necessary business,' he says, winking in the dark. Does that suggest anything to you, Mr. Poe?"

Something curved around his lips; one of his eyebrows went up like a kite.

"To me," he said, "it suggests a woman."

"Ah. A woman, yes. That's an awfully interesting theory. And of course, with the letter being written as it was—in block capitals, as you say—there'd be no good way of knowing the sender's sex, would there? So Leroy Fry may well have set off that evening believing that a woman was awaiting him at the cove by the landing. And for all we know, a woman *was* waiting." Lowering myself onto the bed, I propped a pillow behind me and leaned back against the headboard. I stared at my scuffed boots. "Well," I said, "that's a problem for another day. In the meantime, Mr. Poe, I can't . . . I mean to say, I'm so grateful for your assistance."

If I was expecting him to accept my thanks and quietly leave . . . well, I don't think I ever expected that.

"You *knew*," he said, quietly.

"Knew what, Mr. Poe?"

"The solution to the puzzle. You knew it all along."

"I had an idea, that's all."

He was silent for a long while, and I wondered then if I'd lost him for good. He might bridle at the notion of someone's getting the better of him. He might accuse me of using him for sport (and weren't you, Landor?). Might even sever the tie altogether.

In fact, he did none of those things. His climbing had taxed him more than he let on, and he stayed quite still in his rocker, never once even rocking—and when I sent remarks his way, he answered them simply, with no ill will or need to embroider. We passed an hour in this way, saying very little at first and then, as he got his strength back, talking more and more of Leroy Fry.

I've always regretted that the people most likely to tell you about a dead man are the people who knew him least—that is, the ones who knew him in the last months of his life. To unlock a man's secrets, I've always thought, you must go back to that day when he was six and wet his pantaloons in front of the schoolmistress, or to the first time his hand found its way to his nether parts . . . the small shames driving us on to the big ones.

At any rate, the only thing Leroy Fry's cadet friends could agree on was that he was quiet and had to be drawn out. I told Poe what Loughborough had said about Fry's falling in with his "bad bunch" and then seeking the comforts of religion, and we asked ourselves what sort of comfort he might have been seeking on the night of October the twenty-fifth.

And then our talk turned to other matters . . . sundry topics . . . I couldn't tell you what they were because at around two in the afternoon, I fell asleep. Strangest thing. One minute I was talking—a bit lazy in the head, but talking. Next minute I was sitting in a dusky room—a place I'd never been before. A bat or a bird fluttered behind the curtains; a woman's petticoat grazed my arm. The air was frigid on my knuckles, and something was pricking my nostrils, and a vine was swinging from the ceiling, grazing the bald space on my head, and it had the feel of fingers.

I woke with a gulp of air . . . to find him still watching me. Cadet Fourth Classman Poe, at my service. A look of biding he had, as though I'd been in the middle of a joke or a story.

"Very sorry," I mumbled.

"Not at all."

"Don't know what . . ."

"Never fear, Mr. Landor, I myself must be contented with no more than four hours of sleep a night. The consequences have on occasion been dire. One night, I fell dead asleep during guard duty and remained for a whole hour in a somnambulistic trance, during which I evidently came within a whisker of firing on another cadet."

"Well," I said, standing. "Before I start firing on cadets myself, I should be getting on. I want to get home before nightfall."

"I'd like to see it sometime. Your home."

He spoke lightly and never once looked at me. As though to say whether or not I honored his request was a matter of huge indifference to him.

"It would give me the greatest pleasure," I said, watching him brighten.

"And now, Mr. Poe, if you would please leave by the door and then by the *stairs*, you would spare an old man a great deal of unnecessary worry."

He rocked himself out of the chair, then drew himself up in stages. "Not so very old," he said.

And now it was my turn to brighten: the faintest flush in my cheeks. Who could have guessed I'd be so easy to flatter?

"You're very kind, I'm sure, Mr. Poe."

"Not at all."

I expected him to leave then, but he had other ideas in mind. Once more he reached into his coat. Once more he drew out a piece of paper—a more elegant specimen, folded once—which he opened to reveal a fine regular cursive. He could barely suppress the tremor in his voice as he said, "If it is indeed a woman we seek, Mr. Landor, I believe I may be credited with a sighting of her."

"Is that so?"

It was, I would soon learn, one of his tics, the way his voice dropped in volume as he became more excited, lowering to a buzzing, crackling mutter, veiled and not always intelligible. On this particular occasion, though, I heard every word.

"The morning after Leroy Fry's death," he said, "before I knew anything of what had passed, I awoke and at once began inditing the opening lines of a poem—lines that speak of a mysterious woman and an obscure but profound distress. Here you see the result."

I admit I resisted at first. I had read enough of his poetry by now to consider myself immune to it. It came down to this, I suppose: he insisted. And so I took the paper from his hands, and I read:

> 'Mid the groves of Circassian splendor,
>> In a brook darkly dappled with sky,
>> In a moon-shattered brook raked with sky,
> Athene's lissome maidens did render
>> Obeisances lisping and shy.
> There I found Leonore, lorn and tender,
>> In the clutch of a cloud-rending cry.
> Harrowed hard, I could aught but surrender

> *To the maid with the pale blue eye*
> *To the ghoul with the pale blue eye.*

"Of course, it's unfinished," he said. "For the time being."

"I see." I handed the paper back to him. "And why do you believe this poem is connected with Leroy Fry?"

"The air of concealed violence, the—the suggestion of unspeakable duress. An unknown woman. The *timing* of the thing, Mr. Landor, that can surely be no accident."

"But you might have woken up any morning and written this."

"Ah yes, but *I* didn't write it."

"I thought you—"

"What I mean to say is that it was *dictated*."

"By who?"

"My mother."

"Well, then," I said, a current of laughter bubbling in my voice. "By all means, let's ask your mother up. I'm sure she'll be able to shed no end of light on Leroy Fry's death."

I will always remember the look he gave me then. A look of the deepest surprise, as if I'd forgotten something that should have been as known to me as my own name.

"She's dead, Mr. Landor. Dead nearly seventeen years."

Narrative of Gus Landor

10

November 1st

"No, over here . . . that's right . . . a little more . . . oh, that's fine, Gus. . . . Mmm. . . ."

When it comes to the female mystery, there's nothing like a measure of instruction. I was married for some twenty years to a woman who gave me little more in that regard than a smile. Which was, of course, all a man needed in those days. Patsy, by contrast—well, she makes me feel, at the age of forty-eight, a bit like those cadets who are forever mooning after her. Takes me by the hand. Straddles me as straightforwardly as a teamster mounts his mule and draws me in entire. There's something tidal in her motion—it has that feeling, I mean, of something that's been going on forever. And at the same time, she's so terrestrial in person—a big girl with sprouts of black hair on her arms, strong haunches—heavy in the breast and hips, short in the leg—you can wrap your hand round her and feel, for a moment, that this thigh, this soft floury belly are *yours* and can't be taken away. Only, I would say, in her eyes, which are large and the color of butterscotch and lovely, only there is anything held apart.

Reader, I confess it now: Patsy was the reason I was so eager to leave Poe behind that Sunday. She and I were to meet back at my cottage at six, and she was to stay or leave, depending on how she felt. That night she felt like staying. When I woke, though, around three in the morning, there was no one on the other side of the bed. I lay in the half-glow of the night lantern, feeling the straw where it bunched beneath me, *waiting* . . . and soon enough I heard:

Scroonch. Scroosh.

By the time I got out of bed, she'd scooped out all the ashes and swept the fireplace clean, and she was sitting on the edge of the sawbuck table in the kitchen, scrubbing the life out of an iron kettle. She'd thrown on the nearest thing to hand—my nightshirt—and in the blue kitchen light, her creamy breast, flopping through the vent, was the closest thing to a star. And that sweat-licked aureole, yes, the midnight sun.

"You're out of pine wood," she said. "Brush, too."

"Would you kindly stop?"

"And I've given up on the brass. It's too far gone. You'll need to hire someone."

"Stop. Stop."

"Gus," she said, lifting her voice into a singsong as she sent the horse-hair brush dancing. "You were snoring to wake the dead. It was either go home or see to this room. Which is a disgrace, you know that. Don't worry," she added, "I'm not moving in."

That was the refrain she always fell back on: *I'm not moving in, Gus.* As if that were the thing I feared most in the world, when in fact, there could have been worse things.

"*You* may like setting up house with spiders and mice," she said, "but most people prefer them out of doors. And if Amelia were here—"

The *other* refrain.

"If Amelia were here, she'd be doing the same, believe you me."

So funny to hear Patsy go on this way, as though she and my wife were old comrades working toward a common end. I should resent it, probably, hearing Amelia called by her given name, seeing her mantle snatched up so easily (if only for an hour or two every week or two). But I can't help thinking how much Amelia would have liked this young woman: her industry and calm, her delicate ethics. Patsy thinks through all her positions. Lord knows how she aligns herself round me.

I went back to the bedroom, found myself a tin of snuff, and carried it back to the kitchen. Her brows angled up when she saw me.

"How much you got left?" she asked.

She took a single dip. Her head tipped back as the powder turned to vapor and filtered through her sinuses, and she stayed like that for a while, drawing in the air and releasing it in a long stream.

"Did I mention, Gus? You're out of cigars. And the chimney's smoking again. And the root cellar's got squirrels."

I braced myself against the wall and sank down until I was sitting on the stone tile. It had the same effect as jumping into a lake. A splash of cold rising through the tailbone and scalding my spine.

"While we're awake, Patsy . . ."

"Yes?"

"Tell me about Leroy Fry."

She swept her arm across her brow. In the candlelight, I could just make out the lines of sweat along her jaw, around her collarbone, and the blue veins of her breast. . . .

"Oh, I've talked about him before, haven't I? You must have heard me."

"As if I could sort out every beau of yours."

"Well," she said, scowling a bit, "there's nothing to tell. He never said a word to me, never so much as grabbed. Couldn't hardly stand to look at me, that's how bad it was. He used to come in nights with Moses and Tench, and they'd be telling the same jokes, and he'd be laughing the same way. That's what he was there for, to laugh. Kind of a *peeping* sound, like a wren makes. He drank only beer. Now and again I'd glance over, and he'd be looking at me, and he'd just yank his head away. Like this, Gus. Like someone had a noose round him—"

Too late she caught herself. Her brush froze. Her lips folded in.

"I'm sorry," she said. "You know what I meant."

" 'Course."

"He was, I think, the fastest blusher I ever saw. But maybe I only say that because he was so fair."

"A virgin?"

Oh, the glare she gave me then. "Now, how would I know?" she asked. "No good test for a man, is there?" She grew quiet then. "I could just about see him with a *cow*, maybe. A big, motherly, *pushy* kind of cow. With a fat udder."

"Don't go on," I said. "You'll make me miss Hagar."

She began to dry the pot with a cotton towel. Round and round her arm went, and I found myself staring at those hands of hers, the tiny undulations of skin that the soap and the friction had made. An old woman's hands on a young woman's bare rich arms.

"It seems Fry was going to meet someone the night he died," I said.

"Someone?"

"Man, woman, we're not certain."

Without raising her head, she said, "Are you going to ask me, Gus?"

"Ask you . . . ?"

"Where I was the . . . what night was it?"

"Twenty-fifth."

"Twenty-*fifth*." She eyed me tightly.

"I wasn't going to ask, no."

"Well, never mind, then." Down her eyes went. She plunged the towel into the pot's center and gave it a fierce turn and then mopped her face one more time and said, "I spent the night at my sister's. She's getting those terrible headaches again, and someone has to stay with the baby till his fever passes, and the husband is no earthly use, so . . . that's where I was." She gave her head an angry shake. "I should be there *now*."

But if she were there now, she wouldn't be *here*, and that would be . . . what? Did she want me to say what that would be?

I took another dip of snuff. Such a clean feeling racing through my head. A fellow in such a state could make affirmations, couldn't he? On an autumn night, to a young woman standing not five feet away? But there was something hard and clotted in my head. I didn't know what it was until the image came back to me: two hands clutching the window lintel at the Cozzens hotel.

"Patsy," I said. "What do you know about this Poe fellow?"

"Eddie?"

That was a shock. Hearing him reduced to that little endearment. I wondered if anyone had ever called him that before.

"Sad little thing," she said. "Beautiful manners. Beautiful *fingers,* have you noticed? Talks like a book but holds his liquor like a leaky pail. Now *there's* your virgin, you ask me."

"Something odd about him, that's for sure."

"Because he's a virgin?"

"No."

"Because he drinks a bit?"

"No! He's—he's full of the most senseless fancies and . . . *superstitions*. Imagine this, Patsy. He shows me a poem, claims it has something to do with Leroy Fry's death. Claims it was dictated to him in his sleep by his dead mother."

"His mother."

"Who I'm sure has better things to do in the afterlife—assuming it exists—than go whispering bad poetry in her son's ear."

She drew herself up then. Placed the pot on the wood-block counter. Proudly drew her bosom back inside my nightshirt.

"I'm sure, if she'd known it was bad, she'd never have whispered it."

She was so very solemn I thought she was having me on. She wasn't.

"Oh, Patsy," I said. "Don't. Not you. Please."

"I talk to my mother every day, Gus. More than I did when she was alive. In fact, we were having just the pleasantest chat on the way over here."

"Christ."

"She asked me what you were like. And I said well, he's a bit on the old side, and he talks a lot of bunkum, but he's got these lovely big hands, Mother, and these ribs. I do love feeling his ribs."

"And she—what?—listens? Talks back, does she?"

"Sometimes. When I need her to."

I jumped to my feet. The chill had worked its way right up to my chin now, and I had to walk about the kitchen a few circuits, chaff the blood back into my arms.

"The people we love are always with us," she said, quietly. "You should know better than—"

"I don't see anyone else here," I said. "Do you? As far as I can tell, we're all alone."

"Oh, you can't believe that, Gus. You can't stand there and tell me *she's* not here."

The sky that night was a deep-roasted purple, and the hills couldn't be seen except where a single light winked from Dolph van Corlaer's farmhouse. And somewhere a cock, roused too soon, was in the midst of a long tapering crow.

"It's a funny thing," I said. "I never could get used to sharing my bed. The elbow in my face and, I don't know, someone's hair in my mouth. But now, all these years later, I can't get used to having it to myself. Can't even bring myself to take up the whole bed. I just lie there, on my side, trying not to use up too much blanket." I pressed my hands against the windowpane. "Well," I said, "she's been gone a long time now."

"I wasn't speaking of Amelia, Gus."

"*She's* gone, too."

"That's what you say."

No point in arguing. My daughter *was* gone, that was plain to see. For all anyone could tell, she'd never been there in the first place, and even I, in those days, tended to remember *around* her. I'd recall, for instance, how often my wife used to apologize for never having given me a boy. And how I'd always comfort her by saying, "A daughter suits me better anyway." For who else would fill up the silences so well? The quiet of an evening like this, when I'd be lost in my usual pursuits—my "bachelor moods," Mattie used to call them—and I'd look up suddenly . . . and there she would be, on the far side of the room. My daughter. Slim and straight, her cheeks turned to coral from sitting so near the fire. She'd be, oh, sewing up a sleeve or writing to her aunt or smiling at something Mr. Pope had once written. Once my eyes had found her, they would never permit themselves to leave her again.

And the longer I looked, the more my heart would crack, for it seemed to me I was already losing her. Had been losing her from the day I first held her in my hands, violet and squalling. And there was nothing, in the end, that could stop her from being lost. Not love. Not anything.

"The only one I miss right now is Hagar," I told Patsy. "My coffee could use some cream."

She watched me. Very studiously, like someone poring over a deed.

"Gus, you don't take cream in your coffee."

Narrative of Gus Landor

11

November 1st to November 2nd

Four o'clock is the closest thing West Point has to a magic hour. The afternoon recitals are finished, the evening parade hasn't yet been called, and the cadets have a brief gap in the day's long march, which most of them use to storm the female citadel. At four o'clock on the dot, a regiment of young women, gallantly fitted in pink and red and blue, are already pacing Flirtation Walk. Within minutes come an invading horde of "grays," each offering his arm to a pink or a blue, and if things are very far along—say, a day or two—you may see a gray removing the button nearest his heart and exchanging it for a lock of the pink's hair. Eternal troth is pledged. Tears are shed. It's all over in half an hour. Nothing to beat it for efficiency.

On this particular day, it had another useful result. It cleared the remaining grounds of cadets and left me quite alone, standing by the northern entrance to the icehouse, facing an empty Plain. The leaves fell in a steady draft, and the light, which had been a naked glare until today, lay soft and muted on a rising crest of mist. I was alone.

Then there came a rustle . . . the snapping of a twig . . . the barest of footfalls.

"Ah, good!" I said, still in the act of turning. "My note reached you."

Not stopping to reply, Cadet Fourth Classman Poe danced round the side of the icehouse, wrenched open the door and dropped inside. A gust of cool air spilled after him.

"Mr. Poe?"

From somewhere in the dark came a long croaking whisper: "Did anyone follow me?"

"Well, let me . . . no."

"You're certain?"

"Yes."

He consented then to move closer to the doorway—until the planes of his face were back in the light. A nose. A chin. The glacier of his brow.

"I am baffled by your conduct, Mr. Landor. You *demand* utter secrecy, and then you call me out in full daylight."

"There was no help for it, I'm sorry."

"But suppose I am seen?"

"A very good point. I believe it might be best, Mr. Poe, if you started climbing again."

I pointed to the thatched dome of the icehouse, silhouetted against the sky like a squashed arrowhead. Poe twisted his head round to follow the line of my finger, until at last he stood squarely in the light, squinting into the sun.

"It isn't so high," I said. "Fifteen feet, I'd say. And you're so good at climbing."

"But . . . whatever for?" he whispered.

"Now, I should probably give you a leg up, will that do? You might then try grabbing the top of the door frame—right there, do you see? And from there, you should have no problem reaching the cornice. . . ."

He looked at me as if I were speaking in reverse.

"Unless you're still tired from the other day," I said. "I'll certainly understand if you are."

What choice did he have now? He laid his hat on the ground, rubbed his hands together, gave me a frowning nod, and said, "Ready."

Being small, he could cleave to the icehouse's stone surface rather well, and he slipped only once, as he was climbing onto the cornice. But his right foot held fast, and soon he was drawing himself up and over. Half a minute later, he was crouched like a gargoyle on the crest.

"Can you see me from where you are?" I called up.

Kssst.

"Sorry. Can't hear you, Mr. Poe."

"Yes." A hissing whisper.

"You needn't worry. We're quite alone for the time being, and if anyone hears me, they'll just write me off as insane, which—sorry, what was that, Mr. Poe?"

"Please tell me why I'm up here."

"Oh, yes! What you're looking at is the scene of the crime." With my feet, I sketched out an area roughly twenty yards square. "The *second* crime," I corrected myself. "This is where Leroy Fry's heart was removed."

I was standing now just north and a little northeast of the icehouse door. To the northwest lay the officers' quarters, to the west the cadet barracks, to the south the Academies, and to the east the guard post at Fort Clinton. A very sensible choice our man had made: he'd found the one spot where he might be assured of carrying out his work unseen.

"Funny thing," I said. "I've searched all round this icehouse. Crawled on my hands and knees, got at least two pairs of trousers dirty. It never occurred to me until now to try a—a *different* vantage point."

His vantage point, I meant. The man who'd cut through Leroy Fry's flesh and bone, soaked his hands in the drip and stench of a once-living body.

"Mr. Poe, can you hear me?"

"Yes."

"Very good. I'd like you to look down now, to where I'm standing, and tell me, please, if you see any—any *gaps* in the ground cover. By that I mean, any places where the grass or the soil seems to be broken. Where a rock or a stick might have been driven into the ground."

There was a long pause. Long enough that I was on the verge of repeating myself when I heard a long hiss.

"Sorry, Mr. Poe, I can't—"

"By your left foot."

"By my left . . . by my . . . yes. Yes, I see it."

A small indentation, maybe three inches round. Reaching into my pocket, I pulled out a shiny white stone—I'd collected a mess of them by the river that morning—pressed it into the crevice and stepped away.

"There you are," I said. "Maybe now you can see the value, Mr. Poe, of a God's-eye view. I doubt I would ever have caught that with my—my *mortal* eyes. Now, if you can just tell me where *else* you see gaps. Of roughly the same size and shape."

It was a halting business. He needed at least five minutes before he could begin in earnest. Between sightings, still more time elapsed, and on several occasions he changed his mind and had me remove the stone marker I had just set down. And because he insisted on whispering everything, the task of following his directions was a bit like groping down an alley with only a firefly as a guide.

He fell silent again. And then sent me scurrying in an unforeseen direction, some three yards *away* from the area I'd sketched out for him.

"We're leaving the crime scene, Mr. Poe."

But he insisted I put a stone there. And kept insisting and kept pushing the perimeter outward until it no longer made any sense whatsoever. I felt the stock of stones in my pocket dwindling, and a dismal feeling came over me as I saw the terrain I'd limned so neatly in my head popping its borders.

"Are there any more, Mr. Poe?" I called out wearily.

A good half an hour had passed by this point, and my little gargoyle declared that there *was* one more. Which was, for strange reasons, the hardest to find of all. *Three paces north . . . five paces east . . . no,* six *paces east . . . no, you passed it . . . there . . . no, not there,* there! His scratching whisper trailed me the whole time like a gnat . . . until at last the gap was found and the marker inserted, and I could hear the relief in my voice as I said:

"You may come to earth now, Mr. Poe."

Scrambling down, he jumped the last six feet and landed on his knees in the grass. Then melted once again into the blackness of the icehouse's interior.

"You mentioned the other day, Mr. Poe, how the nature of this crime—the taking of Leroy Fry's heart—drew you back to the Bible. I must admit I was already moving in the same direction. Not to the Bible, exactly—there's not much that would make me do that—but I couldn't help wondering if there weren't something in this business that smacked of *religion*."

His hands flashed in the darkness.

"Well, really, the *whole* business smacks of it," I said. "Leroy Fry falls in with a 'bad bunch' a couple of summers back and then does what? Runs straight to the prayer squad. Thayer sees Fry's body and thinks of what?

A religious fanatic. So then, let's take religion as our starting premise, and let's ask ourselves, might there be some traces left of the original act? Some signs of a rite—I mean, a *ceremony*. Stones or—or candles or some such, placed in an intentional way?"

Poe's hands were folded together now: soft, priestly hands.

"Well, then," I went on, "if such objects *were* used, it stands to reason our man would have removed them the moment he was done. No sense leaving evidence. But what of the—the *impressions* made by the objects? Those would have taken much longer to erase, and there was precious little time as it was, what with the search party already on its way. Not to mention, our man had a *heart* that needed seeing to. Very well, then, he takes away the objects, but he doesn't likely stay to fill the holes the objects made." I smiled at those hands in the icehouse. "That's what we're doing today, Mr. Poe. We're finding the holes he left behind."

I scanned the white stones studded like tiny grave markers amid the pale grass. From my coat pocket, I drew out a pencil and a notebook. Moving in a wave pattern, I began calibrating the distances between the stones, sketching as I went, until the paper held a lattice of dots.

"What have you found?" whispered Poe from the depths of the icehouse.

It was only when I handed him the page, I think, that I really *saw* what was there:

"A circle," said Poe.

Circle it was. Fully ten feet in diameter, by my estimate. Considerably more space than Leroy Fry's body would have consumed. Large enough to hold half a dozen Leroy Frys.

"But the pattern inside the circle," said Poe, his face bending low over the paper, "I can't get anywhere with that."

We both stared at it a little longer, trying to connect the inner to the outer dots. Nothing worked. The harder I looked, the more the dots seemed to scatter . . . until I let my gaze settle on the stones themselves.

"Hmm," I said. "It only stands to reason."

"What?"

"If we missed some of the dots on the circle's circumference—see?—I'd be willing to wager we missed some *inside* the circle as well. Let me just . . ."

I set the paper on top of the notebook and began drawing a line through the dots that were closest together, and then I kept going, barely aware of what I was doing, until I heard Poe say:

"Triangle."

"Yes, indeed," I said. "And from what they told me, I'm guessing that Leroy Fry was right *inside* that triangle. And our man was—he was . . ."

Where?

Years ago, the family of a farrier in the Five Points paid me (with several lifetimes' worth of savings) to look into his death. The fellow had been cudgeled and branded with one of his own irons. On his forehead I found a raised U of flesh, as though a horse had stepped on him. I remember running my hand along that scar and wondering about the person who'd done it and then looking up and seeing—no, I won't say that—*imagining* the killer standing by the door with the iron still smoking in his hand, and in his eyes a *look* . . . rage and fear, I suppose, and a certain shyness, as though he doubted he was worthy of my notice. Well, the *actual* killer, when we found him, was very little as I'd pictured him, but the look in the eyes, *that* was the same. It stayed like that, too, all the way to the gallows.

That particular case made me a believer in, well, *pictures*. But that afternoon by the icehouse, Reader, there was no picture. No one looking back at me. Or maybe it's better to say that whoever was there kept changing position and shape . . . multiplying.

"Well, this has been most helpful, Mr. Poe. You'll need to go off to parade now, and I'm expected at Captain Hitchcock's, so I'll just—"

I turned to find him kneeling in the grass. His face tilted down. Muttering like a crow.

"What is it, Mr. Poe?"

"I saw them from the roof," he said. "They didn't fit, you see. So I didn't . . ." His voice trailed off into more muttering.

"I'm not quite clear yet, Mr. Poe."

"Scorch marks!" he cried. "Quickly, now!"

He tore a page from my notebook and spread it across the grass and began shading the page with the pencil, in brisk sweeping motions that soon filled the paper—or *nearly* filled it. For when he raised the paper to the light, we could see, like a message painted on a misty window:

$$\text{SHⱢ}$$

"It looks like . . . *SHJ*," read Poe. "Society of . . ."

Oh, yes, we ran through all the societies we could think of. Sororities. Schools, spaniels. An ungodly time we spent there, kneeling in the grass, combing our brains.

"Hold off," Poe said suddenly.

He squinted at the paper and, in a low voice, said, "If the individual letters are reversed, mightn't we then expect the whole *message* to be reversed?"

At once I tore off a new page and wrote out the letters in large, bold strokes so they filled the paper from end to end.

$$\text{J H S}$$

"Jesus Christ," said Poe.

I tipped myself back into a sitting position and gave my knees a rub. Then I reached for some tobacco.

"Common enough inscription in the old days," I said. "I don't believe I've ever seen it written backward, though."

"Unless," said Poe, "someone *other* than Christ was being invoked. Someone directly *opposite* to Christ."

I was sitting in the grass, chewing my plug. Poe was studying a train of clouds. A blackbird was whistling, and a tree toad was gargling. Everything was different.

"You know," I said finally, "I've got a friend who might be of some use to us."

Poe only half glanced at me. "Is that a fact?"

"Oh yes," I said, "he's quite the expert on symbols and . . . *rituals* and the like. He's got an extensive collection of books pertaining to the—to the . . ."

"The occult," Poe answered.

And after a few more seconds of chewing, I allowed as how *occult* probably was the right word for it.

"Fascinating fellow," I said. "My friend, I mean. Name of Professor Pawpaw."

"What an extraordinary name!"

I explained to Poe that Pawpaw was Indian by birth, or rather half Indian and, oh, a quarter French and God knows what else. And Poe asked me then if he was a genuine professor. And I said well he's a *scholar*, no doubt about that, in great demand among society ladies. Mrs. Livingston once paid him twelve silver dollars for the pleasure of a single hour of his time.

Poe gave a negligent shrug. "I hope *you* have some means of paying him, then," he said. "I'm in arrears myself, and Mr. Allan won't even send me money for mathematical instruments."

I told him not to worry, I would take care of it. Then I bid him good day and watched his slender figure picking its way (with no great speed) down the Plain.

What I never got around to telling him was this (and didn't the very thought of it make me laugh out loud as I walked back to the hotel?): I had already found the best possible compensation for Professor Pawpaw. I would bring him the head of Edgar A. Poe.

Narrative of Gus Landor

12

November 3rd

Professor Pawpaw's cottage is only a league or so inland from mine, but it lies at the end of a steep climb, and the path is so overgrown you must, fifty yards short of the house, abandon your horse and hack your way through a lane of cedar bushes. You are rewarded then with a piazza wreathed in jasmine and sweet honeysuckle. Oh, and a dead pear tree, with a long cloak of bignonia blossoms and, dangling from every arm, wicker birdcages full of mockingbirds, orioles, bobolinks, and canaries, all of them singing from dusk to dawn without cease. No obvious harmony, but if you listen long enough, either the jangling will take on a pattern or (this is Pawpaw's theory) you'll give up on pattern altogether.

Now, if Poe had got his way, we'd have made the trip to Pawpaw's that very night. I said we'd never find the place in the dark. Besides, I wanted to give the professor a bit of warning. That very night, an Academy messenger was dispatched with a note from me.

The next morning, Poe woke up, chewed a piece of chalk, and then presented his white tongue to Dr. Marquis, who sent him off with a fistful of calomel powders and a note excusing him from duties. Poe then squirmed through a loose fence board in the woodyard and met me just south of the guard post, where we mounted Horse and set off on the high road from Buttermilk Falls.

It was a chill, clouded morning. The only heat seemed to come from the trees, rearing up from pale granite ledges, and from the dead leaves that shone out of pools and glens and beds of spongy moss. The path rose quickly as we crept round bulging faces of stone, and Poe yammered in my ear about Tintern Abbey and Burke's principle of the sublime, and *Nature is America's truest poet, Mr. Landor,* and the more he talked the more I felt the dread wrapping me round. Here I was, smuggling a cadet off the reservation—knowing full well that Hitchcock and his officers made a point of inspecting barracks quarters every day. Woe to the cadet who reported himself "sick" and failed to answer the double knock on the door!

Well, rather than think about those consequences, I told Poe all I knew about Pawpaw.

His mother was a Huron squaw, his father a French-Canadian arms trader. At a young age he was taken in by a tribe of Wyandot Indians, who were massacred in short order by purposeful Iroquois. The lone survivor, Pawpaw was rescued by a Utica bone dealer who gave him a Christian name and raised him on strict terms: church twice a day; catechism and hymns before bed; seventy Bible verses a week. (In all respects, it was the same as my own upbringing, except that Pawpaw was allowed to play cards.) After six years, the bone dealer fell prey to scrofula. The boy then landed in the home of a charity-minded textile titan, who died soon after and left Pawpaw six thousand a year. Pawpaw promptly reclaimed his Indian name and removed himself to a Jersey-freestone house in Warren Street, where he issued monographs on alcoholism, manumission, henbane—and the reading of the human skull. Just as his fame was cresting, he removed himself again, this time to the Highlands. He communicates now mostly by post, bathes twice a year, and regards his past with a certain wryness. Once, upon being called a noble savage, Pawpaw was heard to say, "Why spoil it with the noble part?"

All that Sunday school, you see: he needs to shock people. Which was why, maybe, he'd prepared for our coming by hanging a dead rattlesnake over the door and strewing the front walk with frog bones. The bones crunched softly beneath our feet and stuck in the crevices of our boots so that we were still picking them out when Pawpaw appeared. Compact and heavy-chested, he stood in the doorway with an absent air, as though he'd come out simply to gauge the weather. We stared at him, for Pawpaw is made for staring—it's his cause and his effect. The first time I came, he greeted me in full Indian regalia, waving a flint arrowhead. Today, for reasons beyond me or even him, he was dressed as an old Dutch farmer. Homespun coats and breeches, pewter buckles, and the most enormous shoes I have ever seen: you could have packed a man in them. The only things not quite in keeping were the eagle's claw that dangled round his neck and the skinny line of indigo that ran from his right temple to the tip of his nose (a new touch).

Slowly, those handsome hazel eyes of his began to glimmer with understanding. "Ohh!" He cut straight for Poe. Grabbed him by the arm, hauled him over the doorsill. "You were right!" the professor shouted back to me. "He's perfectly remarkable. Such an enlarged organ!"

By now, he and Poe were half running toward the parlor. Which gave me leave to stroll down the professor's front hall, to see once again the bison rug and the stuffed screech owl, the flails and harnesses hanging on the walls like museum relics. By the time I reached the parlor, a row of apples was spluttering in the hearth, Poe had been flung into a Duncan Phyfe armchair, and over him stood Pawpaw, with his silver-copper skin and potato nose, rubbing his fingertips together and proffering, in lieu of a cordial, the gapped line of his own gray teeth.

"Young man," he said. "Would you do me the favor of removing your hat?"

With some hesitation, Poe took the leather pot off his head and set it on the Brussels carpet.

"This won't hurt in the least," said the professor.

Were I meeting Pawpaw for the first time, I might have doubted. He had the trembling hands of a man pulling up his very first petticoat as he wound a length of string round the densest part of Poe's skull.

"Twenty-three inches. Not so large as I would have guessed. Clearly it is the proportions that are so shocking. Mr. Poe, how much do you weigh?"

"One hundred forty-three pounds."

"And your height?"

"Five feet eight. And one half."

"Oh, one *half*, is it? Now, young man, I wish to feel your head. Don't look like that. There will be no pain, unless rendering up your soul through the medium of fingers be agony. You need only remain still, can you do that?"

Too cowed even to nod, Poe merely blinked. The professor drew in two draughts of air and suffered his twitching fingers to merge with that virgin scalp. A sigh, the barest breath of air, emerged from his gray lips.

"Amativeness," intoned Pawpaw. "Moderate."

He lowered his ear to Poe's cranium, like a farmer sounding for gophers, while his fingers threshed through the matted black hair.

"Inhabitiveness," said the professor, more loudly. "Small. Adhesiveness: full. Intellectual faculties: large—no, *very* large." A smile from Poe there. "Love of approbation: full." A smile from me. "Philoprogenitiveness: very small."

On it went, Reader. Cautiousness, benevolence, hope: trait by trait, that skull was forced to yield up its secrets. Yield them to the *world*, I should say, for the professor roared *out* each finding like an auctioneer; only when his dark-grained baritone began to taper away did I know he was coming to a close.

"Mr. Poe, you have the bumps of a rootless disposition. The portion of your skull devoted purely to animal propensities—by which I mean the lower posterior and the lower lateral—that area is somewhat less developed. However, secretiveness and combativeness are both highly developed. I discern in your character a violent and almost certainly *fatal* division."

"Mr. Landor," said Poe, quailing a little. "You never told me the professor was a seer."

"Repeat that!" barked Pawpaw.

"You . . . you never . . ."

"Yes, yes."

"Told me the—"

"Richmond!" cried Pawpaw.

Pinned to his chair, Poe began to stammer. "That's—that's true, I am . . ."

"And if I'm not mistaken," I put in, "he spent a few years in England."

Poe's eyes were fanned wide now.

"The Reverend John Bransby of Stoke Newington," I explained. "That noted authority on spelling."

Pawpaw clapped his hands. "Ah, very good. *Excellent*, Landor! The

British overtone chimes so easily with the woodland notes of the South. Let me see now, what else can we say about this young man? He is an artist. With those hands, he can be nothing else."

"An artist of sorts," said Poe, blushing.

"He is also . . ." A moment of suspension before Pawpaw thrust his index finger into the young man's face and cried, "An orphan!"

"That is also true," said Poe quietly. "My parents—my *real* parents— died in a fire. The Richmond theater fire of eighteen-eleven."

"And what business did they have going to the theater?" growled Pawpaw.

"They were *actors*," said Poe. "Very fine actors. Renowned."

"Ah, renowned," said the professor, turning away in disgust.

Some awkwardness then. Poe in his chair, achy with resentment. The professor stalking the room, trying to blow all the pathos away. And me: waiting. Until the quiet had stretched so far and no more, at which point I said:

"Professor, I was wondering if we might come to the business at hand."

"So be it," he said, frowning.

He made us tea first of all. It came in a warped silver pot and tasted like tar: spiky on the tongue, gluey in the throat. I drank three cups, one after another, like shots of whiskey. What choice did I have? Pawpaw kept no spirits here.

"Now, then, Professor," I said. "What are we to make of this?"

I brought out the drawing Poe and I had made, of the triangle within the circle, and laid it on Pawpaw's table, which was no more than a steamer trunk laid over with pressed tin.

"Well," said the professor, "it depends on whom you talk to. Summon an ancient Greek, an alchemist, and he would tell you the circle is an *ourobouros*, a symbol of eternal unity. Summon a *medieval* thinker"—his eyes swerved upward—"he would say it is both creation and the void toward which creation must always tend." His eyes settled once more on the paper. "*This*, however—this can only be a magic circle."

Poe and I exchanged a look.

"Yes, yes," continued Pawpaw. "I remember seeing one in *Le Véritable*

Dragon Rouge. If I recall aright, the magician would stand ... *there* ... in the triangle."

"The magician alone?" I asked.

"Oh, he might have a group of assistants, all of them inside the triangle with him. Candles on either side, and in front—*there*, let us say—a brazier. Light everywhere, a festival of light."

I closed my eyes, trying to imagine it.

"The people who performed these ceremonies," said Poe. "Would they have been Christians?"

"Often, yes. Magic was not solely the province of darkness. In your own drawing, as you can see, you have the Christian inscription—"

His finger was resting now on the inverted *JHS*, and you might have thought the letters were speaking straight into his skin, for he snatched his hand away and rose to his feet and backed off two paces. A hard peevish cast came over his face.

"Dear God, Landor, why did you let me go on? You think I have all day? Come!"

Hard to describe the professor's library to one who has never been there. It's a small, windowless room, no more than a dozen feet in any direction, and *all* of it given over to books: folios, quartos, parchment-covered duodecimos, piled vertically, and horizontally, dangling off shelves, sprawled on the floor. Still open, many of them, to whatever page the professor was last reading.

Pawpaw was already scaling the shelves. Within half a minute, he'd bagged his quarry and hauled it down to earth. A massive volume bound in black leather, with silver clasps. The professor gave it a pat, and a plume of dust rose through his fingers.

"De Lancre," he said. "*Tableau de l'inconstance des mauvais anges*. Do you read French, Mr. Poe?"

"Bien sûr."

Poe gently peeled away the first sheet of parchment. Cleared his throat, puffed out his chest. Prepared to recite.

"Please," said Pawpaw. "I cannot bear being read to. Kindly take your book to the corner and read in silence."

Of course, there was no furniture in the corner, or anywhere else. With a shy smile, Poe dropped onto a brocaded pillow, while the professor motioned me gravely to the floor. I chose instead to lean against the shelves as I pulled out a pigtail of tobacco.

"Tell me about this de Lancre fellow," I said.

Wrapping his arms round his ankles, Pawpaw rested his chin on his knees. "*Pierre* de Lancre," he said. "Redoubtable witch hunter. Found and executed six hundred Basque witches over a period of four months, and left behind the remarkable volume that Mr. Poe is now perusing. A pure delight. Oh, but wait! What sort of host am I?"

And he was up on his feet and out the door, to return five minutes later with a platter of apples—the ones I'd seen roasting in the hearth. They were unknowable now: blistery and wounded, oozing sap. Pawpaw looked a bit offended when I declined.

"As you like," he sniffed, cramming one into his mouth. "Where were we? Yes, yes, de Lancre. Now, the book I *wish* I had to give you, Landor, is *Discours du Diable*. Written by one Henri le Clerc, who exterminated *seven* hundred witches before he was done. What makes his story unusual is that he experienced a midlife conversion. Like Saul on the road to Damascus, except that le Clerc was moving in the *other* direction. To the dark side."

A line of apple sap had worked its way down his chin. He fingered it away.

"Le Clerc was himself captured and burned at the stake in Caen in 1603. In his arms, it's said, he held the aforementioned volume, clothed in wolf's skin. As the flames rose higher, he said a prayer to his—his *lord*, and cast the book into the fire. Onlookers swore that it vanished in a trice, as though someone had plucked it from the very heart of the furnace."

"Well, I can see why—"

"The story is not finished, Landor. Word soon spread that le Clerc had left behind two or three other volumes identical to the one that was destroyed. None has ever been conclusively identified, but in the intervening centuries, the task of recovering these lost books has become the *idée fixe* of many an occult collector."

"One of them being you, Professor?"

He grimaced. "I don't especially covet the volume myself, though I can see why others might. It is said that le Clerc left behind instructions for curing incurable illnesses, and even for securing immortality."

Just then I felt the smallest of breezes on my hand. I looked down to find an ant crawling over my knuckles.

"I think I *will* have one of those apples," I said.

And behold, it was good. The black crust tore away like paper, and the inside was a molten wonder, sweet and sticky-clean. I could see Pawpaw smiling at me, as if to say, *You doubted?*

"Perhaps," he said, "we should ascertain our young friend's progress."

Only a few minutes had passed since we left him in the corner, but Poe was so still that a frond of dust had already settled across his shoulders. Even as we approached, he forbore to raise his head. I had to look over him to see what he was studying.

It was an engraving, stretching across both pages: the portrait of a feast. Droopy-breasted hags astride great hairy rams. Winged demons dragging aloft the bodies of still-living babies. Bonneted skeletons and dancing fiends and, rising up in the center—in his golden chair—the master of the feast: a mannerly goat, with fire coming out of his horns.

"Remarkable, isn't it?" said Poe. "One can't stop looking. Oh, Professor, might I have leave to read aloud from just one section?"

"If you must."

"This is from de Lancre's description of the sabbath ritual. Excuse my stumbling, I'm still translating. *It is commonly known among the . . . fraternity of evil angels that the—the* contents *of a witches' sabbath feast are confined to the following sundries—to wit,* unclean *animals such as are never eaten by Christian peoples . . ."*

I felt myself drawing closer.

". . . as well, the hearts of unbaptized children . . ."

Poe stopped and, looking first at the professor, then at me, began to grin.

". . . and the hearts of hanged men."

Narrative of Gus Landor

13

November 3rd to November 6th

We were silent, Poe and I, all the way back to the Point. It was only when he was dismounting, about a quarter mile short of the guard post, that he saw fit to speak again.

"Mr. Landor," he said. "I have been pondering where next we should direct our enquiries. It occurs to me that if we wish to locate a secret enclave of . . ." He hesitated but a second. ". . . Of *Satanists,* well, then, we should address ourselves to those who would be most sensitive to such an enclave's presence. Their *opposite* number, as it were."

I gave it some thought.

"Christians," I said warily.

"Christians, yes. Of the most devout flavor."

"You don't mean the Reverend Zantzinger?" I asked.

"Oh, Lord, no!" cried Poe. "Zantzinger wouldn't know the Devil if it sneezed on his alb. No, I rather had in mind the prayer squad."

It made perfect sense, I recognized that straight off. This was the very squad that Leroy Fry had briefly joined, a voluntary association of cadets who found the West Point chapel too Episcopalian and wanted a straighter road to their God.

Until today, of course, Poe had held this squad in nothing but contempt. "*Now,* Mr. Landor, I think we might put them to good use, if you would permit me."

"Of course. But how do you—"

"Oh, you leave that to me," he drawled. "In the meantime, you and I must find a better means of communicating. From my end, it's relatively simple: I need but slip into your hotel and leave messages under your door. You, however, would be best advised not to leave any notes in my barracks quarters, as my roommates are the nosiest devils. I would suggest instead Kosciusko's Garden, do you know the place? You'll find a natural spring there and, on the southern perimeter of the spring, a loose rock—igneous, I believe—large enough to conceal any piece of paper, provided it's sufficiently folded. Simply leave your missives there in the morning, and I shall take pains to retrieve them in the interval between—. What? Why are you chuckling, Mr. Landor?"

In fact, I was feeling just a little vindicated. No spy of my acquaintance had ever taken to his work with such flair, and I couldn't wait to sing his praises to someone—even if that someone was only Hitchcock. He and I duly gathered in Thayer's parlor late the next day (Thayer, good deity that he was, absented himself), and we drank coffee larded with lumpy cream, and ate dodger cakes and pickled oysters. The scent of Molly's pot roast tickled the air, and Hitchcock talked about a book he was reading—Montholon's *Memoirs of Napoleon*, I think—and it was all very light and full of grace, even if this grace came out of great compression. For the chief of engineers had just demanded a full accounting of my enquiries, and this was to be forwarded to the secretary of war, and it was said that the president himself had taken an interest in the matter—and when the president takes an interest, it can safely be said that things are teetering, and it will take some timely action to set them right again. That was what lay beneath all our pleasantness: a *ticking*, as pronounced as the clock in Thayer's downstairs study, which at the five o'clock hour came chiming through the floor.

I felt for Hitchcock, I did my level best for him. Told him what I knew and didn't know and what I supposed. I even told him about Pawpaw, whose quirks are hardly the sort to warm the military mind. I lived up to every one of our terms, or so I thought, and then I saw Hitchcock rise and peer into a glass cabinet full of war totems, and I realized my job was just beginning.

"So, Mr. Landor. By virtue of some—some *holes* in the ground, you are now persuaded that a diabolical—what should we call it, *society*?"

"That would do."

"Society or—or *cult* is in play somewhere in the vicinity of West Point. Within the Academy's own walls, very possibly."

"It's possible, yes."

"And you're further persuaded that this individual—"

"Or group."

"—or *group* of individuals is under the sway of some medieval—I was going to call it twiddle-twaddle . . ."

"Go right ahead, Captain."

". . . and that consequent to this, Leroy Fry was killed and his heart removed, all to satisfy a bizarre devotional exercise. Is that what you're trying to tell me, Mr. Landor?"

"Now, Captain," I said, smiling gently, "you know me better than that. Have you ever heard me say anything outright? All I can tell you is there's now a chain of possibility. A series of markings at the crime scene that may have occult meaning, and a very specific set of directions—*occult* directions—that could pertain to our crime."

"And from this you deduce . . . ?"

"I don't deduce anything. I only say that Leroy Fry was killed in just such a way as to make his heart *useful* to a particular class of worshipper."

"'Useful,' 'class of worshipper'—those are fine euphemisms, Mr. Landor."

"If you want to call them bloodthirsty demons, Captain, be my guest. It doesn't bring us any closer to learning who they are. Or whether they are working toward larger ends."

"But if we're to accept your—your 'chain of possibility,' Mr. Landor, then it seems increasingly likely that one party *was* behind both crimes."

"As I think Dr. Marquis was the first to theorize," I said.

It was a measure of something—my boredom? despair?—that I felt the need to claim an ally. And in fact, Hitchcock didn't care a rap about Dr. Marquis; he cared only about jabbing holes in my theory. *Peck peck peck,* on and on, until at last I said:

"Go to the icehouse yourself, Captain. Tell me I'm wrong. Tell me the holes aren't there, the letters aren't there. Tell me they don't form the pattern I've described, and I won't trouble you with my theories any longer. And you can find yourself another whipping boy."

It took this—the threat of rupture—to quiet him. To quiet me, too. When I spoke again, my voice was much softer:

"I don't know what you expected, Captain. Whoever took Leroy Fry's heart was in terrible earnest about *something*—why not that?"

Well, it came down to this, Reader: Hitchcock had a report to file, and this report had to have words in it. And so, after a few more questions for the sake of "amplification," and some groping for the right language, we pretty soon had all we needed for the chief of engineers—for now, at least. And since that was the real purpose of our meeting, I was congratulating myself on my escape and preparing to leave . . . when I made the mistake of bringing up my young friend.

"Poe?" cried Hitchcock.

You see, he'd just about got used to the idea of my engaging Poe. But that this same Poe had become an active partner—that I proposed to go on using him in light of these latest developments—these things, Hitchcock hadn't foreseen. It brought him back to his feet, and once again he was cramming my head with in loco parentis and congressionally mandated this and statutory that. Somehow, in the midst of all this, I looked into the heart of what he was saying and came to a realization: Hitchcock was afraid.

"Captain," I said. "All will be well."

Which, come to think of it, was the kind of thing my daughter used to say to me, even in the direst circumstances. I wondered if it sounded as convincing coming from my lips.

"But surely," said Hitchcock (all tracks round the mouth), "surely, if such a—a *society* exists, then its members are not to be trifled with."

"Certainly not. That's why Mr. Poe is tasked only with gathering information. That's the beginning and the end of his responsibility. All other risks will be borne by me."

Oh, these Army men and their stiff quills! Won't take direction from a civilian if they can possibly help it, not even from the president (*especially* not the president). And so they push and push, and finally I had to say:

"Please, Captain. I have told Mr. Poe in no uncertain terms that he's not to place himself in peril, or even the hint of peril."

In fact, I had yet to say such a thing to Cadet Poe, though I fully meant to. Taking advantage of the chink I'd made in the conversation, I added, "As always, he is to make academic duties his first concern."

"Health permitting," said Hitchcock.

The air was most definitely chillier.

"Health?" I asked.

"I do hope you'll wish Mr. Poe a speedy recovery from his recent illness," said Hitchcock.

"He's already on the mend, I believe."

"I'm glad to hear it."

"I'll tell him you asked after him."

"Please do," said Hitchcock. "Please tell him I asked after him."

As we were quitting the superintendent's quarters, Hitchcock paused in the act of shaking my hand and gave me a look of the purest skepticism.

"To the best of my knowledge, Mr. Landor, not one member of our faculty, not a single cadet officer or soldier has ever uncovered evidence of Satanism at the Point. How do you expect Mr. Poe to find what has eluded everyone else?"

"Because nobody else has been looking," I said. "And no one else can look in the way that Poe does."

Always, after I had finished talking to Hitchcock, I made a point of visiting Leroy Fry's body at the Academy hospital. I'm not sure why. I think, in retrospect, I must have been testing my constitution. For Dr. Marquis had, in recent days, begun injecting the corpse with potassium nitrate, a chemical commonly used to preserve ham and sausage. The results were clear: a body growing greener by the day, and a ward that stank overwhelmingly of rank meat. And flies everywhere, shaking with lust.

But when I dreamed about Leroy Fry, that night, he was in much better shape. The noose was still coiled round his neck, yes, but the hole in his chest was gone, and he was no longer in cadet gray but in officer blue. He held a lump of charcoal in one hand, and in the other a cage of blue-eyed birds, and whenever he spoke, his voice was the sound of birds. "I won't tell," they chanted, over and over. And from somewhere behind that sound came another: a woman singing in a high cracking treble. Through it all the West Point drums kept their cadence, and when I woke, the drum was in my chest, and the shades of my dream were still half visible in the dark.

Well, it was a bit of fancy, Reader, nothing more. I mention it only to show some of the problems I faced in trying to get a good night's sleep. Sleep was hard won and easily lost in those days, and I've since wondered if my time at the Point wasn't all one continuous thread: dreaming into waking, waking into dreaming, no intervals. And no end points. Not yet.

The note was waiting for me when I awoke the next morning. Wedged under the door. No salutation, no name . . . but I knew who'd sent it the moment I saw it. He could have written it with his left hand, and I would have known.

> *Mr. Landor. I have made a most important discovery.*

And two inches below that, in smaller but no less urgent lettering:

> *May I call on you at your home? Tomorrow?*

Narrative of Gus Landor

14

November 7th

I was once a newcomer myself here, Reader. So I can imagine what it is to approach this cottage for the first time, as Poe did on that Sunday afternoon. First you cross a brook, twice. Then, you see, beneath the canopy of a tulip tree, a skinny square chimney made of Dutch bricks, and beneath that a roof of old-fashioned gray shingles, projecting over the gables on each side. The house isn't nearly so big as you thought from a distance. Twenty-four feet long and sixteen broad, with no wings. A grapevine has climbed nearly to the roof. There's no bell; you have to knock. If no one answers, make yourself at home.

That's what Poe did: strolled in as if I weren't even there. Not from any rudeness, I could tell that, but out of a need to *see*. Why this place should have loomed so large for him, I can't say, but when a cadet decides to make you the focus of his Sunday afternoon—the only moment in the whole week when he can take his liberty—you mustn't question him.

He moved in straight lines from object to object, fingering the Venetian blinds and the string of dried peaches, pausing before the ostrich egg that hung in the chimney corner. More than once he seemed on the verge of a question, only to be drawn on by something he hadn't expected and had to account for.

Visitors have always been a rarity here, but I can think of no other who has put the place to such a scrutiny. It left me ill at ease. I found myself wanting to apologize for my neglect or give every object its proper context.

Normally, Mr. Poe, these pots would have been full of flowers. My wife was a great one for geraniums and pansies. And that ingrain carpet? A thing of beauty before my boots got hold of it. The windows were all dressed in white jaconet muslin, and yes, that ground-glass lamp came with an Italian shade, but the shade got torn, I forget how. . . .

Poe circled and circled—looked until there was nothing left to see. Then he went to the window, levered the blinds apart with his fingers, and gazed eastward, to the paling where Horse was tied, to the rock ledge farther on, and, farther still, to the Hudson's chasm and the shaggy pelts of Sugarloaf and North Redoubt.

"It's lovely," he murmured to the glass.

"You're very kind."

"And cleaner than I might have expected."

"I have someone who stops by now and then."

How droll that sounded to my ear: *someone who stops by*. Briefly there flashed through my mind the image of Patsy scrubbing pots in my kitchen in the middle of the night, her snow-breast streaked with sweat.

Poe was kneeling by the hearth now, peering into a marble vase. God knows what he expected to find there—twigs? flowers? ashes? Not *this*, I can be certain. He gave a whistle as he drew it out: a '19 model flintlock, 54 caliber, with a 10-inch smoothbone barrel.

"Fertilizer?" he asked, dry as sand.

"A memento, that's all. The last time it was fired, Monroe was president. No balls in it, but there's still powder, if you'd like to make some noise."

Who knows? He might have taken me up on it if something else hadn't caught his eye.

"*Books*, Mr. Landor!"

"I do read, yes."

Not much of a library—a scant three rows in all—but mine. Poe's fingers glided along the bindings.

"Swift, who better suited? The lamentable Cooper. *Knickerbocker's History*, of *course*, every library must . . . must . . . oh, and *Waverley!* I wonder if I could even bear to read that again." He leaned closer. "Well, this is intriguing. *Essay on the art of deciphering*, by John Davys. And there's Dr. Wallis and Trithemius—a whole row of cipher studies."

"My retirement pastime. Harmless, I hope."

"If there's one thing I would never accuse you of, Mr. Landor, it's harmlessness. Let me see now. Phonetics, linguistics, those stand to reason. *Natural History of Ireland. Geography of Greenland.* You must be a polar explorer. . . . Aha!" He grabbed a blue volume from the topmost shelf and wheeled back on me, eyes shining. "You have been found out, Mr. Landor."

"Oh?"

"You gave me to understand you didn't read poetry."

"I don't."

"Byron!" he cried, thrusting the volume straight to the ceiling. "And if you'll excuse me for saying so, it looks terribly well *thumbed,* Mr. Landor. We appear to have more in common than I ever realized. Which is your favorite? *Don Juan* or—or *Manfred*? *The Corsair,* I've a particularly *boyish* attraction to—"

"Please put it down," I said. "It's my daughter's."

I made every effort to keep my tone level, but something must have broken free, for he flushed a deep red and, from pure awkwardness, let the book fall open. In that instant, a brass chain spilled from out the pages, and before he could catch it, it landed with a *ping* on the wooden floor. The air took up the sound and made it repeat.

Face crumpling, Poe knelt down and snatched up the chain. Cupped it in his palm and held it out to me.

"This is—"

"My daughter's, too."

I saw him swallow, hard. I saw him tuck the chain back into the book and set the book back on the shelf. He dusted off his hands. He walked to the maple settee and lowered himself onto the cane seat.

"Your daughter is no longer here?"

"No."

"Perhaps she's—"

"She ran off. Awhile back."

His hands had formed a knot: loosening and tightening, loosening and tightening.

"*With* someone," I said. "You want to know if she ran off *with* someone. She did."

He shrugged, looked at the floor.

"Was it someone you knew?" he asked after a time.

"In passing."

"And she's never to return?"

"Not likely."

"Then we're both alone in the world."

He said this with half a smile on his face, as though he were trying to recollect a joke someone had told him.

"*You're* not alone," I said. "You have your Mr. Allan of Richmond."

"Oh. Well, Mr. Allan is spoken for elsewhere. He has just fathered a pair of twins, in fact. And is on the brink of marrying again—*not,* alas, the woman who bore his twins. It doesn't matter, I'm little to him now."

"And your mother, you still have *her,* yes?" I tried to keep the barb out of my voice, but failed. "She still *speaks* to you, at any rate?"

"From time to time, yes, I do believe that. But never *directly.*" He held out his hands. "I've no real memory of her, Mr. Landor. She died before I was three. My brother, however, was four at the time, *he's* told me things about her. How she carried herself. Oh, and the *scent* of her, she always smelled of orrisroot."

It was here, Reader, that something strange began to happen. I can describe it only as a change in the barometric pressure. I felt for all the world as if a storm was brewing—right over my head. My skin prickled, my eyes pulsed, the hairs in each nostril stood on end.

"You mentioned she was an actress," I said faintly.

"Yes."

"A singer, too, maybe?"

"Oh, yes."

"What was her name?"

"Eliza. Eliza Poe."

Uncanny! To feel this pressure building in my temples. Not pain, not even discomfort. Just a warning that left me braced for the next thing. *Wanting* it.

"Tell me more," I said.

"I don't know where to . . ." His eyes made a circuit of the room. "She was *English,* I suppose that's the first thing to say about her. She came to America with her mother in 'ninety-six, still a girl. Eliza Arnold was her name then. Began in brat roles, moved on to ingenues and leading ladies. Oh, she played everywhere, Mr. Landor: Boston, New York, Philadelphia. . . . Always *rapturously* received. She played Ophelia before she was finished. Juliet, Desdemona. She did farce, melodrama, *tableau vivant*. There was nothing she couldn't do."

"And what did she look like?"

"Lovely, that's what they tell me. I have a cameo of her, I'll show you sometime. Very petite, but of a good figure, with . . . *dark* hair." He fingered his own locks. "And large eyes." He caught himself in the act of expanding his own eyes. Grinned puckishly. "My apologies, it comes over me whenever I talk about her. I believe it's because whatever is good in me, Mr. Landor—in person, in spirit—comes from her. I do believe that."

"And her name was *Eliza* Poe?"

"Yes." A queer look came over his face. "Something is troubling you, Mr. Landor."

"Not exactly. I saw her perform once. Many years ago."

A confession, Reader. I haven't read many fine books. I've rarely been to the opera or the symphony or the lyceum. Haven't traveled anywhere south of the Mason-Dixon. But I have been to the theater—many times over. From the moment I could choose among all the sins my father warned me against, that was the one I chose more than any other. In later years, my wife would say it was the only mistress she ever feared. I would bring home playbills like coquettes' fans, and at night, with Amelia snoring by my side, I would relive the whole bill in my head, from the fire juggler to the burnt-cork comedian to the tragedy queen. In my time on earth, I have been privileged to see Edwin Forrest and a dancing three-legged horse, Mrs. Alexander Drake and a burlesque dancer named Zuzina the Hittite, John Howard Payne and a girl who could wrap her entire leg around her head and scratch her nose with her toes. I knew them all by name, as surely as if I had fraternized with them in the local taverns. And today you need only speak one of those names to call up for me a whole climate of association: sounds, sights . . . *smells*, for there is nothing like a New York theater on a November afternoon, when the smell of candle wax melds with the odors of rafter dust and spit-congealed peanut shells and sweat-heavy wool to make something pure as any drug.

Well, that's what happened when I heard the name Eliza Poe. In a mere instant, I had tumbled back twenty-one years and landed in a fifty-cent seat—eighth row orchestra, Park Street Theatre. It was winter, and the place was cold as charity. The whores hanging from the top gallery shivered in their shawls. During that evening's performance, two rats scuttled over my boot, and a woman ten rows back pulled out her breast to feed her squalling baby, and a small fire broke out in the rear benches. I scarcely noticed: I was watching the play. It was something called *Tekeli; or The Siege of Montgatz*. A melodrama about Hungarian patriots. I recall very little of the plot: Turkish vassals and star-crossed lovers, I think, and men in fur hats named, oh, Georgi and Bogdan, and women traipsing about in Magyar vests with braids of artificial hair that swept after them like brooms. But I do remember the actress who played Count Tekeli's daughter.

She struck you first by how tiny she was—frail shoulders and wrists, a fifelike voice—far too slight a figure, you would have thought, for such fierce labor. I remember the way she ran across the stage and threw herself round the portly middle-aged actor who was playing her lover—she was fairly *swallowed* by him. The stage had never seemed so terrifying a place for a young woman.

And yet as the play went on, I could feel something dauntless coming out of her, and it enlarged her and seemed even to enlarge the other actors around her, so that her chubby lover was slowly changed into the lover of her vision, and this play with all its contrivances and death scenes bore the impress of her spirit. Her conviction carried all, and I ceased to fear for her and began in a way to long for her, to wish her back on stage the moment she left. Nor was I alone in my admiration, for there was a ripple that greeted her whenever she came on, and a couple of outright wails went up over her death (collapsed, like Juliet, atop her dead lover's body). And when the curtain had fallen on poor old Tekeli, bewailing his crimes against a free Hungary, it came as no surprise that the only player called out for an encore was *her*.

She stood in front of the curtain, amber light flickering over her hair and hands. She smiled. And it was then I realized she was not as young as

I'd thought. Her face was gaunt and lined, the skin had shrunk round her hands, her elbows were patched with eczema. She looked altogether too weary for an encore, and her eyes were nearly blank, as if she'd forgot where she was. But then she nodded to the conductor in the pit and, with only two bars of preamble, began to sing.

Her voice was as small as she was. Too slight a voice, surely, for such a vast space as the Park. But this also ran in her favor, for everyone fell silent the better to catch what she was singing—even the whores in the gallery ceased their chattering—and because her voice was so clean and unadorned, it carried farther than a thicker voice might have. She stood entirely still, and when she was done, she dropped a curtsy and smiled again and gave us to know, by certain gestures, that there would be no second encore. And then, as she was about to take her leave, she took a backward step, as though a sudden wind had tugged her by the petticoat. Caught herself quickly—made as though it were a part of her farewell—and walked carefully toward the wings, waving her hand one last time as she disappeared.

I should have known it even then. She was dying.

Well, I didn't say quite all *that* to my young friend, just the nicer parts: sobs, huzzahs. Never have I had a more captive audience. He sat there at my feet, in a trance, practically *watching* the words as they came out of my mouth. And afterward, he questioned me as sharply as an Inquisitor. Wanted me to repeat everything, to call back details I was beyond remembering: the color of her costume, the names of the other players, the size of the orchestra.

"And her song," he said, breathing heavy. "Can you sing it now?"

No, I didn't think I could. It had been more than twenty years. I was very sorry, but I couldn't.

Which mattered not a bit. Poe sang it himself, right there on my sitting-room floor.

> *Last night the dogs did bark,*
> *I went to the gate to see,*
> *When ev'ry lass had her spark,*
> *But nobody came to me.*

> *And it's O! dear what will become of me*
> *O! dear what shall I do,*
> *Nobody coming to marry me,*
> *Nobody coming to woo*
> *Nobody coming to woo.*

I remembered it only when he reached the coda, an ascending scale to the dominant tapering back at the last second to the tonic—most affecting. As Poe himself seemed to know, for he drew out those final three notes. A good lyric baritone he had, and he didn't preen with it as he did with his speaking voice. He seemed to be meeting the notes as he went along. And when that last note had dwindled away, he raised his head and said, "My key, not hers." And then, with more emotion, "How privileged you were, Mr. Landor, to hear it."

It had indeed been a privilege, that's what I told him. I would have said that even if it hadn't been. My motto is never get between a man and his dead mama.

"What was she like on stage?" he asked.

"She was charming."

"You're not just—"

"No, no, she was delightful. Girlish and . . . *clear,* in a very nice way."

"That's what they tell me. I wish I could have seen for myself." He wrapped his chin in his hands. "How extraordinary, Mr. Landor, that Fate should have connected us in such a fashion. I could almost believe that the whole purpose of your seeing her was so that you might one day report back to me."

"And now I have," I replied.

"Yes, and what a—what a blessing it is." Looking down, he wormed his hands together, feeling the friction of finger against finger. "You understand how it is, Mr. Landor—to be so utterly bereft, I mean. To lose the one who is dearer to you than life."

"Yes, I suppose I do," I said, evenly.

"I wonder." He glanced up with an appeasing smile. "Would you mind telling me about *her*?"

"Who?"

"Your daughter. I should be glad to hear, if you wouldn't object."

There was a good question: *did* I object?

It had been so long since anyone had asked me that if I had any objections, I could no longer remember what they were. And so—because he'd asked so nicely and because no one else was there and because the fire had died down to a murmur and the air was growing chill round the edges—and, I suppose, because it was a Sunday afternoon, which was when she always felt nearest to me—I began talking.

In no particular order. I just bounced across the years, landing on one memory, rebounding off another. There she was, falling from an elm tree in Green-Wood Cemetery. And there she was, sitting in the midst of Fulton Market. From the youngest age, she could just be set down in the busiest of marketplaces, and she wouldn't budge, wouldn't complain—she always knew someone would be coming back for her. And there she was, buying a dress at Arnold Constable for her thirteenth birthday and, oh, eating ice cream at Contoit's and giving a hug to Jerry Thomas, the bartender at the Metropolitan Hotel.

Her petticoats always made a certain sound, peculiar to her, like a stream churning against a weir. She walked with her head slightly down, as though she were checking the laces of her boots. Only poets could make her cry; humans, almost never. If someone spoke crossly to her, she would stare right *into* him, as though she were trying to understand the terrible change that had come over him.

And she could do dialects—Irish and Italian and at least three different varieties of German—God knows where she learned them all—the streets of New York, I guess. She might have had a career in the theater herself if she hadn't been so—so *inward*. Oh, and she had this curious way of holding her pen, her whole fist curled round the shaft, as though she were trying to spear a fish. We could never get her to hold it any other way, no matter how much her hand cramped.

Her laugh, too, did I mention that? Such a *private* sound—nothing more than a gust of air through the nostrils—accompanied, maybe, by a tremor of the jaw, a stiffening of the neck. Oh, you had to be *alert* to know when that girl was laughing, or you'd miss it completely.

"You haven't told me her name," said Poe.

"Her name?"

"Yes."

"Mattie," I said.

And something fell out of my voice. I should have given up speaking altogether, but I staggered on.

"*Mattie* is her name."

I laid my arm against my steaming eyes and gasped out a laugh. "I'm afraid you find me a bit out of sorts, I do apologize. . . ."

"You needn't say any more," he said gently. "If you don't care to."

"Maybe I will just stop for now."

It was awkward, yes. I would have tried to pretend nothing had happened, but Poe saw no need. He took what I'd said and stored it away and spoke to me as intimately as if he'd known me all his life.

"I do thank you, Mr. Landor."

And there was in his tone the sweetest form of absolution. I never stopped to ask myself what I was being absolved of. I only knew that whatever embarrassment I'd felt was already seeping away.

"Thank *you*, Mr. Poe."

I gave him a nod. Then I sprang to my feet and went in search of snuff.

"So!" I called back. "In the midst of all this chatter, I believe we've quite forgotten the job we were charged with. You say you've found something?"

"Better than that, Mr. Landor. Some*one*."

Poe had made his move (as expected) on Friday afternoon, right after evening parade but before mess was blown. This interval, he had used to approach one of the leaders of the prayer squad—a third classman by the name of Llewellyn Lee. In a low, entreating voice, Poe had asked whether he might join the group at their next convocation, as Sunday chapel would be too long a wait. This Lee quickly called together several of his squadmates for an impromptu discussion by the gun trestles.

"A dreary tribe, Mr. Landor. Had I voiced to them my true religious principles, they would instantly have banished me from their ranks. As it was, I had to affect a docility and deference quite outside my usual character."

"I do appreciate that, Mr. Poe."

"Luck was on our side, however. Being zealots, they are fundamentally credulous in all matters. As a consequence, they had no qualms about inviting me to their next meeting. And when I informed them that I was in dire need of spiritual counsel, owing to a recent encounter with a fellow cadet—well, I hardly need tell you that this piqued their interest. *Please explain yourself,* they said. I announced then, in fearstruck accents, that certain *overtures* had been made to me by this same cadet. Overtures of a rather dark and, to my mind, un-Christian nature. Upon further prompting, I told them I had been exhorted to query the very grounds of my faith . . . and to apprentice myself in mysterious and arcane practices of ancient provenance."

(Was that really how he put it to them? I don't doubt it.)

"Well, they rose to it, Mr. Landor. To a man, they demanded to know who this importunate cadet was. I told them, of course, that as his confidences had been made to me in private, I was honor-bound not to reveal the fellow's name. They said, *Oh yes, we understand,* but a minute later, they were back at it: *Who? Who was it?*"

The memory of it made his eyes twinkle. "Ah, but I stood firm. I said they could not drag it from me did God himself threaten to smite me with a lightning bolt. It would not be right, I said. Against all the codes of an officer and a gentleman. Well, we went back and forth until one of them, goaded beyond all endurance, at last broke out with: *Is it Marquis?*"

There was a savage grin on his face now. He was pleased with himself, no denying it, and who could blame him? It's not every day a plebe gets the better of upperclassmen.

"*Et alors,* Mr. Landor! Thanks to my little ruse and their callow sensibilities, we now have at our disposal a name."

"And that was all they gave you? A name?"

"They didn't dare do more. The fellow who let it slip was instantly pummeled into silence."

"But I don't understand. Why did they mention Dr. Marquis when you had expressly told them it was a cadet?"

"Not *Dr.* Marquis—*Artemus* Marquis."

"Artemus?"

That grin stretched wider now. All those pearly perfect teeth in full revelry.

"Dr. Marquis' only son," he said. "A first classman. And reputedly a dabbler in black magic."

15

November 7th to the 11th

And from that instant, Poe had a new mission. He was to find some way of getting close to this Artemus Marquis, learn as much as could be learned, and report back to me at punctual intervals. It was here, on the brink of his next adventure, that my young spy blanched.

"Mr. Landor, with all due respects, it's impossible."

"Why is that?"

"Oh, it's undeniable that I—I possess some small local renown, but I've no reason to believe I am *known* to Mr. Marquis. For all that we march in the same cadet company, we've no acquaintance in common, and being a plebe, I've *scant* resources for contracting any sort of social intimacy. . . ."

No, no, he assured me, it wouldn't do. Teasing a name out of the prayer squad, that had been one thing; worming his way into the confidences of a first classman would be quite another.

"I'm sure you'll find a way," I said. "You can be very charming when you set your mind to it."

"But what am I to look for, exactly?"

"Why, I'm afraid I don't yet know, Mr. Poe. It seems to me the first task is to gain Mr. Marquis' trust. Once you've secured that, you need only keep your eyes and ears open."

And when still he caviled, I laid a hand on his shoulder and said:

"Mr. Poe, if anyone is capable of this, you are."

Which I think I must have believed. Why else would I have let an entire week go by without word from him? Although, by the time Thursday night rolled round, I admit I'd begun to despair of our project's success. I was actually in the act of framing my defense before Hitchcock when I heard a thump against my hotel door.

By the time I opened it, the hall was empty. The package, though, that was waiting for me in its plain brown wrapper.

And here was I, expecting scraps of intelligence, the briefest of bulletins. Leave it to Poe to produce an entire manuscript. Pages upon pages! God knows when he'd found the time to write it all out. It's well known what a taskmaster Thayer is: reveille at dawn, morning maneuvers, meals, recitations, drills, parade, tattoo at nine-thirty. Cadets can't get more than seven hours of sleep on any given night. Looking at Poe's account of the past week, I'd say he got by with even less than his usual four.

I read it all in one sitting. And it gave me no small pleasure, partly because, like all narratives, it says so much about the author—though not, of course, what the author himself would say.

Report of Edgar A. Poe to Augustus Landor

November 11th

Enclosed you will find a brief history of my investigations undertaken to the present date.

I have endeavored in every way to be as factual as possible—precision, Mr. Landor!—with none of the lyrical accents that would occasion you pain. Wherever I err toward Fancy, kindly excuse it as not the prerogative—the *reflex* of a Poet, unable to pry his soul free of its vocation.

I believe I impressed upon you the nearly insurmountable challenges I faced in forming an intimacy with Artemus Marquis. Indeed, I spent the better part of Sunday night and early Monday morning turning the problem over in my mind. I came at length to a certain conclusion—namely, that forcing myself on young Marquis' attentions would demand a public display such as would align me with his deepest and, unless I presume too far, his *darkest* sympathies.

Accordingly, as soon as Monday's reveille roll call had finished, I lost no time in making my way to the hospital, where I was able to present myself directly to Dr. Marquis. This good gentleman asked me what it was ailed me. I informed him that I was sick at my stomach. "Vertigo, hey?" cried Dr. Marquis. "Let me feel of your pulse. Pretty quick. Very well, Mr. Poe, keep in the house today and take care of yourself. Matron will give you a dose of salts. Tomorrow, I want you to knock about, take exercise, stir yourself. Nothing better." Armed with salts and a note excusing me from duties, I presented myself next to Lieutenant Joseph Locke, who, in tandem with his cadet commanders, was overseeing the breakfast formation. I could not help but note Mr. Artemus Marquis standing among their ranks.

A brief word about his appearance, Mr. Landor. He is perhaps five feet and ten inches, slender and well knit, with hazel-green eyes and chestnut hair of such a curly disposition that the Academy barbers have yet to tame it. Mindful of his privileges as a first classman, he has even begun to sport a mustache which he trims with great rigor. A smile seems always to play on his lips, which are full and warm. He is reckoned extremely handsome, I believe, and a more susceptible soul might suppose that Byron himself had been reborn in all his beauty.

Lieutenant Locke, upon reading the doctor's note, affected a great scowl. Cognizant now that I possessed an audience—and in particular the young Marquis—I took this advantage to announce that in addition to the vertigo, I was laid under by an even worse ailment: *grand ennui* seizure.

"*Grand ennui?*" expostulated the lieutenant.

"Of a most pronounced character," said I.

At this, a few of the more discerning cadets began to titter amongst themselves. Others, however, impatient at the delay, began to vent their displeasure in no uncertain terms. "What a fast animal it is! Hey, get on with it, Dad!" (I must regretfully supply context for this last epithet. In respect to my fellow classmates, I am considered somewhat older in appearance—nothing to be wondered at, as I am further on in years than most of them. My roommate, Mr. Gibson, by way of comparison, is no more than fifteen. There has even been circulated a scurrilous rumor that my Academy appointment was originally intended for my son and was passed to me upon that hypothetical young man's untimely death.) These imbecile antics were summarily silenced by the cadet adjutant, and I am pleased to report that most of the fellows in my company looked upon the proceedings with no comment. Artemus Marquis was one of these.

By now, Sergeant Locke had begun to grow vexed in spirit. Although I endeavored to make him understand that my condition was serious indeed, he would have none of my justifications and warned me to mind myself or be reported. Protesting my innocence, I cried that he could ask the doctor himself, if he liked. Even as I spoke these words, Mr. Landor, I undertook my rashest act of all. I located Artemus Marquis' eye in the crowd, and in a covert but unmistakable fashion, I *winked* at him.

Had Marquis *fils* been more piously disposed toward his father, he might well have taken great offense, thereby dashing on the spot any hope of my binding myself to him. You may ask, then, why did I see fit to court such a danger? I had already concluded, you see, that a man fain to flout Religious Orthodoxy would be as willing to flout Family Orthodoxy. There is, I acknowledge, no a priori reason for believing so, but my inferences were soon vindicated by the moue of amusement which overtook the young man's face. I heard him then remark, "It's quite true, Lieutenant. My father has told me he's never seen anything like it."

My delight at this turn of events spurred me on toward new transgressions. Thus, as Sergeant Locke was turning to Artemus to chide him for his impertinence, I announced, loudly enough for all to hear, that my spells were most pronounced in liturgical settings. "I fear I shall have to miss chapel," I said, most pointedly. "For the next three Sundays, at the very least."

I saw Artemus' hand pass before his mouth—whether to conceal amusement or consternation I cannot say, for Sergeant Locke was even now fronting me. In a voice unnaturally low, he charged me with "unbecoming brazenness" and opined that an extra tour or two of guard duty would do something to "cure me of that." Fumbling for his ubiquitous notebook, he then awarded me three demerits, adding a fourth for improperly blacked shoes.

(Mr. Landor, I must interrupt my narrative and entreat you most earnestly to speak with Captain Hitchcock in my behalf. I should never have so brazenly courted infractions had the Academy's business not been foremost in mind. I am not so anxious about the demerits, but the guard duty would be an enormous encumbrance to our ongoing inquiries—to my very Health.)

Sergeant Locke commanded me to return directly to my quarters, with the injunction that I had best be there when the officers came round for their morning inspections. I took him at his word and was indeed dutifully seated in Number 22 South Barracks when the knock came, shortly after ten o'clock. Imagine my surprise, Mr. Landor, to find the commandant himself entering my quarters. I immediately rose to attention and was relieved to see that my hat and coatee were properly hung on their wall pegs and that my bedroll was in good order. For reasons unknown, Captain

Hitchcock prolonged his inspection beyond the normal bounds, perusing both the front room and the sleeping room of our suite, and even made a point of commenting on the condition of my blacking brush. His inspection at last complete, he inquired of me, in what I might call an exceedingly ironical tone, how my vertigo was progressing. I forbore to make any but the most noncommittal rejoinder. Captain Hitchcock then enjoined me to avoid any further antagonizing of Lieutenant Locke. I assured him that such had never been my intention. Although not exactly satisfied on that score, he left.

The rest of the day was passed in study of a mostly unfruitful sort: algebra and spherical geometry, neither of which presents any remarkable challenge to one of my attainments, in addition to the translation of a rather mundane passage from Voltaire's *Histoire de Charles XII*. By afternoon, I was so eager for diversion that I even gave myself leave to pen verse. Sadly, I was unable to indite more than a few lines, beset as I am by the memory of this *other* poem—dictated by the unseen *Presence* to which I have already adverted.

My dark ruminations were interrupted sometime toward midafternoon by the sound of a rock thumping against my window. Leaping from my chair, I threw open the casement. What was my astonishment in beholding Artemus Marquis in the assembly yard below!

"Poe, is it?" he cried.

"Yes."

"Hash tonight. Eleven o'clock. Eighteen North Barracks."

Not staying for my reply, he sauntered off.

I was struck most forcibly by the volume of his delivery. Here, after all, was an upperclassman inviting a plebe to partake of an illicit after-hours activity. And for all that, he called up *à gorge déployée*. I can only theorize that being the son of a West Point faculty member must confer (at least in his mind) a certain immunity from reprisal.

I will not tax you, Mr. Landor, with the complicated stratagems by means of which I left my quarters shortly after tattoo. Let it suffice that the two cadets who share my rooms are fast sleepers—and that, by dint of light treading and quick thinking, I was able to present myself to the occupants of Eighteen North Barracks several minutes prior to the appointed hour.

Inside I found the windows covered over with blankets. Bread and butter had been smuggled from the mess hall and potatoes from the officers' mess, a chicken had been hooked from someone's barnyard, and a basket of speckled red apples had been claimed from Farmer de Kuiper's orchard.

Naturally, as a singularly favored plebe, I was the object of some curiosity—though one of the room's occupants made a special point of withholding his approbation. This was Cadet First Classman Randolph Ballinger, of Pennsylvania, who lost no chance to gibe me. "Oh, Dad! Give us more French." "Eddie boy, isn't it past your bedtime?" "I think it's about time we filled the *pot de chambre*." (I need hardly remind you that *pot*, as rendered by the Gallic tongue, is homophonic with my own surname.) Being that no one else appeared disposed to rise to his bait, I could not at first understand why he so served me—until, from various hints, I divined that he was Artemus' roommate. From this I concluded that he had appointed himself guardian of Artemus' inner circle and was, in the execution of this office, as zealous as Cerberus.

Had I come under my own banner, Mr. Landor, I should have made this Ballinger answer for his slights. Being all too mindful, however, of my responsibilities toward you and to the Academy, I resolved to bite my tongue. The others, I am relieved to say, seemed bound and determined to make up for Ballinger's churlish manners. I attribute this in large part to Artemus, who demonstrated unfeigned interest in my humble history. Upon learning that I was a published Poet—not that I in any way volunteered this intelligence (nor did I, except under great duress, disclose the opinion of Mrs. Sarah Josepha Hale, who has seen fit to hymn a sample of my verses as evidencing notable gifts)—upon learning, I say, of my Vocation, he immediately demanded a public reading. What could I do but comply, Mr. Landor? In truth, the only real difficulty consisted in finding a poem suitable to the occasion. "Al Aaraaf" is a bit abstruse for lay audiences and remains, in any event, unfinished, and while I have earned warm praise for the closing stanza of "Tamerlane," it was evident that something in a lighter vein was needed in this context. I allowed then as how I had been moved to panegyrize Lieutenant Locke. I soon learned that more than one of the fellows in the room—Artemus included—had, over the course of their years at the Academy, been reported by this dagger-eyed officer. Thus, they were well primed for my bit of doggerel (composed, I confess at the risk of boasting, on the very spot).

> *John Locke was a notable name;*
> *Joe Locke is greater; in short,*
> *The former was well known to fame*
> *But the latter's well known "to report."*

This provoked a hearty round of laughter and acclamation. I was praised beyond all measure, and was earnestly requested to compose squibs on the subject of *other* officers and instructors. I complied as best I could and even hazarded impersonations of the more colorful specimens. It was generally agreed that I had done particular justice to Professor Davies—"caught old Rush Tush to the life"—and when I aped the professor's habit of leaning forward and crying, "How's that, Mr. Marquis?" . . . well, you never heard such a roar.

Amidst all this revelry, there was but a single abstainer: the afore-mentioned Ballinger. I cannot recall the exact text of his remarks, though I believe there was something to the effect of how much better off I would be entertaining ladies in Saratoga, rather than wasting my exquisite gifts on a place such as this. Fortunately, I was rescued from the necessity of re-plying in kind by Artemus, who shrugged his shoulders and said, "It's not just Poe. We're *all* wasted here."

At this, one of the wags opined that the only good reason to come to the Academy was "to meet all the women." This prompted the most vio-lent and boisterous roar of the evening. Being a man yourself, Mr. Landor, you will find it in no way wonderful that the conversation soon devolved into such sightings of the female form as had been secured in recent weeks. One might have thought twenty years had passed since these poor fellows had beheld a woman, so voracious were they in savoring every last detail.

At length, it was suggested by one of those present that Artemus "take out his telescope." I assumed this at first to be a particularly unfortunate metaphor, but in fact, an actual telescope of modest proportions was soon procured from the mantel, and ere long, Artemus had set it on a tripod and trained it out his window, in a south-by-southeasterly direction. After tactful questioning, I learned that Artemus, while still a plebe, had, in the course of his nocturnal explorations, located a certain far-off domicile wherein a young woman was said to have passed before the window in a state of half undress. No one but Artemus and Ballinger had seen it at the time, no one had seen it since, and yet the mere *possibility* of espying this elusive vision of Woman drove man after man to the eyepiece.

I alone forfeited the chance to view, for which reticence I was soundly ridiculed by Ballinger and, on this occasion, one or two others. I considered myself in no way obliged to answer their ridiculous charges, and once they saw that they would gain nothing more from their efforts than a succession of blushes, Ballinger and his fellow gibers gradually desisted. It may even be that my blushes further endeared me to the evening's host, for after the revels wound to a close, Artemus made it an especial point to invite me to a game of cards on Wednesday evening.

"You'll come, won't you, Poe?"

This was advanced in a tone sufficient to stifle any dissent in its birth. And in the interlude of silence that ensued, it became incontestably clear that Artemus asserted over this group the authority of a monarch, whose crown is no less contested for being so lightly worn.

The only problem I faced in accepting the invitation of young Marquis was the inadequacy of my cash reserves. For reasons too complicated to enumerate, I have nearly run through my twenty-eight-dollar stipend for the month. I briefly considered requesting capital of *you*, Mr. Landor, but in the end, I was rescued by the kindly intervention of my Tarheel roommate, who stepped in *au moment critique* and graciously loaned me two of his private stock of dollars (on top of the three that, as he gently reminded me, he had lent me in October). So it was that on Wednesday evening, with bills in hand, I gamely crept up the stairwell and once again presented myself to the hosts of Eighteen North Barracks. Artemus professed himself delighted to see me and, with a charmingly proprietorial air, showed me round to the fellows who had not been on hand two evenings previous. Introduction was scarce needed, for my feats of *vers de société* had already been bruited about mess hall and parade ground, and those cadets who had not been present were eager to have squibs coined for their own least favored personages. (I'm afraid that Captain Hitchcock was numbered among these ranks. I am unable to recall the quatrain he inspired, other than the accompanying rhyme, which was "kitchen clock.") In one respect at least, this gathering was different to the last: one of the cadets had smuggled in a bottle of Pennsylvania hard whiskey (courtesy of *la divine* Patsy). The very sight of it warmed my blood.

The game, Mr. Landor, was écarté—long a favorite of mine and one I was wont to play ofttimes as a matriculant at the University of Virginia. You will not, I think, be surprised to learn that before two rounds had passed, I had vaulted into a winning position—much to the perturbation of Ballinger, who, warm with spirits, failed to announce that he had the king of clubs and hence forfeited the right to mark it. Happy would I have been to while away the entire evening snapping up his nickels, had I not perceived another unintended victim of my wiles: Artemus. By the increasing frequency of the peevish remarks that escaped him, I was led to believe that this was not the first time he had incurred losses, nor would it be the last. As his irritation grew, so, too, grew my cares. Having worked so hard to seat myself in the cathedral of his affections, I could not bear to see my labor set at naught by something so paltry as cards. And so, Mr. Landor, I took the path away from pride and toward the general amity: I contrived to let Artemus win and closed the evening some three dollars and twelve cents in arrears.

(Mr. Landor, I must here pause and earnestly request that you make good on these debts, which were incurred entirely in the Academy's service. Had Mr. Allan seen fit to make good on his promises, I should have had no need to beg this of you, but my financial embarrassments leave me with no other recourse.)

Well, sir, it is no small thing for a man to throw away even a modest clutch of worldly goods when they lie so near to his grasp. However, my "losses" (for so they would be constructed by amateur eyes) excited no end of pity in my fellow cadets, Artemus most particularly, and left them still better disposed toward me than before. Now, I could see, was the moment for bringing our business to its maturity. And thus it was that, with the greatest care and tact, I caused the subject of Leroy Fry to be introduced into our conversation.

I disclosed to them that *you,* Mr. Landor, had interviewed me under the mistaken impression that I was an intimate of Fry's. This fomented no end of debate on the fascinating subject of Yourself. I will not oppress you with the minutiae, Mr. Landor, except to say that you are now enveloped in a cult of legend comparable to that of Bonaparte or Washington. It was said by one that you had caused a felon to confess his deed simply by clearing your throat, and by another that you had unmasked a murderer by sniffing the residue of his thumb on a candle holder. In the view of Artemus himself—I feel it incumbent to report—you seem an altogether *mild* gentleman, surely more at home apprehending scallops than scoundrels. (If his alliteration is too juvenile for full comic effect, you can at least take comfort, Mr. Landor, in the misconception it betrays of your character.)

The talk subsequently turned to the unfortunate Fry himself. By the testimony of one of the assembled wits, the poor lad had never ranked in the first section of anything—he had failed even to wield a theodolite with notable success—and so had effected, by his death, the one achievement which might have gained him distinction. The prevailing consensus was that Fry had occupied such a small niche in the Academy's firmament that he would therefore have been deemed incapable of such a large and awful act of self-annihilation. Yes, Mr. Landor, it is still generally believed that Leroy Fry visited death upon himself. Interestingly, it is also widely credited that he was in the act of venturing out that evening for an assignation. How these two assumptions can be in any manner reconciled—well, that is outside my poor ken, though one second classman did propound the theory that Fry had hanged himself in despair over being jilted by the lady who had sworn to meet him.

"And what lady would have sworn to meet *him*?" exclaimed one.

Amidst the laughter occasioned by this remark, the smiling Ballinger was heard to say, "What of your sister, Artemus? Didn't she dazzle Leroy?"

The room grew ominously silent, for it seemed that the odious Ballinger was on the verge of impugning a lady's honor, a circumstance which must make any gentleman worth the name rise and demand an accounting. I myself was in the act of doing so when I was arrested by Artemus' hand on my sleeve. His countenance had lightened into a state of strange serenity, and it was with great unease that I heard him say, "Come, Randy. You were closer to Fry than anybody in this room."

Speaking in a level tone, Ballinger replied, "I don't believe I was so near to him as *you*, Artemus."

As the young Marquis made no riposte, the room once again fell quiet—a silence so deep and so suspenseful that none dared speak. It was then that Artemus confounded us all by collapsing into laughter, in which condition he was soon joined by Ballinger. Theirs was not, though, the merry peal that gladdens a listener's heart; no, Mr. Landor, it was laughter of an altogether more hysterical order, exemplary of nerves tautened to their limit. Only by Artemus' own exertions were we able to renew the spirit of revelry with which the evening had commenced. Even so, no one dared presume to raise the specter of Leroy Fry, and as the time crept well past the midnight hour, we relapsed into such banalities as could be safely essayed by fatigued minds.

Shortly before one o'clock, I became aware that our numbers had one by one dropped off until four only remained together. I thereupon determined to take my leave. Artemus rose with me and offered—nay, all but demanded—to serve as my escort out of barracks. Lieutenant Case, he explained, had taken of late to walking the halls in caoutchouc overshoes. In this way he had maneuvered, over the course of a week, to hive five cadets, break up three hashes, and confiscate six meerschaums. I might be hived "perfectly frigid," I was informed, unless I employed an escort.

Thanking him profusely, I assured him that I would gladly take any risks on my own head.

"Well, good night, then, Poe." His hand clasped mine and then he added, "Come to my father's house this Sunday for tea. Some of the other lads will be there, too."

What next transpired, I fear, pertains at best indirectly to Artemus. I have thus debated the propriety of recounting it to you, Mr. Landor. Remembering, however, my Charge—to recount *all*—I proceed.

I soon found that the stairwell of North Barracks was beset by a darkness nearly impenetrable. In the act of groping my way to ground level, I managed to catch my heel on one of the risers, and might have tumbled headmost down the remaining steps had I not grabbed hold of a sconce just over my head.

Holding fast to the banister, I made my way down the remaining steps with no further mishap until my hand touched the door, at which time I was arrested by a terrifying premonition. To my benighted faculties, it seemed that *somebody was there*—lurking in the ebon shadows.

Had there been a lantern at my disposal, I might have had the means to put my fears to rest. Alas, with vision so effectually stymied, I had only the evidence of those *other* senses, which, by way of compensation, had been stimulated into overacuteness, so that there came to my ears a low, dull, quick sound, such as a watch makes when enveloped in cotton. In that instant, I was seized by the distinct and ineradicable impression that I was being *watched*—*marked*—in the way prey is measured by a beast in the depths of the jungle's penumbrae.

He will kill me. That was the naked thought which seized me at that moment. And yet I could not have said before whom I trembled, nor why he might have wished me ill. Stranded there in the pitch blackness, I could but await my Fate—with the despair of heart that characterizes the Doomed Man.

There was a long and obstinate silence; and I was once again applying my weight against the door when I felt a hand close round the front of my throat—another hand clutch the back of my neck—in a perfect chain of constriction.

I should add that it was not so much the force as the *surprise* of this assault which left me helpless to embark on any positive course of defense. In vain, yes, in vain did I struggle—until the hands, as suddenly as they had materialized, were withdrawn, and I fell to the ground with a sharp cry.

Supine, I gazed upon a pair of bare feet shining with an unearthly pallor in the Plutonian darkness. From above me came the softly insinuating snarl:

"Why, what a woman it is."

That voice! *The odious Ballinger*—lording it over me!

For a few seconds longer he stood, breathing heavily. He thereupon made his way back up the stairs, leaving me in a state of near-perfect agitation and—I will confess it—consuming rage. Such injuries, such insults, are not to be borne, Mr. Landor, even in the pursuit of higher Justice. Mark me! There will come a day when the lion shall be devoured by the lamb—when the Hunter shall himself be *hunted*!

My Aristotelian unities must now be compromised, Mr. Landor, for I see I have forgot to mention the last remark Artemus made to me. As I was standing in the hall, I heard him say that he desired me to meet his sister.

Well, that's Poe's version. Of course, you never can be sure about what someone tells you, can you? That encounter of his with Lieutenant Locke, for instance: I'm willing to bet he didn't pull it off with quite the coolness he'd like us to believe. And that business of letting Artemus win at écarté—well, it's my experience that young men don't play cards but are played by them. I'm willing to be proven wrong.

I should say that of all the things in Poe's account, the part that seemed least clouded by the narrator—the part, at any rate, I kept returning to—was that cryptic exchange between Artemus and Ballinger:

You were closer to Fry than anybody. . . .

I don't believe I was as near to him as you. . . .

Those words: *closer, near*. I had to ask myself, what if those two jovial fellows were talking about *actual* distance? Jesting, in their coded way, about how *near* they'd been to Leroy Fry's dead body?

It was a straw, yes, but I was in a mood to grasp. And so, before dinner, I made a point of stopping in the cadet mess.

Reader, have you ever seen Ourang-Outangs set loose from their chains? Such is the picture I'd have you keep in mind as we enter the mess. Imagine hundreds of famished young men marched in silence to their tables. Imagine them standing at attention behind their seats, waiting for just two little words: "Take seats!" Listen to the buzzing roar that follows as they fling themselves on pewter plates and dive for viands. Tea is gargled still hot, bread is swallowed whole, boiled potatoes are torn like carrion, slabs of bull beef vanish in the blink of an eye. For the next twenty minutes, the raging of the Ourang-Outangs fills the air, and it is no surprise to learn that here, as nowhere else, fights break out—over nothing more than pork and molasses. The only wonder is the beasts don't eat the tables, the very chairs on which they sit, and then hunt down the stewards and the mess-hall captain.

All of which is to say that I was virtually ignored when I stepped into the room. Which gave me leave to talk up one of the stewards, a highly intelligent Negro who had seen and learned a great deal in his ten years here. He could tell you which cadets pinched bread and which ones pinched beef, which were the best carvers and which had the worst manners, which ones took their meals at Mammy Thompson's and which ones dined on cookies and pickles from the soda shop. His insights went beyond food, for he also had a deep sense of which cadets would actually graduate (not many) and which of these would remain brevet second lieutenants for half their lives.

"Cesar," I said. "I wonder if you wouldn't point out some of these fellows for me. Gently, now, I don't want to be rude."

To be more sure of him, I asked him first to identify Poe. Cesar found him straight off—hunched over a plate of mutton, picking with distaste at a mound of turnips. I then threw out some meaningless names, belonging to cadets I'd heard of but never talked to. And then, taking care to keep my voice light, I said, "Oh, and Dr. Marquis' son. Where would he be?"

"Why, he's one of the table commandants," said Cesar. "Over there in the southwestern corner."

And that was my first glimpse of Artemus Marquis, seated at the head of the table, swallowing a forkful of boiled pudding. His posture was Prussian, his profile clean enough for a coin, his body tapered exactly where the uniform tapered. And unlike some of the other table commandants, who would jump to their feet or bark warnings, he ruled over his ravenous boys much as Poe had already noted: without in any way seeming to rule. I saw two of his cadets get into an argument over who should be pouring the tea. Far from putting his oar in, Artemus unlocked his spine, slouched back in his chair, and *watched,* with a look that steered just north of indolence. He gave them all the tether they wanted and then, without a sound or a sign, snapped it back—for didn't they stop bickering as suddenly as they'd started? And didn't they each give Artemus a quick appraising glance before returning to their business?

The only person Artemus actually spoke to was the fellow on his immediate left. A blond warrior—a hearty, jawy sort who talked with the food still in his mouth, his cheeks puffing out like gills—with a neck so large it seemed to be feasting on his head. His name (as the great Cesar soon informed me) was Randolph Ballinger.

You might have watched the two of them from start to finish, watched them for many dinners to come, and found nothing out of the way. They spoke in clear masculine cadences. Their smiles were candid, their manners free. No menace hid in their joints. They laughed at each other's jokes and stood when the time came to stand and marched when it was time to march. There was nothing—nothing, I suppose, but Artemus' good looks—to set them apart from their peers.

And yet they *were* apart, I felt it in my nerves. I felt it when I turned them over in my head.

Artemus, yes. Artemus, why not? Carving away Leroy Fry's heart.

It made such perfect sense I almost couldn't trust it. A surgeon's son, with a straight path to his father's instruments and textbooks—his father's *brain*. Who better to perform such a tricky business in such a trying environment?

I forgot to mention. There came a point in that mess-hall dinner when Artemus Marquis turned his head, very slowly, and met my gaze. No trace of embarrassment. No urge to pacify me or anyone. A pair of hazel-green slates, wiped clean.

In that moment, I felt him bracing his will against mine, daring me on.

That, at any rate, was the idea that troubled me as I left the mess hall. The sun was bright enough to scratch tiny hairs across my retinas. In the artillery park, a bombardier was shining the brass barrel of an eighteen-pounder; another was hauling a barrow of pine logs toward the woodyard. A horse was drawing an empty cart up the steep hill from the boat landing, and the cart was rattling like a bushel basket of peas.

In my pocket was a note for Poe: *Well done! I want to hear all I can about Ballinger. Widen the web.*

I was carrying it to our hiding place in Kosciusko's Garden. There is nothing much to this garden, Reader, at least to name. It's only a small terrace gouged out of the Hudson's rocky bank. You'll find some piled rocks, a bit of greenery, a couple of hardy chrysanthemums . . . and, yes, just as Poe said, a clear spring welling up in a stone basin . . . and etched in that stone, the name of the great Polish colonel who oversaw the building of West Point's fortifications. It was to this hidden nook that he is said to have retreated from his cares. These days, there's not much retreat to be had—at least in the warmer months, when the place is overrun by tourists—but on a November afternoon, if you fix things right, you can make it answer in much the same way it answered for Kosciusko.

So, at least, had been the impulse of the two people who were seated there now on a stone bench. A man and a woman. The woman was small-boned, with a girl's waist and nearly a girl's face, only the slightest pouching of skin showing around the jaw. She was grinning from ear to ear—*fearfully* grinning—and somehow managing to speak *through* her grin to her companion. Who was Dr. Marquis.

I didn't recognize him at once, but then I'd never come across him— or anyone, really—in quite that attitude before. I doubt I can convey the thing's strangeness. He had pressed his thumbs into his ears. Not like a man shutting out a terrible din but like a man trying on a hat. His fingers lay draped along the sides of his head, like an otter's pelt, and from time to time, he would waggle them a little, as if to find a better fit. His eyes stared into mine—big wide veiny eyes that seemed to be trembling on the brink of an apology.

"Mr. Landor," he said, rising to his feet. "May I introduce to you my charming wife?"

Well, Reader, you know how it is. A person can, in the space of one second, be magnified several times over by association. I looked at this grinning woman with her draining attentiveness, and suddenly she contained her husband and her son and a wardrobe of secrets—all submerged in that tiny bird-frame.

"Why, Mr. Landor," she said, in a softly nasal voice. "I have heard so much about you. I'm so delighted to make your acquaintance!"

"All mine," I said. "The *pleasure*, I mean. All—"

"I understand from my husband that you are a widower."

The sally came so quickly it caught me in the throat.

"That is so," I managed to say.

I looked to the doctor, waited for him to—what?—blush, maybe. Look askance. But his eyes were shiny with interest, and his big ruined lips were already rehearsing the words to come.

"All due sympathies," he said. "All due . . . goes without—without . . . May I ask, Mr. Landor, was it *recent*?"

"Was what?"

"Your wife going to her reward. Was it—"

"It was three years ago," I said. "Only a few months after we came to the Highlands."

"A sudden illness, then."

"Not sudden enough."

He had to blink away his surprise. "Oh, I'm—I'm—"

"She was in great pain toward the end, Doctor. I could have wished her a faster reward than she got."

This was deeper, I think, than he wished to go. He turned his face to the river, muttered his consolations to the water.

"Must be . . . almighty lonely and all that, where you . . . if you should ever . . ."

"What my husband *means* to say," said Mrs. Marquis, smiling like the sun, "is that we should be honored to have you in our house. As our esteemed guest."

"And I'd be delighted to accept," I said. "In fact, I was going to propose the same thing myself."

How I expected her to react, I can't say, but I never expected this: her face—every part of her face—sprang open, as if it were held together by trip wires. And then she squealed—yes, I think *squealed* is the right word—and even as the sound came out, she was slapping it back into her mouth.

"*Propose?* Why, you sly devil. Oh, what a devil you are."

Then, lowering her voice, she added:

"I believe you are the gentleman charged with inquiring into Mr. Fry's death, is that so?"

"It is."

"How fascinating. My husband and I have just been discussing the matter. Indeed, he now informs me that despite his own"—she squeezed his bicep—"*heroic* efforts, the body of that unfortunate Mr. Fry has been judged too far along for public display and has at last been shut away, in accordance with all decent sensibilities."

This I knew already. Word of Fry's death had been late getting to his parents, and the decision had been made to shut him up for good in his six-sided pine box. Before sealing the lid, Captain Hitchcock had asked me if I wanted one last look.

I did. Though, for the life of me, I can't say why.

No longer bloated, Leroy Fry's body had shrunk back on itself. He floated in a swamp of his own fluid, his arms and legs were black cream, and even the maggots had taken their fill of him, they came scurrying out of every cavity, leaving the rest to the newly hatched beetles that stirred beneath his skin like new muscle.

One thing else I noticed before they sealed the box: the final reservoirs of fluid had swelled into Leroy Fry's eyelids. His yellow eyes had, after eighteen days, closed.

And now I stood in Kosciusko's Garden and stared into the bright brown irises of Mrs. Marquis' eyes, which were open as wide as they could be.

"Oh, Mr. Landor," she said. "This whole affair has left my husband quite shaken. It's been many years since he has had to witness such carnage. Not since the war, I think. Isn't that so, Daniel?"

He nodded in grave assent and slowly curled his arm round her tiny waist, as though to reassert his claim over this—this *trophy*, this wren of a woman, with her crinkling, overawed brown eyes and her calico pockets.

I mumbled something about needing to get back, but my two companions declared themselves ready to walk me as far as my hotel. And so, having failed to leave my message for Poe, I found myself carted back to

Mr. Cozzens', the good doctor following behind and his wife alongside me, her hand coiled round my arm.

"You won't mind, I hope, if I lean on you just a little, Mr. Landor? These slippers have given my poor feet such a pinching. How the female sex tortures itself in the name of fashion."

Spoken like a post belle at her first hop. And if I were a young cadet at such a hop, I would say . . . I would say . . .

"You may be sure your sacrifices aren't lost on me."

She looked at me then as if I had uttered the most original sentence ever conceived. Which, I seem to recall, is how young women look at you when you're a young man. And then out of her mouth came the strangest laugh I have ever heard, high and echoing and broken into even segments, like stalactites dripping in a vast cavern.

"Why, Mr. Landor, if I *weren't*. And that's all I will say, if I *weren't*!"

Saturday night, I went back to my cottage, where Patsy was waiting for me. Of all the pleasures she promised, the one I think I looked forward to the most was the chance she would give me to *sleep*. I figured, you see, that a stretch of lovemaking might ease me out of that half-waking state of mine. What I'd forgotten was how much she *awakened* me, even as she spent herself. Once she was done with me, she just . . . glided off to dreamland, didn't she? . . . with her head resting on my breastbone. And me? I lay there, still aflame with her, marveling at the thickness of her black hair, the *strength* of it, like nautical roping.

And when I could draw my thoughts from Patsy, I found them returning of their own accord to the Point. The evening tattoo would already have sounded, I thought, and the moon would have left its tracks everywhere. And from my hotel window, I would have been able to see the year's last steamers bearing south, leaving a train of glitter. Mottlings of shadow on the mountain slopes . . . the ruins of old Fort Clinton smoldering like the end of a cigar. . . .

I heard Patsy's voice, slurry with sleep.

"Are you going to tell me, Gus?"

"Tell you what?"

"About your little investigation. Are you going to tell me, or will I have to . . . ?"

Catching me off guard, she swung a leg over me. Gave me just the softest pulse and waited for me to pulse back.

"Maybe I forgot to mention," I said. "I'm an old man."

"Not so old," she said.

Which was the very thing Poe had said to me, I remembered. *Not so old*.

"So what have you found out, Gus?"

She fell back on her side, gave herself a nice scratch on the belly.

Strictly speaking, I wasn't to tell her anything. Total discretion, that had been my vow to Thayer and Hitchcock. But having already broken one vow—abstinence—made it much easier for me to break another. Without any more encouragement, then, I started talking about the markings by the icehouse and the visit to Professor Pawpaw and Poe's encounters with the mysterious Cadet Marquis.

"Artemus," she murmured.

"You know him?"

"Oh, certainly. Glorious look to him. He'd almost *have* to die young, wouldn't he? You wouldn't want him to age even a fraction."

"I'm surprised you haven't—"

She looked at me sharply. "You're about to embarrass yourself, aren't you, Gus?"

"No."

"Good." She nodded firmly. "Can't say I would've picked him for the violent sort. Always very cool."

"Oh, I don't know, maybe he's not our man, there's just—there's a *quality* to him. To his whole family."

"Explain yourself."

"I came across his mother and father yesterday in the midst of a very private talk, and they acted—oh, it sounds childish, they acted like people who were *guilty* of something."

"All families are guilty," said Patsy. "Of something."

And in that moment, I thought of my father. To be specific, I thought of the birch he used to take to my hide at regular intervals. Never more than five strokes at a time—never a need for more. The sound was all it took: the screaming whistle, always more shocking than the blow. To this day, the memory of it can set me sweating.

"You're right," I admitted. "But some families are guiltier than others."

I did manage some rest that night. And the next evening, back at Mr. Cozzens' hotel, I fell asleep the moment my head touched the pillow. Only to be awoken again at ten minutes before midnight by a soft rap on my door.

"Come in, Mr. Poe," I called.

There was no one else it could be. He opened the door with great care and stood there, framed in the blackness, loath to take even a step into the room.

"Here," he said, setting another sheaf of foolscap on the floor. "My latest installment."

"Thank you," I said. "I look forward to reading it."

He might have nodded, there was no way of telling, for he carried no candle, and my lantern was out.

"Mr. Poe, I hope you're not ... I'm a bit worried, you see, that your studies are being neglected."

"No," he said. "They're just beginning."

A long pause.

"And how are you sleeping?" he asked me finally.

"Better, thank you."

"Ah, you're a lucky man, then. I can't seem to sleep at all."

"I'm sorry to hear it."

Another pause, even longer than the one before.

"Good night, then, Mr. Landor."

"Good night."

Even in the dark, I recognized the symptoms. Love. Love had carved out the heart of Cadet Fourth Classman Edgar A. Poe.

Report of Edgar A. Poe to Augustus Landor

November 14th

It may hardly be conceived, Mr. Landor, with what fervor I anticipated my Sunday-afternoon tea with the Marquis household. My last encounter with Artemus had left me more than ever persuaded that seeing him embosomed in the comforts of hearth and home would go further toward determining his guilt or innocence than any other trial. And should he fail to incriminate himself in his boyhood domicile, I had every hope of snatching clues from those near relations whose unwitting utterances might bear more fruit than they themselves knew.

The family residence is situated among the stone houses that line the western rim of the Plain—"Professors' Row," so runs the bucolic sobriquet. There is nothing to distinguish the Marquis home from its neighbors— nothing, I should say, but the sampler on the front door which bears the inscription "Welcome Sons of Columbia." I was admitted not, as I should have expected, by the housemaid but by Dr. Marquis himself. Whether or not he *knew* of the uses I had lately made of his name, I cannot say, but any qualms I might have experienced at the sight of his rubicund complexion were at once allayed by the air of abiding concern with which he inquired about my vertigo. Upon being apprised that I had made a full and complete recovery, he smiled in the most indulgent manner and expostulated, "Ah! Do you see, Mr. Poe, what a little knocking about will do?"

The excellent Mrs. Marquis was previously unknown to me, though I have heard sundry aspersions cast against her character, to the effect that she is of a highly unsettled and high-strung disposition. Against this judg- ment I must interpose my own observations, which found in her nothing that was neurotic and much that was enchanting. Upon making my acquaintance, she was, from the start, wreathed in smiles. It was a source of amazement to me that a plebe could prompt such a dentate effluence, and I was all the more amazed to learn from her that Artemus had spoken of me in terms reserved only for those of Highest Genius.

Two others of Artemus' class were also present for this occasion. One of these was George Washington Upton, the distinguished cadet captain from Virginia. The other—and how my heart sank at the sight!—was the belligerent Ballinger. Recalling, however, my duties to God and country, I resolved to put out of mind his shabby behavior and craven assault, and greeted him with nothing but fellow feeling. Soon a wonder came to light! This Ballinger had either undergone a marked change of heart or, more likely, had been instructed to show me a more fitting deference. I will say only that his conversation was easy and courteous and in keeping with a gentleman's upbringing.

The dismal fare purveyed by Mr. Cozzens in the cadet mess had left me in a state of high anticipation regarding the Marquis victuals. In this respect, I was not to be disappointed. The hoe cakes and waffle cakes were of the first order, and the pears, I was delighted to ascertain, were liberally spiked with brandy. Dr. Marquis proved himself to be the most congenial of Hosts and derived a particular enjoyment from showing us his bust of Galen, as well as some of the more curious and intriguing monographs which bear his authorial imprint. Miss Marquis—Miss *Lea* Marquis, that is, Artemus' sister—performed on the pianoforte with a becoming fluency and sang a selection of those sentimental ditties which have laid waste to our modern culture—sang them, nevertheless, to charming effect. (It must be admitted that her voice, a natural contralto, was stretched rather too high by the prevailing keys. Her performance of "From Greenland's Icy Mountains," for instance, would have been the more exquisite for being transposed down a fourth or even a fifth.) Artemus had demanded that I sit beside him during his sister's recital, and at punctual intervals, he darted inquiring looks in my direction to assure himself of my admiration. Indeed, that admiration was mitigated only by the necessity of hearkening to his ongoing commentary: "Wonderful, isn't she? . . . Natural musician, you know. Playing since she was three. . . . Oh, that was a pretty run, wasn't it?"

Eyes and ears far less attentive than mine might have perceived all there was to know about the nature of a young man's attachment to his older sister. And by certain signs he was given during the recital's interludes, by certain smiles that were vouchsafed for his eyes alone, it became apparent that his affection was wholly reciprocated, and that there indeed existed between them a sympathy—a sibling *rapport*—such as I have never been blessed to know (raised as I was in a household separate entire from those in which my brother and sister were reared).

You, Mr. Landor, have doubtless experienced sufficient of these afternoon entertainments to know that when one performer has done, another is more often than not called up to plug the breach. So it was that upon the conclusion of Miss Marquis' performance and at the vociferous urging of her mother and brother, I was exhorted to favor the assembled guests with a sample of my own humble verse. I confess that I had half expected such an eventuality and had taken the liberty of preparing a brief selection, composed during last summer's encampment and titled "To Helen." It is not my prerogative here to share with you the entire text (nor do I suppose it to be anything you desire, O great Poetical-Inimical!). I pause only to remark that it is my own favorite among my efforts in the lyrical line, that the Woman of the title is likened variously to Nicean barks, Greece, Rome, Naiads, etc., etc., and that upon reaching the closing lines—"Ah! Psyche, from the regions which/Are Holy Land!"—my labors were remunerated with the sound of a pervasive and well-nigh percussive sigh.

"Hang it!" cried Artemus. "Didn't I tell you the Beast was a prodigy?"

The response of his sister was altogether more subdued, and as I already felt a deep solicitousness for her on Artemus' account, I made a point of seeking her out in private to ascertain if by chance my little offering had offended. She at once put me at my ease with a smile and an unequivocal shake of her head.

"No, Mr. Poe, it was lovely. I'm only a little sad thinking upon poor Helen."

"Poor Helen?" I echoed. "How poor?"

"Why, standing up in that window niche, day and night. *How statue-like*, didn't you say? How tiresome, you mean. Oh, dear, now it is *I* who have offended *you*. I do apologize. I was only thinking that a healthy girl like Helen should want to come out of her window niche now and again. Walk in the woods and chat with friends and go to a ball, even, if she feels up to it."

I answered that Helen—the Helen of my vision, that is—had no need of walking about, nor of dancing, for she had something far more precious: Immortality, as conferred upon her by Eros.

"Oh," she said, smiling gently, "I can't think of any woman who wishes to be immortal. A good joke might be all she desires. Or a single caress. . . ." No sooner had she spoken than a small tincture of red began to irrigate her marble cheek. Biting her lip, she hurried down a less fraught avenue of conversation and came at length to—well, to myself, Mr. Landor. She had been moderately intrigued, it seems, by my allusions to "a perfumed sea" and a "weary, way-worn wanderer" and inquired whether she might infer from these phrases that I had myself traveled and seen much. Her powers of logic, I answered, were unassailable. I then limned for her in general terms my sojourns at sea and my peregrinations across the European continent, culminating in St. Petersburg, where I became embroiled in covert difficulties of so complex a nature that I had to be extricated at the eleventh hour through the exertions of the American consul. (Ballinger, happening to pass by at this juncture, asked me if the Empress Catherine herself had served as my advocate. His tone was sardonic, and I was left to conclude that his reformation in regard to me was, at best, piecemeal.) Miss Marquis heard my narrative with an air of perfect openness and unstinting encouragement, interrupting only to query me further surrounding this or that particular detail, and through it all, she evinced such a pure and abiding interest in my paltry affairs that—well, Mr. Landor, I had forgot what a beguiling thing it is to place one's deeds in the safekeeping of a young woman. It is, I rather think, one of the world's least reckoned wonders.

But I see I have not yet taken pains to describe this Miss Marquis. Was it Bacon, Lord Verulam, who said, "There is no exquisite beauty without some *strangeness* in the proportion"? Miss Marquis would bear out the truth of that sagacious remark. Her mouth, to take but one part, is irregularly formed—a short upper lip, a soft, voluptuous under—and yet it composes a triumph of sweetness. Her nose has perhaps too perceptible a tendency toward the aquiline, and yet its luxurious smoothness and harmoniously curved nostrils rival the graceful medallions of the Hebrews. Her cheeks are over-ruddy, yes, but her brow is lofty and pale, and her brown tresses are glossy, luxuriant, and naturally curling.

As I am enjoined by you to practice strict and scrupulous honesty in all matters, I should add that most observers would consider her a shade past her full bloom. In addition, there is about her person a lingering *tristesse*, which (if I do not presume too far) bespeaks the thwarting of Hope and the blighting of Promise. And yet how this sadness becomes her, Mr. Landor! I would not trade it for a thousand of those giddy effusions which are the province of so-called marriageable girls. Indeed, I find it scarcely to be fathomed that when so many insipid females are dragged straight from their fathers' mansions to the altar, a pearl such as this should rest unclaimed in the seabed of her girlhood home. It is true, then, what the Poet says: "Full many a flower is born to blush unseen / And waste its sweetness on the desert air."

I do not believe that my interview with Miss Marquis lasted more than ten or fifteen minutes, and yet what a gamut of themes we traversed together! I have not the time to enumerate them all (could I even recollect them), for the eloquence of her low, musical language possessed a charm that surpassed mere disputation. Being a woman, she is not so steeped in the moral, physical, and mathematical science as a man, and yet she is every bit as fluent in French as myself and has, to my astonishment, some modest proficiency in the classical tongues. Having used Artemus' telescope to her own profit, she was able also to discourse quite knowledgeably on a star of the sixth magnitude to be found near the large star in Lyra.

More than any of her intellectual acquisitions, however, what most confounded and beguiled me was her *natural* intelligence, which had the effect of cutting straight to the heart of any subject, no matter its abstruseness. I well remember with what lucidity she heard me out on the subject of Cosmology. At her prompting, I told her that the universe was, in my opinion, an eternal "revenant" returning to fullness from Material Nihility, swelling into existence and then subsiding into nothingness, this cycle being repeated ad infinitum. So, too, the Soul: a residue of diffused god-head, undergoing its own eternal cycle of cosmic annihilation and rebirth.

To any other woman, Mr. Landor, I might have conceived my speculations to be thoroughly repugnant. In Miss Marquis, however, I could find no trace of revulsion and much to testify to amusement. The very wryness of her expression seemed to imply that I had just executed the most complicated and dangerous gymnastic maneuver—and done it for no better reason than that I had been *dared*.

"You must take care now, Mr. Poe. All that diffusion will end by diffusing *you*. And then, of course, if you wish to flirt with . . . material nihility, is it? . . . why, then, you must also flirt with spiritual nihility."

"Oh, Private Poe never flirts!"

It is a measure of our mutual engrossment that we so utterly failed to remark Artemus' presence until he so brusquely announced it. Then again, I consider it more than possible that Artemus had every *intention* of startling—stole toward us on cat's feet for that very purpose—for having delivered himself of his jape, he pinioned Lea's arms behind her, as though to take her captive, and with the point of his chin gently jabbed her shoulder.

"Speak then, sister. What do you think of my little protégé?"

Frowning, she prised herself from his grip. "I think," she said, "that Mr. Poe is beyond being anyone's protégé." Artemus' face fairly collapsed with dismay—he had not expected to be chided—but with her exquisite aversion to causing harm, Miss Marquis at once absolved him of his crime with a peal of laughter.

"He is certainly not to be corrupted by the likes of you," she blurted.

This remark had the effect of leaving *both* of them bound hand to foot in Laughter's chain. Their hilarity was, in truth, of such an expansive and consuming nature that I gave up any suspicions of being its butt and joined my own quieter laugh to theirs. Nevertheless, I was not so disarmed by Thalia's wiles that I failed to keep my wits about me, nor did I fail to discern that Lea ceased to laugh well in advance of her brother, and that through her eyes pierced a look—entirely missed by Artemus in his prostration to Comedy—of the deepest penetration. In that moment, I believe, she was peering into Artemus' very soul, to see what lay brushed across its canvas. What comfort or desolation she found there, none but a metaphysician could say. I can report only that her merriment did not return in the same abundance as before.

Fate provided me with no further occasion to speak with Miss Marquis. Artemus had challenged me to a game of chess (a pastime normally forbidden by the Academy), and Miss Marquis had been inveigled by Ballinger and Upton into a private concert, which was soon drowned out by those Cadets' strenuously unmusical vocal accompaniments. Dr. Marquis meanwhile took up his pipe and contemplated us benignly from the ramparts of his rocking chair, as Mrs. Marquis contented herself with rather desultory needlepoint—which exercise she shortly broke off in a passion, declaring herself afflicted with the most frightful Migraine and requesting leave to sequester herself in her bedchamber. When her husband made to stay her departure with the gentlest of remonstrances, she cried, "I don't see why you should care, Daniel—I don't see why *anybody* should care," and at once fled the room.

In the wake of such an abrupt leave-taking, it was but a matter of time before the guests murmured their regrets and began the necessary rituals of departure. These rituals, however, were summarily abrogated by Artemus, who gave me a parting press of the hand before loudly calling upon Ballinger and Upton to escort him back to barracks. I was sorely puzzled by his precipitous action, for it left me with no polite means of making my departure, save by my own devices (Dr. Marquis having absented himself to comfort his afflicted spouse). As I waited in the foyer for the maid to fetch my cloak and shako, I chanced to catch Ballinger's parting glance in my direction—a stare of such naked malignity that I stood fairly dumb before it. Thankfully, I was able to retain sufficient of my faculties to intuit that this look only *partly* included me. I turned my eyes then back to the parlor, where I found Miss Marquis, framed by her pianoforte, abstractedly performing a simple motif in the uppermost register.

Ballinger had by now followed Artemus out the door, but that *expression* of his remained powerfully *present*, and before long, the meaning of it came flashing upon my mind: this fellow was jealous—yes, jealous! overcome by purple rage!—at the prospect of my being left alone with Miss

Marquis. From this I could conclude only that he regarded me as, *mirabile dictu,* a contender for her attentions!

Oh, it is a sweet and a fitting irony, Mr. Landor, that in treating me as his arch-rival, Ballinger should have given me the courage to regard myself for the first time in that light. Otherwise I should never have had the temerity in that moment to address Miss Marquis. No, I would sooner have faced down an onrushing horde of Seminole or hurled myself into Niagara's thunderous Abyss. But confident now of the *threat* I posed, if only in Ballinger's jaundiced eyes, I found myself able—somehow—to speak.

"Miss Marquis, I fear it would be the grossest imposition on your graciousness to request an audience with you tomorrow afternoon. And yet there is nothing, nothing in the world that would afford me greater pleasure."

The moment the words had left my lips, I was seized by a paroxysm of self-reproach. That a mere Plebe (though no Boy, Mr. Landor) could presume to stake even the smallest claim upon a Woman of such ineffable grace—how could this be viewed as any but the barest effrontery? And yet I felt *you,* Mr. Landor—*you* foremost of all—urging me onward. For if we seek to plumb the depths of the enigmatic Artemus, what better plumb *line* than his beloved sister, by virtue of whose esteem he sinks or sails? Nevertheless, it was with an all too perfect sense of my fault that I awaited the justifiable reproach that was hers alone to make.

Her countenance, however, betrayed an altogether differing vein of feeling. With that wry smile of hers—I had already become tolerably familiar with *that*—and a gleam in her eye, she begged to know if she was to meet me at Flirtation Walk or Gee's Point or any of those other secluded venues beloved of amorous cadets.

"None of these places," I stammered.

"Where, then, Mr. Poe?"

"I had in mind the cemetery."

Her astonishment was considerable, but she recovered herself in good time and bestowed upon me an expression of such severity that I nearly blanched before it.

"Tomorrow," she said, "I am engaged. I am free to meet you at four-thirty on Tuesday afternoon. You will have fifteen minutes of my attention. Beyond that, I promise nothing."

As this was fifteen minutes more than I had dared hope for, I had no need of promise beyond that. It was enough to know that before another forty-eight hours had passed, I should once again be in her presence.

In perusing the above lines, Mr. Landor, I see that I may have given the impression of being quite overborne by Miss Marquis' manifold charms. Nothing could be further from the truth. If I am sensible to her virtues, I am still more sensible to the imperative of drawing these investigations to a successful close. My lone purpose in furthering my acquaintance with her, therefore, is to glean from her such insights into her brother's character and propensities as might advance the ultimate end of Justice.

Oh! I nearly forgot to include perhaps the most intriguing detail pertaining to Miss Lea Marquis. Her eyes, Mr. Landor! They are of an exquisite and a decidedly pale blue.

Narrative of Gus Landor

17

November 15th and 16th

When we first went into business together, Captain Hitchcock and I had mapped out a wide range of eventualities. We'd talked about what we'd do if the guilty parties were cadets or soldiers. We'd even discussed what to do if Leroy Fry's assailant should turn out to be a faculty member. But *this* possibility had somehow slipped between the crevices: a faculty member's *son*.

"Artemus Marquis?"

We were sitting in the commandant's own quarters. Strictly a bachelor affair, fairly shabby by Army standards, with dried-out quills and a clock of cracked marble and the scent of amiable decay hanging in every brocaded curtain.

"Artemus," Hitchcock repeated. "Dear God, I've known him for years."

"And would you vouch for his character?" I asked.

This was, I knew, the most impertinent query I'd yet made. Artemus was, by virtue of being a cadet, *vouched* for. He'd been appointed by a United States representative, hadn't he? He'd passed his entrance exams and had borne up under nearly four years of Sylvanus Thayer's pounding and, barring any disaster, was due to take up his brevet commission the following summer. Such feats were, by their very design, guarantors of character.

But curiously, it was not Artemus' character that Hitchcock rushed to defend, but rather his father's. Dr. Marquis, I was given to know, had caught a musket ball in the Battle of Lacolle Mills, had been personally commended by Colonel Pike for his extreme diligence in tending to the wounded, had never, through all his many years at the Academy, known a breath of scandal. . . .

"Captain," I said, feeling the wave of pique that came over me whenever he talked on top of me. "I don't believe I even mentioned the good doctor. Did I mention the good doctor?"

Well, he just wanted me to know that Artemus Marquis came from a fine family, a *distinguished* family, and his collusion in such inconceivable acts was—was *inconceivable*. Yes, Reader, he was starting to repeat himself . . . until something rose up in his head and left him, for a short time, mute.

"There *was* an incident," he said at last.

I stayed perfectly still in my chair.

"Yes, Captain?"

"I remember, yes, it was some time ago, well before Artemus was a cadet. It had to do with Miss Fowler's cat."

More rummaging now.

"This cat," he said, "vanished under circumstances I can't recall, but I *do* recall it met a bizarre end."

"Dissection?" I guessed.

"Vivisection. Yes, I'd completely forgotten that. And it was—" His eyes went light with wonder. "It was Dr. *Marquis* who assured Miss Fowler that the cat had been dead *prior* to—to being quartered. I remember how deeply affected he was by the incident."

"Did Artemus ever confess to the deed?" I asked.

"No, of course not."

"But you had reason to suspect him?"

"I knew he was intelligent, that's all. Not malicious, not by any stretch, but *prankish*."

"And a doctor's son."

"Yes. A doctor's son."

Newly agitated, Captain Hitchcock drew himself out of the candlelight. I could see him rolling something—a marble? a ball of clay?—in his palm.

"Mr. Landor," he said, "before we go any further toward impugning anyone, I wish you would tell me whether you've discovered anything to tie Artemus to Leroy Fry."

"Precious little, as it stands. Artemus was a year ahead of Fry, we know that. There's no sign of their having fraternized in any way. Never sat at mess together, never shared a section. Never, as far as I can tell, marched together or sat together in chapel. I've interviewed several dozen cadets by now, and I've yet to hear any of them mention Artemus' name in connection with Fry."

"What about this Ballinger fellow?"

"That's a little more promising," I conceded. "There's some evidence that Ballinger and Fry were friendly at one time. They were seen together a couple of summers ago, pulling tents down on a bunch of new plebes. Both were also, for a brief while, members of the . . . oh, damn, what's the . . . the Amo—Amo-soapic—"

"Amo*sophic* Society."

"The very one. Fry, being a quieter soul, didn't take to debating as naturally as Ballinger, and he soon quit the place. No one can recall having seen them together after that."

"And is that all?"

I almost let it rest there, but something in his voice—a note of retreat, maybe—egged me on.

"There is one other link," I said, "though it's nothing but innuendo. Ballinger and Fry both appear to have had a hankering for Artemus' sister. Indeed, from what I hear, Ballinger considers himself the prime candidate for her affections."

"Miss Marquis?" echoed Hitchcock, arching a brow. "I think that unlikely."

"How so?"

"You may ask any of the faculty wives. Miss Marquis is well known for discouraging the overtures of even the most importunate cadets."

All but *one*, I thought, grinning to myself. Who would have guessed my little bantam would be rushing in where other cocks feared to go?

"Aha!" I exclaimed. "She's a prideful thing, I suppose."

"The exact opposite," he answered. "So exceedingly modest as to make one doubt whether she has ever seen herself in a mirror." The slightest reddening came over the captain's cheek. So he *was* open to the calls of the flesh, after all.

"Then what explains her withdrawing from the world?" I asked. "Is she so awfully shy?"

"Shy! You must engage her on the subject of Montesquieu sometime and see for yourself how shy she is. No, Miss Marquis has ever been a puzzle and even, among certain circles, a consuming pastime. Now that she has attained the ancient age of twenty-three, she is no longer much spoken of. Except, I am sorry to say, by nickname."

Politeness, I guess, would normally have kept him from venturing further, but seeing my curiosity, he moved to slake it.

"They call her the Sorrowing Spinster," he said.

"And why 'sorrowing,' Captain?"

"I'm afraid I couldn't tell you."

I smiled and folded my arms across my chest and said, "Knowing how carefully you choose your words, Captain, I'll have to presume you don't use the word *couldn't* when you actually mean, maybe, *wouldn't*."

"I choose my words with care, yes, Mr. Landor."

"Well, then," I said, cheerful as a shower, "we may come back to the business at hand. Which, unless you object, leads us in the direction of Artemus' quarters."

Oh, how grim he looked in that moment! For he was already heading down the same path.

"Shall we inspect them first thing tomorrow morning?" I suggested. "Ten o'clock, why don't we say? Oh, and Captain, if we could keep this between the two of us. . . ."

It was cold as blazes, that I remember. The clouds were low and sharded like icicles, and the stone edifices of North and South Barracks, standing at right angles to each other, made a whetting stone for the hard flat single-minded wind that drove in from the west. We felt it, didn't we, standing in that L-shaped assembly yard, preparing our little raid? Shivered like fish on a line.

"Captain," I said. "If you don't mind, I'd like to look first at Cadet Poe's quarters."

He never asked me why. He'd gotten tired, maybe, of digging in his heels. Or else he had his own suspicions about this young man of mine, who so freely clothed himself in myth. Or else he just wanted to get in out of the cold.

My, but it was small enough, this room where Cadet Fourth Classman

Poe and his two roommates passed their days and nights! *Room* is no word for it—*bandbox*. Thirteen by ten, and halved by a partition. Numbingly cold, smoky, close, with a smell like whale guts. There were a pair of candle sconces, a woodbox, a table, a straight-backed chair, a lamp, a mirror. No bedsteads, not in Thayer's monastery: you sleep on a narrow pallet on the floor, which you roll up each morning with your blanket. Oh, it was a bare gray mean space—not to be owned by anyone. There was nothing in Number 22, South Barracks, to announce that somebody here had once swum the James River or written poems or been to Stoke Newington or was in any way different from the other two-hundred-odd boys that the Academy was squeezing into men.

Well, the soul will out, I suppose, even against large odds. So it was that after a cursory look at the room, I came to Poe's trunk and, unlatching it, found—there on the underside of the lid—an engraving of Byron. As fugitive and damning as a love letter.

From another pocket, I drew out a tiny bundle layered in black crepe. The crepe fell away in an instant to reveal the cameo portrait of a young woman in an Empire gown and ribboned bonnet. An almost aching girl-ishness to her sweetly huge eyes, her frail shoulders. She looked nearly the same as she had looked at the Park Street Theatre, all those years ago, singing "Nobody Coming to Marry Me."

The very sight of her left a clot in my throat. A familiar sort of tightening—it was, I realized, the same feeling I got whenever I thought too long about my daughter. I remembered then what Poe had said, sitting there in my parlor:

We're both alone in the world.

Breathing out, I closed the trunk and clicked the hasp.

"He keeps a neat room," said Hitchcock, grudgingly.

That he did. Should he care to, I thought, Cadet Fourth Classman Poe could go on keeping a neat room for another three years and a half—three years and a half of bedrolls and tight-buttoned collars and shiny boots. And for his reward, he would get—what? A posting on the Western frontier, where, in between hunting Indians, he could recite his poems to military men and their neurasthenic wives and wasting daughters? Oh, what a figure he would cut in those small bright parlor-graves.

"Captain," I said, "I no longer have the heart for this."

The rooms in North Barracks were at least larger—twenty-five by nineteen—a sop for the upperclassmen. The *only* sop, so far as I could see. Artemus' quarters, though warmer than Poe's, were even drearier: the pallets patched, the coverlets hard used, the air sneezy, and the walls pouched and streaked with soot. Because it faced west, the room had to make do with whatever light broke over the mountains, and even at midmorning, the gloom was so deep we were reduced to using matches to peer into some of the tighter corners. It was in this way that I found Artemus' compacted telescope, tucked between a water bucket and a chamber pot. No other signs of old revels: no cards, chickens, pipes, not even the stray aroma of tobacco (though the windowsill bore scattered grains of snuff).

"The woodbox," said Hitchcock. "That's always the first place I look."

"Then by all means, Captain."

Surprise! He could find only wood at first. Oh, and an old lottery ticket from Cuming's Truly Lucky Offices and a scrap of book-muslin handkerchief and a half-empty packet of Brazil sugar—one by one, he dragged them to the surface, and I was just about to pocket the sugar when I heard a sound behind us.

A clicking, like a latch being slid into place. And then an even fainter sound coming from behind *that*.

"Captain," I said, "I'm beginning to think we were expected."

The sun by now was just starting to carom off the blue rocky slopes to the west, and for the first time that morning, waves of hard yellow light were flooding into that dank chamber, and it was the *light*, really, that made me understand what was happening, more than anything else.

"What's wrong?" called Captain Hitchcock.

He had drawn a small brown-paper bundle from the woodbox, and he was holding it out to me like an offering, but I was already throwing myself against the door frame.

"It won't open," I said.

"Step aside," he shouted.

He set down his bundle and charged, gave the door two good kicks. It shuddered but held firm. Another two kicks: the same. We were *both* kicking now, slamming our boots sole-first into the wood—a perfect racket of thumps and counterthumps. But even through that din, the sound on the *other* side of the door could still be heard.

A sound with no equal. A queer damp sputter, like a half-extinguished candle.

And something else now: a *light,* flickering through the door's lower crevice.

Hitchcock was the first to act. He grabbed one of the cadet trunks and hurled it at the door. The wood sagged just a little—enough to give us hope. On the next attempt, we both held the trunk, and we threw our combined weight against it, and this time the door wrenched clear of its frame, leaving a space of maybe three inches, enough to poke an arm through. One more kick from Hitchcock, and the latch on the other side at last tore off, and the door groaned away, and we were standing in the hallway, looking down on a black ball the size of a cantaloupe, with a long yarny fuse that was streaming with fire.

Hitchcock grabbed the shell and took three long strides to the nearest window. Yanked open the casement and, after checking to see no one was there, tossed the ball with no further comment into the yard below.

And there it lay, studded in the grass, smoking and fuming.

"Stand back, Mr. Landor."

But I couldn't, any more than he could. We watched that bristly fuse burn down and down—who would have thought it had so much distance still to travel?—and it was like trying to read a book over somebody's shoulder, waiting for the page to turn.

And then it turned, but there was no climax, only the slow dying of the spark, followed by . . . nothing. No explosion or cloud of sulfur, just silence. And a few hoops and vines of smoke, and the smack of my traitor heart. And a thought, real as a wound, that someone had once again danced ahead of us.

Minutes later, when the last of the smoke had cleared and the shell still slumbered in the yard below, Captain Hitchcock went back to the woodbox, picked up the bundle he had dropped, and slowly, with the care of someone unwrapping a dead pharaoh, peeled away the brown paper.

It was a *heart*. Oozing rust. As raw as life.

Narrative of Gus Landor

18

November 16th

It was good fortune, I guess, that Dr. Marquis, when we brought him a heart to identify, never thought to ask us where we'd found it. The sight was too thrilling for him: a by-God *heart*, still in its wrapping, lying on a blacksmith bed in Ward 3-B just as Leroy Fry had once done. It might have been a Park Avenue matron with corns, judging from the way Dr. Marquis' fingers stole toward it. He clucked his tongue, he cleared his throat. . . .

"Not too badly decomposed," he offered at last. "Must have been kept in a cold place."

"It *was* cold, yes," I said, remembering the chill of Artemus' quarters.

Slowly the doctor circled the bed, scratching his chin, squinting hard.

"Mmm," he muttered. "Yes, gentlemen. I can see why you might have thought it was a man's heart. Nearly identical, isn't it? The atria and ventricles, the valves and the arteries, all where they should be, yes."

"*But?*"

His eyes were aglitter as they met ours. "The *size*, gentlemen. That's what gives it away. *This* whippersnapper"—he worked his fingers under the bundle, gave it a speculative lift—"weighs upwards of five pounds, I'd wager. Whereas a *human* heart seldom gets above nine or ten ounces."

"No bigger than a fist," I said, recalling our last conversation in this room.

"Exactly," he said, beaming.

"Then tell us, please," said Hitchcock. "If it's not a human heart, what sort of creature did it come from?"

The doctor hooked his brows over his eyes. "Hmm, yes, that's a bit of a puzzler. Too big for a sheep. A *cow*, that's my best guess. Yes, almost certainly a cow." His face brightened in a flash. "I don't mind telling you, gentlemen, it calls me back to my youth, seeing one of these specimens. Many was the cow heart I used to dissect in Edinburgh. Dr. Hunter used to say, 'If you can't find your way round a *cow's* heart, you've got no business with a man's.'"

Captain Hitchcock's hands were tented over his eyes. His voice was weary as suds.

"Haverstraw," he said dully. "The heart must have come from Haverstraw."

And because I didn't respond as quickly as he wished, he pulled the tent from his eyes and glared me down.

"Do I need to remind you?" he asked. "The two dismembered animals we read about in the paper a fortnight ago? One of them, you may recall, was a *cow*."

"I do remember," I said. "And I consider your theory as likely an explanation as any."

A slow leak of breath from his clenched jaw.

"Mr. Landor, mightn't you just once find something definitive to say? Just *once*, mightn't you come down on the *positive* side of an equation?"

The thing is, I sympathized with him. Here we sat in his musty office, with drums beating in the distance. We had in our possession the most tangible sort of evidence, but we were no further along than when we started, and maybe a distance back.

But what about the *heart*? you might ask. Surely that was proof enough? Well, to the best of our knowledge, nobody had seen Artemus put it in the woodbox; as Hitchcock was the first to point out, *anyone* could have put it there. Cadet rooms were never locked. Which also meant that anybody could have jammed that piece of stovewood into the door latch to keep me and Hitchcock from leaving.

But what of the bomb itself? Surely that would have been hard to procure? Well, no. The powder magazine was but lightly guarded at best, almost never at night, and the shell hadn't been charged.

Someone, though—*someone* had lit the fuse. Someone had been standing outside in the hallway while Captain Hitchcock and I were in Artemus' barracks, between thirty and thirty-five minutes past ten.

And here was the most damnable thing of all: Artemus Marquis had an alibi. He had been in recital from nine o'clock to noon—sitting alongside Ballinger, as it turned out, and giving every show of interest in Artillery and Infantry Tactics. Neither cadet, their professor swore, had left the section room for even half a second.

And so we really *were* back to where we began—save for one thing. It was well nigh impossible that anyone *outside* the Academy could have made it into Artemus' barracks in that five-minute interval. None of the sentinels had reported seeing anyone come from outside the grounds, either that morning or the previous evening. While a stranger might have slipped through the guard posts, his presence—in broad daylight, in a particularly well-trafficked area of the Academy, would almost surely have been noticed.

So, amid all the bristling ends and dangling fringes, all the feints and taunts, the only clear inference we could draw was this: our man—our *men*—came from within.

You can see now, Reader, why I was prepared to weep for Captain Hitchcock. He'd let himself hope, you see. Cadet fatalities had so far been limited to one. The local journals had contained no more accounts of savaged livestock. There was every reason to believe that the madman who'd attacked Leroy Fry had since set himself to terrorizing *other* communities. Who were to be pitied, of course, but who lay outside Ethan Allen Hitchcock's sphere.

All that had changed in the ten seconds it took him to carry that bomb from the hall to the window.

"What I fail to understand," he said now, "is why Artemus, if he is our man, would have been so stupid as to leave the heart in the woodbox. He knows how regularly we inspect barracks quarters. Surely he could have found a better place to secrete it."

"Unless . . . ," I said.

"Unless what?"

"Unless someone else put it there."

"And toward what end?"

"Why, to incriminate Artemus, of course."

Hitchcock looked at me for a long while.

"Very well," he said at last. "Then why would someone plant a bomb—a bomb with no *powder*—outside Artemus' door? While Artemus was in recital?"

"Why, to give him an alibi," I said.

Hard deep crescents carved themselves out on either side of his mouth.

"So you're suggesting, Mr. Landor, that some—some *fellow* out there wants to clear Artemus' name, while some *other* fellow wants him to hang?" He made a vise of his hands and squeezed his head through. "And where does Artemus himself fit into all this? By God, this is the most—the most infernal damned muddle I've ever . . ."

Reader, I don't want you to think that Captain Hitchcock was averse to hard thinking. He was, as anyone could have told you, a learned man. On easy terms with Kant and Bacon. A Swedenborgian, if you can believe it, and an alchemist. But I think he preferred to take his thinking on his own terms, in the quiet of his own quarters. When it came to the Academy, he wanted things to run like water through a mill: according to agreed-upon laws, with no chance of intervention, human or otherwise.

"Very well," he said again. "I accept that we can arrive at no positive declarations on one side or another. What do you suggest we do, then?"

"Do? Why, nothing at all, Captain."

He stared at me, almost too wrought to reply.

"Mr. Landor," he said, in a deceptively calm voice. "A *heart* has been found in cadet quarters. A United States officer and a private citizen have been threatened with a bomb, and you are telling me I may do nothing?"

"Well, we can't place Artemus in arrest, we know that much. We can't arrest anyone else. So I'm afraid I don't see what we *can* do, other than ask the quartermaster to fix Artemus' door."

Gently, he ran one of his dried quills along the edge of his desk, and I watched his eyes drift by slow degrees toward the window. In that moment, with the late-afternoon light flaring along his profile, I could almost *feel* the weight that was pressing on him.

"Any day now," he said, "we are expecting Mr. Fry's parents. I have no illusions of being able to offer them comfort or solace. But I would like to look them both in the eye and make a solemn vow that what happened to their son will never happen to another cadet. Not while I'm commandant." He set both hands on his desk. Stared me down. "Will I able to promise them that, Mr. Landor?"

A rill of something—something like old tobacco juice—piled up at the corner of my mouth. I wiped it away.

"Well, Captain," I said. "You can certainly promise them, if you like. But just to be on the safe side, don't look them in the eye when you do it."

Think of a greyhound standing on two legs, and you will have a rough idea of the height and heft of Private Horatio Cochrane. He had narrow down-cast eyes and baby's skin, and the ridge of his spine could be seen through his shirt, and he was slightly bent, like a bow that hadn't released its arrow. I interviewed him in the shoemaker's shop, where he had gone to get his right boot repaired for maybe the tenth time that year. There was a large gap between the boot's toe and its sole, and this gap resembled nothing so much as a toothless mouth, which talked whenever Private Cochrane talked and went silent whenever he went silent. His boot was, in fact, the most expressive thing about him. Nothing else flickered in that planed boyish face.

"Private," I said. "I understand you were the one who stood watch over Leroy Fry the night he was hanged. Is that so?"

"Yes, sir," he said.

"The funniest thing, Private. I've been going through all the—" I chuck-led softly. "—all this damned *paper*, you know, all these statements and . . . affidavits from the night of October the twenty-fifth. And I've come across a bit of a problem, which I was hoping you could help me with."

"If I can, sir, I'll be glad to."

"I'm much obliged, I'm really . . . now, if we could just start by walking through the events in question. When Mr. Fry's body was brought back to the hospital, you were detailed to the room . . . this Ward B-3."

"Yes, sir."

"And you were asked to do what, exactly?"

"They requested me to look out for that body, sir, and make sure no harm come to it."

"I see. So it was just you and Mr. Fry?"

"Yes, sir."

"And he was covered? With a blanket, I'm thinking?"

"Yes, sir."

"And what time was this, Private?"

A slight pause. "I'd say it was one o'clock when I was first detailed there."

"And did anything happen while you were on watch?"

"Not till . . . not till around two-thirty, it was. That's when I was relieved of my duty."

I smiled at him. I smiled at his boot, which smiled back.

"'Relieved,' you say. Now, that's what brings me to this—this *problem* I've been having. You see, Private, you made two statements. In the first—oh, dear, I don't seem to have it with me, but I believe it was taken shortly after Mr. Fry's body disappeared—you said you'd been relieved by Lieutenant Kinsley."

The first sign of life then: a slight flexing of the muscles round his jaw. "Yes, sir."

"Which is a very curious thing, because Lieutenant Kinsley was accompanying Captain Hitchcock all night. I have that from both of the officers in question. Now, I'm guessing you *realized* your mistake, Private, because in your next statement—a day later—and again, forgive me if I have it wrong, but I think you said simply 'the *lieutenant*': 'I was relieved by the *lieutenant*.'"

A tiny agitation in the column of his throat. "Yes, sir."

"So maybe now you understand my confusion. I'm just not certain *who* it was relieved you." I smiled at him. "Maybe you can clear that up for me, Private."

A twitch of a nostril. "I'm afraid I can't tell you, sir."

"Oh, now, Private. I can assure you anything you tell me will be held in private. You won't be made to suffer any consequences for any of your actions."

"Yes, sir."

"And you do understand that I have full authority from Colonel Thayer to conduct these inquiries?"

"Yes, sir."

"Well, then, let's try this again, shall we? *Who* relieved you, Private?"

A tiny trickle of sweat along the hairline. "I can't tell you, sir."

"And why not?"

"'Cause—'cause I never got his name."

I eyed him for a few moments. "The name of the officer, you mean?"

"Yes, sir."

His head was bowed now. The reproach he'd been awaiting so long was about to rain down.

"Very well," I said, as gently as I could. "Maybe you can tell me what this officer told you."

"He said, 'Thank you, Private, that will be all. Please report to Lieutenant Meadows' quarters.'"

"Something of an odd request, wasn't it?"

"Yes, sir, but he was very definite on the point. 'Off you go,' he said."

"Well, that's most interesting. Now, the funny thing about Lieutenant Meadows' quarters is, I believe they lie directly south of the hospital."

"That's correct, sir."

And *away* from the icehouse, I remembered. Hundreds of yards away.

"What happened next, Private?"

"Well, I lost no time in making for the lieutenant's quarters. I was no more than five minutes in passage. Lieutenant Meadows was still asleep, so I banged on his door until he come down, and that's when he told me I wasn't sent for."

"He hadn't sent for you?"

"No, sir."

"So then you . . ."

"I went back to the hospital, sir. To be better certain of my orders."

"And when you got back to Ward B-Three, you found what?"

"Nothing, sir. I mean to say, the body was gone?"

"And how long would you say you'd been away from the body?"

"Oh, no more than half an hour, sir."

"And once you found the body was gone, what did you do then?"

"Well, sir, I ran straight to the guardroom in North Barracks. I told the officer on duty, and he told Captain Hitchcock."

The rap of the cobbler's hammer began to sound from the next room. A slow steady pulse, like the reveille drums. Without even thinking, I was on my feet.

"Well, Private, it's certainly not my purpose to add to your troubles. But I'd be glad if you could tell me more about this officer who ordered you to quit your post. You didn't recognize him?"

"No, sir. I've only been here but two months, though, so . . ."

"Can you tell me what he looked like?"

"Oh, it was terrible dark in the room. I had but the one candle, you see, and that was next to—next to Mr. Fry, and this officer had a candle, too, but his face was in shadow."

"So you didn't see his face?"

"No, sir."

"How did you know he was an officer, then?"

"The bar, sir. On the shoulder. He was holding the candle in such a way I could see it."

"That was very thoughtful of him. And he never otherwise identified himself."

"No, sir. But then I wouldn't expect it of an officer."

I could see it so clearly at that moment. Leroy Fry's shrouded body. The quailing private. The officer: shoulder bathed in light, voice coming out of the long shadows.

"How did this officer *sound*, Private?"

"Well, he didn't say so very much, sir."

"High voice? Low?"

"High. Medium to high."

"What about his shape? His form? Was he tall?"

"Not so tall as you, sir, I wouldn't think. Maybe two or three inches shorter."

"And his frame. Was he slender? Heavy?"

"Slender, would be my guess. But it was hard to say."

"Do you think you'd be able to recognize him again? In the light?"

"I doubt it, sir."

"What about his voice?"

He scratched his ear, as if trying to scratch the sound back in. "It's possible," he allowed. "It's just possible, sir. I could give it a try."

"Well, then, I'll see if we can arrange it, Private."

It was when I stood to go that I noticed, on the wall behind Cochrane, two piles of garments. Underdrawers and blouses and pantaloons, rearing up on every side, reeking of sweat and mold and grass. . . .

"Well, now, Private," I said. "That's quite a lot of clothing you've got."

He leaned his head to one side. "Oh! That's Cadet Brady's, sir. And that pile there is Cadet Whitman's. They pay me to clean their laundry once a week." I must have looked puzzled, for he quickly added, "A private can't live, sir. Not on what Uncle Sam pays you."

Amid all the day's unruliness, I never had a spare thought for Poe. Not until I got back to my hotel late that night, after taking a long walk around the reservation, and found the brown-paper parcel by the door.

How the sight of it made me smile. My little bantam! Hard at work all this time. And though he didn't know it—though *I* didn't know it—moving toward the heart of things.

Report of Edgar A. Poe to Augustus Landor

November 16th

Have you remarked, Mr. Landor, how early in the day—and with what singular swiftness—Dusk comes to these Highlands? It seems to me that the sun has only just inaugurated its reign when, as suddenly, it absconds, leaving the invading gloom to descend like Judgment. Night's cruel tyranny comes hard on—and yet, here and there, a prisoner may find commutations of his sentence. As his eye traces upward, he may be delighted by the full orb of the retreating sun, confronting him from the turreted clefts of Storm King and Cro' Nest, shedding a glorious effulgence as it goes. Now, as at no other time of the day, the broad aisle of the Hudson stands revealed in all its glory—this profound and mighty torrent, which, in its thundering passage, draws the Imagination down every ravine and shadow.

And no venue affords a purer vantage on this blessed scene than the West Point cemetery. Have you found your way there, Mr. Landor? It is a small enclosure about half a mile distant from the Academy, situated on a lofty riverbank and almost entirely obscured by trees and shrubbery. If one had to be buried, Mr. Landor, one might do far worse. To the east lies a shaded walk with exquisite views of the Academy. To the north, a sloping alluvial expanse, bounded by rugged heights, behind which lie the fertile valleys of Dutchess and Putnam.

This cemetery, then, is a space twice hallowed—by God and by Nature—and of a character so quiet and immured as to make even the most reverentially disposed think twice before trespassing. Certain it is, however, that *my* thoughts were all jointly taken up with one still living.

She it was who had consumed my sleeping and waking. *She* it was whose imminent arrival had prostrated every energy of mind.

Four o'clock had come, Mr. Landor. *She* had not. Five, ten minutes elapsed—still she had not come. A less faithful attendant might have despaired, but my devotion to you and to our joint cause determined me to wait all evening if needed. It was, by the evidence of my watch, precisely thirty-two minutes past four when my vigil was at last rewarded with the sound of swishing silk and a glimpse of a pale yellow bonnet.

Not so long ago, Mr. Landor, I should have been the first to deny that ever a thought arose within the human brain beyond the utterance of the human tongue. And yet Miss Marquis! The majesty, the ease of her demeanor; the incomprehensible lightness and elasticity of her footfall; the luster of her eye, more profound than the well of Democritus—all these aspects of her lie outside the compass of language. The pen falls powerless from my shivering hand. I could inform you that she arrived slightly out of breath from her climb; that she wore an Indian shawl; that her ringlets were tied in an Apollo knot; that she had absently wound the drawstring of her reticule round her index finger. What would these *signify*, Mr. Landor? How could they convey the unthought-like thoughts that stirred from the abysses of my heart?

There I stood, Mr. Landor, groping for words ample to the occasion, and finding only these paltry syllables:

"I had feared the cold might keep you away."

Her reply was every bit as succinct.

"It did not," she said. "As you may see."

That her manner toward me was greatly altered from our last encounter, I could discern at once. Indeed, there could have been no mistaking the desiccated coolness of her tone, the aggrieved attitude of her alabaster jaw, the calculated refusal of her eye—lovely eye!—to connect with mine. Every movement, every intonation gave sign that she was chafing beneath the obligation I had imposed upon her.

Well, Mr. Landor, I confess that I am little schooled in the ways of Woman. I could therefore see no way of bridging the mysterious impasse that now divided us, nor could I fathom her reasons for honoring an engagement which was so patently distasteful to her. She, on her side, contented herself merely with twirling her reticule and making repeated circuits of the Cadet Monument.

The sight of this column served to turn my thoughts upon those unfortunate Cadets who had (like Leroy Fry) been taken away in the dawning of their usefulness. I gazed upon the clusters of dark green cedars, which stood like sentries over this camp of Death; upon the snow-white gravestones, composing so many tents for those who, in the height of their manly beauty, had been called from Life's daily drills. In momentary thrall to these conceits, I even made so bold as to confide them to my restless companion, in the hope that they might endow some common fund of discourse—only to see them dismissed with a cut of her head.

"Oh," she said, "there's nothing so very poetical about Death, is there? I cannot think of anything more *prosaic*."

I answered that quite to the contrary, I considered Death—and in particular, the death of a beautiful woman—to be Poetry's grandest, most exalted theme. For the first time since her arrival, she gave me the full gift of her attention—and then exploded into a paroxysm of laughter more discomfiting by far than the coldness which had preceded it, and much akin to that hilarity which had seized her in Artemus' presence. She suffered it to travel through her frame before, wiping the merriment from her eyes, she murmured, "How well it sits on you."

"What?" I asked.

"*Morbidity*. It suits you even better than your uniform. See, now, your cheeks are all aglow, and there is a positive glitter to your eye!" Shaking her head in wonder, she added, "The only one to match you is Artemus."

I replied that I had never, in my avowedly brief acquaintance with that gentleman, known him to dwell in the realms of Melancholy.

"He does consent," she said, pensively, "to visit our world for long intervals. You know, Mr. Poe, I believe it's possible to dance on broken glass for some length of time. But not forever, I think."

I retorted that if one knew *only* the sensation of broken glass—that is, if one had been raised from earliest infancy to tread upon it—one would count it no worse than the gentlest sward of turf. This observation, I was flattered to see, occupied her thoughts for no small interval, at the close of which she replied, in a lower tone, "Yes. I can see you two hold much in common."

Availing myself of this incremental thaw in her demeanor, I endeavored then to draw her attention to the divers points of interest that presented themselves to the inquiring eye: the views of the landing and the siege battery; Mr. Cozzens' hotel; the remains of old Fort Clinton, whittled down by the tempests and wintry blasts of half a century. These spectacles excited in her nothing so much as a shrug. (In retrospect, Mr. Landor, I should have expected that one reared in these climes, as Miss Marquis has been, would regard them in the fashion of the faeries who abide all their lives in palaces of diadems and so consider those treasures no more worthy of notice than gorse bushes.) I no longer had any shadow of hope that Joy might be extracted from our misbegotten encounter, and so resolved to bear my sufferings with fortitude. *Small talk,* Mr. Landor. How much valor is needed to perpetrate it under such unpropitious circumstances! I inquired after Miss Marquis' health. I commended her taste in dress. I expressed the belief that blue looked well on her. I asked her if she had been privileged to attend any dinner parties of late. I asked her—yes!—if she believed the frigid climate to have settled in for good. Upon making this last comment, which I considered the height of banality and the very pinnacle of inoffensiveness, I was astonished to see her wheel upon me in a perfect fury of clenched teeth and stabbing eye.

"Oh, let us *not* . . . Do you—Mr. Poe, do you suppose I consented to come here in order to talk of the *weather*? I have done with that, I can assure you. For many years—too *many* years, Mr. Poe—I was one of the 'four o'clocks' waiting down by Flirtation Walk. You have seen them, I'm sure. Doubtless you have escorted one or two. There is considerable talk of weather, as I recall, talk of boat rides and dances and dinner parties, and before very long—time being of the essence—someone is protesting undying love. It never matters *who*, of course, for it all comes to naught. The cadets leave—they always do *leave*, don't they, Mr. Poe?—and there are always more to take their place."

I had thought that speech of such a vehement character would soon spend itself down or would, at the least, effect some diminution in its author's rage. Quite the opposite, Mr. Landor: the longer she continued, the higher leapt the tongues of her ire's flame.

"Ah, but you still have all your buttons, Mr. Poe! Does that mean you have never once torn off the one closest to your heart and proffered it for a lock of your mistress' hair? In my time, Mr. Poe, I have given away so many of my tresses, it's a wonder I'm not bald. I have heard so many troths plighted that had they all come to pass, I should now have as many husbands as Solomon had wives. Proceed, then, by all means. Declare your undying love, so that we may both return home and be none the worse."

At last, her fury did abate, by slow degrees. Passing her hand across her brow, she turned away and, in accents of the heaviest dullness, muttered, "I'm sorry, I'm being a horror, and I've no idea why."

I assured her that I required no apology, that my sole concern was for her welfare. Whether she derived solace from this, I cannot say, but she sought no more comfort in my direction. The minutes passed like days. Oh, yes, Mr. Landor, it was a situation peculiarly uncomfortable, and I could scarcely summon the resolution to end it—until, that is, I became distinctly aware of a change in Miss Marquis' manner. She was, for the first time since her arrival, shivering.

"You are cold, Miss Marquis."

She shook her head; she denied it; nevertheless, she shivered. I inquired if she wished to borrow my cloak. No answer did she make. I repeated my offer. No answer. Her shivering had by now increased tenfold, and there was, stamped on her exquisite visage, an expression of unutterable fright and awe.

"Miss Marquis!" I cried.

Amid the fevered calls of *her own* disordered fancy, my plaintive treble might have emanated from the remotest cavern, so little did she mark me, so rapt was she in the contemplation of her private, her all too palpable terror. Fright being, in its way, as communicable a disorder as leprosy, I soon felt my *own* heart pound, my *own* limbs stiffen, and at length I became persuaded—merely on the evidence of Miss Marquis' terror-struck countenance—that *another was there*, a personage of such vile depravity that before him, our very souls lay in mortal peril.

I turned on my heel and scanned the near and far horizons for this figure—this *malignity*—which so oppressed my lovely companion. In the full fury of my monomania, I inspected every stone, peered behind every cedar, made three more circuits of the monument. No one was *there*, Mr. Landor!

Mollified, though by no means *pacified*, by this intelligence, I turned back to my companion, only to discover that the spot upon which she had last been standing now stood vacant. *Miss Marquis had vanished.*

The urgency which now seized me was so utter and entire that I ceased any longer to regard myself as a being separate and enclosed from the one who had disappeared. Never once did it occur to me that I should be late for evening parade. Fain would I have given up *all* parades, *all* duties, for one more glimpse of her angelic aspect. I ran—from tree to tree, from stone to stone—I sprinted along the shaded walk—canvassed every log and stump—searched turf and moss, meadow and stream for her. I shouted her name to the tree toads and the cock robins; I shouted it to the westerly wind and the sinking sun and the very mountains. No answer came back. In the depths of my agony, I even—you may imagine at what cost—dragged myself to the precipice of the cemetery bluff and called down the craggy slope, expecting every second to find her broken, lifeless body laid out on the rocks below.

I had quite despaired of finding her, Mr. Landor, until, at length, I passed a rhododendron bush—not fifty yards from where I had last seen her—and beheld, through the tracery of the nearly denuded branches, a single foot, encased in a lady's boot. Squinting through the overgrowth, I came to see that this foot was connected with a leg, this leg with a torso, this torso with a head—composing in sum the pallid and inert form of Miss Lea Marquis, prostrated on the bitter, hard, rocky ground.

Kneeling before her, I remained for some time both breathless and motionless. Her blue eyes were turned up in the most alarming fashion, so that her irises fairly disappeared behind the canopies of her eyelids. A line of saliva had materialized round those tender and voluptuous lips, and her whole person was suffused with a trembling so pronounced and generalized in its character as to make me dread for her life!

She spoke no word, and I—not for worlds could I have uttered a syllable—until at last—at last!—the fit of ague began to recede. And still I waited, until my vigilance was rewarded with the swell of her breast, the scarcely visible flutter of her eyelashes, the soft dilation of her nostrils. She was not dead. She would not die.

Her face, however, was of the ghastliest pallor. The knot of her hair had come unraveled, and the ringlets of her jetty hair now tumbled over her brow in promiscuous confusion. Her *eyes,* Mr. Landor. Her pale blue eyes *stared* into mine, with a wildness and a wantonness—a too, too glorious effusion. These alterations to her appearance, being organic in nature, were not, in themselves, worrisome. There was no gainsaying, though, the disturbances to her person which bore an external, a human—nay, I will go further, an *inhuman*—imprint. Her dress, Mr. Landor, had been torn above the shoulder. Brutish nails had gouged her wrists; the blood still ran from her wounds. A brutish fist had left a bruise on her right temple—sacrilege against the spiritual placidity of her noble brow.

"Miss Marquis!" I cried.

Had I a thousand years, Mr. Landor, and words innumerable, I could not portray the smiling raiment in which her lovely, battered face was then clothed.

"I'm so sorry to have troubled you," said she. "Do you think you might walk me home? Mother does tend to worry when I'm gone too long."

Narrative of Gus Landor

19

I can't blame Poe for not recognizing the symptoms. He'd never had a clergyman in the family, you see, and clergymen are the physicians of choice for this particular disorder. Even my father, who was more about freezing the soul than healing it, even *he* would be called upon more often than he liked. One family I specially remember. They lived in the farmhouse in the next glen. Each time their boy had a spell of falling sickness, they'd come galloping into our hollow, carrying that arched, thrashing body, demanding a miracle. Hadn't Jesus done it for that boy in Mark 9:17–30? Couldn't the Reverend Landor do the same?

And Father would always try. He'd set his hand on that child's convulsing frame and command the spirits to come out, and by the looks of things, they *would*—only to come back the next day or the week after. After a time, the boy's family ceased to trouble us.

Possessed, that was the word I remember the boy's father using. But possessed by what? I wondered. All I could see was absence. A shell where a human being had once lived.

Of course, I had only Poe's account to go by. But if I was right about Lea Marquis' illness, she had *reason,* suddenly, to be a sorrowing spinster. And though I had yet to meet her, I confess I sorrowed in her behalf, for who knew how much longer her body could last under such a dire sentence?

Poe's own words came back to me on a draft of cold air: *The death of a beautiful woman is Poetry's grandest, most exalted theme. . . .*

Well, I couldn't get behind that myself. But then, I was on my way to a funeral.

This was the day on which Leroy Fry's body was to be committed to the earth. What cerements he wore, I couldn't tell you, for his coffin was never opened from the moment the six bombardiers hoisted it from the hearse to the moment the earth closed it round.

Poe had been right about this, at least: you couldn't find a much better place to be buried than the West Point cemetery. Or a better time than a November morning, with fog rolling like surf around your shins and the wind hissing among the stones and brambles . . . and leaves raining down, the year's last leaves, massing in scarlet drifts round the white crosses.

I was standing not ten feet from the gravesite, listening to the muffled drum, watching the procession of banners and black plumes. I remember how the bier creaked under the coffin's weight and the way the cord grated as the coffin was lowered into the ground. And yes, the sound of dirt clods on that stark pine box—a sound that seemed to come up through the ground, right through the spikes of grass. Most of the rest is a muddle now. Leroy Fry's father, for instance—I must have seen him, but I don't recall. *Mrs.* Fry I remember. A freckled, stooped woman in black crepe, with a doe's eyes and ears, emaciated in the arms and shoulders, plump only in the cheeks, which were puffed and pink. She coughed out little pellets of air and kept rubbing away tears that weren't there—her fists left trenches of red alongside her nose—and she gave no sign of listening to anything, least of all the Reverend Zantzinger's sermon, a long parade of shouting dragoons and thundering hooves.

Once Leroy Fry was in the ground, I would never again dream of him. Or else I was dreaming round the clock now. Because the horses, drawing away the empty hearse, weren't they moving at half their usual speed? And the chaplain—surely, he took upward of an hour to brush one speck of dirt from his sleeve. And why was it that after the bombardiers fired their volleys over Leroy Fry's grave, the mountains caught the report and refused to part with it? It kept echoing, I mean, and building, like a trapped storm front.

And what, finally, could explain *this*? Leroy Fry's mother, standing before me. Scarred with sun, pinched with grief.

"You're Mr. Landor, aren't you?"

There was no getting round that one. Yes . . . yes, I was. . . .

She hesitated for a long while. Unsure of the etiquette, maybe. In her normal life, she would never have gone up to a man as she was doing now.

"You're the one who's looking into . . ."

"Yes, that's so," I answered.

She nodded vigorously, without meeting my eyes. And I nodded, too, because I couldn't say the things that were expected of me: how sorry I was, what a terrible loss it was . . . for you, for all of us. . . . Nothing like that would come out, and it was a great relief to see her giving up on speech as well and instead fumbling through her reticule, from which at last she drew a tiny clothbound volume with gilt edges.

"There's something I'd like you to have," she said, pressing the book into my hand.

"What's this, Mrs. Fry?"

"Leroy's diary."

My fingers closed round it, then fell slack. "Diary?"

"Yes, indeed. I believe it goes back at least three years."

"I'm not—" I stopped. "I'm sorry, I don't recall any diary being found with his personal effects."

"Oh, no, it was Mr. Ballinger who gave it to me."

For the first time, she sought out my gaze, and held it.

"Mr. Ballinger?" I asked, keeping my voice low.

"Yes, can you imagine?" A smile stirred on her lips. "He was a good friend of Leroy's, and he said as soon as he heard what—what happened with Leroy, why, he went straight to Leroy's quarters to see what could be done, and that's how he came to find this diary, and he knew there should be nobody looking at such a thing but Leroy Fry's own mother, and that's how he came to give it to me, and he said, 'Mrs. Fry, I want you to take this back home to Kentucky with you, and if you feel like burning it, you go right ahead, it's up to you, but it's not right anyone else should look at it.'"

That's how it came out: one long sentence, each word diving after the next.

"Oh, it was awful considerate of him," she said. "But look here, I've been thinking it over, Mr. Landor. Seeing as how *you're* the one what's looking into the whole business, and the whole Army is practically depending on you, well, then, it seems only right that you should have it. What would I do with it, anyway? I can hardly *read* the thing. Well, look for yourself, it's all twisty and gnarly, isn't it? Can't make head nor tails myself."

Which was, in fact, the very idea. Leroy Fry had taken the usual precaution of crosshatching his entries—running vertical columns across horizontal ones—the better to foil the prying eye. It was a practice that could leave such a jumble of letters that even the original author might have trouble transcribing it. You had to have an eye trained for such things. An eye like mine.

And in truth, my eye jumped right in, and my brain followed straight after, and I was already sorting out the patterns when I heard Mrs. Fry's voice—*felt* it, I should say, like a drop of hail on my scalp.

"He should be caught."

Looking up from the pages, I peered into her eyes, and I knew then she wasn't talking about her son.

"He should be caught," she said again, a little louder. "What Leroy did to himself, that was one thing. But nobody ought to have gone and done what they did to his poor little body. That's a crime, or should be if it's not."

What was there to do but agree? Yes, yes, a terrible crime, I said, fumbling, wondering if I should take her hand, lead her somewhere. . . .

"Thank you, Mrs. Fry. You've been a great help."

She nodded, absently. Then, turning halfway round, she watched her youngest son's coffin disappear under the last spadefuls of dirt. Nothing for the Army to do now but mark the site with one of those spotless crosses, blazing white in the red and gold leaves.

"It was such a nice service," said Mrs. Fry. "Don't you think? I always told Leroy, I said, 'Leroy, the Army will *do* for you.' And you see? I was right."

If I thought I'd be rewarded for my find, I would have to think again. Hitchcock gave it his best full-dress frown when I waved it in front of him. Couldn't bring himself to trust it or even touch it. Crossed his arms like bayonets and asked me how I knew it was Fry's diary in the first place.

"Well, Captain, I guess a mother would know her own son's handwriting."

He asked me what would have kept Ballinger from tearing out any incriminating pages. I said he likely wouldn't have known where they were. Fry had not only crosshatched his entries in microscopically tiny letters but also written some in reverse, Hebrew-style, making the whole thing about as penetrable as a cuneiform.

But here was what Captain Hitchcock really wanted to know: Why hadn't Ballinger just thrown the whole thing away? If the diary was worth taking, why risk letting anyone see it?

And to that I had no good answer. Maybe, I ventured, Ballinger had nothing to fear from these pages. Ah, but why then would he have taken such a risk in the first place? Interfering with an Academy inquiry was serious business, grounds for dismissal or worse. (It was all I could do to keep Hitchcock from keelhauling him on the spot.) No, the only explanation I could come up with was the one that was least likely.

"And what's that?" asked Captain Hitchcock.

"That whatever's in there, well, Ballinger wants it to be known. Someday. By someone."

"Meaning?"

"Meaning, he may have a conscience."

Well, Hitchcock scoffed, and who was I to stick up for the young man? I didn't know him, and what I came to know of him wouldn't have put me on his side. But I do believe there's something about the human soul that wants to be known, even in its ugliest corners. Why else does a man—myself included—bother putting words to paper?

16 June. Today begins a grate Adventuere.

That's how Leroy Fry's diary starts. Adventure it was, though not for me, not at first. Nothing but drudgery. With a pen in one hand and a magnifying glass in the other, I worked steadily by the dwindling taper light, the diary on my left, a transcribing notebook on my right. The letters swarmed over me, up and down, backward and forward. On occasion,

I had to lift my eyes from the page just to blink them clear, or close them altogether.

Oh, it was a slow business ... maddening ... an agony. I had only about two pages finished when Poe came knocking. So softly I almost didn't hear. The door tickled open, and there he stood, in his shabby boots and his cloak newly torn at the shoulder, bearing still another brown-paper parcel.

Texts, I thought. *I'm drowning in texts*.

"Mr. Poe, you needn't have rushed it over tonight. I'm quite occupied, as you can see."

"It was no great difficulty," he said, softly, in the dark.

"But all this- –all this *writing* you're doing," I said. "You'll wear yourself out before you're done."

"It doesn't matter."

He dropped straight to the floor, and in the sputtering light from the tapers, I could see him staring up at me, with an air of deep expectation.

"What is it, Mr. Poe?"

"I'm waiting for you to read it."

"You mean now?"

"But of course."

He never asked me what the *other* document was, the one in my lap. He must have imagined I was simply biding my time until he could report back to me. Maybe I was.

"Well, then," I said, taking the pages from him and stacking them lightly in my lap. "Not quite so long as the last one, I think."

"Perhaps not," he agreed.

"Can I—might I *get* you something? A nip of something, if you're ..."

"No. Thank you. I'll just wait for you to finish."

And so he did. Sat there on the cold floor, watching every word rise from the page to my eye. And whenever I glanced his way, he was in the same position, *watching*. ...

Report of Edgar A. Poe to Augustus Landor

November 17th

My previous encounter with Miss Marquis had been of so inconclusive a nature as to make me wonder if I should ever again set eyes upon her. A stranger was she to me still,—and yet the prospect of being forever segregated from her was beyond sufferance, and it was with heavier heart than usual that I plied myself once more to the Sisyphean round of mathematics and French. How sterile seemed to me the picaresque antics of Lesage, and the logical flights of Archimedes and Pythagoras. I have heard that men deprived of all light and sustenance may slumber for more than three entire days and deem it of no greater duration than a catnap. Happily would I have exchanged their lot for mine! Yoked within the span of each new day lay an endless caravan of days. Seconds elapsed like minutes, minutes like hours. Hours? Were these not Eons?

Dinner came—I lived still. But to what avail? Every energy of mind lay in abeyance; shades of the deepest melancholy darkened my path. On Wednesday evening, as I listened to the beat of tattoo calling all cadets to their slumbers, I dreaded lest the insufferable gloom which pervaded my spirit should succeed in swallowing me whole, leaving behind nothing more than my bedclothing and the musket which hangs—with what forlornness!—on the wall above my head.

Onward came the dawn, and the beating of reveille. Shaking myself free of Sleep's gossamer web, I found one of my roommates, young Mr. Gibson, standing before my pallet with an expression of reptilian glee.

"A message for you," he cried. "And in a woman's hand!"

True enough, there was a slip of paper with my name inscribed upon the back. And yes, the lettering gave every evidence of the graceful arabesques and curlicues so widely associated with the weaker sex. I did not dare presume, however, that the hand in question might belong to *her*—though every truncheon beat of my heart cried it to the icy dawn air: It is She! It is She!

> *Dear Mr. Poe:* [it read]
> *Would you be so good as to meet me this morning? I believe you have a brief interval of liberty between breakfast and the day's first recitals. If that be the case, and if you can forbear to look kindly on my petition, I shall be waiting for you at Fort Putnam. I promise I will not keep you long.*
> *Yours,*
> *L.A.M.*

I ask you, Mr. Landor, *who* could resist such a summons as this? The gentle importunity of these words, the unaffected elegance of her penmanship, the faintest effluvium of perfume from the stationery. . . .

Mistress Time, in all her mercurial vanity, now saw fit to make the remaining hours pass as quickly as a dream. Upon being released from the squalid confines of mess, I took silent leave of my gray confreres and, without another thought, launched myself up Mount Independence. I was alone now. Alone, yes, and *happy*, for could there be any doubt that *she* had preceded me through this tangled brake and woodland path? It was no hardship, then, to climb over the soft spangled moss and splinters of rock, to scale the ruined ramparts of that ancient fortification which housed the unfortunate Major André during his final days on Earth, for *her* dainty boots had blazed the trail.

Passing beneath an arched casemate overgrown with vines, I came to a fringe of cedar bushes and there discerned, on a broad table of granite, the half-reclining figure of Miss Lea Marquis. She turned her head as I approached, and there appeared on her face a smile of the most unforced and most infectious enthusiasm. All the vexation which had disfigured her person during our last encounter had been superseded entirely by those native fires and graces which had so commended themselves in our first meeting.

"Mr. Poe," she said. "I'm so happy you could come."

With a slight and graceful motion, she indicated that I might seat myself alongside her, a position I assumed with all due alacrity. She informed me then that her sole intention in arranging our interview had been to thank me for my ministrations toward her in her hour of need. Although I had no recollection of any extraordinarily chivalrous conduct on my part, such acts of *caritas* as I had performed in guiding her safely home had, I soon found, been more than amply recompensed. For upon learning that I had missed evening parade on her account (and been duly reported, by the three-headed dog of Locke), Miss Marquis had hastened at once to her father and assured him that without my kind intervention, she might well have come to harm.

Well, as soon as the good Dr. Marquis received these tidings from his only and beloved daughter, he wasted no time in petitioning Captain Hitchcock in my behalf, relaying to him the entire history of my magnanimous acts. The commandant, to his everlasting credit, not only absolved me of demerit but excused me from the additional round of guard duty which Locke had assigned me and, in closing, let it be known that my conduct would do justice to any officer of the United States Army.

Neither did the amiable Dr. Marquis confine himself to this single charitable office. He further intimated that he should be glad of a chance to express his gratitude toward me in person and could imagine no better means of accomplishing that end than to receive me once more as an honored family guest at some date in the very near future.

What a reversal of fortunes was this, Mr. Landor! I, who had despaired of ever again beholding Miss Marquis, was to be vouchsafed still one more chance to revel in her company, under the benign and approbatory supervision of those who held her . . . I was going to say *more* dear than I . . . I find I cannot.

The air, as I have reported, was chill at that early hour, but Miss Marquis, wrapped in a pelisse and cape, gave no evidence of undue hardship. Instead, she applied herself entirely to the scene which lay before us, lofty Bull Hill and old Cro' Nest and the rugged range of Break Neck, stopping now and then to finger the ribbon-strap of her sandal.

"Ugh," she said at last. "It's all so bare now, isn't it? How much nicer in March, when one can at least be *sure* there's life on the way."

I replied that to the contrary, it was my belief that the Highlands, to be apprehended in the full extent of their glory, must be seen immediately after the fall of the leaf, for neither Summer's verdancy nor Winter's rime can then conceal the minutest objects from the eye. Vegetation, I told her, does not improve, but rather obstructs, God's originating design.

How I seem to amuse her, Mr. Landor—the more so when I have the least design to amuse.

"I see," she said. "A Romantic." And then, smiling broadly, she added, "You do enjoy talking of God, Mr. Poe."

I remarked that in matters of human and natural provenance, I could imagine no more appropriate entity to invoke, and inquired if she knew of a more suitable authority.

"Oh," she said. "It's all so . . ." Her voice trailed away, and her hand made a gentle fanning motion, as if to send the topic sailing on the next easterly wind. In our too-brief acquaintance, I had never known her to be so vague on any point, so averse to taking up the dangling thread of discussion. Not wishing, however, to arouse her suspicions with a more concerted inquiry, I permitted the matter to drop and contented myself instead with the aforementioned view—and with such occasional sidelong glimpses of my companion as I might, in good conscience, purloin.

How precious did her lineaments seem to me in that moment! The lovely soft green of her bonnet, the voluminous, billowing pool of her skirts and petticoats beneath her. The delicious contour of her sleeve and her puffed white undersleeve, out of which peeped fingers of delectable whiteness and vigor. Her scent, Mr. Landor! The very aroma which had lain pent within that slip of stationery—earthy, sweet, lightly pungent. The longer we sat, the more it imposed itself upon my consciousness— until, driven near to distraction, I asked her if she would be so good as to identify it for me. Was it *eau de rose*? I wondered. *Blanc de neige*? *Huile ambrée*?

"Nothing so fashionable as those," said she. "It is only some orrisroot."

This intelligence had the effect of summarily silencing me. For several minutes altogether, I found myself incapable of even the most rudimentary speech. At length, growing anxious for my welfare, Miss Marquis begged to know what was the matter.

"I must ask your pardon," said I. "Orrisroot was my mother's favorite fragrance. I used to smell it on her clothes, long after she had died."

I had intended it only as a passing remark; it was certainly never my purpose to speak of my mother in any greater detail. I had not reckoned, however, on the countervailing force of Miss Marquis' curiosity. She at once "brought me out" on the subject and succeeded in extracting from me as thoroughgoing an account as my constrained circumstances might afford. I told her of my mother's national renown, of the many proofs of her extraordinary artistry, of her joyous and abject devotion to husband and children . . . and of her tragic and untimely end in the fiery abyss of the E----- Theatre, scene of so many of her thespian triumphs.

My voice trembled as it passed over certain events, and I doubt I would have had the strength to carry the narrative to its full conclusion had I not enjoyed, in Miss Marquis, an audience of such surpassing empathy. I told her *all,* Mr. Landor, or at least as much as could be compressed into ten minutes' duration. I told her of Mr. Allan, who, being most affected by my orphaned state, had taken it upon himself to make me his heir and raise me as the Gentleman my mother should have wished me to be. I spoke of his wife, the late Mrs. Allan, who had, until her own recent demise, been a *second* mother to me. I spoke of my years in England, my peregrinations across Europe, my service in the artillery—and more, I spoke of my thoughts, my dreams, my fancies. Miss Marquis listened to *everything,* good and ill, with a near-sacerdotal equanimity. In her person I found embodied the principle enumerated by Terence: *Homo sum, humani nil a me alienum puto.* Indeed, her spirit of indulgence so emboldened me that after a very short time, I felt free to confess that my mother has maintained a kind of supranatural presence in my sleepings and awakenings. No living memory did she bequeath me, I avowed, and yet she persists with mysterious doggedness as *spirit*-memory.

Upon hearing this, Miss Marquis looked at me with great intentness. "You mean to say she *speaks* to you? What does she say?"

For the first time that morning, I grew reticent. How I longed to tell her, Mr. Landor, of that mysterious poetical fragment—I could not. Nor did she seem in any way to demand further elaboration. After posing the question, she abandoned it as quickly and concluded by murmuring, "They never leave us, do they? The ones who come before us. I wish I knew why."

Haltingly, then, I spoke of the Theories I had propounded on this very question. "There are times," I declared, "when I believe the dead haunt us because we love them too little. We *forget* them, you see; we don't mean to, but we do. All our sorrow and pity subside for a time, and in that interval, however long it lasts, I believe they feel most cruelly deserted. And so they clamor for us. They wish to be recalled to our hearts. So as not to be murdered twice over.

"Other times," I continued, "I believe we love them *too* much. And as a consquence they are never free to depart, because we carry them, our most deeply beloved, within ourselves. Never dead, never silent, never appeased."

"*Revenants,*" she said, eyeing me closely.

"Yes, I suppose so. But how can they be said to *return* when they have never gone away?"

Her hand passed in front of her mouth—for what purpose, I could not ascertain until I heard the eructation of merriment spilling through her lips.

"Why is it, Mr. Poe, that I would sooner spend an hour with you in the"—again she laughed—"in the *gloomiest* contemplations than spend another minute speaking of dresses and baubles and the things that make most people happy?"

A solitary gleam now struck the base of the mountain on which we gazed. Miss Marquis, however, turned her attention away, and, with the assistance of a blunt stick, began idly to sketch abstract figures on the granite ledge.

"The other day," she said at length. "In the cemetery . . ."

"We need not speak of that, Miss Marquis."

"But you see, I *want* to speak of it. I want to tell you . . ."

"Yes?"

"How grateful I was. To open my eyes, I mean, and find you there." She chanced a glance in my direction, then withdrew it at once. "I looked deep into your face, Mr. Poe, and I found there something I never would have expected. Not in a thousand years."

"What did you find, Miss Marquis?"

"Love," she said.

Ah, Mr. Landor! You will scarcely credit that until this moment, I had never once entertained the notion of being in *love* with Miss Marquis. That I admired her—*greatly*, yes—I would never have disputed. That she intrigued—nay, fascinated—me was beyond argument. But never, Mr. Landor, did I dare venture any more exalted construction of my sentiments.

And yet as soon as this—this sacred *word* had passed her lips, I could no longer deny the truth that lay locked within it, the truth that she, with her exquisite clemency, had now sprung from its straitened cell.

I *loved*, Mr. Landor. In despite of all my protestations, I *loved*.

And with that, a change came over all things. Sturgeon, rising in a great commotion of smacks and slaps, burst through the surface of the Hudson, and out of the bosom of that haunted river issued, little by little, a melody more divine than that of Aeolus' harp. I sat, motionless, as upon the golden threshold of the wide-open gate of dreams, gazing far away to where the prospect terminated—only to realize that it terminated in *her*.

"I see I've embarrassed you," she said. "You needn't feel that way. You must have seen—" Her voice caught, but she went on. "You must have seen the love that was in *my* heart, too."

How suddenly it comes, this benison of Love! And how it eludes us even in the moment of its birth! Although we may scale the very heavens to grasp it, we cannot close it round. No, no, it must always escape us. We must fail—FALL—

In short, I fainted dead away. And might, without a single qualm, have missed the morning recital. And might have missed many more, might even have suffered Atropos herself (cruel daughter of Themis!) to shear the thread of life, so happy—so exorbitantly, *inhumanly* happy—was I in that moment.

It was *her* face I beheld upon returning to my senses—*her* heavenly orbs, exuding rays of holy light.

"Mr. Poe," she said. "I suggest that during our next meeting, we both remain conscious for the entire duration."

I heartily concurred with her suggestion and vowed that I would never again so much as close my eyes if she lay framed therein. I then implored her at once to seal our covenant by referring to me ever after by my Christian name.

"Edgar, is it? Oh, very well, Edgar, if you like. And I suppose you must then call me Lea."

Lea. Lea! What a ravishing residue does that name deposit within my ear's inner chamber! What a world of happiness is foretold within those two brief and euphonious syllables!

Lea. Lea.

Narrative of Gus Landor

20

November 21st

This was the oddest part of all: Poe had nothing to add to what he'd written. As soon as I was finished reading, I waited for him to pick up where he'd left off. To quote another Latin poet or walk me through some etymology, expound on the unsurvivability of love. . . .

But all he did was bid me good night. And after promising to report further when he could, he slipped away as easily as a wraith.

I didn't see him again until the next evening—and might never have seen him again at all but for chance. Poe himself would call it something grander, but for now, I'll stand by my word. It was *chance* that made me halt in the midst of toiling over Leroy Fry's diary and gave me a sudden hankering for air. Sent me spilling out the door into the charcoal dusk, swinging my lantern in slow arcs to keep from losing my footing.

It was a dry piney night. The river was noisier than usual, and the moon could have cut you just to look at it, and the ground seemed to crackle with each step, so that I walked with great care, as if I were on the brink of offending. I paused by the ruins of the old Artillery Barracks and stood within sniffing distance of the Plain, casting my eyes along the long incline of night-purpled grass.

And then stopped.

Something was moving. Something by Execution Hollow.

I lifted my lamp higher, and as I drew closer, the figure's strangeness, the jangle of its borders, resolved into something clearer. I was looking at a man—a man on all fours.

Which from a distance, seemed a dire, an unhealthy pose for anyone to be in—the prelude to a full collapse. But as I drew still closer, I could see there was a *meaning* behind this position. For just beneath that first figure lay a second.

The one on top, I recognized straight off. I had seen enough of him in cadet mess to know the flaxen hair, the farm-boy *mass* of him: Randolph Ballinger, if you please. *Astride* his opponent, using his heavy legs to pin the fellow's arms to the ground and plying the full weight of his mighty forearm against the other's windpipe.

And who was on the receiving end of that onslaught? It wasn't until I'd circled round and got the necessary vantage—seen the outsized head and the brittle whippet frame and, yes, the cloak with its torn shoulder—that I could be certain.

And now I was running. For I knew in my bones how unequal this contest was: Ballinger was a good half foot taller than Poe, forty pounds heavier, and more than that, he had in his actions a clean line of *intent* that suffered no reversal. He would not turn back.

"Leave off, Mr. Ballinger!"

I heard my own voice, rock-steady, shrinking the distance between us.

His head jerked up. His eyes—white pools in the lantern light—met mine. And without letting up one bit from Poe's throat, he said, calm as a pond:

"Private business, sir."

It was Leroy Fry who came echoing back in that moment. Calling out merrily to his companion on the landing: *Necessary business. . . .*

And there *was* a necessity to this business, to judge by Ballinger's flat, unruffled brow, his air of studious attention. He had seen his course, and he would follow it out. And he would do it without another word of explanation. Indeed, the only sound I could make out now was the gargling in Poe's throat, a wet, mangled frequency—worse than any scream.

"*Leave off, Mr. Ballinger!*" I cried again.

And still he pressed down with that heavy, heavy arm, squeezing the last drops of air from Poe's lungs. Waiting for the cartilage of Poe's trachea to give way.

I swung my boot and caught Ballinger square on the temple. He grunted, shook the pain from his head . . . and kept pressing.

The second kick caught him on the chin and sent him sprawling onto his back.

"If you leave now," I said, "you can keep your commission. Stay, and I can guarantee you'll be court-martialed by week's end."

He sat up. Gave his jaw a rub. Looked straight ahead, as if I weren't there.

"Or maybe," I said, "you're not familiar with Colonel Thayer's opinions on attempted homicide."

It came down to this: he was no longer in his element. Like many bullies, he was able to enforce his will within a finite enclosure, but no further. As first assistant to the carver at Table Eight, he could stare down anyone who demanded roast beef before his turn. Outside the orbit of Table Eight, outside of 18 North Barracks, he had no system to gird him up.

Which is to say, he left. With as much dignity as he could muster, but knowing still that he'd been *stopped,* and that knowledge trailed behind him in fumes.

Reaching down, I pulled Poe to his feet. He was breathing more easily now, but his skin was a mottled copper color in the lamplight.

"Are you all right?" I asked.

He winced as he tried a test swallow. "I am quite well," he gasped out. "It will take more than a . . . craven . . . underhanded assault to . . . cow a Poe. I hail from a—a long line of—"

"Frankish chieftains, I know. Maybe you can tell me what happened."

He took a single tottering step forward.

"I can hardly say, Mr. Landor. I'd stolen out of my chambers with the intent of visiting you . . . having taken all the . . . all the usual precautions. Careful as ever to . . . I can't explain it . . . he was able to surprise me."

"Did he say anything?"

"The *same* thing. Again and again. Under his breath."

"And what was that?"

"*'Little beasts—ought to know their place'.*"

"And that was all?"

"That was all."

"And how do you interpret that, Mr. Poe?"

He shrugged, and even this tiny motion sent a new line of pain up the column of his throat.

"Arrant jealousy," he said at last. "He is . . . manifestly distraught . . . that Lea prefers me to him. He seeks to frighten me away from her." From somewhere inside him came a high, squirrelly laugh. "He can scarcely . . . *gauge* . . . the depths of my resolve on this matter. I am *not* to be frightened."

"So you think he wished only to scare you, Mr. Poe?"

"What else?"

"Well, I don't know," I said, gazing once more at Execution Hollow. "From where I was standing, he looked awfully set on killing you."

"Don't be ridiculous. He hasn't the nerve. He hasn't the imagination."

Oh, Reader, I had half a mind to tell him about the killers *I'd* met in my day. Some of the least imaginative men you'd ever want to meet. Which was what made them so dangerous.

"All the same, Mr. Poe, I wish you'd . . ." I shoved my hands into my pockets, gave the turf a light kick. "You see, the point is, I've come to *depend* on you in a fashion, and I'd hate to think you might lose your life over a young woman, however pretty she may be."

"I shan't be the one to lose his life, Mr. Landor. You may be certain of that."

"Who, then?"

"Ballinger," he said simply. "Before I let him come between me and my heart's desire, I will kill him. Yes, and it will be the purest pleasure and the most—the most *moral* act of my career."

I took him by the elbow and walked him gently up the slope toward the hotel. A minute passed before I dared speak again.

"Oh yes," I said, as lightly as I could, "the morality part is easily squared. But as for taking pleasure in it, Mr. Poe, I can't imagine you doing that."

"You don't know me, then, Mr. Landor."

And he was right: I didn't. I didn't know what he was capable of until it was already done.

We stood at last in front of the colonnade. Poe's breathing was coming steady now, and his face had regained something of its usual pallor. Never had that pallor looked so *healthy*.

"Well," I said. "I'm glad I happened along when I did."

"Oh, I think I should have had an answer for Ballinger in the end. But I'm grateful you were standing by in reserve."

"Do you think Ballinger knew where you were going?"

"I don't see how he could have. The hotel wasn't even in view."

"So you don't believe our little arrangement has been disclosed."

"Nor shall it be, Mr. Landor. Not to anyone, not even . . ." He paused to let the tide of feeling crest inside him. "Not even to *her*." Rousing himself then, he declared in a bright voice, "You have failed to ask me why I was coming to visit you in the first place."

"I assume you have some fresh news to deliver."

"Indeed I do."

All hands now, he began to ransack his pockets. It took him a minute to find the thing: a single sheet, which he unfolded as reverently as he might've unpacked a chalice.

I should have guessed. The glint in his eye alone should have told me, but no, I took the paper in all innocence and so was completely unprepared to read:

> *In the shades of that dream-shadowed weir,*
> *I trembled 'neath Night's loathsome stole.*
> *"Leonore, tell me how cam'st thou here*
> *To this bleak unaccountable shoal*
> *To this dank undesirable shoal."*
> *"Dare I speak?" cried she, cracking with fear.*
> *"Dare I whisper Hell's terrible toll?*
> *"Each new dawn brings the memory drear*
> *Of the devils who ravished my soul*
> *Of the demons who ravaged my soul."*

The words revolved in the lantern light, and I found I could call up no words to answer them. Over and over, I dredged my brain for something, and each time I came up empty, and in the end, all I could find to say was:

"It's nice," I said. "Really, Mr. Poe. Very nice."

I heard his laugh then in my ear—full and sweet and ringing.

"Thank you, Mr. Landor. I shall tell Mother you said so."

Narrative of Gus Landor

21

November 22nd to 25th

Later that night, I heard a knock on my hotel-room door. Not the shy tap that was Poe's trademark, but a more urgent summons that had me leaping from my bed, fully expecting to find—who could say?—Judgment itself.

It was Patsy. Wrapped in double bands of wool, her breath steaming in the cold hallway.

"Let me in," she said.

I waited for her to dissolve. Instead, she stepped into the room—all three dimensions, solid as my hand.

"I was just dropping off some liquor for the boys," she said.

"Anything left for me?"

That was as casual as I could be in the face of such temptation. Indeed, I think it fair to say I sprang on her . . . and she, angel that she is, suffered me to. Lay there with the most amused look on her face as I undressed her. Of all the stages, this is the one I like best: the peeling away of layers— stockings, shoes, petticoats—each one more suspenseful than the last. For will she be there at the end of it all? The eternal question. Your hands tremble as you undo the final row of buttons. . . .

And there she lies, shiny and white and prosperous.

"Mmm," she says, dictating to the last. "Yes, indeed. Right there."

It was a longer business than usual—Mr. Cozzens' bed had never made so many squeaks from so many corners—and when we were done, we lay there for a while, her head on my arm. And then, in her usual way, she fell asleep, and after listening for some time to the cataract of her breathing, I gently lifted her head from my chest and slipped out of bed.

Leroy Fry's diary was waiting for me by the window. Lighting the taper, I spread the pages on my lap and placed the notebook on the table and once more set to work, unwinding the long skeins of letters. I'd been working for more than an hour and a half when I felt her hands on my shoulders.

"What's in the book, Gus?"

"Oh." I set down my pen, gave my face a good rub. "Words."

She pressed her knuckles into the knotted ridges above my collarbones. "*Good* words?"

"Not really. Although I'm learning quite a lot about, oh, firing theory and Congreve rockets and Lord, wouldn't it be grand to be back home in Kentucky where the cold don't—don't scratch at your bones so. Amazing how boring a diary can be."

"Not mine," said Patsy.

"You—" My eyes flared open. "*You* keep one?"

After a long pause, she shook her head. "But if I did," she said.

Well, why shouldn't she? I thought. Wasn't I already walled round with texts? Poe with his poems and prose, and Professor Pawpaw with his notebook, and Sergeant Locke with *his* notebook . . . even Captain Hitchcock was rumored to keep a journal. I thought of the scrap in Leroy Fry's balled-up fist and the engraving of that devils' sabbath and the newspapers on Thayer's breakfast table and the newspapers next to Blind Jasper's elbow—all these *texts,* do you see? Not gathering into meaning, as you might expect, but *erasing* one another, until one word was no truer than the next, and down we would all go, down this rabbit hole of *words,* clanging and shrilling like Pawpaw's birds. . . .

So yes, I thought. *By all means, Patsy. Keep a diary.*

"Care to come back to bed?" she whispered in my ear.

"Mmm."

I gave it some thought, I will say that for myself. Gave it serious consideration. And fool that I was, chose to stay where I was.

"I'll be there soon," I promised.

Except that I fell asleep in my chair. And when I woke up, it was morning, and she was gone, and in my notebook, the following words had been scrawled: *Bundle Up, Gus. It's Cold Outside.*

It *was* cold—all through Tuesday and Tuesday evening.

On Wednesday morning, Cadet First Classman Randolph Ballinger failed to return from his guard posting.

A search was immediately mounted, but the men left off after twenty minutes because an ice storm had begun to sweep through the Highlands. The chill and damp were extreme, the views had shrunk to nothing, and after a time, the horses and mules could make no headway, so it was agreed that the search would be remounted as soon as the weather permitted.

But the weather didn't permit. The ice kept falling through the morning and the afternoon. It tickled the roofs and pattered on the leaded casement windows and made a crazing chatter on the eaves and walls. Down, down it came, never stopping, never changing. I spent the whole morning listening to it scratch like a hungry cur in the gutters, until I realized that if I didn't throw on my coat and stagger outside, I would go mad.

Early afternoon, and the whole land lay prisoner. Ice had formed in thick brittle crusts over Captain Wood's obelisk and the brass eighteen-pounders in the artillery park and the water pump behind South Barracks and the downspouts on the stone buildings of Professors' Row. Ice had lacquered together the gravel on the walkways and ambered over the rock lichens on their rocks and clamped the wide expanses of snow into beds hard as quartz. Ice had dragged down the boughs of the cedar trees into wigwams that shuddered at each kiss of wind. Pure democracy, this ice, falling on blue and gray alike, silencing everything it touched. Except for me. My boots, as they picked their way through, made a sound like clanging armor, and the sound seemed to sing from one end of the Point to the other.

Back I staggered to my room and, for the rest of the afternoon, dozed in and out in the endless twilight. Sometime around five, I woke with a start and ran to the window. The ice had stopped, and there was a peal of quiet now, and through the bolls of mist, I could just make out a single dugout toiling downriver with a bare-armed oarsman. I hurried on my trousers and a shirt and coat and closed the door quietly after me.

The cadets had come out of their holes and were already lining up for parade. The crackling ice magnified each step a thousand times over, and in that din, I passed with no interference to Gee's Point. I'm not sure what took me there. I suppose it was the same idea that had come over me my first day there, the notion that I—or, if not me, *someone*—could just keep going. Take that river to somewhere he'd never been.

Behind me came footsteps, crunching down the path. A soft, deferential voice.

"Mr. Landor?"

It was Lieutenant Meadows. Who was, by coincidence, the officer who'd been escorting me the last time I stood here. He was positioned ten feet behind me now, just as he'd been then, and he was *braced,* as though he were getting ready to leap a moat.

"Good evening," I said. "I hope you're well."

His voice was stiff as a quill. "Captain Hitchcock has asked me to come for you. It pertains to the missing cadet."

"Ballinger's been found?"

Meadows said nothing at first. He'd been instructed, clearly, to say no more than was needed, but I took his silence to mean something else. Half under my breath, I spoke the word he couldn't.

"Dead," I said.

His only assent was silence.

"Hanged?" I asked.

And this time, Meadows did consent to nod.

"The heart," I said. "The heart was—"

He cut me off then, as brusquely as if he were carving a joint. "The heart is gone, yes."

It might well have been the cold that made him shiver and set his feet dancing. Or else he'd seen the body.

The moon, just rising over Breakneck Hill, was sending down a soft gauzy light that caught the planes of his face and gilded his eyes.

"There's something else," I said. "Something you haven't yet told me."

Under normal circumstances, he'd have fallen back on the usual refrain: *Not at liberty to say, sir.* But something in him *wanted* to say it. He stopped and started and stopped again and then, after great effort, confessed:

"An additional infamy was perpetrated against Mr. Ballinger's person."

Absurd wording—formal, empty—and yet it seemed to be his only hedge against the thing itself. Until it couldn't be hedged anymore.

"Mr. Ballinger," he said at last, "was castrated."

A silence fell over us then, broken only by the distant sound of ice crunching beneath cadet boots.

"Maybe you'd better show me," I said.

"Captain Hitchcock would prefer if you met him there *tomorrow*. The day being so far along, he considers there's not enough light to—to—"

"To examine the scene, I see. Where is Mr. Ballinger's body being held for the time being?"

"In the hospital."

"Under full guard?"

"Yes."

"And what time does the captain wish to meet me tomorrow?"

"Nine A.M."

"Well, then," I said. "The only thing I now require is a place. *Where* are we to meet?"

He paused, to do the name proper justice, I think.

"At Stony Lonesome."

There is, it's true, a good bit of stone and lonesomeness to all of West Point. But at least when you're looking out from Mr. Cozzens' hotel or standing on Redoubt Hill, you're in view of the river, with all the freedom it promises. Venture out to Stony Lonesome, and you leave behind all signs of settlement, and your only companions are trees and ravines and maybe the low hiss of a stream . . . and the hills, of course, crowding out the light. It's the hills that make you feel like an inmate. Many cadets, I'm told, after two hours of sentinel duty here, come to believe they will never leave Stony Lonesome.

If Randolph Ballinger was one of those, he was right.

The search for him had picked up again the moment the storm stopped. No one was counting on the ice to start melting almost as quickly as it had come. The spell blew off like chaff, and it was just a few minutes after four o'clock when two privates, filing back to the commandant's quarters to make their report, were stopped by a noise like a thousand hinges. A nearby birch tree was shaking off its cloak of rime and springing open to reveal—huddled inside, like the pistil of a lily—the naked body of Randolph Ballinger.

A skin of ice had sealed him round and knitted his arms to his sides, but it failed to keep him from gyring, ever so slightly, in the onrushing wind.

By the time Lieutenant Meadows led me there, Ballinger had been taken down, and the branches that had formerly cocooned him had sprung back to their full height, and the only thing left to see was the rope, which hung now to its full length, stopping somewhere about my chest. Stiff and bristly and a fraction askew, as though some magnet were pulling it off track.

All round us, melting ice was falling—in pebbles and in large ragged sheets—and the sun was laying a dazzle on the earth, and the only things you could look at after a while, the only things that weren't swatting the light right back to you, were the rhododendrons, still in full leaf.

I asked, "Why a birch tree?"

Hitchcock stared at me.

"I'm sorry, Captain, I was only wondering why, if you're going to hang someone, you'd use such a *bendy* sort of tree. The branches aren't nearly as thick as an oak's, say, or a chestnut's."

"Closer to the ground, perhaps."

"Yes, I suppose that would make things easier."

"Easier," agreed Hitchcock.

He had passed into some new realm of tiredness. The sort that swells your eyelids, pulls down your ears. The sort that roots you in the ground because all you can do is either stand perfectly straight or drop.

I like to think I was kind to him that morning. I gave him any number of chances to retire to his quarters, where he'd have plenty of space to gather his thoughts. And when he needed me to repeat a question, I did, no matter how many times it took. I remember, when I asked him what had distinguished the condition of Randolph Ballinger's body from that of Leroy Fry's, he looked straight at me, as though I'd confused him with someone else.

"You were there," I prompted, "when both bodies were found. I was curious, you know, what made the—the look of *this* body different."

"Oh," he said at last. "Oh, no. *This* one . . ." He stared up into the branches. "Well," he began, "the first thing I noticed was how much higher he was. Relative to Fry."

"So his feet weren't touching the ground?"

"No." He took off his hat, put it back on. "There was no subterfuge this time. Ballinger had all his wounds on him when he was found. Which is to say he was killed, he was cut open—and *then* he was strung up."

"No chance, I guess, that the wounds could have been inflicted—"

"Afterward? No." He was warming up now. "No, not from that height, it would be nearly impossible. Impossible just to keep the body still." He thumbed at his eyes. "A man can't take such injuries and then go hang himself from a tree, that's obvious. Therefore, the whole pretense of suicide is voided."

He stared at the tree for a good long time, his mouth hanging just slightly open. Then, remembering himself, he added:

"We're a good three hundred yards from Ballinger's sentinel post. We don't know if he came here willingly, or if he was even alive when he came. He may have walked, or he may have been dragged. The storm, as you see . . ." He shook his head. "It's made a hash of everything. Mud and snow everywhere, dozens of soldiers traipsing through. Footprints all over the place, yes, and no way to tell one from the rest."

He put an arm against the trunk of the birch and let his body tilt a foot or so.

"Captain," I said, "I'm very sorry. I understand what a blow this must be."

I don't know why, but I gave him just the slightest pat on the shoulder. You know the gesture, Reader; it's the sort of thing men do to comfort one another—the *only* thing they do sometimes. Hitchcock didn't take it that way. He jerked his shoulder away and wheeled on me with a fury-blanched face.

"No, Mr. Landor! I don't think you *do* know. Under my watch, two cadets have been murdered and savagely *desecrated,* for reasons that beggar understanding. And we are no closer to finding the monster who did it than we were a month ago."

"Well, now, Captain," I said, still soothing. "I think we *are* closer. We've narrowed our field, we're moving apace. Yes, I think it will only be a matter of time."

He scowled and ducked his head. From his tightly pressed lips came the low but unmistakable words:

"I'm glad *you* think so."

I smiled. I squeezed my arms against my chest.

"Maybe," I said, "you'd care to explain that remark, Captain."

Undaunted, he turned on me the full force of his gaze. "Mr. Landor, I don't mind telling you that Colonel Thayer and I have serious reservations about the progress of your inquiries."

"Is that so?"

"I should be only too glad to be corrected. Indeed, you now have a golden opportunity to defend yourself. Why don't you tell me if you've found more evidence of satanic practices? Anywhere on the reservation?"

"I haven't, no."

"Have you found the so-called officer who persuaded Private Cochrane to abandon Leroy Fry's body?"

"Not as yet."

"And having now held Mr. Fry's diary in your possession for nearly a week, have you yet found a single clue that might be of use in these investigations?"

I could feel the muscles tightening round my eyes.

"Well, let me see, Captain. I know how many times Leroy Fry diddled himself on a given day. I know he liked women with heavy buttocks. I know how much he hated reveille roll call and analytical geometry and—and *you*. Will any of that do?"

"My point is—"

"Your point is that I'm not competent to undertake this investigation. And maybe never was."

"It's not your competence I question," he said. "It's your allegiance."

Such a soft sound that I couldn't place it at first. Then I realized: it was the grinding of my own teeth.

"And now I'm going to have to ask you to explain yourself again, Captain."

He studied me for a long while. Wondering, maybe, how far he could go.

"It's my suspicion, Mr. Landor—"

"Yes?"

"—that you are protecting someone."

Laughter. That was the only response I could manage at first. Because it was too funny, wasn't it?

"Protecting someone?" I repeated.

"Yes."

I flung up my arms. "*Who?*" I cried. And the word rang out to the nearest elm tree, rattled its branches. "*Who* in this whole godforsaken place could I possibly want to protect?"

"Perhaps now," he said, "is the time to talk of Mr. Poe."

The tiniest knot, forming in my stomach. I shrugged, made a show of confusion.

"And why should we do that, Captain?"

"Begin with this," he said, glancing down at his boots. "Mr. Poe is, so far as I know, the only cadet who ever threatened Mr. Ballinger's life."

He looked up just in time to catch the ripple of surprise on my face. I will say this: there was nothing cruel in the smile he gave me then. It looked more like a twisted sympathy.

"Did you really think you were the only one he confided in, Mr. Landor? Just yesterday, at dinner, he was regaling his tablemates with heroic accounts of his epic tussle with Mr. Ballinger. Every bit the equal of Hector and Achilles, to hear Mr. Poe tell it. Interestingly enough, he concluded his account by declaring that he fully intended to kill Mr. Ballinger should they ever cross swords again. To those listeners present, he could not have been any less equivocal."

No indeed, I thought, remembering once again Poe's words on the Plain. Hard to mistake his meaning. *I will kill him . . . I will kill him. . . .*

"See here," I said. "This wouldn't be the first time Poe's made a silly threat. It's—it's part of his nature. . . ."

"It *would* be the first time that his proposed victim turned up dead within twenty-four hours of the threat's being uttered."

Oh, there was no wheedling this fellow. Hitchcock would hold to his opinion as skin hugs a bone. Maybe that's why notes of desperation were starting to creep into my voice.

"Come, now, you've *seen* Poe, Captain. Can you honestly tell me he *subdued* Ballinger?"

"There would have been no need. A firearm would have turned the trick, don't you think? Or a surprise assault? Instead of Hector and Achilles, perhaps we might better ponder David and Goliath."

I gave a chuckle, scratched my head. *Time,* I was thinking. *Buy time.*

"Well, then, if we're going to seriously consider your little theory, Captain, we'll have to admit one problem. Whatever his relations with Ballinger, there's no sign of any link between Poe and Leroy Fry. They didn't even know each other."

"Oh, but they did."

Silly me, thinking he had only one card to drop. When in fact he had a whole deck up the sleeve of that spotless blue coatee.

"It has come to my attention," he said, "that Poe and Fry had a tussle of their own during last summer's encampment. It appears that Mr. Fry, in the usual manner of upperclassmen, decided, along with two of his fellows, to make sport of Mr. Poe, who apparently took such offense at their treatment that he hurled his musket directly at Mr. Fry—bayonet forward. Another inch or two and he might have seriously damaged Mr. Fry's leg. Mr. Poe was then heard to say, by more than one listener, that he would suffer no man—*no* man—to use him in such a way."

Hitchcock let the news sink in for a few seconds. Then, in a softer voice, he added, "I don't suppose he ever volunteered that bit of information to you, did he?"

Oh, there'd be no getting past the captain today. The best I could hope for was a draw.

"Call in his roommates," I suggested. "Ask them if Poe ever left his quarters on the night Ballinger was killed."

"And if they say no, what will that prove? Only that they're sound sleepers."

"Arrest him, then," I said, as lightly as I dared. "Arrest him, if you're so persuaded."

"As you well know, Mr. Landor, it's not enough to demonstrate motive. We must find direct evidence of the crime. I'm afraid I don't see any evidence; do you?"

As we stood there, a raft of ice came plunging from a tulip magnolia and landed with a shudder just six feet behind us. The sound was enough to scare a flock of sparrows from a nearby white oak. They came at us now, boiling like bees, crazed by ice-glare.

"Captain," I said. "You can't really believe this little poet of ours is a killer?"

"How curious you should ask that question. When *you* are the man best disposed to answer it." He took a step toward me, the barest trace of something on his lips. "Tell me, Mr. Landor. *Is* your little poet a killer?"

Report of Edgar A. Poe to Augustus Landor

November 27th

Abject apologies, Mr. Landor, for my delinquency in reporting back to you. The widespread alarums attending upon Ballinger's murder have produced an atmosphere so rife with Rumor, Scandal, and the basest form of Conjecture that I find my motions scrutinized as never before. Were I of a more credulous nature, I might suppose that I myself were laboring under the mantle of suspicion—yes, I!—so queerly do some of my fellow Cadets eye me as I pass.

Ah, what human language can adequately portray the horror which seized me at the news of Ballinger's brutal end? That the churl who has been such an everlasting torment to me should be so effectually removed from this earthly vale—and with such terrifying suddenness! Each time I venture to contemplate the implications ... I find I cannot. For if our murderer could extinguish someone so intimate with the Marquis family, what is to prevent him from turning his sinister attentions to Artemus or even—mark how I tremble, Mr. Landor!—that conduit of my Soul? Oh, it seems to me that our inquiries cannot proceed quickly *enough*. . . .

In the meantime, Mr. Landor, the arrant and ungallant hysteria manifested in this Corps of Cadets continues to grow beyond all bounds. Many a fellow has spoken of sleeping with his musket. Several of the more fancifully inclined have even speculated that Fry's and Ballinger's assailants are none other than the walking incarnations of ancestral Indian spirits, come to avenge their extermination by the European race. Mr. Roderick, a singularly weak-minded third classman, claims to have witnessed just such a spirit along Flirtation Walk, sharpening its tomahawk in the cleft of a British elm.

Word now has it that Mr. Stoddard has petitioned Colonel Thayer to cancel the remainder of the term—final examinations included—as it is well nigh impossible for Cadets to apply themselves to their studies with sufficient vigor and adhesion while they tremble in fear for their very lives.

With what disgust do I behold these craven boys and their unmanful sniveling! How will they bear up under the trial of *combat*, when all is *sauve qui peut*, and blood lies spewn on every side? To whom will they appeal *then* for a stay of Judgment? Oh, it does not augur well for America's soldiery, Mr. Landor.

Nevertheless, our superiors have granted us one accommodation. At evening parade, it was announced that guard post had been doubled, so that no Cadet may now venture abroad without a companion affixed to his side. Under normal conditions, an order of this sort might have occasioned untold grumbling, as it requires us to report for sentinel duty twice as often. Such is the fear that has germinated within this Corps, however, that every man considers his burden his blessing, if it may purchase him some small increase in safety.

My larger purpose in communicating with you, Mr. Landor, is to apprise you of certain developments relating to Lea and Artemus. This afternoon, finding myself in a state of agitation and with some few minutes at my disposal, I at once betook myself to the Marquis family home, there to console myself that Ballinger's fate had not proven overly injurious to Lea's female sensibilities.

Rapping on that now-familiar door, with its "Hail, Sons of Columbia" sampler, I was dismayed to learn that no one was at home—no one, that is, but Eugénie, the maid. I was considering my next course of action when my thoughts were arrested by the vague sound of *voices*, issuing from a quarter that, upon closer inspection, proved to be the rear of the Marquis plot. I hesitated but for an instant; then, stepping round the corner of that stone edifice, I at once beheld Lea and her brother Artemus in their own backyard, engaged in the most animated of dialogues.

Their mutual engrossment permitted me to pass, as best I could determine, unnoticed by them. Seizing my chance, I at once retired to the privacy of a nearby crabapple tree, whence I might overhear the substance of their discourse.

Oh, Landor, you must not think me free of qualm in undertaking such an ignoble reconnaissance of my own beloved. More than once, I determined to abandon them to their private colloquy. However, each time I made that resolution, I recalled my obligations to *you*, dear Mr. Landor, and yes, to the Academy. On *your* account, then, I persevered. And on your account only—not from any unseemly curiosity of my own—I might have wished the tree to be ten feet closer. The Marquis siblings, for the most part, attempted to confine their communications to the level of a whisper. *Attempted*, I say, because as you yourself know, the human voice will not long sustain such a brake. Some innate equilibrium goads it periodically into a more natural register, where, though it remain low, it becomes, in a flash, intelligible, just as the sporadic irruption of a familiar word or phrase in the intercourse of foreigners may disclose the speakers' meaning even to one largely unacquainted with that tongue. Thus was I able, in a fashion, to snatch up divers threads of their conversation, without, however, acquiring enough to weave a coherent narrative tapestry.

I gleaned at once that the theme of their interview was the tragic demise of Mr. Ballinger, for I heard Artemus, in more than one instance, advert to "Randy," and heard him assert also, "My God, that was my best—my dearest friend." Artemus, I should say, spoke in cadences more patently aggrieved than did Lea, whose utterances partook of her own even and serene character—until, that is, in reply to one of her brother's whispered confidences, she was heard to ask, in harshly rising accents that admitted of no small urgency, "*Who else?*"

"*Who else?*" echoed Artemus, his own voice ascending in direct ratio to hers.

From there, the dialogue subsided once again to whispers, and such words as escaped their circumscribed sphere were either too faint or too indistinct to be apprehended. There was, though, a brief exchange during which their excited sentiments once again raised their voices—all too eva-nescently!—into the range of hearing.

"You told me yourself he was weak," said Lea. "You told me he might have—"

"And so he might have," returned Artemus. "That doesn't . . ."

There ensued more words of an indistinct nature . . . more whispers . . . more mystification . . . and then I heard Artemus speak as if he were, for the first time, heedless of any listening ear.

"Darling girl," he said. "My darling."

All other words thereupon ceased, as, lifting my eyes, I beheld the pair, through the interval of crossed branches, fall into each other's arms. Which of the siblings had assumed the part of comforter, and which the part of *comforted,* I could not ascertain. From the Gordian knot of their bodies no sound could escape—no word—no sigh. I can recount only that their embrace was singular both in its filial intensity and in its duration. Some two or three *minutes* had elapsed before the pair betrayed any inclination to be riven, and they might well have tarried longer had they not been recalled to their senses by the sound of approaching footsteps.

It was Eugénie, the maid, laboring toward the water pump—bent, as anyone could see, not on espionage but on the mild and menial office of filling her pail. That I was not instantly descried by her I owe to Providence (or to the air of half-bestial dullness with which Eugénie had taken up her chore), for though I remained hidden from Artemus and Lea, one glance from their servant might, in a trice, have penetrated my arboreal curtain. Eugénie, however, "labored on," impervious to any cares but her own. By the time she reached her self-appointed destination, Artemus and Lea had, for all intents and purposes, *vanished*. Finding no value to biding in concealment, and no ready likelihood of playing audience to any further of their exchanges, I stole straight away and made for my barracks quarters, where I gave myself over to meditations—fruitless, in the main—on their strange encounter.

Will you be "at home" soon, Mr. Landor? I do not cast my lots with the frenzy that prevails about me, but I do find myself, yes, succumbing to a species of nervous apprehension entirely alien to my nature. My thoughts form direct channels to Lea—to whom but Lea? Again and again, I scan *that poem*—which you scorn—in whose lines I read so much danger. How fervently do I pray that the Spirit which sees fit to use me as its conduit will—soon! soon!—make me the Oedipus to its Sphinxlike enigmas. Speak to me! Speak to me, maid with your pale blue eye!

Narrative of Gus Landor

22

November 28th to December 4th

As soon as I had finished reading Poe's latest installment, I went to Kosciusko's Garden and left a message under our secret rock, asking him to meet me in my hotel room after Sunday chapel. He came, all right, but I gave him no greeting, no answer, just let the quiet pile up round us—until the fidgeting in his hands became too much for either of us to bear.

"Maybe you could tell me where you were on the night of November twenty-third," I said.

"The night Ballinger was killed, you mean? I was in my quarters, of course. Where else?"

"You were asleep, I guess."

"Oh!" His face fractured into a crooked grin. "How can I *sleep*, Mr. Landor? When every minute, my mind teems with thoughts of that—that precious creature, more divine in aspect than the most fantastical houris of—of—"

It was the way I cleared my throat, maybe, or the way my eyes hardened over—he stopped suddenly and re-examined me.

"You are vexed, Mr. Landor."

"You might say."

"Is there . . . might I be of some use . . . ?"

"You certainly might, Mr. Poe. You might explain why you lied to me."

His cheeks puffed like gills. "Come, now, I think you've—"

I cut him off with my hand. "When I first asked you to take this job, you told me you'd never had dealings with Leroy Fry."

"Well, that's . . . that wouldn't be entirely . . ."

"I had to hear the truth from Captain Hitchcock. You can imagine my embarrassment. Normally, you see, I'd never ask someone to investigate a crime if there was a good chance he'd *committed* it."

"But I didn't—"

"So before I throw you out on your ear, Mr. Poe, you have one more opportunity to redeem your good name. Tell me the truth: did you know Leroy Fry?"

"Yes."

"Did you have words with him?"

A brief pause. "Yes."

"Did you *kill* Leroy Fry?"

The question hung there for a good long time before he seemed able to interpret it. Dazed, he shook his head.

I pressed on. "Did you kill Randolph Ballinger?"

Another shake of the head.

"Did you have anything to do with desecrating their bodies?" I asked.

"No! May I be struck dead in my tracks if—"

"One body at a time," I said. "You don't deny, I guess, that you *threatened* both men?"

"Well . . . you see, as it relates to *Ballinger*, that was . . ." His hands began to twitch by his sides. "That was my *choler* speaking. I never meant it, not really. And as to Leroy Fry, why . . ." His chest swelled like a pigeon's. "I never *once* threatened him, I merely . . . I declared my prerogatives as a man and as a soldier. We parted ways, and I never gave him another thought."

I squeezed my eyes into buttonholes. "Mr. Poe," I said, "you have to admit, it's a very disturbing pattern. Men who cross you somehow end up on the wrong end of a noose. With rather important organs carved out of their bodies."

He thrust out his chest again, but something must have popped inside him, for it wouldn't swell quite as far this time. His head tipped to one side, and he said, in a soft and fatigued voice:

"Mr. Landor, if I were to kill every cadet who had abused me during my brief tenure here, I'm afraid you would find the Corps of Cadets reduced to less than a dozen. And even those would remain on the barest sufferance."

Well, Reader, you know how it can be. You tilt with a man, you *whang* him with your lance, and then, out of nowhere, he throws off all his armor—as though to say, *Here I am*—and you see at once there was never any point in tilting. A whole world of pain has already been inflicted.

Poe dropped into the rocking chair. Made a close study of his fingernails. The quiet once more climbed round us.

"If you must know," he said, "I have been a figure of fun from my very first day here. My manner, my person, my—my *aesthetics*, Mr. Landor—everything that is purest and truest in me has, without fail, been held up to scorn and ridicule. Had I thousand lifetimes, I could not begin to redress all the injuries that have been done me. A man like me . . ." He paused. "A man like me soon gives up any thought of retribution and contents himself with *aspiration*. With *rising*, Mr. Landor. In that quarter alone lies solace."

He looked up at me, grimacing.

"I know," he said. "I am guilty of speaking out of turn. I'm sure I am guilty of a great many things—intemperateness, flights of fancy—but never *that*. Never murder."

And now his eyes bored into mine, *sounding* me as never before.

"Do you believe me, Mr. Landor?"

I drew a long breath. Stared at the ceiling for a time, stared at him again. Then folded my hands behind my back and made a single turn of the room.

"Here's what I believe, Mr. Poe. I believe you should take better care with what you say and do. Do you think you might manage that?"

He nodded: the faintest pulse.

"For *now*," I said, "I can probably hold off Captain Hitchcock and the rest of the hounds. But if you tell me one more lie, Mr. Poe, you're out in the cold. They can clap you in irons, and I won't lift a finger to defend you, do you understand?"

Again he nodded.

"Well, then," I said, casting my eyes about the room. "There's no Bible to be had, so the oath will just have to be between ourselves. *I, Edgar A. Poe* . . ."

"I, Edgar A. Poe . . ."

"*Do solemnly swear to tell the truth* . . ."

"Do solemnly swear to tell the truth . . ."

"*So help me Landor.*"

"So help me . . ." The laugh caught him midthroat. "So help me Landor."

"Well, that's done, then. You may go now, Mr. Poe."

He stood. Took a half step toward the door and then surprised himself by taking a half step back. His face grew flushed, and a timid smile began to trouble those thin lips.

"If it's all the same to you, Mr. Landor, might I stay for a short while?"

Our eyes met for a second, but it was a long second. Too long for him: he turned to the window and began to stammer into the cold air.

"I've no particular *purpose* in staying. Nothing . . . particularly *germane* to add to your inquiries, I've just—I've come to enjoy your company more than anyone's, really—except for *hers,* I mean. And lacking *her,* why, it seems the next best thing would be to . . ." He shook his head. "I'm afraid words are failing me today."

They failed me, too, for a short while. I remember looking everywhere I could—everywhere but at him.

"Well, if you'd like to stay," I said, airily, "that would be all right. I'm a bit strapped for company myself these days. Maybe . . ." I was already moving to retrieve my little cache from beneath the bed. "Maybe you'd care for a little Monongahela?"

Impossible to miss it: the light of hope that sprang up in his eyes. The same light, probably, in mine. We were both of us men who needed to dull the sore spots.

And that was how we rose to the next level of closeness: on fumes of whiskey. We drank each time he came, and in that first week, he came every night. Crept out of South Barracks and stole across the Plain to my hotel. The route might change, but once he reached my room, the ritual was the same. He would knock—just once—and then push the door open with great deliberateness, as though he were shouldering aside a boulder.

And I would have his drink waiting for him, and we would sit—sometimes on furniture, sometimes on the floor—and we would talk.

Talk for many hours in succession. Almost never, I should say, about the inquiries. And freed of that burden, we could wend in any direction, argue any point. Had Andrew Jackson been wrong to reload his gun during that long-ago duel with Dickinson? Poe said yes; I took Jackson's side. And that aide of Napoleon's who killed himself because his promotion was late? Poe said he was noble; I took the view he was an ass. What was the handsomest color on a brunette? Me: red. Poe: aubergine. (He would never have said "purple.") We argued over whether Iroquois were fiercer than Navaho and whether Mrs. Drake was seen to best advantage in comedy or tragedy and whether the pianoforte was more expressive than the clavichord.

One night, I found myself having to defend the position that I was without a soul. I wasn't even aware it was my position until I declared it, but that's what happens when two men are talking the dark into a truce: they take hold of a line, and they follow it all the way to the end. And so I told Poe we were all just bundles of atoms, crashing against one another, retreating and advancing and then finally stopping. Nothing more.

He advanced any number of metaphysical proofs against me. I was impressed by none of them. At last, driven to distraction, he began to wave his hands. "It's there, I tell you! Your soul, your *anima*, it exists. A little rusty from disuse, yes, but . . . I see it, Mr. Landor, I *feel* it."

And it was then he warned me it would rise up one day and confront me head on, and I would realize my error, ah, too late!

Well, he could go on in that vein for hours. But we were keeping our tongues quite pickled with the Monongahela. And under its cool fire, I could let go at times and listen, with a kind of relief, to Poe venturing down his tangents: the Beautiful and the True, the transcategorical hybrid, Saint-Pierre's *Etudes de la Nature*—oh, it makes my head throb now to think of it all, but at the time, it passed through my hair like a zephyr.

I don't know when it happened exactly, but at some juncture, we ceased to refer to each other as "Mister." The titles simply dropped away, and we became "Landor" and "Poe." It sounded to my ear like two old bachelors renting adjoining rooms—harmless madmen living off the remnants of our family fortunes, lost in a kind of unending speculation about things. True,

I had never known anyone to do that except in books, so over time, I began to wonder about this book Poe and I were writing. How long could it go on? Wouldn't the Army step in at some point? Wouldn't his superiors catch Cadet Poe some night as he floated back to South Barracks? Trap him just as Ballinger had done? Or, at the very least, ask questions?

Poe had the usual bravado about such things, but he listened with interest when I informed him there was a young enlisted man who was itching for pocket change. The very next morning, with my blessing, he took a hoard of quarters to Private Cochrane, and from that night on, he had an Army escort to steer him safely to and from my hotel. In the execution of this duty, Cochrane showed gifts we would never have suspected. He could crouch like a panther and scout terrain like an Indian, and once, when he saw a cadet guard approaching, he dragged Poe straight into the nearest hollow, where they both lay, flat as alligators, until the danger had passed. Poe and I were always trying to show our gratitude, but every time we asked Cochrane up for a nip of whiskey, he declined on account of laundry.

You may imagine, Reader, that jawing on as we did night after night, Poe and I were bound to exhaust the world's subjects and turn, like cannibals, on one another. And so I asked him to tell me about swimming the James River and serving in the Junior Morgan Rifleman and meeting Lafayette and studying at the University of Virginia and going to sea to seek his fortune and waging war for Greece's freedom. There was no limit to his fund of stories, or maybe there was, for every so often he would, by way of resting, inquire after *my* humble history. That was how he came to ask me, one night:

"Mr. Landor, why did you ever come to the Highlands?"

"For my health," I said.

It was true. Dr. Gabriel Gard, a Saint John's Park physician with an income earned largely from never-quite-dying invalids, had diagnosed me with consumption and told me my only hope of living another six months was to leave the miasma and travel up—*up*—to the Highlands. He told me of a Chambers Street land speculator who had, in the eleventh hour, heeded the same advice and was now plump as a turkey and giving thanks on his knees every Sunday in the Cold Spring chapel.

I was more inclined to die where I was; it was my wife who agitated for a move. The way Amelia figured it, her family bequest would pay for the new house, and my savings would cover the rest. And so we found our cottage by the Hudson, and it was Amelia who, by some quirk of fate, grew ill—very ill—and died before another three months had passed.

"And to think," I said, "we came here for *my* health. Well, Dr. Gard was right, after all. I got better and better, and today"—I tapped my chest—"today I'm nearly clear. Just a little bit of rot in the left lung."

"Oh," said Poe, dark as tar. "There's a bit of rot in all of us."

"And for once," I said, "we're in agreement."

Poe, as I've said, could hold forth on many subjects, but he had only one Subject: Lea. And how could I blame him for wanting to talk about her? What point was there in telling him how *compromising* love could be, how it kept a man from doing his job? And what possible point could there be in revealing the truth about her condition? He would learn it soon enough, and until then, wasn't it just as well to leave him his illusions? Illusions die hard in any case, and Poe was, like every young lover, supremely uninterested in what anyone else had to say on the subject—unless it agreed with his own findings.

"Have you ever *loved* someone, Landor?" he asked one night. "The way I love Lea, I mean? Purely and—and inconsolably and . . ."

That was as far as he could go. He fell into a kind of trance, and I had to speak a little louder to be heard.

"Well," I said, tapping the rim of my whiskey glass, "do you mean *romantic* love? Or love of any sort?"

"Love," he answered, simply. "In all its incarnations."

"Because I was going to say my daughter."

Funny that *her* face should have presented itself. Before Amelia's. Before Patsy's. And it was a sign of something—trust? drunkenness?—that I could allow myself to climb out on that particular limb. And feel safe there! For a few seconds.

"Of course," I added, "it's a different sort of feeling when it's your child. It's total, it's . . ." I stared into my glass. "It's helpless, it's doomed . . ."

Poe watched me for several moments, then leaned forward and, with his elbows jabbing his knees, threw a whisper into the dark.

"Landor."

"Yes?"

"What if she were to come back? *Tomorrow?* What would you do?"

"I'd say hello."

"No, don't evade me now, you've come too far. Would you forgive her? On the spot?"

"If she came back, I'd do much more than forgive her, I'd . . . yes. . . ."

He was delicate enough to leave it there. Only much later in the evening did he raise the topic again. In a voice hushed with awe, he said:

"I believe she *will* come back, Landor. I believe we create . . . magnetic *fields* for the people we love. So that no matter how far they travel—no matter how much they resist our pull—they must come back to us in the end. They cannot help themselves, any more than the moon can stop orbiting the earth."

And I said—because it was the only thing I could think to say—"Thank you, Mr. Poe."

God knows how we survived, getting so little sleep. I could at least steal some winks the next morning, but Poe had to be up at dawn. I don't think he ever got more than three hours. Sleep, if it wanted him, would have to come and get him. Some nights it took him in midsentence. His head would wobble, his eyelids would slam down, his brain would be snuffed like a wick . . . but the glass would never stir from his palm, and he might wake up ten minutes later, ready to finish the thought just where he had left off. One night, while I was sitting in the rocking chair, I saw him fall asleep on the floor right in the middle of reciting "To a Skylark." His mouth dropped open, his head rolled to one side and came to rest on my foot, pinning it to the ground. Here was a quandary: to wake him or leave him lie?

I took the latter course.

The tapers had dwindled down by now, the fire had died, the shutters were closed . . . but it was warm there in the dark. *All that talk,* I thought, *stoking the furnace.* I looked down at that sleeping head with its thin, rumpled hair, and I realized then that I had come to organize my days around—around Poe, I guess, or at least around these moments. They had become part of my mind's calendar, and I *depended* on them, the way you depend on seasons to follow one another or the back door to stick or your cat to grab the same splash of sunlight every afternoon.

He woke twenty minutes later. Sat up, rubbed the sleep from his eyes. Gave the room a bleary smile.

"Were you dreaming?" I asked.

"No. I was thinking."

"Still?"

"I was thinking it would be delightful if we could all leave this infernal place. You and I and Lea."

"And why would we do such a thing?" I asked.

"Oh, there's nothing to keep us here any longer. I have no great affection for this Academy, any more than you do."

"And Lea?"

"She will follow Love, won't she?"

I didn't answer. But I couldn't pretend that I myself had never thought of leaving. Or that I hadn't thought—from the very moment I found the Byron engraving in his trunk—that Cadet Fourth Classman Poe might be better served by new masters.

"Well, then," I said. "Where should we go?"

"Venice."

I raised an eyebrow at that.

"Why *not* Venice?" he carried on. "They understand poets there. And if a man *isn't* a poet, Venice will make him one. I swear, Landor, before you've spent even six months there, you'll be penning Petrarchan sonnets and epics in blank verse."

"I'd settle for a nice lemon tree."

He was striding round the room now, trying to corner his vision. "Lea and I will be married—why not? We could find one of those old mansions, one of those wonderfully decaying Faubourg Saint-Germain sorts of places, and we'd all live together. Just like this, with the shutters closed. Reading and writing . . . *endless* conversation. Creatures of the Night, Landor!"

"Has a gloomy ring to it," I said.

"Oh, there would still be crimes, old soul, you needn't fear. Venice has plenty of that, even their *crime* has poetry, it has passion! American crimes are all *anatomy*." He brought his hands together in a decisive motion. "Yes, we must leave this place."

"You forget one thing: this little job of ours."

It *would* keep intruding, this Academy business, no matter how much we tried to ignore it. Poe actually welcomed the interruptions more than I did. There was, I remember, a florid, almost greedy look to him when he asked me if I'd seen Ballinger's body. He most definitely wanted to know what it had looked like.

I told him that the body, when last I'd seen it, was lying on a blacksmith bed in Ward B-3 of the West Point hospital. The ice storm had slowed its decay: the skin had just the slightest flush of blue, and if you could have seen nothing more than the head, you would have thought it a fine specimen indeed, more imposing by far than Leroy Fry's body. But for all that, it was every bit as dead, every bit as empty; if anything, the cincture round the neck was even deeper, the crater in the chest even more jagged, *more* splintered.

And that black rind of blood in the crotch, nearly hidden by the still-swollen penis. No way of getting round that. The person who'd done it was in no way disinterested. He'd had something deeply personal in mind.

Narrative of Gus Landor

23

December 4th to 5th

Captain Hitchcock had been badgering me all week about Leroy Fry's diary. Had I found anything yet? Names of suspicious cadets? New angles to pursue? Wasn't there *something*?

To pacify him, I began bringing him the transcribed pages each morning. "Here you are, Captain," I'd say in a high, bright voice as I dropped the stack on his desk. Without even pausing to dismiss me, he got straight to reading. He really seemed to believe that each new installment would hold the key to everything. When in fact every one just held more of the same: litanies of woe; trivia; sexual itch. I felt almost sorry for the commandant. It could have been no great joy for him to see how little went on in a cadet's brain.

Poe stayed in his quarters on Saturday night. The calls of sleep had grown too pressing even for him to ignore.

That very evening, just before eleven, it began to snow. A thick bestial slouching sort of snow. Only Patsy, normally, could have drawn me from the comforts of my hotel room to plash about in the stuff—and Patsy hadn't sent for me. Well, it didn't matter, I had Mr. Scott's latest, I had a good fire, food, tobacco. Oh, I might have dug in for many days altogether, but the next morning, I received an invitation.

Dear Mr. Landor,

Forgive the inexcusably late notice, but might we prevail upon you to grace our humble home for a modest dinner party this evening at six? Mr.

*Ballinger's death has cast such a pall over our happy little clan, and your
company would be the ideal tonic. Please say you will!!*
   With fondest hopes,
       Mrs. Marquis

Hadn't I been waiting for just this chance to break the Marquis family
enclosure? Wasn't there every likelihood that seeing Artemus "embosomed" (as Poe would have it) in his boyhood home would give me the
glimmer—the *picture*—I'd been lacking?

It was an invitation, in short, I couldn't decline. So it was that at fifteen
minutes to six, I was pulling on my Hessians and actually reaching for my
cloak when the single knock came.

Poe, of course. Shaggy with snow, holding his sheaf of paper. He
handed it over in perfect silence and drifted back down the corridor, and if
the hallway's acoustics hadn't been so good, I might have missed what he
said as he disappeared into the stairwell.

"I've just had the most extraordinary afternoon of my life."

Report of Edgar A. Poe to Augustus Landor

December 5th

The first Snow, Landor! Rare bliss it was to awaken and to find every tree and rock overrun with snow; to find the snowflakes still spilling like hoarded coins from the sky's cloud-purses. If you could only have seen me and my brothers in arms this morning, Landor. You might have thought a crowd of rosy-cheeked shavers had just been set free of their schoolhouse! Several of our company vied for the honor of throwing the first snowball, and in short order, our little skirmish bid fair to devolve into combat every bit as gory as Thermopylae, until the timely intervention of the cadet company commanders restored some small semblance of order.

Morning mess featured several helpings of ice soup, and the singing of "O Thou Who Camest from Above" during Sunday chapel was accompanied by baptismal showers of white powder. Amidst all this revelry and shrieking, it was left to more poetic sensibilities to remark upon ... the supernal *silence* which lay just outside the realm of our tiny conflagrations. Overnight, it appeared, our little Academe had been transformed into a fay's kingdom—a bejeweled realm in which the thundering tramp of boots was changed to pipsqueaks—the loudest invective muffled in a woolen white embrace.

Following chapel, I retired to my quarters, where I lit a fire in the grate and immersed myself in Coleridge's *Aids to Reflection*. (During our next encounter, Landor, we must discuss Kant's distinctions between "understanding" and "reason," as I am reasonably sure that you and I are the respective embodiments of these antipodal principles.) It was some ten minutes after one o'clock when there came an unexpected knocking on my door. Presuming it to be an officer on his inspection rounds, I at once concealed the contraband book beneath my coverlet and rose to attention.

The door opened by small degrees to reveal—no officer—a *coachman*. Ah! how poorly that word suffices to convey the bald outlandishness of his appearance. A coat of dark green, he wore, lined through with scarlet and ornamented richly with silver aiguillettes. His waistcoat was scarlet, and his breeches likewise, with silver lace garters. These articles alone would have rendered him, in these austere climes, a specimen of ripe exoticism, had he not also been wearing the most anomalous of hats. *Beaver-skin,* if you may conceive it, set on a head of ebony hair so luxuriant that one might have thought a Gypsy ruffian had quit the employment of the fifth Duke of Buccleuch and offered his services directly to Daniel Boone.

"Mr. Poe, sir," said he, in a gruff tenor voice that betrayed undertones of *Mitteleuropa.* "I've been sent to fetch you."

"On what errand?" I asked, astounded.

He pressed a gloved finger to his mustachioed lip. "You're to follow me."

I hesitated to comply, as who would not? In the last reckoning, I believe it was naked curiosity (which, along with perversity, I judge to be the *prima mobilia* of human endeavor) that impelled me to follow.

This coachman led me into the assembly yard and thence set a steady course due north. As we wove our way amidst divers gamboling cadets, it was well nigh impossible to ignore the looks of wild surmise excited by my companion's appearance. Still less was it possible to ignore the deteriorating condition of my boots, which, after a morning's immersion in these Highland steppes, were quite soaked through. (The rather fine Hessians which I brought here from Virginia, I was lamentably forced to sell to Mr. Durrie, my fellow plebe, in order to satisfy a debt owed to Major Burton.) In fear lest I should contract frostbite, I begged the coachman to disclose our destination. Nary a word did he utter.

Presently this strange fellow, dragging his fine lace garments through foot-high drifts of snow, disappeared behind the tailor's shop. I made haste to follow, spurred onward by a thousand vague fancies—fancies which corresponded but little to the reality that was to confront me. For as I rounded the corner of the building, I found myself gazing in wonder at . . . a sleigh.

It was an Albany cutter, its swelled sides giving the vehicle the graceful arabesque profile of a gigantic swan. The enigmatic coachman drew up the reins with one hand; with the other, he beckoned me to take the seat next to him. Something there was about his insinuating smile, the extraordinary forwardness and familiarity of his manner—and, most particularly, the singularly skeletal motion of those long, gloved fingers—which imparted the iciest of chills to my frame. I could well have believed that Pluto himself had come to convey me to his infernal and pestilential Netherworld.

Run, Poe! Wherefore did you not run? I can but assume that the anxiety which pervaded my soul was exactly counterweighted by the curiosity to which I have already alluded, leaving me, in effect, motionless, my eyes riveted upon the coachman.

"Driver," I said at last, my voice rising to asperity, "I will not consent to go another step until you tell me our destination."

Answer came there none. Or was I to take *these* for an answer, these attenuated, emaciated fingers, flexing and curling?

"I will not, I say! Not until I know where you mean to take me."

At length his hand ceased to beckon, and with a cryptic smile, he proceeded to tug the gloves from his hands. These gloves he dropped onto the floor of the sleigh, and then, in an extravagantly violent motion, he flung away his beaver-skin hat. And before I could sufficiently recover myself, he began to peel the mustache from his face!

Nothing more was needed to disclose the visage and form that had lain so artfully submerged beneath that *outré* costume. It was my own, my beloved Lea!

At the sight of her dear countenance, so adorably smudged by the awn and spirit gum, so unutterably feminine amid these masculine habiliments, my soul trembled with joy. Once more, Lea beckoned—her fingers no longer the cadaverous talons of Hades' emissary, but the sweet, tender, ineffably precious digits of the divine Astarte.

I set my foot on the runner and hurled myself into the sleigh coach with such unmitigated force that our bodies came into ecstatic collision. Laughing gaily, she fell back and closed her hands round mine, drawing me by graceful degrees closer. Her long jetty lashes folded down. Her lips—those ravishingly irregular lips—parted. . . .

And on this occasion, Landor, I did not swoon. I dared not! To be separated from her for the veriest second—though it were to dwell in the most resplendent and crystalline caverns of Dream—*this* I could never have borne.

"But where are we going, Lea?"

The snow had ceased to fall, the sun had risen in all its fiery eminence, and the land round us gleamed with a rare dazzle. Only now did I have adequate mastery of my faculties to apprehend the depths of Lea's ingenuity. *Somehow* she had secured this conveyance. *Somehow* she had acquired this flamboyant costume. *Somehow* she had reconnoitered this sylvan setting, so ideal in its seclusion. Faced with such an intelligence—infinitely flexible, strategic in its cunning—what could I do, Landor, but resign myself to the part of spectator, awaiting the next stage of the spectacle?

"But where are we going?" I asked again.

Had she answered "Heaven" or "Hell," it would have made no difference. I should have followed.

"Never fear, Edgar. We shall be back in time for supper. Father and Mother are expecting us *both*, you know."

Ah, was this not the diadem on the crown? Stretching before us lay not just an afternoon but an entire evening, and the whole length of it to be spent *together*!

Of the remainder of that wintry excursus I shall write no more, except to say that when the Albany cutter had paused on the hill commanding Cornwall, when the tintinnabulation of the horse's harness bells had subsided into silence, when Lea had set down the reins and granted me the privilege of laying my head in her lap, when the fumes of her orrisroot had risen round me like the holiest incense—then my Happiness passed into a new realm—beyond fancy—beyond belief—beyond even Life itself.

I *did* contrive, Landor, to introduce the subject of the lately deceased Cadets into our conversation. In regard to Ballinger, she gave me to know that she had considered him no more than an intimate of Artemus'—and was, as a consequence, more saddened in her brother's behalf than by any loss *she* had endured. Turning the conversation to Leroy Fry proved a more complicated matter. I did suggest, in the course of proposing future destinations for our Albany cutter, that we might venture once more to the cemetery, if that hallowed ground did not hold too many taxing associations for her. I added that it might be of interest to see Mr. Fry's newly dug grave, assuming that the snow had left any traces of it.

"But why should you concern yourself with Mr. Fry, Edgar?"

Anxious to placate her, I confessed that I had understood Mr. Fry to be an admirer of hers, and that in my present character of *innamorato,* I felt honor-bound to pay respects to any gentleman who had ever pretended to that exalted state.

Tapping her feet on the carpet, she shrugged and, in an offhand tone, said, "He would never have served my purposes, I fear."

"Who *would,* I wonder?"

In response to this simple query, all imprints of emotion or thought drained from her countenance, leaving that treasured canvas a veritable tabula rasa on which I could not so much as etch a line.

"Why, *you,* of course," she answered finally.

She gave the reins a brisk shake and, with a long and gladsome laugh, drove the long road home.

Oh, Landor. I can no longer believe it of Artemus. It beggars the mind that any kinsman of Lea's—one who shares so much of her birthright, so many of her features, who has recited the same treble prayers from beneath the same counterpane—could be capable of such an inhuman, an inconceivable brutality. How can it be that two seedlings from one tree, twining themselves so tenderly round each other, could tend in such shockingly opposed directions . . . the one toward Light, the other toward Darkness? It cannot be, Mr. Landor.

Heaven help us if it can.

Narrative of Gus Landor

24

December 5th

Oh, Poe should have known better. Thinking, I mean, that people tend only to light and dark, and not both ways. Well, it would make for a lively debate some evening, I thought, but right now there was this to consider: Poe and I would be attending the same dinner.

It took me the whole way to Dr. Marquis' residence to decide that it was a good thing. For if nothing else, I would learn just how good an observer my little spy really was.

The door was opened by a wall-eyed girl with chaffed skin and spirits. Wiping her nose with one arm, she grabbed my cloak and hat with the other, dropped them on the hat stand, and sprinted back to the kitchen. She had no sooner vanished than Mrs. Marquis poked her rabbity head into the foyer. In that moment, her features seemed frozen in place, as though she had just been dragged from one of the snowbanks, but as soon as she saw me banging my boots on her mat, she came hard on in her black crepe mourning dress, hands fluttering like pennants.

"Oh, Mr. Landor, what sport! We are all refugees from the cruel elements! Yes, please, come in. It won't do to linger a moment by that door." With a surprisingly strong grip, she took me by the elbow and led me out of the foyer, only to be momentarily blocked by the small, half smiling figure of Cadet Fourth Classman Poe, slender and erect in his best dress uniform. He must have got there a few minutes before me, but in that moment, he became for Mrs. Marquis a newcomer again. She had to stare long and hard before she could account for him.

"Why, of course! Mr. Landor, have you met Mr. Poe? Just once? Well, *once* cannot be enough in this young gentleman's case. No, I forbid you to blush, sir! He is quite the gallant, Mr. Landor, and has the most exquisitely tuned poetical ear. You must hear him go on about Helen sometime, it is really not to be . . . but what's become of Artemus? Oh, his lateness is beyond habitual, it is perfectly *criminal*. Leaving me with two such handsome gentlemen and no one to entertain them. Well, I have a remedy for that. Follow me, if you please."

Did I expect her to be bowed with grief over Ballinger's death? Probably not. I was th 'own a bit, nevertheless, by the vigor of her tread as she led us down an oak-paneled hallway lined with samplers—"God Bless This Home," "How Doth the Little Busy Bee," etc.— and, after brushing away a spiderweb from the grandfather clock, pushed open the parlor door. This parlor, Reader—maybe you know what I mean—it was the kind of room that seems to house all of a family's hopes: the maple American Empire armchairs, with their scrolled feet and horn-of-plenty legs, the chiffonier and the glass cabinet filled with the porcelain tigers and elephants, the snapdragons and gladioluses in the vase on the mantel . . . and a fire, of course, large enough to topple a city. And sitting next to the fire, a young woman, hot-cheeked, embroidering on a tambour. A young woman named Lea Marquis.

I was on the point of introducing myself when Lea's mother let loose with a gasp.

"Oh, me! I have quite forgot about the seating order. Mr. Poe, may I throw myself upon your mercy? It will require but a few minutes, and you do have such an eye for things, and I would be so eternally grateful. Thank you so much! Lea, if you would . . ."

Would *what*? She never said. Just crooked her hand round Poe's elbow and dragged him from the room.

This is to explain why Lea Marquis and I were never formally introduced. It may also account for the spottiness of our conversation. I did my best to make things easy for her. I set my ottoman at a discreet distance and, remembering well her horror of weather topics, avoided any mention of the snow. And when the talk failed, I contented myself with smelling the damp, sweet reek of my boots and listening to the hiss of the oak logs and peering through the stoles of snow on the parlor window. And when that failed to charm, there was always Lea to look at.

Silly of me, expecting Poe's portrait to be lifelike. Some mote had clearly got in his eye, for she—well, she stooped a bit; and her mouth, *I* would have called overripe; and in almost every way, I'm afraid, she suffered by comparison with her brother. *His* jaw looked lumpen on *her*; the brows that arched so agreeably on *his* face were too square, too heavy for hers. And yet those eyes were every bit as enchanting as Poe had said; her figure was fine; and *this* he hadn't quite got across: the strange fluid vitality of her. In the most languid of her movements—in repose, even—there was something alert and primed, a continual and never quite realized potential. I suppose what I'm saying is that there was not a trace of surrender about her.

I didn't mind that she avoided my eye, nor did I care that every sentence seemed to die on us. It felt oddly domestic, as if we had been ignoring each other for many years in perfect comfort, and I was more jangled than I expected when we were at last interrupted—not by Poe or Mrs. Marquis but by Artemus himself, striding into the parlor with squeaking soles.

"Woman," he called to his sister. "Fetch me my pipe."

"Fetch it yourself," she answered.

This was the extent of their greeting. Lea bounded from her chair and set upon him, shaking and squeezing and pummeling. It took the arrival of the servant girl with her dinner bell to bring them back to the world at large. Only then did Artemus give me a nod and a handshake. Only then did Lea permit me to take her by the arm and escort her into the dining room.

Why Mrs. Marquis should have needed help with the seating plan, well, that was anyone's guess. We were a small party that night. The hostess herself sat at one end of the table, and Dr. Marquis at the other (squaring his shoulders like a draft animal). Lea was seated next to me, Poe next to Artemus. Dinner, I recall, was roasted canvasback with cabbage, peas, and stewed apples. There must have been bread, too, for I have a distinct memory of Dr. Marquis cleaning his plate with it, and I remember, too, the way Mrs. Marquis, prior to eating, removed her gloves inch by inch, as though she were sliding out of her own skin.

Throughout the meal, Poe refused to look at me, doubtless fearing that even a half second's eye contact would give us away. He was nowhere near so cagey, of course, with Lea. She, for her part, never met his gaze, though it yet found an answer in her: a bow of the head, a play of the lips. Oh, no, I wasn't too old to have forgot *those*.

Fortunately for them, the lovers had other people's agitations to hide behind that night. Dr. Marquis was carrying on a colloquy with his cabbage, and Artemus was humming a measure of ... Beethoven, I think it was, the same measure again and again. Amid all these crosscurrents, something useful at least emerged: a family history. By dint of quiet questions and leading remarks, I learned that the Marquis family had resided at the Academy for eleven years. I learned that Artemus and Lea had adopted these hills as their own and had, between them, discovered so many secret recesses they could probably, if they wished, gain employ as British spies. Indeed, by virtue of being thrown into each other's company so often, they had forged a bond that Dr. Marquis could mention only in terms of great awe.

"And do you know, Mr. Landor? When it came time to decide what Artemus was to do, there was no question. 'Artemus!' I said. 'Artemus, my boy, you'll have to become a cadet, by God. Your sister won't allow for anything else!'"

"I believe Artemus has always been free to do as he likes," said Lea.

"And he always does," answered her mother, stroking the sleeve of her son's gray coat. "Don't you find my son exceptionally handsome, Mr. Landor?"

"I would—I would judge *both* of your children to have been blessed in that regard," I replied.

My tact was lost on her. "Dr. Marquis looked just the same way when he was young. I'm not embarrassing you, am I, Daniel?"

"Only a bit, my dear."

"What a figure he cut, Mr. Landor! Bear in mind, of course, my family consorted with a great many officers in those days. I remember my mother always told me, 'You may dance with a leaf, and flirt with a bar, but reserve your best smile for the eagle and star.' Well, that was my intention. I would settle for nothing less than a major. But then who should come along but this dashing young surgeon? Oh, I needn't tell you, he had charms. He might have had his pick of all the surplus females in White Plains, so I really can't fathom why he chose me. Why *was* that, dear?"

"Oh," said the doctor, swelling into a laugh. Such a laugh! The jaw opened and shut as if it were being yanked by a ventriloquist.

"Well," Mrs. Marquis went on, "as I explained to my parents, 'Dr. Marquis may not be a major, but his potential is simply limitless.' Why, he had already been one of the personal physicians to General Scott, did you know that? And of course, the University of Pennsylvania was longing to hire him as lecturer. But then the Chief of Engineers came knocking with this Academy appointment, and there you are. Duty *beckoned*, didn't it?" She trailed her knife in absent lines across her plate. "Of course, it was only supposed to be a *temporary* post. A year or two at the utmost, and then back to New York. But we never did get back, did we, Daniel?"

Dr. Marquis confessed that they had not. At which Mrs. Marquis grinned like a tiger. "We still *might*," she said. "It's conceivable. The moon might rise in place of the sun tomorrow. Dogs might write symphonies. Anything might happen, mightn't it, dear?"

I will say this about her smile: it never collapsed, but it never fixed itself, either. Infinite in its nuance. I could see Poe's eyes widening as he watched her—trying to *track* her, in the way you might track a funnel cloud.

"You mustn't think I mind, Mr. Landor. It's terribly remote here, that's true, one might as well live in Peru, but one does, on rare occasion, meet fascinating people. Think only of yourself, Mr. Landor."

"I know *we* think of you," chimed Artemus. "All the time."

"Oh!" cried his mother. "That is only because Mr. Landor is a personage of rare intelligence, a quality in such ridiculously short supply here. I do, of course, exempt the faculty, but the *wives*, Mr. Landor! Not a modicum of wit, not a particle of taste. You will never in your life meet less ladylike ladies."

"Their manners *are* bad," Artemus allowed. "West Point is probably the only place they could still be taken up. I can't think of a drawing room in New York that would have them."

Lea frowned into her dish. "I'm sure you're both being dreadful. We have received a great many kindnesses at their hands, and I have spent many happy hours in their company."

"Knitting, you mean," answered her brother. "Endless knitting." Leaping to his feet, he began darning the air with his fingers and affecting a drawl that was, if I may say so, a pretty fair approximation of one of those faculty wives, Mrs. Jay. "*Do you know, my dear, I believe this October is just a shade cooler than last October. Yes, yes, I know it, for, you see, Koo-Koo—have you met my dear, sweet little parrot from the Azores?—why, he's been* shivering, *poor dear, from the moment he wakes up. I never should have taken him to the violin recital the other night, he can't abide the wind, you know. . . .*"

"Stop!" screamed Mrs. Marquis, squealing through her fingers.

"*Why, I'm quite certain it gave him chilblains.*"

"Naughty boy!"

Thus rewarded, Artemus flung himself back down in his chair with a grin. I let a space of silence fall before I cleared my throat and said, as softly as I could:

"I expect that Mrs. Jay has other topics on her mind these days."

"And what would those be?" asked Mrs. Marquis, still chuckling.

"Why, Mr. Fry, of course. And your friend Mr. Ballinger."

No words then, only sounds. The tender crack of Poe's knuckles, the flick of Artemus' finger against the side of his plate. The slurping of Dr. Marquis' bread as it chased an errant pea round the circuit of his plate.

And then a low snigger from Mrs. Marquis, as she tossed back her head and said, "I hope she will not overstep her bounds by launching her *own* inquiries, Mr. Landor. Such feminine interference could in no way be welcome to you."

"Oh, I'm grateful for any help I can get," I said. "Especially if I don't have to pay for it."

A ghost of a smile stole over Poe's face. Incriminating, I thought, by its very smallness. But when I shot a look at Artemus, I found him too busy with his own amusement to notice.

"Mr. Landor," he said, "I hope when you've finished with your official business, you'll assist me with a little puzzle of my own."

"Puzzle?"

"Yes, the strangest affair! While I was in recital Monday, it appears someone tried to break my door down."

"Terrible people are abroad," intoned Dr. Marquis.

"Really, Father? I was inclining toward the theory that the fellow was simply rude." Artemus smiled at me once again. "While having, of course, no idea who he was."

"All the same, darling, you must be careful," said Mrs. Marquis. "You really must."

"Oh, Mother, he was probably just some tiresome old fellow with nothing better to do and no life of his own to speak of. A rustic sort of cottager who likes to—to *tipple* on the side and hang about in sordid taverns. Don't you think, Mr. Landor?"

I saw Mrs. Marquis flinch; I saw Poe rearrange himself in his chair. The air seemed to crackle round the table. Artemus must have felt it, too, for his eyes opened into pools.

"Oh, you have a cottage, too, don't you, Mr. Landor? Well, then, I'm sure you know the type I'm speaking of."

"Artemus," said Lea in a warning voice.

"You may even have some very *near* relations who fit the pattern."

"Stop it!" his mother yelled.

And everything did stop. We were all looking at her now, staring helplessly at the grooves around her mouth and the taut cords of her throat and her skinny little fists, which had come together in a trembling knot.

"I hate it!" she screamed. "I positively hate it when you take on this way!"

Eyeing her with a bland curiosity, Artemus said, "I don't think I follow your drift, Mother."

"Oh, no, you don't, of course you don't. Follow my *drift*? I might drift clear to the other side of the Hudson, and no one would . . ." For the first time, the corners of her mouth turned downward. "No one would *follow*, would they, Daniel?"

They looked at each other now, husband and wife, with such a depth of feeling that the eight feet separating them shrank to nothing. Then, slowly, with a darkling gleam in her eye, Mrs. Marquis raised her plate above her head . . . and let it drop. A canvasback bone flopped free, the stewed apples flew straight up, and the plate blew into a dozen pieces scattered across the red linen tablecloth.

"Ha! You see! A china plate should never crack unless it is kept too close to the fire. I shall have to speak with Eugénie." Her pitch rising, she slapped at the china fragments, as though she were thrashing them. "I am perfectly furious with her, you know. How she can . . . when she's not even French! If only you could find a decent servant here, but you can't, God help you. Never mind persuading one to wear livery or treat you as—as an *employer*, oh, no! Well, the time has come to speak. The time has come to say, we will *not* be treated this way!"

Her chair tipped back, and she was, shockingly, on her feet, clutching her hair, and before any of the gentlemen could rise, she had staggered from the room, the napkin still pinned to her dress. I heard a swish of taffeta . . . a moan . . . a rattle of boots on the stairs. And with that everything went quiet, as one by one, we turned back to our plates.

"You'll have to excuse my wife," said Dr. Marquis, to no one in particular.

And that was the only thing said on the matter. With no further apology, no explanation, the rest of the Marquis clan tucked right back into their food and kept eating. They were no longer to be shocked. Too many other dinners had come to ruin on this same shoal.

Poe and I, by contrast, had lost what was left of our appetites. We set down our forks and waited as first Lea finished, then Artemus, and finally Dr. Marquis, who rose and, after having a leisurely go at his teeth with a pocket knife, inclined his head in my direction and said, "Mr. Landor, I wonder if you'd care to join me in my study."

Dr. Marquis closed the dining room door behind him and bent toward me, his eyes teeming, his breath steamy with onions and whiskey.

"My wife's nerves," he said. "This time of year. A bit overworked, as you can see. The winter and the cold. Very confining. Sure you understand."

He nodded as if to assure himself he'd done his duty, then motioned me into his study—an exceedingly narrow room, with a smell like burnt caramel and a single burning taper, doubled by the reflection of a looking-glass in a tarnished gold frame. From atop the central bookcase frowned the lordly head of Galen. In a niche between two other bookcases hung an antique oil portrait, no more than two feet high, of a clergyman, robed in black. Just below it was a pillow—coarse and gray and musty—upon which a cameo portrait lay, flat on its back, as though it had been sung to sleep.

"Tell me, Doctor, who is this charming creature?"

"Why," he sputtered, "that's my beloved bride, of course."

More than twenty years had passed since the portrait was first committed to ivory, but very little of Mrs. Marquis' frame or face had slackened. If anything, the advancing years had merely *concentrated* her, so that the round buoyant liquid eyes of this portrait bore as much relation to their present-day counterparts as dough to bread.

"She quite undervalues her own beauty, doesn't she?" said the doctor. "None of the *amour propre* which is, you know, the province of the female. Ah, but I haven't yet shown you my monographs!" Thrusting his hands into the shelf just below, he came away with a stack of thin, yellowing paper that stung the air like pepper. "Yes, yes," he chuckled, "just the thing! *An inaugural essay on blisters.* I was invited to read this at the College of Physicians and Surgeons. Inaugural essay on fistula in ano, very well received at the University of—oh, but now *this,* well, I think it's fair to say this made my reputation, such as it is. *A short account of the most approved method of treating the putrid bilious yellow fever, vulgarly called the black vomit.*"

"A most impressive range of interests, Doctor."

"Oh, that's just the way the old cranium works. Hither and yon, that's my *modus.* But the paper I really *must* show you, Mr. Landor . . . my observations on Dr. Rush's work on diseases of the mind. Published in the *New England Journal of Medicine and Surgery.*"

"I'd be fascinated to see it."

"Would you really?" He grimaced at me, half believing. I must have been the first human being ever to respond to this overture. "Well, that's . . . oh, but it's not . . . do you know, I believe I was perusing it in bed last night. Shall I fetch it?

"By all means."

"You're certain?"

"Of course! Why, I'll even escort you, if you don't mind the company."

His jaw swung open, his hand came forward. "It would be a—a distinct privilege. It would be a delight."

Yes, a little kindness went far with Dr. Marquis. I remember how brightly his boots rang going up the stairs—the sound echoed through the whole house, that's how small these government quarters can be. Everything that happens in one room becomes the property of *all* rooms.

Which meant that from his dining room roost, Artemus could track every step of our progress, would know the exact moment we reached the second-story landing. But would he know this? That his father would forget to bring a candle? And that the first light to present itself to us should be a night-lantern fixed high on the wall of a small, shuttered bedroom? A strange barren curdled space, where the only things visible were a wall clock (stopped at twelve minutes past three) and the outlines of a plain brass bed, stripped of everything but its mattress.

"Your son's room?" I asked, turning on Dr. Marquis with a smile.

He allowed that it was.

"How nice for him," I said. "A little retreat from the hurly-burly of cadet life."

"As a matter of fact," said the doctor, scratching his cheek, "Artemus stays here only on holidays. More credit to him. He told me once, he said, 'Father, if I'm going to be a cadet, then by God, I'm going to *live* like one. No running home to Mother and Father every night, that's not how a soldier makes his way. I shall be treated the same as all my comrades.'" Dr. Marquis tapped his chest and smiled. "How many men can lay claim to having such a son, eh?"

"Few indeed."

Once again he leaned into me; once again the air grew bitter with onions. "I needn't tell you, Mr. Landor, how my heart . . . *swells* to see him grown to such a man. Not cut from my cloth, no. Born to *lead*, anyone can see that. Yes, but we were looking for the monograph, weren't we? This way, please."

At the end of the hallway was Dr. Marquis' bedroom. He stopped—made as if to knock—then retracted his hand.

"It has just occurred to me," he whispered, "that my good bride is resting. Perhaps I'll just tiptoe inside, if you don't mind waiting here?"

"Not at all, Doctor. Please take your time."

As soon as the door had closed after him, I took three long strides back down the hallway and ducked into Artemus' room. Lifting the lantern from the wall and working at top speed, I surveyed the bed frame, then felt under the mattress and behind the headboard. I trained my light on the childhood totems that lay strewn, with bizarre carelessness, round the floor: a pair of cast-off sled runners, a waxen man with clove eyes, the remnants of a box kite and an old hand-cranked miniature carousel.

Not here. I knew that, somehow. *Not here.* And then the lantern light, matching the arc of my thought, swerved toward the closet in the room's far corner.

Closets. What better place for secrets?

The door opened into a darkness so deep my light could scarcely make a hole in it. Smells of bergamot and frangipani came at me, and twining through everything else, the sweet-sharp scent of mothballs. The rustle of satin and organdy and taffeta, stiff with cold.

Artemus' closet was now the holding pen for a woman's excess wardrobe. A perfectly practical thing to do with a young man's abandoned closet, but under the conditions, I couldn't help seeing it as another of Artemus' gibes. (And wouldn't he have tracked the pattern of my tread on the overhead ceiling? Wouldn't he know precisely where I was standing?) Stung, I drove my arm straight through and found, to my surprise, no back wall, nothing to bar my way. Only more darkness.

With my lantern in hand, I squeezed through the massed garments and found myself standing suddenly free of encumbrance, in a hot black lozenge of air. No smells here, no outlines. But something more than emptiness. I had only to take a step forward and feel the soft blow against my forehead to know what was there: a bare clothes rod.

Even this was not quite bare. My hands, ranging along its length, came to rest on a wooden hanger . . . then moved down to find the ribbed cinch of a collar . . . the rough track of a shoulder . . . and beneath that an expanse of dampish wool, descending in bounded segments.

I laid my hands round the garment, dragged it to the floor and raised the lantern to it.

It was a uniform. An officer's uniform.

The real thing, or a very good facsimile. The blue pantaloons with their gold piping. The flourishes of gold on the blue coatee. And there, on the shoulder (I had to bring the lantern closer to make it out), a faint rectangle of shorn thread. Where a bar had once been sewn on.

My mind flashed to—what else?—the mysterious officer who had ordered Private Cochrane to abandon Leroy Fry's body. And at the same instant, my hand, passing along the coatee, came to rest on a small raised patch just above the waist: some sort of substance, faintly sticky, faintly raspy. I ran my finger through it, but just as I was raising the finger to the lantern light, I heard a footfall.

Someone had come into the room.

I blew out my lantern. Sat there in the steaming darkness of Artemus' closet, listening to the unseen presence on the other side take another step . . . another . . .

And then stop.

Nothing for it now, I could only *wait*. For what came next.

And what came was, at first, just one more sound—rending the wall of clothes that lay before me. And by the time this sound had resolved itself into a *thing*, it had already glanced off my ribs and driven through my frock coat and pinned me to the back wall.

Ah, yes. The uniform's missing accessory: a saber.

In those initial moments, it was easier to *feel* the thing than to see it. The shaft of beveled steel, of such a ridiculous sharpness that the air seemed to part before it.

Struggle though I might, it held me fast in my frock coat. I drew my arm from the sleeve and began to wriggle free. Just then the blade loosed its grip . . . only to come surging forward once again, even faster. As I lunged clear, I could see the blade striking the very section of the wall where my heart had lately been, pinning my empty coat in a death blow.

I might have cried out, yes. But I knew no sound would ever escape this dark little cupboard. And I might, yes, have flung myself at my attacker. But that barricade of dresses had left him nothing more than a *possibility*. One wrong guess, and I'd be even more thoroughly at his mercy than I already was. But this was equally true: he couldn't fling himself at me without losing *his* advantage.

The rules, then, had been set down. Our little game could begin.

Back drew the blade . . . forward it charged . . . *whing!* came the answering cry of the wall as the saber caught the section of plaster by my right hip. A second later it was springing back, probing the darkness once again, hungry for flesh.

And me? I kept moving, Reader. Up and down, side to side, a new target for each new thrust. Trying in my own bleak way to read the mind that lay *behind* this blade.

The fifth thrust just missed my wrist. The seventh passed like a breeze through the hairs along my neck. The tenth found the crook between my right shoulder and my rib cage.

Faster and faster it came—*maddened* by all its missed chances. No longer did it crave an outright kill; the crippling thrust was its new object. Inch by inch it descended, from the region of my heart to the region of my legs. And my legs, in reply, leapt into Highland reels, dancing for their very life.

It was a dance that would soon have to end, I knew that much. Even if my lungs could keep pumping air, there wasn't enough oxygen left in this tiny space to draw from. It was exhaustion, then—not strategy, not any hope of reprieve, just bone-*tiredness*—that dropped me to the floor.

And there I lay, on my back, watching that length of steel make a silhouette of me against the plaster. The closer it came, the colder I grew through my sweat. For it seemed to me I was being fitted—*measured*—for my own coffin.

My eyes slammed shut as, one last time, the blade came roaring back. One last time the wall sang its protest. And then . . . silence.

Prying open my lids, I found the blade poised exactly one inch above my left eye. Not still, no . . . twisting and writhing with a pure rage . . . but not withdrawing, either.

I knew then what had happened. The force of the thrust had been so great that the blade had been wedged into the masonry.

It was my last, my only, chance. Sliding out from beneath the saber, I seized one of the dresses from the clothes rod, threw it round the blade, and began to *pull*. Plying my strength, such as it was, against the strength on the other end.

For a while, we were equal. But my assailant had a tight grip on the saber's handle, with all the leverage that supplied. And I? I had only my bare hands, pulling as hard as they could. For several long seconds, we struggled there in the darkness—unseen to each other but no less present.

The blade had now pulled free of the wall. No longer a prisoner, it was once again an instrument of blind will, sliding *away* from me. The strength was ebbing from my fingers, my wrists, my arms, and the only thing that kept me gripping was this thought, chiming over and over in my brain: *If I let go now, it will be the end of me.*

And so I held on, though my hands were sizzling with pain, though my heart was melting into my lungs. I held on.

And in the very moment I had given it all up for lost, the force on the other end of the saber gave way, and the blade went limp. Sank into my bruised hands like an offering from the sky.

I stared at it in dazzlement, waiting for it to spring to life again. It didn't. And still I remained there for another whole minute, unwilling— *unable*—to let it go.

Narrative of Gus Landor

26

Stuffing the uniform under my arm and dragging my frock coat and lantern after me, I pushed through the wall of clothes and stood once more in the chill half-light of Artemus' bedroom, searching myself for signs of violence—and finding none. Not a scratch, not a drop of blood. The only sounds were my own panting and the soft drip of my sweat on the floor.

"Mr. Landor."

It was by his voice I knew him. But standing there in the doorway's shadows, without a candle, he might have been his son's double. I hesitated for just a moment, wondering whether to trust the evidence of my eyes or my ears.

"Very sorry, Doctor," I said. "I'm afraid I tore my coat"—sheepishly, I pointed to the garment that lay in deltas of light on the floor—"and I thought I might borrow one of your son's."

"But your coat is . . ."

"Yes, I did quite a job on it, didn't I? All the same," I added, laughing and brandishing the uniform, "I don't think I could in good conscience impersonate an officer. Having never served in harm's way myself."

Mouth ajar, he came toward me, staring at the garment in my hands.

"Why," he said, "that must be my brother's!"

"Your brother?"

"Joshua was his name. Died shortly before the Battle of Maguaga. Influenza, poor puppy. The uniform's all we have to remember him by." Kneeling down, he gave the fabric a few long strokes, then rubbed his fingers together under his nose. "Funny," he said. "The blue's faded, and the shoulder straps, well, they're a mite old-fashioned, but otherwise, eh? Could almost pass for new."

"My very thought," I said. "Oh, but see? The bar has gone missing."

"Why, there never was a bar," he said, frowning. "Joshua never made it higher than second lieutenant."

The frown now curled upward. A soft rush of air issued from his nose.

"Something amusing, Doctor?"

"Oh, I was—I was remembering how Artemus used to wear this around the house."

"Did he, now?"

"When he was the barest tadpole. I wish you could have seen it, Mr. Landor. His arms gave out a foot or two before the sleeves did, and the trousers! Why, they'd just drag after him in a—in a *most* comical fashion." He gave me a sidelong grimace. "Yes, I know, I should have begged him to show more respect for his country's uniform, but I couldn't see the harm in it. He'd never met Joshua, you see, and he'd always had such a profound respect for his uncle's service."

"*Your* service, too," I put in. "How could he fail to respect that?"

"Oh. Yes. Well, perhaps. He's never—he's never much taken after me. All the better for him, eh?"

"You are too humble, sir. Do you mean to tell me that after all these years of seeing you practice your art, he hasn't absorbed some small amount himself?"

Those ruined lips of his twisted to one side. "I suppose he has, that's true. Why, he could name all the bones and organs from the time he was ten! Knew how to use a stethoscope. Once or twice he helped me set a broken bone. But I don't think he ever cared much for the—"

"*What on earth?*"

No uncertainty *this* time about who was standing in the doorway. Mrs. Marquis' face was thrown into a sharp relief by the taper she held in her hands, and this light played up all the bird-bones of her face and turned her eyes into great abysses.

"Ah, my dear!" said Dr. Marquis. "Recovered so soon?"

"Yes, it appears I was in grievous error. I had feared I was in for one of those horrid migraines, but it seems a moment's rest was all I required, and

I find myself quite cured. Now, Daniel, I see you are on the verge of boring Mr. Landor with one of your journal articles. You must return it to where you found it, and Mr. Landor, you must put away that dreadful old military coat, I am quite sure it won't fit you, and would you both kindly escort me back downstairs before the others begin to wonder where we've gone? Oh, and Daniel, please douse the fire in the parlor, Mr. Landor is perspiring from all the heat!"

We were a few paces outside the parlor door when we heard the pianoforte, kindled into life, and the sound of stomping feet and a single high suppressed giggle. Humor! How had that broken loose? But the evidence was there for all to see. Lea was playing a quadrille on the pianoforte, and under its influence, Poe and Artemus were marching across the parlor floor and swaying as they went. And laughing—laughing like angels.

"Oh, Lea, let me play!" screamed Mrs. Marquis.

Lea needed no more injunction than that. Quit her place at the piano and hied herself straight to the back of the column, wrapped her hands round Artemus' waist, and set to swaying. Mrs. Marquis, proudly perched on the piano bench, pounded out a dance tune recently imported from Vienna, playing it double-time with an almost frightening virtuosity.

And there I sat smiling, coatless and damp, asking myself, *Which of the people in this room just tried to kill me?*

Faster came the notes, louder came the feet, and the laughter was now general—even Dr. Marquis allowed himself to chuckle and wipe his eye— and all the sour undertones of half an hour ago had, in this moment, been banished, and I could almost have believed I'd dreamed the whole business in the closet.

And then Mrs. Marquis, as quickly as she had taken up her task, abandoned it. Slammed her hands down on the keyboard and sent a knife of discord through the room, stopping everyone in place.

"You must forgive me," she said, rising and smoothing her skirt. "What sort of hostess am I? I am quite sure that Mr. Landor wants no more of me on the piano and would much rather listen to *Lea.*" How she drew that name out! Stretched it as far as it could go. "*Leee-aaa?* Would you do us all the favor of a song?"

A song was the last thing on earth Lea wished to undertake, but no matter how she begged off, Mrs. Marquis would have none of it. She wrapped both hands round her daughter's wrist and gave a series of ungentle tugs.

"We must beg, is that it? Very well, everyone, down on your knees. We must all *implore*, it seems."

"Mother."

"Perhaps if we did a salaam or two. . . ."

"There is no need," said Lea, staring at her shoes. "I should be only too glad."

At which Mrs. Marquis broke into a silvery peal of laughter. "Well, isn't that fine! Now, I must warn you all, I have always found my daughter's taste in music rather dowdy and mournful. I have thus taken the liberty of suggesting a selection from the Lady's Book."

"I'm not sure Mr. Poe would—"

"Oh, I'm sure he *would*. Wouldn't you, Mr. Poe?"

"Whatever Miss Marquis would see fit to grace us with," said Poe, half trembling, "would be a benediction to the—"

"Just as I thought!" cried the mother, lashing him away with her hand. "You will not put us off another moment, Lea." With a low undertone, audible to everyone within twenty feet, she added, "You *know* Mr. Landor won't care for it."

Lea looked at me then. Ah, yes, with the most undivided attention she had given me all evening. Then she set the music on the stand. Lowered herself onto her bench. One last glance, she gave her mother—impossible to read—not pleading, not resistance; *curiosity*, maybe. She was wondering what would happen.

Then she cleared her throat and began to play. And sing.

> *A Soldier's the lad for my notion,*
> *A Soldier's the lad for my notion.*
> *We girls must allow that his row de dow dow*
> *Sets the hearts of his hearers in motion. . . .*

Strange that Mrs. Marquis should have found it in the Lady's Book. It was the sort of song you might have heard many years ago at the Olympic Theatre, on a bill with burnt-cork comedians and French ballerinas. It would have been performed by a girl named Magdalena or Delilah, and she would have worn blue-beaded ostrich feathers or, more daringly, a sailor's suit, and her cheeks would have been as red as her lips, and her knees redder still, and her kohl-smeared eyes would have been screwed into an uglifying wink.

Delilah would at least have taken to her task with some zeal. But then I'd guess even galley slaves would've shown more enthusiasm than did Lea Marquis that December evening, sitting bolt upright on her bench, her arms rigid as muskets. Once, just once, her hands lifted off the keyboard, as though she would stop. But then she (or someone) thought better of it, and down came the hands, and up climbed the voice.

> *With his row,*
> *With his dow,*
> *With his row de dow . . .*

She was, as Poe had reported, a natural contralto, singing in a too-high key, and her voice, as it neared the top of the clef, began to cloud over, until it was just a burst of steam through clenched lips, scarcely to be heard but weirdly resilient all the same. Nothing would quite still it.

> *Dow de dow,*
> *Dow de dow, dow . . .*

I suppose, in that moment, I thought of Pawpaw's birds, calling through their iron bars. What would I not have given—what would all of us not have given, I think—for the key to this particular cage. But the song rolled onward (easier to call the tide back than stop it), and as it went on, the bottom fell out of Lea's voice, and her hands took on a strange new energy, began to flog the keys, and with each flog, some note went spinning off its rhythm—landed in another measure entirely—and the piano itself, stunned by the pounding, seemed ready to rise up in protest, and still Lea sang on:

With his row,
With his dow . . .

For the first time all evening, Poe was looking *away* from her, as though she might be found somewhere down the hall, and I could see Artemus dragging his fingers down his cheek, and there was Mrs. Marquis, the author of it all, in a trance of pleasure or was it fear, her eyes glinting in different directions, her throat rippling with swallows. *Please,* I thought, *please. . . .*

Oh, a Soldier's the lad for my notion!
Oh, a Soldier's the lad for my notion!

She sang three choruses, and the whole production lasted some four minutes, at the close of which we all sprang to our feet, clapping as though our lives depended on it. Mrs. Marquis clapped louder than anyone. Her feet beat a tarantella on the floor, and her voice rang out with such a vengeance that Dr. Marquis had to drive a finger into his ear.

"Oh, my dear, *yes!*" she shouted. "Wasn't it? I only wish, my dear—and this is *all* I will say, and you will never hear me broach the subject again, I promise—but I do wish you wouldn't grow so faint of heart when you approach those F's and G's. You must think"—she jabbed the air with a long saber thrust—"you must think *out,* not up. It is not a climb, it is a journey into—into *resonance,* I have told you this, Lea."

"Please, Alice," said Dr. Marquis.

"I'm sorry, have I said somehing to offend?" Receiving no reply from her husband, she turned a querying eye on each of us in turn before settling on her daughter. "Lea, dear, you must tell me, have I done anything to *bruise* you?"

"No," said Lea coolly. "I have told you before. You would have to do a great deal more to bruise me."

"Well, then, why is everyone so morose? Why have a party at all if we can't be gay?" She took a step back. Her eyes began to well. "And the snow-light is so charming, and here we *are,* and why aren't we happy?"

"We are, Mother," said Artemus.

Though there was nothing particularly gay in his tone just then, only the clang of obligation, shouldered for the thousandth time. But it was enough, wasn't it, to fire a new spirit in Mrs. Marquis, who became from that moment a relentless organizer. She put us through several rounds of checkers and charades, and she demanded that we wear blindfolds while eating the cake, so that we might guess all the flavors that Eugénie (darling Eugénie!) had smuggled into it. And it was only when we had finished our chocolate truffles and crept back into the parlor, and Dr. Marquis, no mean musician himself, was playing "Old Colony Times" in blue accents, and Artemus and Lea stood with their arms wrapped round each other, rocking back and forth, and Poe sat on the ottoman, gazing up at them as if they were condors . . . only *then* did Mrs. Marquis turn her attentions back to me.

"Mr. Landor, you are quite full? You're certain? Well, that's a blessing. I wonder if you wouldn't mind sitting next to me. Oh, I'm so glad you were able to come. I only wish that Lea had been in better form. I assure you if you were to come back another time, you would not be disappointed."

"I am . . . I have no right to . . ."

"Well, of course, that's just the sort of man you are. It is a perfect wonder to me, Mr. Landor, that you have not been subject to more intrigues since coming to the Point."

"Intrigues?"

"Oho! Don't think I am blind to the ways of women. Their maneuvers have slain more men than all the world's cavalries combined. Surely at least one of these dreadful Army wives has introduced you to at least one of her dreadful daughters?"

"I don't—I don't believe they—"

"Now, if they had girls like *Lea,* there'd be no stopping them. Lea, as you know, has always been considered quite the 'catch.' If she weren't so very particular, she might have had, oh, *lots* of—but you know, she has a great many *ideas,* and I've always thought she would be so much better off with a man of, shall we say, more mature sensibilities? Someone who might guide her, through gentle persuasion, toward her proper sphere in life."

"I would have thought your daughter herself might be the best judge of—"

"Oh, yes!" she interrupted, her voice a high locusty shrill. "Yes, I thought the same thing when I was her age. And look at me now! No, Mr. Landor, in these matters, one's mother really does know best. And that is why whenever I have the opportunity, I tell Lea, 'An older man's the one for you. A *widower*, that's who you ought to set your cap for.'"

And as she said it, she reached over and tapped me twice on the cuff link.

The merest gesture, that was all it took, and suddenly it was *me* in the cage, and the bars had slammed down, and I couldn't even sing my way to freedom.

And here was the final joke. Mrs. Marquis had, as usual, spoken loudly enough for everyone in the room to hear. And now they were all peering through the bars at me. There was Artemus, with that peculiarly blank look of his, and there was Lea, dry-eyed, dry-mouthed. And there was Cadet Fourth Classman Poe, his cheeks reddened as if by a slap, his lips pruny with outrage.

"Daniel!" screeched Mrs. Marquis. "Fetch me champagne! I wish to be twenty again!"

And for some reason, that was the moment I chose to look down at my hands, only to see the coppery, granular residue I had wiped from the officer's coat in Artemus' closet—preserved, as in amber, on the skin of my finger.

Blood. What else but blood?

Narrative of Gus Landor

27

December 6th

So here's how it was, Reader. I had gone to the Marquis home hoping to solve one mystery, and I came away with three.

Starting with this: who had tried to kill me in Artemus' closet?

Only Artemus himself and Dr. Marquis would have had the strength to wield a saber with such might, but they were both, so far as I knew, accounted for elsewhere: the doctor tending to his wife, the cadet downstairs in the parlor. It was next to impossible that someone from outside could have entered the house without anyone's knowing. *Who*, then? Who had driven that blade against my tenderest points?

And the next mystery was this: if the uniform in Artemus' closet was the same one Private Cochrane had seen that night in Ward B-3—and I fully believed it was—then who had been wearing it?

Artemus was, of course, the prime candidate. And so, the day after my dinner at the Marquises', I had Captain Hitchcock call him into his office on the pretext of inquiring about the broken door in his barracks. A very pleasant chat they had, and the whole time, Private Cochrane was standing in the adjoining room, his ear to the door. When the interview was over, and Artemus had been dismissed, Private Cochrane screwed his mouth to one side and allowed as how that *might* have been the voice he heard, but then he might also have heard the voice somewhere else, and then again, it might have been someone else's voice altogether.

We were, in short, at sea. Artemus was still our first choice. But had I not seen with my own eyes how easily Dr. Marquis could ape his son in the dark? And here was a new wrinkle. From Poe's last account, I now knew that *Lea* Marquis could play the part of a man with some success.

It all added to the unease that had begun to steal over me: this feeling that the Marquis family had no *center*—no magnetic north, as it were. Peering into my mind's compass, I might find the needle pointing to Artemus . . . but then I would recall how tamely he yielded to every last one of his mother's moods, how *resigned* he sounded whenever he was around her.

Very well, then, let the needle find Mrs. Marquis. But for all her skill in pressing herself on the general mood, she could only go so far, couldn't she? Lea had, in her own way, stood up to her—even in the act of bowing to her wishes. How to account for that?

Lea, then. Try Lea. But the needle wouldn't stay there, either, not when every memory of her left me with the impression of someone being dragged off to the lions.

Which led me to the third mystery: Why would Mrs. Marquis want to fob off her daughter on a spent clock like me?

Lea Marquis was still perfectly marriageable. Too old to land a cadet, it was true, but then she'd never really wanted one, by the sound of it. And weren't there bachelor officers aplenty? Loitering in their cramped quarters? Had I not heard a trace of longing even in Captain Hitchcock's voice when he spoke of her?

Well, of all the mysteries, this alone seemed to admit of a solution. For if Lea's illness was what I guessed, then her parents might well have come to view her as damaged goods, to be awarded to the first claimant who presented himself. And was this not, in its own way, happy news for Poe? For what stronger claimant could there be? No one better disposed than he to see Lea Marquis through sickness and health.

My thoughts, then, had already gathered round him by the time he came to my hotel room. Came, I should say, like someone who *knew* he was being weighed. Most nights, you see, he wore only a shirt and vest under his cloak; tonight it was best dress—sword and cross belt, even—and instead of creeping in as he usually did, he took two long strides into the center of the room and whipped off his shako and bowed his head.

"Landor, I wish to apologize to you."

Smiling a little, I cleared my throat and said, "Well, that's awfully decent of you, Poe. May I ask . . . ?"

"Yes?"

"What are you apologizing for?"

"I am guilty," he said, "of imputing unworthy motives to you."

I sat on the bed. I gave my eyes a rub.

"Oh," I said. "Lea, yes."

"I cannot defend myself, Landor, except to say that there was something discomfiting about the manner in which Mrs. Marquis drew you into her confidences. I'm afraid I assumed—*wrongly*, it goes without saying—that you had welcomed and . . . perhaps even abetted her stratagems."

"How could I, when—"

"No, please." He put up his hand. "I will not impose upon you the indignity of defending yourself. And besides, there is no need. Anyone with a speck of mental faculty would recognize that the idea of your courting or—or *marrying* Lea is, frankly, too absurd even to be entertained."

Ah. Too absurd, was it? Well, as I had a peculiar male vanity of my own, I came close to resenting his remark. But hadn't I just been ridiculing the idea myself?

"So I'm very sorry, old turtle," said Poe. "I hope you'll . . ."

"Of course."

"You're sure?"

"Positively."

"Well, that's a relief." Laughing, he threw his hat on the bed and ran a hand across his brow. "Having made my clean breast, I hope we may now move on to matters of far greater moment."

"Indeed we may. Why don't you begin by showing me Lea's note?"

His eyelids fluttered like moth wings. "Note," he said dully.

"The one she slipped into your pocket while you were putting on your cloak. You probably didn't even notice it until you got back to barracks."

His cheek grew perceptibly pinker as he stroked it with his hand.

"It's not a . . . I'm not sure *note* is the best name for—"

"Oh, let's not worry about what to call it. Just show it to me. If you're not too embarrassed."

For his cheeks were giving off an actual heat now . . .

"Far from—far from embarrassing me," he stammered, "this missive is a source of everlasting pride. To be the recipient of this—this . . ."

Well, he really *was* embarrassed, for after pulling the scented paper from his breast pocket, he set it down on the bed and turned away as I read:

> *Ever with thee shall my glad heart roam—*
> *Dreading to blanch or repine.*
> *Gather our hearts in a green pleasure-dome,*
> *All wreathed in a rich cypress vine—*
> *Richer still for that you are mine.*

"Very sweet," I said. "And very clever, too, the way she—"

But he had no need for testaments. He was already talking over me.

"Landor, I scarcely know what to do with a gift such as this. It is too—it is . . ." He smiled, a bit sadly, as he ran his fingers around the rim of the paper. "Do you know, this is the first poem anyone has ever written for me."

"Well, then, you're one poem ahead of me."

All those tiny white teeth came blazing forth at my expense. "Poor Landor! Never had a poem of your own, eh?" He cocked an eyebrow. "Nor *written* one, that we may be sure of."

I stood on the verge of correcting him. Because, you see, I *had* written poems. For my daughter, when she was very little. Silly rhyming things I'd leave on her pillow: *Sandman here/Wishing you cheer. Here's a kiss/There's more of this.* Not exactly shining examples of the form. In any case, she outgrew them.

"That's all right," Poe was saying. "I shall write a poem for you someday, Landor. Something that will send your name down through the ages."

"I'd be awfully grateful," I said. "But first, I suppose, you should finish the one you've started."

"You mean . . ."

"That business about the girl with the pale blue eye."

"Yes," he said, watching me closely.

I watched him back. Then, groaning, I said:

"Very well. Out with it."

"What?"

"The latest verse. You must have it somewhere about you. Right behind Lea's, probably."

He grinned, shook his head.

"How well you read me, Landor! I doubt there is a secret in the entire universe that you could not, with your extraordinary perceptions, divine in the space of—"

"Yes, yes. Bring it on."

I remember how carefully he spread it across the bed, as if he were unfurling Jesus' shroud. Smoothed all the creases out of it, then stood back and regarded it like a nun, in a hush of faith. And then beckoned me to read.

> Down—down—down—came the hot thrashing flurry
>   Of wings too obscure to descry.
> Ill at heart, I beseeched her to hurry . . .
> "Leonore!"—she forbore to reply.
> Endless Night caught her then in its slurry—
>   Shrouding all but her pale blue eye.
> Darkest Night, black with hell-charneled fury,
>   Leaving only that deathly blue eye.

He was glossing it for me before I'd even finished reading.

"We've already had occasion, Landor, to note how close the names are: *Lea . . . Leonore*. We've noted, in addition, the common feature of blue eyes. We've noted the suggestion of unspeakable distress—fully in keeping with Lea's deportment in the cemetery. We glimpse now—" He stopped. His hand trembled as it pressed the paper. "We see a conclusion, Landor. An imminent demise. What greater urgency can there be? The poem is *speaking* to us, you must see that? It is all but *announcing* that an end is come."

"What must we do, then? Send the girl to a cloister?"

"That's the hell of it!" he cried, flinging his hands toward the ceiling. "I don't know. I can only be the conduit for the poem, I cannot fathom its deeper meanings."

"Oh, 'conduit'," I growled. "Would you like to know something, Poe?

You are the author of this poem. Not your mother, God rest her soul. Not some supernatural scribbler. *You.*"

He folded his arms across his chest, sank into the rocker.

"Use some of that analytical rigor of yours," I said. "You have Lea on your brain day and night. You have reason, given your brief history with her, to fear for her safety. This fear, naturally enough, has found its way into your most favored form of expression: a poem. Why look any further than that?"

"Then why can't I summon it whenever I wish? Why should I not be able to pen a fourth stanza here and now?"

I shrugged. "You fellows have *muses,* I believe. Muses are reckoned to be fickle."

"Oh, Landor," he said, twitching his head away. "You should know me well enough to know I don't believe in muses."

"Then what do you believe?"

"That I am *not* the author of this poem."

It made for an impasse, Reader. There he sat, hard as shale, while I circuited the room, doing nothing more, I thought, than feeling the play of light and shadow on my face, wondering why the light was no warmer than the shadow. In fact, I was coming to a decision.

"All right," I said at last. "If you insist on taking it all that seriously, then let's look at the whole thing. Do you think you might recall the first two stanzas?"

"Of course. They're ingrained in my memory."

"Would you mind writing them down? Just above this one?"

He complied at once, scratching away without a single falter until the top half of the paper lay submerged in ink. Then he sat himself back down.

I studied the paper for a time. I studied *him* for an even longer time.

"What is it?" he asked, his eyes getting larger.

"Just as I expected," I said. "The whole thing is an allegory of your mind. A bad dream, that's all, dressed up in meter."

I let the paper slip from my hand. It rocked back and forth in the air, I remember, like a toy boat riding a trough of water, and even after it landed on the bed, it seemed to pulse for a second more.

"Of course," I said, "speaking strictly as a reader now, I do think a few editorial changes might improve the thing. Provided your mother doesn't object."

"Editorial changes?" he answered, half laughing.

"Well, this 'ill at heart' business, for instance. What does that mean? Heartburn? Indigestion?"

"To a—to a literalist, perhaps."

"And this other phrase of yours, 'harrowed hard.' Strikes me as bit of piling on, if you know what I mean."

"Piling on?"

"Oh, and please defend, if you can, this name. This *Leonore*. Honestly, what sort of name is that?"

"It is . . . mellifluous. It is anapestic."

"No, I'll tell you what it is, it's the kind of name that exists only in poems. If you'd like to know why a fellow like me reads so damned little verse, it's because of names like *Leonore*."

Jaw awry, he snatched the paper from the bed, and jammed it into his coat pocket. There was a steam rising from him now—like a mangle touching wet trousers.

"You continue to surprise me, Landor. I had never supposed you to be such an authority on language."

"Come, now."

"I had thought you had no time for such trifles. Now I see that your intellect encompasses everything. There is no *end* of improvement to be found in your company, it seems."

"I was only throwing off a few—"

"You have—you have *thrown* quite enough, thank you," he said, patting the paper where it lay against his bosom. "I shan't trouble you any further. In the future, you may be sure, I shall take care to keep my verses to myself."

He didn't stalk out. Not right away. Stayed another hour, if I recall aright, but it was almost as if he *had* left. And I now think that's why I never told him of my encounter in Artemus' closet. Because why bother pouring such news into a deaf ear?

(Or else there was something else at work in me. Something that *wanted* him to stay just a little bit in the dark.)

Very quickly, we fell into a thick deep silence, and I was thinking, with a spark of irritation, that I needn't have come all the way to West Point to be alone, I might have just stayed in Buttermilk Falls . . . when, out of nowhere, he rose and, without a word, strode from the room.

Didn't slam the door, I'll say that for him, but left it half open. It was still open when he came back, an hour or so later. His chest was shivering, his nose was clicking from congestion, his bare head was pearled with sleet. He stepped softly, almost on tiptoe, as if he were afraid of waking me. And then gave me that pickled smile and, with a lordly twirl of fingers, said:

"It galls me, Landor, but it appears I must apologize twice in one evening."

I told him there was no need. I told him it was all my fault, I had no business intruding on what was a perfectly delightful little poem—well, not *delightful,* that was the wrong word, but . . . highly poetical . . . oh, he took my meaning, didn't he?

Well, he let me go on a bit, it was probably not unpleasing to him, but it wasn't (to my surprise) what he was after. Nor was he after another tumbler of Monongahela—*that* he turned down with the barest flick of his wrist. Sat himself on the floor, didn't he, with his hands wrapped round his knees. Stared into the cotton rug, with its swirling gold and green fleur-de-lis, and said, soft as could be:

"Confound it, Landor, if I lose you, I might as well lose everything."

"Oh," I said, smiling, "you'd still have plenty of reasons to live, Poe. Plenty of admirers."

"But not *one* who has been as good to me as you have," he said. "No, it's true! Here you are, a distinguished man, a man of substance, yes! And you've—you've let me drone on for hours on end on all conceivable subjects. I've spilled out every last content of my heart and mind and soul, and you've"—he cupped his hands—"*kept* it all in your safekeeping. You've been kinder than any father, and you've treated me like a *man.* I shall never forget that."

He gave his knees one last embrace, then sprang to his feet and made for the window.

"I will spare you more mawkishness," he said. "I know you don't care for it. I will only make a vow: never again will I suffer jealousy or—or *pride* to imperil our friendship. It is too precious a gift. Next to Lea's love, it is the *most* precious gift I have received since coming to this accursed place."

The wages of decency, I thought. I knew then that if I were ever to shake him off me, I would have to do much worse than criticize his mother's poetry. I would have to find something unpardonable.

Before he left that night, I said:

"One more thing, Poe."

"Yes?"

"While I was upstairs with Dr. Marquis, did Artemus ever leave the parlor?"

"Yes," he said slowly. "To check on his mother."

"And how long was he gone for?"

"No more than a few minutes. I'm surprised you didn't see him."

"Did he look any different when he got back?"

"A bit flustered, yes. He said his mother had been beastly and he'd had to step outside to clear his head. Yes, that's right, he was still wiping the snow from his brow when he got back."

"You saw snow on him?"

"Well, he was wiping *something*. Although . . . yes, that *was* curious. . . ."

"What?"

"There was no snow on his boots. Come to think of it, Landor, he looked much the same as *you* did when you came down."

Narrative of Gus Landor

28

December 7th

Having spent far too many hours confined in one hotel room, Poe and I agreed one night to something rash. We would meet under cover of darkness at Benny Havens'. Weeks had gone by since I'd last been to Benny's, but such is the way of the place that nobody shows much surprise when you stop in, no matter how long it's been. Benny's jaw muscles may betray a faint tremor, Jasper Magoon may especially want you to read to him from the *New York Gazette & General Advertiser,* Jack de Windt may, in the midst of planning his assault on the Northwest Passage, raise his chin in your direction, but otherwise, there's no fuss made, no questions asked, come in, Landor, let's forget you were ever gone.

I was the only one who'd felt my absence, probably. All the familiar things seemed new again. The colony of mice living in the alcove just by the dartboard—I couldn't remember their making such a racket before. And the bargemen's wet boots on the flagstone floor, had they always scraped like that? And all the dank smells—mold and candle wax and things secretly fermenting on floors and walls—rushed in on me now, as though I were dipping my head down an unused well.

And there was Patsy, swiping the remains of some ham hocks into her apron and quietly finishing off a mechanic's hard cider for him. I could almost believe I was watching her for the very first time.

"Evening, Gus," she said, evenly.

"Evening, Patsy."

"Landor!" cried Benny, leaning over the counter. "Have I told you the one about the fly? Which lands in the three gentlemen's drinks? Well, mind you, the first gentleman is *English*, so he just pushes his drink away, being a priggish sort of fellow. . . ."

Benny's voice, too, that felt new. Or else it was working on me in a different way, not through my ears but through my skin, a sort of razzing prickle.

"Now the *Irishman*, why, he just shrugs his shoulders and drinks the beer anyway, doesn't he? What does he care if it had a fly in it?"

I tried to hold his eyes, but I couldn't, they were too hot. So I stared down at the counter, and I waited, with a dire patience.

"But the *Scotsman*," cried Benny in his grave raucous voice, "why, he picks up that fly, and he screams, 'Spit it out, you bastard!'"

Jasper Magoon roared so hard he coughed up a finger of gin, and a bargeman caught the laugh and threw it to the outer part of the room, where it was taken up by the Reverend Asher Lippard and passed round, from hostler to drayman. The tin ceiling and the flagstone floor rang, and the laughter spread until it was a *weave* of sound, flawed only by a single off-color thread, a high thin squiggly laugh that burst through the others like the call of a famished turkey. A laugh I spent some time trying to identify before realizing it was mine.

Poe and I had planned to meet as if by accident, so when he got there, at some twenty minutes to midnight, it was all "Why, Mr. Poe!" and "Why, Mr. Landor!" and looking back, I'm not sure why we bothered. Patsy already knew he was working for me, and the rest of them wouldn't have cared. Indeed, they would have been hard pressed to distinguish Poe from all the other sodden, red-eyed cadets who rolled in night after night. No, the only person who could have troubled us would have been another cadet, and Poe was, fortunately enough, the only one to stop by that evening. Which meant that instead of lurking in some dark corner with a snuffed-out lantern, he and I could sit by the fire and help ourselves to Benny's pot of flip, and we could approach the feeling we enjoyed in my hotel room: the mutual ease of two old bachelors living out their term.

That night, Poe chose to talk of Mr. Allan. The inspiration for this,

I believe, was a recent letter in which Mr. Allan had made mention of visiting—provided, of course, he could find a boat to take him up the river and a boatman who wouldn't skin him of half his fortune.

"Do you see?" Poe cried. "It's always been like this, from the time I was a child. *Every* expense to be spared. Or if not spared, then scrutinized and—and interrogated and *begrudged* for the remainder of time."

From the day he had taken Poe into his house, Allan had refused to clothe or educate him in the manner of a gentleman. In a million ways, large and small, Allan had denied him, and when Poe had needed help publishing his first volume of verse, hadn't Allan been the one to say, "Men of genius ought not to apply to my aid," and when he'd had needed fifty dollars to pay his Army replacement, hadn't Allan balked and hedged for so long that to this day, Sergeant Bully Graves was demanding payment (as relentless as any creditor, was Bully), and it wasn't right, it wasn't *just,* that a sensitive young man should be plagued in such a way.

Said Poe, taking another taste of flip:

"I tell you, Landor, there is no consistency in the man. He teaches me to aspire to eminence, then sets about blasting my every hope of advancement. Oh, yes, it's always 'Stand on your own two feet' and 'Never fail to your duty,' but really, Landor, *really,* it's 'Why should *you* get what I did not?' Do you know, Landor, when he sent me to the University of Virginia, he left me so impoverished I was forced to leave after only eight months!"

"Eight months," I said, smiling thinly. "You said you'd studied there three years."

"I did not."

"You did, Poe."

"Landor, please! How could I have been there three years, when the man was already *squeezing* me from the moment I arrived? Do you see this drink in my hand? I tell you, if Mr. Allan had been the one to buy me this, he would now be demanding it back in the form of urine."

I thought then of Benny's Scotsman, trying to get his beer back from the fly, and I had some idea of repeating the joke to Poe, but he was already standing and, with a boy's smirk, announcing that he had to excuse himself. "To add my bit," he said, "to the river tide."

He tittered then and took a long stride toward the door, nearly colliding with Patsy, to whom he apologized at great length and to whom he made to tip his hat before remembering he *had* no hat. Patsy, ignoring him, made straight for our table and, after a moment's pause, began clearing away the thousands of crumbs and small puddles that had piled up in the short time Poe and I had been there. She wiped with long placid strokes, the same industrial precision she had shown in my kitchen. I had forgot what an enchantment it was.

"You're quiet tonight," I said.

"I hear better that way."

"Oh," I said, "why bother with hearing when you can"—my hand groped under the table—"when you can *feel*. . . ."

I was stopped by her arm. Not the piece of her I was seeking, and yet it was enough—just the one square of skin—to set me aching from toe to ear. The memory of our last time came over me . . . her ripe white fullness . . . her cedar scent, never to be mistaken. I will know it a thousand years on, if I still have a nose. I sometimes think that what people—people like Poe—call a soul comes down to nothing more than this. A smell. A cluster of atoms.

"Christ," I said, under my breath.

"Sorry, Gus, I can't stay, there's . . . the kitchen's a terror tonight. . . ."

"Could you at least *look* at me?"

She raised those lovely chocolate irises toward mine. In a second, she drew them away again.

"What's wrong?" I asked.

Her shoulders formed a ridge against her neck. "I don't think you should have taken that job," she said.

"Don't be ridiculous," I answered. "It's a *job,* that's all. Like any other."

"No," she said, half turning away. "It's not." She cast a look at the bar. "It's changed you. I can see it in your eyes, you're not there anymore."

The quiet came over us like a wind, and there we were, and you see how it can be, don't you Reader? You think something has settled into a certain position, and then it turns out it was never in that position at all. . . .

"Well, then," I said. "The change must lie in *you,* not me. I don't pretend to understand it, but I can—"

"No," she insisted. "It's not me."

I studied her averted head. "I suppose that's why you haven't sent for me."

"I've had my hands full with my sister, you know that."

"And your *cadets*, Patsy. Have they had their hands full, too?"

She didn't flinch. In a voice so soft I could scarcely hear, she said:

"I would have figured you for being too busy yourself, Gus."

I half rose in my chair. "Never so busy I can't—"

And that was as far as I got before Poe sprang on us. Giggling with cold and burning with spirits, heedless of everything and everyone beyond himself. He straddled the back of his chair and rubbed his hands together and groaned, "Good Lord! My Virginia blood shall never be thick enough for these winters. Praise God for flip. And praise God—just a splash or two, many thanks—praise God for *you*, Patsy! How you brighten these dreary, wasted hours. I must write you a sestina sometime."

"*Some*body should," I said.

"Somebody," she agreed. "You're right. That would be lovely, Mr. Poe."

He watched her go with a long whistling sigh. Then he bent his face over his glass and muttered:

"It's no good. Every female I meet, no matter how—how pulchritudinous, only sends me spiraling back to Lea. I can think of no one but *her*, I can *live* for no one but her." He let the liquid bubble for a moment in his throat. "Oh, Landor, I look back on the poor benighted creature I was before I met her, and I see a dead man. Marching in all the right directions, answering when spoken to, fulfilling all his appointed rounds, but *dead* all the same. And now this woman has awakened me, and I am alive at last, and at what cost! What pain it is to be among the living!"

He lowered his head into the cradle of his hands.

"Would I ever conceive of returning, though, Landor? Never! Better to have this agony multiplied a thousandfold than to be led back to the land of the dead. I *cannot* go back, I *will* not. And yet . . . oh, God, Landor, what am I to do?"

I emptied my glass. Set it on the table and pushed it away.

"Stop loving," I said. "Don't love anyone."

He would have been insulted if he'd been soberer, or if he'd had more time to answer. But it was at that moment that the Reverend Asher Lippard came bursting through the back door.

"Officer! Landward!"

With that, Benny Havens' establishment . . . I was going to say *erupted,* but that wouldn't convey the orderliness of it. This was at least a weekly event at Benny's. One of Thayer's "blues" would swing by on a surprise raid, and whoever was stationed closest to the door—tonight it was Asher— would sound the alarm, and whichever cadets had chosen that night to "run it" would be bundled out the front door and herded straight up the riverbank. So it was with Poe on this night. Patsy threw him his cloak and hauled him to his feet, Benny dragged him from the fireplace to the door, and Mrs. Havens gave him one final push and slammed the door after him. He was borne along like a stone skipping over water.

The rest of us had our own part in the drill. We were to remain in our places until the officer appeared, and we were to present him with fat dumb faces when he asked if any cadets had been there. The officer, if he was new to this, would mumble darkly at us and leave the premises on his own time. (One or two might have a drink before going.)

We waited, then, for *tonight's* officer . . . but the door never budged. It was Benny himself who finally pushed it open—from the inside. Took a step into the night, craning his head.

"No one there," he said, frowning.

"You don't suppose they cut him off at the river, do you?" cried Jack de Windt.

"Oh, we would have heard something. Come, now, Asher, tell us, what made you think you saw an officer?"

Asher's mouse eyes sharpened. "What made me *think*? Christ, what do you take me for, Benny? You don't think I can recognize a *bar* as well as anyone?"

"A bar, you say."

"Why, certainly. He was holding his lantern up—like this—and the bar, why, it was plain as a pimple. Right there on his shoulder."

"And did you see anything else?" I asked. "Anything but his shoulder?"

The sureness began to leak from Asher's face. His eyes flicked from side to side. "No, Gus. It was the lantern. The way he was holding it, I mean. You could only see the bar. . . ."

         *   *   *

A fine-bladed, icy rain had begun to fall—the same rain that had been falling the night Ballinger was killed. It had already sheathed the knob on Benny's door and beaded the hemlock branches . . . and formed a glistening skin on the steps leading up to the main road.

I set my foot on that first step. I waited. Or maybe just listened, for the night was silvery with sound. The sifting sound of the wind and a batlike rustle in a sugar tree, and, just above me, in a half-bald birch, a crow—black against black—knitting and creaking.

Dark! The only light came from the torch outside Benny's door and the torch's reflection in a puddle of frozen water, captured by a clump of juniper. A near-perfect mirror, that puddle: I found Landor soon enough. I was still staring at him when the sound came clattering down the steps like a rolling marble.

Not a noise Nature would make. Too human. Too much like someone running away.

And maybe if I'd been trained for some other trade, if I hadn't worked half my life as a constable, I wouldn't have given chase. But when you've done what *I* did for a living, and a fellow's running from you, why, there's nothing for it but to follow.

I crawled up those ice-bound steps on all fours and stood once more on the road to West Point. To the north, I could see—no, it was nothing like seeing—I could *feel* a stirring, a *commotion* within the darkness. Legs and arms and head. No more than a hunch, really, but as I crept up the road, I was soon given all the proof I needed: a squelch of boots.

With no lantern at my call, I had only this sound to lead me, but it was as sure a guide as any. I stole along, trying to keep that dark figure in my scope, trying to match my tread to his. I must have been drawing closer, for the sound was growing louder . . . and then, above the tramping, came the snort of a horse, not twenty feet off.

Hearing that changed everything. I knew once he'd climbed on that horse, there'd be no bringing him to ground.

And I knew this, too: I'd be a fool to jump him now. Best to wait until the exact moment of mounting—the point when any rider is most vulnerable—before taking my chances.

This time, at least, I wasn't as blind as I'd been in Artemus' closet. My eyes had won a few minutes to adjust to the dark, and I could see now the purple flanks of a horse, shaking ice from its withers, and the outlines of another figure, more human, bracing itself against the pommel.

And something more: a white stripe, splitting the dark.

And because it was the most definite part of the picture, it was this stripe I threw myself at and I wrapped my hands round. And when I felt the stranger's body give way beneath mine, this stripe became my anchor.

For now we were rolling—down a steep hill. The road had chosen that exact spot to fall away, and we were in its grip. The mud sucked me down, ice crystals flew into my face, stones scored my back. I heard a quick groan—not mine—and felt the heel of a hand pressing into my eyes. Stars of pain burst from my sockets, and from behind me came a light patter like straggling rocks. And when the rolling had stopped—when at last we had reached the bottom of the hill—I groped once more for the white stripe and found only more darkness.

But a darkness so different from the night's that I could do nothing but sink into it. When I came out again, I was lying across the road, with a head angry as a trapped fly. In the distance I could hear hooves, galloping northward.

Welcome, I thought. *To your latest failure.*

It was my own fault, I knew, for thinking I had only one fellow to contend with. Somebody else had been there the whole time. Somebody with a talent for clobbering brains.

Not until half an hour later, after I'd staggered back to Benny's and had my head seen to by Mrs. Havens—and been treated to a free round of drinks by my sympathetic friends—did I notice the thing that had wrapped itself, without my knowing, round my coat sleeve. The sole prize I'd taken away from my struggle: a band of starched cloth, now smeared with dirt and twigs. The white collar of a priest.

Report of Edgar A. Poe to Augustus Landor

December 8th

My dear Landor, I thought you should like to know how I effected my retreat from Mr. Havens' establishment last night. My escape, as you might have supposed, lay entirely along the river shore. The prevailing icy conditions, however, had made this narrow margin treacherous in the extreme. On more than one occasion, I stumbled and barely escaped plunging into the frigid Hudson's embrace. It required the full concatenation of my strength, agility, and wits to keep myself erect and in continual motion.

I confess I should have taken greater care with my passage had I not, in my fevered fancy, believed myself to have been "found out" by the authorities. I had, of course, taken the usual precaution of stuffing my bedclothes, but I knew it would need but a single turning down of my coverlet to expose my crude counterfeit. From that moment, I would be in arrest—dragged in short order before Colonel Thayer's tribunal, my divers misdemeanors arraigned in monotonal litanies, my everlasting sentence pronounced in sonorous and thundering cadences.

Dismissal!

Oh, I cared not, Landor, for the status of Cadet. My *career*? I would fain have abandoned it with a snap of my finger. But to be eternally banished from the lodestone of my heart! Never again to bathe in the coruscations of her eye—no! no! This could never be!

I therefore lengthened my stride and redoubled my speed. It was, by my estimation, one-thirty or two o'clock in the morning when I was at last rewarded with the sight of Gee's Point. As my exertions had drawn me to the very precipice of exhaustion, I rested awhile before betaking myself up the steep ascent to the main grounds. With no further incident, I arrived at the door of South Barracks, congratulating myself on my good fortune.

Pausing one last time to reconnoiter the grounds, I stepped into the stairwell. The door closed behind me with a great rush. The ebon air surged round, benighting the very Night, and it seemed to me that I could hear— yes! once more!—the low, dull, quick sound, the throbbing pulsation so akin to, and yet so at variance with, the palpitations of a human heart. Was it my *own* heart? I wondered. Or had my still-audible panting touched off a corresponding rhythm in the tensile air, much as the drummer's stick finds answering reverberations in the tautened hide of his tympan?

Nothing stirred, and yet I felt, on every side—*witness*, Landor. *Eyes*, searing me with their unholy flame.

With what silent fury did I remonstrate with myself! How sternly did I prod my unwilling body into motion! A single step—succeeded by another—still another. And then, like the summons from another world, came the sound of my own name:

"Poe."

I cannot say how long he had been lying in wait. Only *this* can I report, that as he approached, I became sensible of the soft and metrical sound of his *own* panting, giving me reason to believe that he had been traveling at nearly as great a speed as I.

Besieged as I was by a thousand conflicting sensations, I yet retained sufficient presence of mind to ask him what he purposed in coming here at such an advanced hour, and to a barracks that was not his own. No answer made he—no closer did he come—though I could yet *feel* him, yes, agitating the veriest molecules of this black chamber with his rest- less peregrination. In this way alone was I able to infer—with what *frisson* of dread you may well imagine—that he was *orbiting* me, like a cold and maleficent moon.

Once again I inquired, with as much civility as I could assume, what business he had with me and whether it might not wait until morning. At last, in a cool, dry, insinuating voice, he said:

"You *will* be good to her, won't you, Poe?"

Oh, how my heart leapt at the sound of that simple personal pronoun. *Her*. He could be adverting only to that light of my bosom! Emboldened by the sentiments that swelled through me, I announced in no uncertain terms that I should sooner—I nearly said "tear my heart from my chest," Landor!—sooner saw off my *limbs* than comport myself in such a manner as might occasion pain in his sister's breast.

"No," he said, patiently. "No, what I mean is, you're not the sort to take undue advantage of a lady? There's none of the *cad* about you, is there? Behind those sad eyes of yours?"

I informed him then that to a sensibility such as mine, whatever physical charms might adhere to any single woman must always pale alongside those ineffably enticing *spiritual* charms which compose the true locus of the Feminine Allure, and which tend more effectually toward lasting concord between the sexes.

This heartfelt declaration prompted nothing more than a dry laugh from Artemus. "I thought as much," he said. "I daresay . . . of course, I don't mean to embarrass you, Poe, but it's my suspicion you've not yet, oh, *given* yourself, shall we say? To a woman."

How grateful was I then for the cover of darkness! For were not my blushes of such a vehemence and fire as to outshine Ra's golden chariot?

"Please," said Artemus, "don't misunderstand me, Poe. It is one of the qualities I find most endearing in your character. There is about you a kind of . . . an implacable *innocence* which commends itself to all who hold you dear. And naturally, in that latter company," he added, "I number myself."

For the first time I could perceive his features well enough to see that his lips trembled, that his eyes were bent fixedly before him, and that his head, from time to time, tipped to one side. What, indeed, had I been fearing at his hands? Throughout his countenance there reigned only mildness and benignity.

"Poe," he said once more.

It was then that he touched me, but not in the way I should have expected, not in the manly fashion of comrades—no, he took me by the hand and spread my several fingers before him. Then, speaking in accents of mournful wonder, he murmured:

"Such beautiful hands you have, Poe. Why, they're as pretty as any lady's." He drew them closer to his face. "Priest's hands," said he. And then—I shudder, yes, shudder! as I write this—he pressed his lips to them.

*   *   *

Oh, Landor, I scarcely know to pose the inquiry without wreathing Artemus in fresh clouds of suspicion, and yet proceed I must. Can it be conceivable that on the night of his death, Leroy Fry was venturing out of his familiar haunts for the purpose of—once again, my pen quavers at the very suggestion—for the purpose, I mean, of rendezvousing—not with a young woman, as we supposed—but with a young *man?*

Narrative of Gus Landor

29

December 8th

Leave aside Poe's question for the moment, Reader. I've another one for you. Why did I expect any sympathy from Captain Hitchcock?

Why, after telling him of my close calls in Artemus' closet and outside Benny Havens' tavern, did I expect him to inquire after my health? Express fears for my safety? I should have known he'd be too busy grappling with the *message* to worry overmuch about the messenger.

"What I fail to understand," he began, pulsing his fist against the desktop, "is why our man—if it is our man—should have followed you off the reservation. For what purpose?"

"Why, to track me, I suppose. As I've been tracking him."

Although even as I said it, another possibility was forming in my head. What if our mystery man hadn't been tracking *me* at all? What if he'd been tracking *Poe*?

And if he had, he would have seen Poe go into the tavern. He would have learned I was in the tavern at the same time. And from there, he might have drawn some interesting conclusions about just what Cadet Poe was up to after tattoo.

But of course, I couldn't share any of this with Hitchcock, because it would have meant confessing I'd taken one of his cadets off the reservation and, what was worse, drunk spirits with him. Which would have set me even lower in Hitchcock's esteem than I already was.

"It still makes no sense," the captain was saying. "If it really was the same man you encountered in the Marquis home, why should he have tried to kill you in the one instance and simply left you unconscious in the next?"

"Well," I said, "that might be where our second man comes into the picture. Maybe he has a *calming* influence on his comrade. Or maybe they're just trying to scare me senseless."

"But if you truly believe Artemus is involved with all this," Hitchcock said, "how can we possibly delay in arresting him?"

"Captain, I don't pretend to know how your military justice works, but back in New York, we can't arrest someone unless we have cold evidence against him, and begging your pardon, we just don't have that yet." I ticked off the items on my fingers. "We have a priest's collar, which means nothing without a priest. We have some blood on Joshua Marquis' uniform, but that could be anyone's—Christ, it could have come from the Battle of Maguaga, for all we know. And Private Cochrane won't be able to identify that uniform, I promise you, any more than Asher Lippard will. All they saw was a *bar*."

Hitchcock did something that I'd yet to see him do: he poured himself a sherry. Actually let it slosh around his teeth.

"Perhaps," he said, "the time has come to call in Artemus for direct questioning."

"Captain. . . ."

"Surely if we applied enough pressure . . ."

I knew enough by then to know you don't dismiss any idea proposed by an Army officer, not out of hand. No, you sift through as if it were high-grade ore, only to find to your deep regret that it isn't *quite* the ore you were looking for. So I made a show of sifting.

"Well, of course, it's your decision, Captain. From my side, I'm thinking Artemus is too cool a customer for such a stratagem. He knows full well we don't have any tar to feather him with. All he has to do is deny it over and over again—and sound like a gentleman doing it—we won't be able to touch him. At least that's how it looks to me. And I wonder if we might not just strengthen his hand by calling him out in public."

Do you see how tactful I can be, Reader, when I try? It made not a lick of difference. Hitchcock's eyes narrowed and his chin rose as he set the empty glass back on the desk.

"So these are your only reasons for holding off, Mr. Landor?"

"What other reasons could there be?"

"Perhaps you're concerned that someone else might be incriminated."

A long silence then, crackling with old tensions. I heard the low growl spilling from my throat as I dropped my head back.

"Poe," I said.

"By your own account, there were *two* men present that night."

"But Poe was—"

Poe was running back to the Point.

Yes, once again, I'd backed myself into a corner. I couldn't provide Poe with an alibi because I couldn't admit he'd been there in the first place. And also because another vagrant thought had sidled forward to snag me.

How could I be sure *where* Poe had been?

I let the air out of my lungs. I shook my head.

"I can't believe you're still after that boy's scalp, Captain."

Hitchcock leaned toward me. "Let me enlighten you on one point, Mr. Landor. The only scalp I'm *after* adheres to the man—or men—who killed two of my cadets. And lest you think I am alone in this, I can assure you that my objective is shared by everyone in the chain of command, right up to and including the commander in chief."

Nothing for it now but to put up my hands in mock surrender. "Please, Captain. I'm on your side. Really."

Who knew if he was really mollified? But he stayed quiet for a full minute, as I unknotted the muscles in my back.

"I'll tell you why I'm holding off," I said at last. "There's a piece missing here. And I know, as soon as I find it, everything will tumble into place, and we'll have everything we need. And *until* I find it, nothing is going to make sense, and nothing is going to stick, and no one will be satisfied—not you, not me, not Colonel Thayer, not the president."

Oh, it took a good deal more back and forth but at last we agreed on this: Hitchcock would assign someone (*not* a fellow cadet) to track Artemus' comings and goings, as discreetly as possible. That way he could at least ensure the safety of the cadet corps without compromising my inquiries. He never told me who he had in mind for that mission, and I never asked—didn't want to know—and once we'd come to our agreement,

Hitchcock had no more use for me. Dismissed me, in effect, with the following words:

"I trust I'll get the next installment of Mr. Fry's diary tomorrow morning."

I should have just said yes.

"Actually, Captain, you'll get it a little later tomorrow. Tonight I'm expected for dinner."

"Is that so? May I ask where?"

"Gouverneur Kemble's."

If he was impressed, he made no show of it. And to do him credit, I don't think he was.

"I went there once," he drawled. "That man talks more than a Methodist."

Whereas Poe, if asked to describe Gouverneur Kemble, would draw something from his bag of myths: Vulcan in his smithy, maybe, or Jove with his thunderbolts. Me, I know too little of mythology, and too much of Kemble, who is one of the least mythical people I've ever met. He is merely someone who acquired secrets and money in roughly the same proportion and figured out how to sow one to harvest the other.

He first got the knack in Cadiz, where he learned a thing or two about making cannons. Coming home, he made straight for Cold Spring, and there, on the banks of Margaret Brook, Gouverneur Kemble built himself a foundry. A gnashing steaming screaming thing, with mill wheels and forcing pumps and casting houses. A place of magic. Uncle Sam's dollars pour in, and out pour cannon and cannonade, grapeshot and round shot, shafts, cranks, pipes, gears. If there's a piece of iron between Pennsylvania and Canada that Gouverneur Kemble *didn't* make, well, that iron is not to be trusted. It's to be thrown out, that's what, cast from this blessed vale, if it doesn't bear the imprimatur of the West Point Foundry.

The foundry has been here long enough that you no longer notice it so much, or maybe I should say, you notice it the way you notice streaks of feldspath in a boulder. It becomes part of your idea of the place. The roar of that blast furnace, the mighty ring of Gouverneur Kemble's eight-ton trip hammer—why, these things must have been going on for centuries. And even the forests that get fed, day by day, into Kemble's charcoal kilns—so many taken, and so quickly, that the hillsides seem to be shaking them off like burrs—surely this has been going on forever, too.

Well, this same Gouverneur Kemble, being an old bachelor, has a hungering for human company. Once a week, he holds an open house and calls over fellow souls to sample the fruits of his bounty. These are mostly other bachelors, but at some time or other, everyone who *counts* must make the trip to Marshmoor. Thayer, of course, is a regular guest. Likewise Thayer's officers and the members of Thayer's Academic Board and Thayer's Board of Visitors. And pretty much every passing comet: landscape painters, Knickerbocker authors, thespians, the occasional bureaucrat, the occasional Bonaparte.

And me. Having many years ago helped Kemble's brother worm free of a land swindle in Vauxhall Gardens, I'd been invited some half a dozen times since coming to the Highlands and, before this evening, had gone . . . once. Oh, I was happy to be asked, yes, but I *don't* hunger so much for company, and the horror of people usually beats out the honor of going to Marshmoor. But that was before I began to molder inside the spanking-clean walls of Mr. Cozzens' hotel. Before I started spending my days and nights with men in stubbled woolen uniforms. Before visions of Leroy Fry and Randolph Ballinger began to dance in my head. The dread of strangers had begun to ebb before the dread of *this place*, this Academy, and so it was that when the latest Kemble summons came, I nearly fell over myself in my haste to accept.

And this explains why I was sliding on my ass down a hill of ice when, by all rights, I should have been poring over Leroy Fry's diary, and why, upon reaching the landing and hoisting myself to my feet, I found myself scanning the waters and asking the private on duty if the weather might force Kemble to cancel. For the ice was still coming, steady as the mail.

I needn't have feared. Twenty yards offshore lay Kemble's barge, only a few minutes past its appointed time. Six oars on the thing! Kemble is never one to do things in a small way. No choice but to lower my wet bottom onto one of those wet benches and let myself be . . . transported.

I closed my eyes for a time and pretended someone *else* was being ferried across. And this brought me closer to the rhythm of the river, which was roiling and breathing sulfur. A choppy, bucking ride I had of it that night. In another two months, I knew, the river would be frozen over, and I would have been ferried across in a horse-drawn carriage. Tonight, I could see nothing but the flickering points of torches through the mist, and I only knew I was getting closer because the water turned calm and the shore curved away and the oarsmen didn't dig so deep as before. Even so, they kept dragging up platefuls of silt and algae—an old eel pot—the lid from a tobacco box—and the boat, every so often, would shift without warning on the jostling tides.

From nowhere came the dock, a mere blur in the twilight, no more real than the mist until an outstretched glove made it definite.

The glove belonged to Kemble's coachman. Shining like money in his clean vanilla livery, and driving a large-wheeled tilbury headed by two white horses, standing still as marble, fogged round with the steam of their own breath.

"This way, Mr. Landor."

A team of servants had already hacked the ice from the wharf, and the carriage went up without a lurch, rose as if being *assumed*. Tucked itself under a portico and rocked to a stop. And there, on the top step, stood Gouverneur Kemble.

Stood, somehow, as though he were on horseback, with his big, stout-whiskered head erect and his legs slouching beneath him. Feet big as pumpkins. Big, jowly, ugly face, red with pleasure. He was cackling from the moment he set eyes upon me, and when he smothered my one hand in his two, I could have believed I was disappearing into him.

"Landor! You've stayed away too long. Now come inside, man, this weather isn't fit for dogs. Oh, but you're soaked, aren't you? And this *coat*! Why, it's got holes in it! Never mind, I keep an emergency supply, just for situations like this. They're not in my size, never fear, the proportions are strictly human, and if you don't mind my saying, they have a bit more *ton*. What a silly word that is, *ton*. But stop, let me get a look at you: too *thin*, Landor. The Academy gruel must not agree with you, but then it agrees only with rats. Never mind, you shall eat well tonight, my friend. Until you're bursting the seams of *all* my coats!"

Twenty minutes later, I was installed in a sparkly new frock coat and a waistcoat with a delightful roll collar, and I was standing in Kemble's study, which was about four times the size of Pawpaw's and paneled with some of the very same trees that Kemble had fed into his charcoal kiln. One servant smacked the fire back to life, a second arrived with a decanter of Madeira, and a third brought the glasses. I took *two* glasses, to make up for lost time, and drained them at my leisure while Kemble took his one glass to the picture window and gazed down the lawn to the broad gleaming plain of the Hudson. *His* Hudson, so serene at this remove you might have mistaken it for a lake.

"Snuff, Landor?"

There were no pipes to be had in Gouverneur Kemble's mansion, but there *were* snuff boxes. None quite as handsome as this one, however: a little gold sarcophagus, with the Fall of Man inlaid around the sides and a golden cannon bisecting the lid.

Kemble smiled to see me dive in. "Thayer always declines," he said.

"Well, it's his nature. Renouncing."

"He's not renounced *you*, has he?"

"He may soon," I said, "the way this inquiry drags on. Who knows when it will end?"

"It's not like you, Landor, taking such a time with things."

"Well." A wan smile. "I'm out of my element, I suppose. Not cut out for military life."

"Ah, but here's the rub. *You* fail, it's simply a blow to your professional pride. You need only return to that charming little house of yours and have another glass of Madeira or—or *whiskey*, is it, Landor?"

"Yes, whiskey."

"Whereas if *Thayer* falls, people fall with him." One gigantic thumb wormed into his ear and pulled itself out again with a resounding pop. "It's a delicate time, Landor. The South Carolina legislature has passed a resolution calling for the Academy's abolition, did you know that? And don't think they lack for allies in the Congress. Or the White House." He raised his Madeira to the light of a coppered lantern. "I believe Jackson's merriest pastime must be reinstating every cadet Thayer dismisses. He's *waiting* for his chance to have Thayer's head, and I mean to tell you, he'll get it if we can't make this business go away. I tremble for the Academy."

"*And* your foundry," I added.

Strange, I hadn't meant to say that out loud. But Kemble didn't bridle. He stepped away a pace, drew himself up taller, and said, "A strong Academy means a strong nation, Landor."

"Of course."

"Now, I happen to think that one death, however bizarre the circumstances, doesn't matter so much in the grand scheme of things. *Two*, though, is another matter."

And what could I say to that? Two *was* another matter. *Three* would be another matter still.

Kemble frowned, took a gargle of Madeira. "Well, I hope, for all our sakes, you'll find your man and put this whole dreadful business behind— Oh, but look at you, Landor, your hands are shaking. A little closer to the fire, I think, and another Madeira and—ah, do you see? The rest of our guests, unless I mistake! Nosing into the wharf. Do you know, Landor, I've been cooped up so long I've half a mind to greet them in person. You wouldn't care to . . . you *would*? Are you sure? Very well, if you insist, but wrap up warm. We don't want you catching pneumonia, your country depends on you, you know. . . ."

Two carriages were dispatched to meet the boat party. Kemble and I sat in the second one, wrapped in our several folds, a little purple with spirits. Silent. Or, if *he* was talking, I wasn't attending. I was considering, as I had never done before, the costs of failure.

"Ah!" cried Kemble. "Here we are."

He set one foot on the ground and went down before anyone could blink. His servants, it seemed, had not been able to clear away every last patch of ice. Oh, it was an epic fall, all two-hundred-odd pounds of him slamming to earth. He became, in that instant, pure topography: his belly a highland, tapering down to a head-hamlet, with two hard-blinking eye-ponds. Four servants rushed to his aid. He waved them off with a smile. Made a show of hoisting himself to his own by-God feet. Then, clapping his stovepipe back on his head and brushing the crystals from his shoulders and elbows, he raised a single shrubby eyebrow and said:

"I do hate being comedic, Landor."

The first one to step off the landing was Lea Marquis. This was a surprise, yes, though the greater surprise was in seeing how well turned out she was. The spinster-maiden of the Marquis family parlor had fixed her hair in an Apollo knot, bound herself into a lilac taffeta dress with the fullest skirt I had ever seen, and powdered herself all over with pulverized starch, most of which had survived the river crossing, none of which could hide the pinking of her cheeks in the sharp night air.

"My dear Lea!" cried Kemble, beaming and throwing out his arms.

"Uncle Gouv," she answered, smiling. She took a single step toward him ... and then stopped, aware that his eyes had swerved toward the figure standing just behind her in the boat.

An Army officer, that was the only thing you could say about him from this distance. No clear rank. Face averted. By now, of course, I knew all the West Point officers, and it was a point of pride for me to recognize them before they recognized me, but this one, for some reason, would not reveal himself. It wasn't until one of the coachmen's lanterns cast a spray of light his way, catching him just as he was setting foot on the dock, that I knew him.

Knew him at once. Through all the false clothes and airs and facial adornments. It was Cadet Fourth Classman Poe. Wearing the uniform of the late Joshua Marquis.

Narrative of Gus Landor

30

Well, I've got ahead of myself. I didn't at first have any idea *whose* uniform it was. Then Poe whipped off his cloak and wrapped it round Lea and stood there in his lagoon of lantern light, and I knew at once what I was looking at. In only one detail had it changed since last I saw it: it now bore on its shoulder a single yellow bar.

"Mr. Landor!" cried Lea, with widening eyes. "Allow me to present to you a dear friend of our family's, Lieutenant le Rennet. *Henri* le Rennet."

I scarcely heard the name at first. No, all I could see was that uniform. More to the point, all I could see was how beautifully it fitted Poe. A tailor could have done no better.

And because I had already spent so much time trying to put a face and a body to that uniform, seeing *Poe's* face and *Poe's* body in it . . . made me feel as if I were tumbling down a long spiral. The spiral of Poe's *words*, all those loving texts on which I had staked so much—how could I know, now, if they were to be trusted? Hitchcock's suspicions aside, how did I *know* Poe had been telling me the truth? That he hadn't crossed paths with Artemus and Lea Marquis *months* before he said he had? Come to that, why couldn't it have been *Poe* crouched on the Plain that night, carving the heart from Leroy Fry's chest?

It was madness, I knew that. I tried to argue myself out of it. *He's just wearing a costume, Landor. He doesn't know it has any special meaning. He's playing a game, for Christ's sake. . . .*

And *still* I found myself staring into that face, trying to reassure myself that nothing could have changed so very much in the space of one minute. He was wearing a uniform, that was all.

I swallowed. I said, "Very pleased to meet you, Lieutenant."

"The pleasure is mine entirely," returned Poe.

He had adopted for this occasion a slight accent, a Mediterranean breeze with a faint whisper of M. Bérard. But what struck me most was the change to his face. Lea (or someone else) had patched together a horsehair mustache for him, smeared it with shoeblack and gummed it to the normally hairless region just above his lip. Crude, yes, but there was a kind of genius to it, too, for under its influence, Poe looked easily thirty or thirty-two. Handsomer, as well: the thing actually became him.

The second boat had brought over a larger crowd, and more were pulling up in carriages. I wish I could recall the names of all the guests, Reader. One of the publishers of the *New York Mirror* was there. A painter by the name of Cole and a Shaking Quaker woodworker and a woman who composed hymns. Male or female, Kemble treated them all the same. Clapped them on the elbow and worked their hands like one of his forcing pumps and demanded they take coffee and Madeira or empty his wine cellar if they liked (as if they could!), offered them emergency cloaks and emergency frock coats, and in this way blew on them like a bellows, *driving* them from his atrium to his parlor.

I alone held back—always the last to be blown. I stood in the atrium, listening to the stamp of feet on Kemble's glorious oak floors, the tip-tip-tip of his grandfather clock (quite the largest one I'd ever seen), and the sound of my own feet tapping on the parquet floor. Before a minute passed, my ears began to pick out still another rhythm, this one a light patter, like the dancing of mice. Lifting my head, I found Lea Marquis standing not ten feet away, tapping her feet in counterpoint to mine. Smiling.

"Miss Marquis, I—"

"Oh, you won't denounce us, will you?" she implored. "No one will be harmed by our little masquerade, I assure you."

"No one but Mr. Poe," I said, gravely. "You must know Academy officials dine here on a regular basis."

"Oh, yes, we are *en garde* for that eventuality. In the meantime . . ."

Against my will, my judgment, I felt my lips tickling. "In the meantime," I said, "I won't do anything to get in your way. And I'm delighted to find you here, Miss Marquis. I'd thought I was in for another evening of men."

"Yes, this appears to be the one night a year when females may safely tread through Marshmoor. Our annual night of enfranchisement, historic in its implications."

"But surely, as his niece—"

"Oh, 'Uncle' is just a term of endearment. I've known him since I was a girl, you see. He's an old friend of the family."

"And where, then, are the rest of the Marquises?"

"Well," she said, breezily, "you will not be surprised to learn that Mother has taken to her bed again."

"Migraine?"

"Wednesday is *neuralgia*, Mr. Landor. My father is staying with her, my brother is immured in geometry, and I am the sole family emissary."

"Well," I said, "we are all the happier as a result."

Even as I heard myself say it, I felt the heat steal into my cheeks. Weren't these the words of a suitor? I took a step back. Crossed my arms.

"I must say, Miss Marquis, I've always wondered why there aren't *more* women here. The place could use some."

"Uncle Gouv hates us," she answered simply. "No, don't look that way. I know he professes merely to be *mystified* by my sex, but what more damning confession can there be? One fails to understand only what one fails to esteem."

"You have many admirers, Miss Marquis. Do they all understand you?"

Her eyes ambled away from mine. When she spoke again, it was with a heavy sort of lightness.

"I've always been told some woman broke Uncle Gouv's heart long ago. But I rather think he's *never* had his heart broken." She looked at me. "Not like you, Mr. Landor. Not like me." She smiled then, and tilted her head. "It appears we have been abandoned. Shall we throw in our lots with the rest of them?"

On the subject of his dinner table, Gouverneur Kemble had very clear ideas. Women (on the rare occasions when they were present) must sit at one end, men at the other. Of course, in any such arrangement, there must always be two members of each sex rubbing shoulders with their opposites. So it was that the female hymnist sat next to the Shaker woodworker, and I was placed alongside one Emmeline Cropsey.

Married to an unstable Cornish baronet, Mrs. Cropsey had been banished to America on a small allowance and had become a kind of wandering critic, lighting from state to state, deriding all she saw. Niagara had bored, Albany had appalled, and with her Highlands tour nearing an end, she was even now waiting for her husband to send more money so she could find more country to hate. Before we had even picked up our forks, she informed me that she was composing a volume, to be titled *America: The Failed Experiment*.

"On the assumption that you take no share in the prevailing ethos of this frightful land, Mr. Landor, I freely avow what I could not confess to any of your tobacco-spitting brethren: West Point will be the principal case in my docket."

"How interesting," I said.

From there she went on about, oh, the myth of Cadmus and something about Leroy Fry and Randolph Ballinger's being lambs on the altar of the American demigods. It was a bit like listening to Poe, except not so restful. I'm not sure when, exactly, but at some point Mrs. Cropsey's drone—and indeed the whole welter of accents that crisscrossed Gouverneur Kemble's table—began to give way before one particular voice. No louder than the others but with a natural authority as good as a thousand trumpets. Lieutenant Henri le Rennet—in his absurd mustache and borrowed costume—was taking hold.

"It is true, yes," he said. "France is my *pays natal*. But I have been a soldier in your country's army long enough to become tolerably well acquainted with your English literature. And I regret to inform you that its condition is dire. Yes, dire, I say!"

The painter, edging out on a shaky limb, asked, "Mr. Scott seldom disappoints, I suppose?"

Poe shrugged, speared a turnip. "If one has sufficiently low expectations, no."

"Mr. Wordsworth?" ventured another.

"He shares the same failing as all the Lake poets: he insists on edifying us. When in fact—" He broke off. Held the turnip aloft like a torch. "When, in fact, the whole end of Poetry must be the rhythmical creation of beauty. Beauty and pleasure, those are her highest callings, and the death of a beautiful woman, that is Poetry's most exalted theme."

"But what of the writers within our shores?" tried one. "Mr. Bryant, let us say?"

"I grant you, he has eschewed the poetical affectations which hobble the majority of our modern poetry. But I cannot say that his work betrays a single *positive* excellence."

"Mr. Irving, then?"

"Much overrated," said Poe, flatly. "If America were *truly* a republic of the arts, Mr. Irving would be considered nothing more than a backwater tributary."

Here he overstepped. Irving was a divinity in these parts. More to the point, he was a boon companion of Gouverneur Kemble. Even if you hadn't known that, you couldn't have missed (unless you were Poe) the rippling motion of heads as diner after diner hazarded an anxious reading of Kemble's face, desiring to know if offense must be taken. Kemble never looked up—left it to the *New York Mirror* publisher to do his work for him.

"Lieutenant," said this publisher, "I am beginning to fear you abuse our host's generosity by so freely venting your spleen. Surely there is at least one literary light whom you read with pleasure?"

"There is *one*." He paused here. Scanned the faces of his listeners, as if to ascertain whether they were worthy. Then, with his eyes narrowed and his voice lowered for prime effect, he said, "I don't suppose you have heard of . . . Poe?"

"Poe?" cried Mrs. Cropsey, like a deaf invalid. "*Poe*, do you say?"

"Of the *Baltimore* Poes," he said.

Well, no one had heard of either Poe *or* the Baltimore Poes. Which filled our lieutenant with a deep and dark sadness.

"Can it be?" he asked, softly. "Ah, my friends, I am no prophet, but I can safely foretell that if you have not heard of him yet, you *shall* in time. Of course, I myself have never met the fellow, but I am told he hails from a long line of Frankish chieftains. As do I," he added with a modest lowering of his head.

"And he's a poet?" asked the woodworker.

"Calling him a mere poet is, to my mind, like branding Milton a merchant of doggerel. Oh, he is young, this Poe, of that there is no doubt. The vine of his genius has yet to bear its ripest fruit, but there is harvest enough, my friends, for any refined palate."

"Mr. Kemble!" exclaimed Mrs. Cropsey. "Wherever did you find this charming *soldat*? I believe he is the first man I've encountered in your country who is neither imbecilic nor demonstrably insane."

Her remark sailed right over Kemble, for the Irving gibe had cut deeper than anyone might have guessed. In tones stiff with resentment, he voiced his belief that Miss *Marquis* was answerable for the lieutenant.

"Indeed!" cried Lea from her end of the table. "Lieutenant le Rennet is an old war comrade of my father's. They stood side by side in the defense of Ogdensburg."

An approving murmur ran across the table, stopping dead with Mrs. Cropsey, who frowned and said, "Surely, Lieutenant, you are far too young to have fought in the War of Eighteen-Twelve."

Poe smiled at her. "I was a mere *garçon* at the time, madame. Fighting alongside my adoptive father, Lieutenant Balthasar le Rennet. My mother, she tried, yes, to keep me at home, but I said, 'Pah! I will not abide with women while there is fighting to be done.'" He gazed up at the chandelier. "Thus, my friends, I was present for duty when my father took a cannonball to the breastbone. It was I who caught him as he fell. It was I who laid him on the patch of ground that would, all too soon, become his grave. It was I who bent down to hear his dying whisper: '*Il faut combattre, mon fils. Toujours combattre. . . .*'" He took a long breath. "In that moment, I knew what my destiny was. To be a soldier as brave as he. To be an officer in Columbia's army, fighting for the land that has been a . . . a . . . *second* father to me."

His face sank into his hands, and a silence fell over the table as Kemble's guests took up his tale like a dropped handkerchief and held it before them, wondering whether to keep or return it.

"I cry whenever I think of it," offered Lea.

She wasn't, in fact, crying, but she did tip the scales in Poe's favor. The hymn composer brushed something from her eye, and the painter cleared his throat, and the Newburgh headmistress was so affected as to let her hand rest for a second or two on the sleeve of her woodworker neighbor.

"Well," said Kemble, sullenly. "Your career does . . . the highest possible honor to—to your father's memory. And to your adopted country." Gathering himself, he twisted his wince into a straight line. "May I toast you, sir?"

Up went the glasses. Out came the smiles. It was all *clink-clink* and "Hear, hear" and "Well said, Kemble," and I watched as a fine claretlike blush stole across the pale proud cheeks of Lieutenant le Rennet.

And that was how a lowly West Point plebe came to be hated and, in short order, saluted by one of America's great men. Poe's triumph was complete, and like all such triumphs, doomed to end. For in the act of burying his head, he had managed somehow to tear off nearly half his mustache. I didn't notice at first; it was Lea, semaphoring madly in my direction, who sounded the alarm. Then I saw Mrs. Cropsey staring at Poe with a look of groggy shock, as if he were crumbling before her eyes. I had only to follow the line of her gaze to see the hank of black horsehair dangling from his lip—*switching* in the streams of his breath, like a baby skunk's tail.

I stood at once. "Lieutenant le Rennet? I must beg a brief word with you. In *private,* if—if you can spare yourself."

"Not at all," said Poe, with some regret.

I led him from room to room, looking for a place that didn't have a servant within listening distance. That takes doing in Gouverneur Kemble's house. I was reduced to dragging him through the study and out onto the front verandah.

"Landor, what are you up to?"

"*Up* to?" I snatched off the dangling black hank and held it aloft with my thumb and forefinger. "A little more gum arabic next time, Lieutenant."

His eyes jumped from their holes. "Oh, God! Did anyone see?"

"Only Lea, I think. And Mrs. Cropsey, who is, lucky for you, despised."

He fumbled through his pockets. "There must be some . . ."

"What?"

"Some *snuff* left over from—"

"Snuff!"

"Surely, the—the *juice* is adhesive, isn't it?"

"If you don't mind smelling like a cuspidor. Come, now, Poe, you've had your show. Time to bring down the curtain and—"

"And abandon Lea?" His eyes made a wolf-flare. "On the first night we've ever spent alone together? I'd sooner resign my commission on the spot. No, I'm in it for the duration, Landor, whether you help me or not."

"Then it will be *not*. And before I get any angrier, tell me where you found that uniform."

"This?" He looked at the garb on his body as if it had just now settled over. "Why, Lea gave it to me. It belonged to a dead uncle, something like that. Fits me like a charm, doesn't it?" His grin slowly faded as he studied my face. "What is it, Landor?"

I grabbed the bottom of his coatee—ran my finger along the square of bloodied cloth I had discovered in Artemus' closet. The finger came away clean.

"What's wrong, Landor?"

"Did you wipe it off?" I asked in a simmering voice. "Give it a little *scrub*, maybe, before you started out?"

"But why would I do that? It's quite clean enough, isn't it?"

"Oh, then maybe *Lea* did it for you."

His lips began opening and closing. "I haven't—I haven't the slightest . . . Landor, what's the *matter* with you?"

I opened my mouth to reply, only to be stopped by a voice that came from behind us. A voice that was neither Poe's nor mine. But familiar all the same.

"Mr. Landor."

The intruder was standing in the doorway, still in his cloak, his boots rimed with ice, his frame silhouetted and, at the same time, fully hidden by the light from the study.

Trust Ethan Allen Hitchcock to make such an entrance.

"I was hoping to find you here," he said.

Oh, he was grim as a cow.

"And so you do," I said, waving at Poe behind my back. "So you find me, yes."

"I wish I had happier news to—"

He stopped then. Knitted his brows and considered the small, slender figure that had wheeled itself toward the river and was even now trying to squeeze itself into the night's folds.

"Mr. Poe," said the commandant.

I suppose, if Poe could have jumped straight from the verandah into the Hudson, he would have done it. If he could have heaved himself over the nearest mountain, he would have done that, too. But he had never felt so small, I'd guess, as he did in that moment. So far from superhuman.

His shoulders shook. His head drooped on its stalk. He turned slowly round.

"How well you look in your uniform," said Hitchcock, widening his gaze to enclose both of us. "And what an ingenious entertainment you and Mr. Landor have devised."

Poe stepped forward—I will always remember this—bowed his head, like a vassal to his liege.

"Sir, I must tell you, on my honor, Mr. Landor had nothing to do with this. He was as surprised and—and as dismayed as you, sir. It was . . . believe me, sir, it was entirely my own initiative, and I fully deserve—"

"Mr. Poe," said Hitchcock, his jaw going hard. "I find I am in no humor just now to administer to you. I have, as it happens, far more important matters to attend to."

He came toward me now, his face flat and blank. Not to be read, except for the eyes, which were tiny and blazing.

"It appears that while you have been availing yourself of Mr. Kemble's hospitality, another cadet has vanished," he said.

I barely listened to what he said. No, I was far more conscious of the fact that he was *saying* it in the full hearing of Poe, someone he might as easily have sent away with one wave of his hand. Something had changed, that was clear enough. The rules of decorum that guided Hitchcock from the moment he woke to the moment he fell asleep had been swept aside.

"No," I answered, strangely calm. "That's impossible."

"I only wish it were," he said.

Poe's head drew back. A quick shiver took hold of him from heel to crown.

"But which one?" he asked.

A long pause before Hitchcock answered:

"Mr. Stoddard."

"Stoddard," I echoed, dully.

"Yes. Don't you relish the irony, Mr. Landor? The last cadet to see Leroy Fry alive may now himself have met the same fate."

"Ah!" came the cry from the doorway.

And now it was Hitchcock's turn to be surprised. Hitchcock's turn to spin round and find a silhouetted figure. The figure of Lea Marquis.

She didn't faint, I won't go that far, but she dropped, yes. Dropped to one knee. The wide skirt of her dress turned to aspic round her, but her eyes—her eyes stayed fixed the whole time. Never so much as blinked.

Poe was the first to rush to her side. Then me. Then Hitchcock, more flustered than I had ever seen him.

"Miss Marquis, please accept . . . I had no idea you were . . . I should have . . . you must . . ."

"They'll keep dying."

That was what she said. Under her breath—and over it, too, somehow. Said it with her blue eyes blazing. Said it as though there were no one else on that verandah.

"One by one," she said. "They'll keep dying until nobody's left."

Narrative of Gus Landor

31

December 8th to 9th

By the time tattoo came round that night, word of Stoddard's disappearance had spread to every cadet, bombardier, and instructor. Theories blazed like fireflies. Mrs. Cutbush continued to insist that Druids were involved; Lieutenant Kinsley said the answer lay in the stars; Mrs. Thompson, the boardinghouse proprietor, was putting her money on Democrats; and more and more cadets were subscribing to the idea of a vengeful Indian spirit. No one went easefully to bed. Several of the faculty wives had already announced their intention to spend the remainder of the year in New York (one even stayed up until dawn supervising the packing). The cadets who held sentinel duty that night stood back to back so nothing could catch them by surprise, and at least one upperclassman woke in a terror, screaming and grabbing for his musket on the wall.

Yes, fear was abroad, but you wouldn't have known it by the appearance of the West Point commandant. When I stopped by his quarters shortly after ten the next morning, Hitchcock was sitting at his desk, looking serene and maybe a bit forgetful, as if he were trying to locate his crossbelt. The only sign that something was amiss was his right hand, which had set off on a mission all its own, combing the Hitchcock hair in endlessly repeating strokes.

"We sent out another search party at dawn," he said, "though I can't imagine what they might find that the last one didn't." His hand paused. His eyes closed. "No. No, I *can* imagine."

"Oh, now, Captain," I said. "I wouldn't give up hope just yet."

"Hope," he repeated in a lower register. "I'm afraid it's too late for that, Mr. Landor. I'd settle for a good night's sleep."

"Then please get some," I said. "I've just been to Mr. Stoddard's quarters."

"Yes?"

"And I made an interesting discovery."

"Yes?"

"Mr. Stoddard's trunk was empty."

He looked at me with an air of suspension, as though the rest of my sentence had been sheared off in midflight.

"There were no clothes in it," I prompted. "No civilian clothes."

"And what are we to make of that?"

"Well, for one thing, I don't think we have another corpse on our hands, Captain. I believe Mr. Stoddard has run off on his own two legs."

He sat up. Drew his hand from his hair. "Go on," he said.

"Well, I'm sure you'll recall that Mr. Stoddard was one of—no, he was the *only* cadet petitioning to cancel the term. Isn't that so?"

He nodded.

"Now, I know," I said, "believe me, I *know* you've got some anxious fellows running about. Why, you've got young men seeing Iroquois in bushes! But to the best of my knowledge, only Stoddard has begged to be sent home. Why?"

Hitchcock regarded me for a few seconds. "Because he had a particular reason to fear for his safety," he said.

"That's my thinking, too, yes. As you remember, Captain, we had occasion to talk to Mr. Stoddard very early on in our inquiry. He was the one who told us of running into Leroy Fry in the stairwell. That strange meeting, that remark of Fry's about *necessary business*."

"So you think he may have seen something that night? Something *else*?"

"Well, it's possible, that's all I'll say."

"But why would he have held it back, when we gave him every chance to tell us?"

"All I can think is he had more to fear from *telling*."

Hitchcock sat back in his chair. His eyes drifted toward the leaded casement window.

"You mean to suggest that Stoddard might be implicated in the other deaths?" he asked.

"Well, he's deep into something or other. Deep enough, at any rate, that he thought it better to run away than confess."

Suddenly he was standing. Making straight for the bookshelf, as if he had a specific title in mind, but then stopping a yard short.

"We know that Stoddard was an intimate of Fry's," he said.

"Yes."

"But we don't know of any connection between Stoddard and Ballinger."

"Oh, we do, actually. You'll find it in the next transcription of Fry's diary. Two summers ago, both Stoddard *and* Ballinger were good mates with one Leroy Fry."

His eyes took on a damp, avid cast. "But how is Stoddard connected with Artemus Marquis?"

"That's not clear as yet. One mystery at a time. In the meantime," I said, "it's most important that we find Mr. Stoddard. I can't stress that too highly, Captain. We must track him down wherever he's gone."

He watched me for a time. Then, speaking low and firm, he said:

"If Mr. Stoddard is hiding on the reservation, we shall find him soon enough."

"No, Captain," I said, kindly. "I think he's probably left us for the time being."

I began to wriggle into my cloak—then thought better of it. Draping the cloak back on its hook, I settled into my chair and looked into Hitchcock's one candle and said:

"Captain, if you don't mind . . ."

"Yes?"

"I'd like to beg mercy for Mr. Poe."

One corner of his mouth tilted down; his eyes began to glitter.

"Mercy?" he said. "Do you mean for his little *coup de théâtre* last night? That would seem a bizarre request, Mr. Landor, when you, better than anyone, can enumerate all his infractions. Begin with leaving the Academy reservation after hours. Continue with the imbibing of spirits—a goodly quantity, by the looks of him. Let us not forget presenting himself under an assumed name."

"He wouldn't be the first cadet to—"

"He is the first in *my* tenure, Mr. Landor, to have the temerity to impersonate an officer of the United States Army. You may imagine how I regard that particular subterfuge."

Strange. I couldn't help feeling—as I always did in Hitchcock's presence—that I was myself on trial. I bowed my head over my hands, and the words came jittering out, like spasms of sin.

"I believe—I believe he was—under a certain impression."

"Which was?"

"That he was helping me."

Hitchcock eyed me coldly. "No, Mr. Landor. I don't believe that was the impression he was under. I believe I *know* the impression he was under."

I might have begged him then to recall what love can do to a young man. But this was Ethan Allen Hitchcock. Against *his* hide, Cupid's whole arsenal had made scarcely a nick.

"As you know," he continued, "this is far from being Mr. Poe's first infraction. I have not even mentioned the dozen or so occasions over the past few weeks alone when he left his quarters after tattoo for the purpose of . . . well, why don't you tell me, Mr. Landor, what *is* it that draws him to Mr. Cozzens' hotel night after night?"

Oh, my.

Well, in the end, I had to smile, Reader. Thinking how clever Poe and I had believed ourselves in hiring a paid Army escort and shutting ourselves behind closed doors, drinking and chattering until dawn. Poe hadn't *seen* anyone following him, had he? And so we trusted the evidence of our senses, when we should have relied on our history with Thayer and Hitchcock. These were men who had to know everything. Hence, they knew everything.

Hitchcock laid his hands on his desk and drew himself toward me. "I never had him intercepted, Mr. Landor. I granted you *both* that latitude and never cried foul and never once demanded an explanation. Nor did I ever hold you to account for frequenting Mr. Havens' establishment. You will see, perhaps, that I am not so rigid a man as you believe. And should you need further confirmation, I will gladly inform you that the only person to be disciplined for last night's fiasco is Lieutenant Kinsley."

"Kinsley?"

"Of course. He was the officer detailed to watch South Barracks last night. He manifestly failed in his duty."

"But Poe was—"

"Indeed he was. However, my running into him must fall under the category of an unfortunate accident. Had I not been preoccupied by business, I might well have toasted his good health and congratulated him on his pluck. Even now, I cannot in good conscience punish a fellow simply because fate contrived against him."

I waited for all the physical signs of relief—the uncoiling in my shoulders and chest, the lightening of my heartbeat—but none of them came. I couldn't believe it, you see. I couldn't believe we were in the clear, and in fact, we weren't. Stealing after us came Hitchcock's voice, a straight line through the dark.

"Nevertheless, Mr. Landor, I can no longer consent to Poe's being your agent in this affair."

I stared at him.

"I don't see . . . we've made . . . Captain, we've made great *progress* thanks to him. He's been a great help to me."

"I don't doubt it. But with two cadets dead and a third missing, I cannot even *think* of placing another young man in harm's way."

The oddest sensation then, Reader: a kind of searing in my face and my neck. Shame, I now suspect. For until very recently, how little care I had ever given to Poe's safety! I had followed his meetings with Lea and Artemus as a *reader* would, never once thinking that behind the yarn lay a real person, with real flesh and blood—which might at any second be forfeited.

"That's not the only reason," I said.

"No, it's not," he allowed. "I've told you before, I believe your proximity to Poe has cost you a certain amount of objectivity. Perhaps when you're no longer in regular contact with him, you may be better equipped to . . ."

He didn't finish. He didn't have to. I straightened myself in my chair; I took a deep breath; I said:

"Very well. You have my word. Poe will no longer be part of the investigation."

There was, at least, no triumph in Hitchcock's manner. His eyes were turned inward, and his hand was brushing the top of his desk, clearing away shadows.

"You should know," he said. "Colonel Thayer has reported Mr. Stoddard's disappearance to the chief of engineers."

"The chief won't be pleased. Coming right on top of Ballinger's death. . . ."

"Yes, I think it fair to say he will *not* be pleased. And so long as we are playing soothsayer, I think it fair to expect that Colonel Thayer will be reprimanded for the unconventional manner in which he has pursued this matter."

"They can't blame him, surely, for—"

"He will be reminded that from the very outset, he should have engaged an *officer* to conduct these inquiries, not a civilian."

Something in the way he said that, something rigid and rehearsed, gave it a trailing echo in my mind. I felt as if I were eavesdropping on conversations that had taken place days earlier, in closed rooms.

"I'm sure *you've* been reminding him, too," I said, calmly. "But then you never wanted me here in the first place. It was Colonel Thayer's idea from the start."

He didn't bother denying it. Kept his voice as even as the horizon.

"It scarcely matters now, Mr. Landor. Colonel Thayer and I must both take responsibility for what will doubtless be perceived as a want of judgment. I fully anticipate that as a consequence, the chief of engineers will send his own investigator here posthaste. Someone with carte blanche to see this business to its end." His hand started up again: clearing the desk, clearing the desk. "Now, if the chief of engineers acts as precipitately as is his wont, I believe we can expect this investigator to arrive in, oh, three days' time." His lips worked for a few seconds, checking his figures. "We find ourselves, then, with something we did not have before: a term of expiration, Mr. Landor. You have three days to find the perpetrator of these crimes." He paused, then added, "*If* it is still your desire that he be found."

"My desire doesn't enter into it," I answered, shifting in my chair. "I agreed to take it on, Colonel. We shook hands on it. That's all that matters."

He nodded, but his eyebrows had sharpened at the corners, and when he laced his hands together and leaned once more over his desk, I could tell he was far from appeased.

"Mr. Landor," he said. "I hope I don't presume too far when I suggest that you harbor a latent hostility toward this Academy. No, wait." He put up a finger. "This animus, I have intuited from my very first meeting with you. Until today, I never thought it a fit subject for inquiry."

"But now?"

"Now I fear that it might present yet another obstacle to the prosecution of your inquiries."

Oh, I was boiling then! I remember actually *looking* for something to fling—an inkwell, a paperweight—but nothing seemed equal to my anger. Which meant I had only words to toss back at him.

"In Christ's name!" I growled, jumping to my feet. "What more do you want from me, Captain? Here I am, working with no compensation—"

"By your own request."

"—working like a *dog*, if you must know. Thanks to you, Captain, I have been . . . I've been bludgeoned, nearly *filleted*. I've risked my *life*, all in behalf of your precious institution."

"Your sacrifices are duly noted," he answered dryly. "Now, if you could return to my earlier question. Are you intrinsically hostile to this Academy?"

I ran my hand across my brow. I let out a scoop of air.

"Colonel," I said, "I've no quarrel with you. I hope you and your cadets will thrive and flourish and—and *kill* and do whatever soldiers must do. It's just . . ."

"What?"

"This little monastery of yours," I said, holding his eye. "You know it doesn't make saints."

"Whoever said it did?"

"Nor does it always make soldiers. Now I don't align myself with the president or any of your enemies, but I *do* believe when you take away a young man's will, when you fence him round with regulations and demerits and—and deprive him of his use of reason, well, I think you make him less human. And more desperate."

The slightest flare just then in Hitchcock's nostrils. "You must assist me here, Mr. Landor. I'm trying to follow your train of logic. Do you mean to imply that the *Academy* is to blame for these deaths?"

"Someone connected with the Academy, yes. Hence the Academy itself."

"But that's ridiculous! By your standard, every crime committed by a Christian would be a stain on Christ."

"And so it is."

It may have been the first time I ever caught him off guard. His head drew back and his hands came together again and he was, for a short while, without words. And in the silence that spilled over us, I came to a clear reckoning.

Captain Hitchcock and I would never be friends.

We would never drink Madeira together in Gouverneur Kemble's study. We would never play chess or listen to concerts, we wouldn't stroll up to Fort Putnam or read newspapers over grapefruit. We would never, from this moment on, spend a minute in each other's company that wasn't strictly required by our jobs. And all for the simple reason that we would never forgive each other.

"You have three days," said Hitchcock. "In three days, you'll be done with us, Mr. Landor."

I was just walking out the door when he thought to add, "And we with you."

Narrative of Gus Landor

32

December 10th

Well, Captain Hitchcock could have said a great many things about me, but not that I was wrong about Cadet Stoddard. The very next morning, a local fisherman, name of Ambrose Pike, came forward to say he'd been flagged down by a young cadet who'd offered him a dollar to be oared downriver. Pike took him as far as Peekskill, then watched as the young man drew another couple of dollars from his leather pouch and booked passage on the next steamer to New York. Pike would have thought nothing more of it, but his wife had told him the cadet might be a fugitive, in which case Pike himself could be sent to Ossining for abetting a criminal unless he came forward, and so here he was, ready to tell anyone who'd listen that Ambrose Pike was no abettor.

How had Pike known it was a cadet he was transporting?

Well, the lad was still in his uniform, wasn't he? It was only when they got downriver that he put on his homespun shirt and his neckerchief and his fur cap and became just another river rustic.

What explanation had the young man given for wanting to leave the Point in such hurry?

Said there was a crisis back home. Said he couldn't wait for the Academy longboat. And that was all he said until they got to Peekskill. Not even a farewell.

Was there anything else he could tell us about the young man?

He was plenty pale in the face, that much Pike had noticed. And though the sun was strong and the boy was mighty well bundled, he would now and again break into a fit of shivering.

What did Pike take that to mean?

Well, it was hard to say. But he looked like he had Old Scratch on his tail.

That same day, I got in the mail an interesting package from my New York correspondent, Henry Kirke Reid.

Dearest Gus,

Always a terrific pleasure to hear from you—even if business must protrude its ugly head. I must beg you, the next time you give me an assignment, grant me a little more than four weeks to accomplish it. The dispatches from Richmond have only just arrived, and with another week or two at my disposal, I might have gleaned a good deal more about your man. In any event, I am duly enclosing what I have, which includes the results of inquiries in Boston, New York, and Baltimore.

Your Poe is many things, Gus. I'll leave it to you decide if he is any one thing in particular. I will only say that while his past is as littered with dead bodies as anybody's, none of these departed souls has yet risen up to arraign him. Nor is there a warrant on his head. All of which means, as you know, exactly nothing.

In your letter, you mentioned my compensation. Would you do me the favor of forgoing that? The inquiries were not overstrenuous, and it would be my own humble way of honoring Amelia's memory. I never did send adequate condolences.

New York is not quite so merry a place without you. But I expect we'll survive until the next Landor sighting. What choice do we have?

With fondest wishes,

H.K.R.

That night, I sat down and read Henry's dispatches—read them over and over again, with a mounting sadness. I could feel things coming to a breach, you see. And when I heard the familiar rap on my hotel-room door, I congratulated myself for having turned the key in the lock. The door knob jiggled, gently at first, then with greater insistence, before at last falling still. I heard the sound of retreating steps. I was alone again.

Report of Edgar A. Poe to Augustus Landor

December 11th

Landor, where were you last night? I found your door unexpectedly barred and, upon knocking, received no answer. I was the more bewildered as I was nearly certain that I had glimpsed a light in your window. You must take greater care, you know, to extinguish your tapers when you go out. You wouldn't want to burn down Mr. Cozzens' magniloquent hotel when it has only just been built.

I wonder, though, will you be "at home" tonight? I am quite beside myself in regard to Lea. She has resisted all my best efforts to see her, and I am left to suppose that the fresh horrors occasioned by Mr. Stoddard's disappearance have wrought havoc with her exceedingly delicate sensibilities. Perhaps she wishes to conceal from me all evidence of feminine infirmity? Alas, then! How little she knows me, Landor! I should love her still more in weakness than in strength; I should prize her more at Death than at Love's Nativity. She must know! She must!

Landor, where are you?

Narrative of Gus Landor

33

December 11th

He was back again that night. A frigid night, I remember. I had opened Leroy Fry's diary, but the symbols seemed to fly away from me, and in the end, the book just lay there in my lap like a sleeping cat. The embers were dying in the grate, and my fingers were white-tipped with cold because I couldn't, for some reason, manage to throw another log on the fire.

This, too, I failed to do: lock the door. Shortly after eleven, I heard the soft rapping . . . saw the door open . . . spied once more that familiar head. . . .

"Good evening," said Poe, as he'd always said before.

Except that we stood now on changed ground. Neither of us could have defined the difference, exactly, but we both felt it. Poe, for instance: he couldn't sit, couldn't stand. Wandered through the room, in and out of shadows, glancing out windows, tapping rhythms on his flanks. He was wishing, maybe, that I'd offered up my usual bottle of Monongahela.

"Private Cochrane wasn't there to escort me tonight," he said at last.

"Yes, I think Private Cochrane has another master now."

He nodded, not truly attending. "Well," he said, "it doesn't matter. I know the terrain well enough now. I won't be caught."

"You *have* been caught, Poe. We *both* have. And now come the consequences."

We looked at each other for some time before I said, "Maybe you'd better sit down."

He forsook the rocker, his usual seat. Perched himself instead on the edge of the bed and let his fingers dance over the counterpane.

"Listen to me, Poe. In exchange for looking mercifully upon your conduct at Mr. Kemble's, Captain Hitchcock has asked that you step down as my assistant."

"He cannot do that."

"He can," I said. "He does."

The fingers were pirouetting now. Large wheeling moth arcs. "Well, now, Landor. Did you tell him all the—the—all the *myriad* ways in which I've been of assistance to you?"

"I did."

"And it made no impression upon him?"

"He's greatly concerned for your safety, Poe. As he should be. As I should have been."

"Perhaps we might appeal to Colonel Thayer. . . ."

"Thayer agrees with Hitchcock."

He gave me his boldest smile then. The smile of a Byron.

"Well, what do we care, eh, Landor? We may meet as before. They can't stop us."

"They can dismiss you."

"Let them! I will take Lea and shake off the dust of this cursed place forever."

"Very well, then," I said, crossing my arms. "*I* dismiss you."

Just the slightest flicker in his eyes as he studied me. No words, though. Not yet.

"Tell me," I said. "What was the oath you made me? In this very room? Do you remember?"

"I swore to—to tell the truth."

"The *truth*, yes. It's a word that no one apparently has ever defined for you, Poe. Which presents me with a bit of a problem, you see. I can do business with a poet all right. But not with a liar."

He eased himself onto his feet and, after studying his hands for a bit, said in a low voice, "You had better explain yourself, Landor. Or I shall have to demand satisfaction from you."

"I don't need to explain myself," I said coolly. "You may cast your eyes on this."

Reaching into the side-table drawer, I drew out Henry Kirke Reid's stack of yellow sheets, bound with cord. Threw the packet halfway across the bed. Eyes wary, he asked me what it was.

"I had a friend of mine look into your history," I said.

"Why?"

"I was hiring you for a job," I answered, shrugging. "I had to know what sort of fellow I was dealing with. Especially if the fellow likes to talk of killing people. Of course, the report was compiled at great speed, so it's not as complete as it might be. But 'tis enough, 'twill serve."

He shoved his hands into his pockets and took another tour of the room. And when he spoke again, I could hear the brittleness: a card player piling up bluffs.

"Well, Landor, I am glad I have given you an occasion to cite Shakespeare. You're not one for allusions, as a rule."

"Oh, I used to go to the theater quite a lot. As you know." Reaching across the bed, I gathered up the pages again. "But what are you waiting for, Poe? Don't you want to read it? If someone had taken the same trouble with me, I'd be bursting to see what was there."

A very large shrug then. A drawl:

"The usual tissue of lies, I'm sure."

"Tissue of lies, yes. That's the very phrase that came to my mind as I read it." I made a show of flipping through the pages. "By the time I was done, the only question left was this: what *haven't* you lied about, Poe?" I caught his eye for the merest second, then went back to scanning the pages. "It's hard even to know where to begin."

"Then don't," he said, quietly.

"Well, let's start small. You left the University of Virginia not because Mr. Allan cut off your funding but because you . . . let's see, how did Henry word it? . . . *accrued ruinous gambling debts,* yes. Does that jog your memory, Poe?"

No answer.

"I can certainly see," I went on, "why you like to tell people you spent three years there instead of only eight months. But that isn't the only thing that's got inflated. That old swimming feat of yours? Seven miles and a half up the James River? Appears it was closer to five."

He sat now. Sat on the very edge of the rocker. Utterly still.

"Never mind, that's just a bit of enlarging," I went on. "No harm in that. No, it gets really interesting right around . . ." My finger dropped like a meteorite. "*Here*. Your European adventures, yes. I'm afraid I just can't figure out where you fit them all in, Poe. Your whole life has been spent living with Mr. Allan or going to school or serving in the U.S. Army, with no breaks in between. So, let's see, where does that leave us? Fighting for the Greeks: a lie. Traveling to St. Petersburg: a lie. No diplomat ever had to rescue you because it's a safe bet you've never been anywhere but England. As for sailing the seas, I'm guessing you borrowed that from your older brother. Henry, I believe, is his name: Henry Leonard. Or is it *Henri*?"

He did just what I would have expected then. Took his finger and rubbed the region between his nose and upper lip, where that horsehair mustache had so lately resided.

"These days, of course, Henry's awash in other things," I said. "Booze, mostly. No one's expecting much from him but an early grave. Must be an awful disappointment, too, for a family like yours, with such a distinguished lineage. Frankish chieftains, wasn't it? And, oh, a Chevalier le Poer and maybe a British admiral or two thrown in." I smiled. "Shanty Irish, more like. Oh, I used to see plenty of your kind in my New York days. On their backs, usually: they always land on their backs. Just like Henry."

Even in the room's dim light, I could see the color rising in his cheeks. Or maybe I could *feel* it, like the heat from the grate.

"The funny thing is, you really do have a distinguished family member, and yet you never speak of him. Your grandfather, Poe. An actual general, for God's sake! Stalwart of the Quartermaster Department. Warmly remembered—shall I read it, Poe?—*warmly remembered for his valiant efforts to clothe and requisition Revolutionary troops*. An intimate of Lafayette's, it seems. I can't imagine why you wouldn't mention him. Unless . . ." I buried my head in the pages once more. "Well, now, I suppose his life after the war wasn't quite so heroic. A dry-goods store, I see, among other businesses.

None of them coming to much. And from there, let me see . . . *Declared insolvent in 'oh-five. Died penniless in 'sixteen.* Very sad." I looked up with a frown. "A *bankrupt,* I guess that's what we'd call him. And to think, Poe. You were so ashamed of him you preferred to let people think Benedict Arnold was your grandfather."

"That was a game," he said, shaking his head. "Having a bit of fun, that was all."

"Hiding a bit of truth, too. As it pertains to General David Poe and, of course, the *Baltimore* Poes. Who, as best I can tell, have never had more than two cents to rub together."

His head was beginning to sink now. Inch by inch.

"Which brings us to the final lie," I said, raising my voice. "Your parents."

And now I lifted my gaze from the paper. For I knew this bit by heart.

"They didn't die in the Richmond theater fire of eighteen-eleven. Your mother was two weeks dead by the time that fire broke out. Some sort of infectious fever, I believe, though the records are a little fuzzy on the subject."

I stood now. Advanced on him, brandishing the paper like a cutlass.

"And your father wasn't even on the scene, was he? Ran off two years before that. Left your poor mother in the lurch, the bounder, with two young children. Nobody ever saw him again. Nobody much missed him, either. Terrible actor, I'm told, never got the notices his wife did. And already drinking himself to an early grave. But then, in your family, that would seem to be a common—oh, how did you describe it, Poe?—*medical* condition. Corroborated by several eminent physicians."

"Landor, I beg you."

"Well, my heart does go out to your poor mother. All alone in the world. First husband dead, second one gone, and two children to feed. No, I'm sorry, did I say 'two'? I meant *three.*" I riffled through the sheaf of papers. "Yes. Yes, that's right. A third child, name of Rosalie—*Rose,* as she's now called. Grown up into rather a *vague* girl, I'm told. Not quite . . . not quite all . . . oh, well, that's strange." I squinched my brows together. "Seems she was born in December eighteen-ten. Which was—let me think now—more than a *year* after your father left. Humm." I smiled, shook my head. "Doesn't that beat all? I've never known a baby to take a whole *year* to be born. What do you make of that, Poe?"

His hands had curled round the arm of his rocker. The air was coming in slow, deep drafts.

"Oh, well," I said, lightly. "We must be modern about all this. What more can you expect of an *actress*? You know the old joke, Poe. The difference between an actress and a whore? The whore's job is done in just five minutes."

And now he sprang from his chair. Hands like claws, eyes like clouds, he came at me.

"Sit down," I said. "Sit down, *poet*."

He stopped. Dropped his hands to his side. Took a few steps back and resumed his place in the rocker.

Safe now, I turned and walked to the window, drew aside the curtains, and looked straight into the night: clear and even and purple-black, punched with stars. The moon hung flat and white and whole in the hollow of the eastern hills, and its light came at me in slow waves, first hot, then cold.

"There was only one matter," I said, "that my little inquiry couldn't resolve: are you a murderer, Poe?"

My own fingers, I was surprised to see, were trembling. The fire, maybe, I'd let the fire die down.

"You're certainly many things," I said, "but *that*? I couldn't credit it. No matter what Captain Hitchcock said." I turned round and stared at his ashen face. "But then I thought about that conversation you had with Lea at Fort Putnam. Shall I quote you? I know the words by heart, I think."

"You may do what you like," he answered, dully.

I licked my lips. Cleared my throat. "Words of Cadet Fourth Classman Edgar A. Poe, as addressed to Miss Lea Marquis: *The dead haunt us because we love them too little. We forget them, you see; we don't mean to, but we do. . . . And so they clamor for us. They wish to be recalled to our hearts. So as not to be murdered twice over.*" I looked down at him. "Your very words, Poe."

"What of it?" he snarled.

"Why, that's as close to a confession as a fellow can come. The only thing left to find was your victim. And even that took but a few moments." I began circling his chair now. Just as I used to do in my New York days, when I was interviewing a suspect: cinching him round. "It's your mother, isn't it?" I leaned over his shoulder. Whispered in his ear. "Your mother, Poe. Every time you forget her—every time you throw yourself into the arms of *another* woman—why, it's like killing her all over again. Matricide, yes. One of the gravest crimes in all creation."

And now I was up again and walking. Completing the last hoop of the circle.

"Well," I said, facing him head on, "you needn't worry, Poe. Forgetting someone isn't a hanging offense. Which puts you in the clear, my friend. It turns out you're not a murderer after all. You're just another little boy who can't stop loving his mama."

Again he sprang up . . . and again he faltered. Why, I couldn't tell you. Was it the difference in our sizes? (I could have laid him flat, I suppose, if I'd had a mind to.) More likely it was the difference in our power, which is another thing altogether. There comes a time, I think, in every man's life when he is forced to see his utter helplessness. He spends his last penny on a drink, or the woman he loves sweeps her plate clean of him, or he learns that the man he has trusted with everything wishes him only evil. And in that moment, he is *bare*.

That's how Poe stood now in the middle of that room, as though every last strip of skin had been peeled away. His bones wobbled inside him.

"I assume you are finished," he said, finally.

"For now. Yes."

"Then I will bid you good night."

Dignity, yes, that would be his last redoubt. He would hold his head high as he made his way to that door for the last time. He would carry this pose all the way into the hall and beyond.

Or he would try to, at any rate. Something, though, would make him turn back one last time. Something would make him speak, in a scalded voice.

"You will one day *feel* what you have done to me."

Narrative of Gus Landor

34

December 12th

I was still awake when the morning drumbeat came. Awake, but with a curious feeling of shuffled senses. It seemed to me, sitting up in my bed, that the cinder of dawn outside my window had a *smell*, like boot blacking, and that the coverlet tasted of mushrooms, and that the very air around me had the substance of clay. I was, in short, somewhere between clarity and exhaustion, and after a time, the exhaustion held sway. I fell asleep still sitting up, and woke a little after noon.

Dressed in a hurry and stumbled over to the mess hall and stood for a moment watching the cadet-animals devouring their dinner, so lost in my several thoughts that I didn't notice Cesar the steward approaching. He greeted me like an old friend and asked if I wouldn't rather eat with the officers in the ordinary upstairs, yes, sir, the ordinary was a much better place for a gentleman like me. . . .

"And I'd be most obliged," I told him, smiling. "But I was looking for Mr. Poe, would you know what happened to him?"

Oh, Mr. Poe had told the mess-hall captain he was feeling poorly and might he be excused to report to the hospital. That was some half an hour ago.

Report to the hospital? Well, I thought, he'd used that ploy before. He hadn't prepared for his sectional, maybe. Or else he was haunting Lea's doorstep, begging for an audience.

Or . . .

Yes, it was an idea that might have been lifted from one of Mrs. Poe's melodramas. But in my defense, I had very little experience in breaking other people's hearts, and it threw me out of whack, I think—the idea that Poe might take the Romantic way out. And so I hurriedly thanked Cesar and pressed a coin into his palm and heard him say as I was turning:

"You don't look good, Mr. Landor."

I didn't stay to argue. I was already hurrying toward South Barracks. Bounding up the stairs to the second floor, taking ten long strides down the hallway. . . .

There, just outside Poe's door, stood a man I'd never seen before. An older man, three inches shy of six feet, lean and bristly with a long proud hawk nose and a pair of shaggy brows that looked to belong to someone much older. His arms were crossed like swords, and he was . . . *lounging*, I was going to say, but though he inclined against the wall, his body didn't bend an inch, any more than a ladder would bend if you leaned it in a corner.

Seeing me, he tipped himself perpendicular. Inclined his head and said:

"I wonder if you could tell me where I could find a Mr. Poe."

A high flinty voice, with the ghost of a Scottish burr rising up through every *r*. I stared at him, I'm afraid. He didn't belong here! No uniform, no notion of the Academy's schedule. And a testiness about the place, as though it were a maze thrown in his path by an evil djinn.

"Do you know," I answered at last, "I was wondering the same thing."

And what sort of business would you have with Mr. Poe? That was the question that beetled from his pale high-boned face. It was the question, anyway, that I fell over myself answering, like a plebe before the Board of Examiners.

"He's been . . . I suppose you'd call it *assisting* the Academy in some—some inquiries I'm undertaking. Or he *was* assisting. . . ."

"Are you an officer, sir?"

"No! No, I'm just . . . I'm a fellow they keep around. For the time being." Stuck for words, I extended a hand. "Gus Landor," I said.

"How do you do? I'm John Allan."

I don't know how to describe it, Reader, except to say it was a bit like watching a fairy-tale figure crawl from the page. I knew him only through the medium of Poe, you see, and like all the figures in Poe's past, he had a fantastical quality in the telling, and I would have no more expected to meet him than get knocked down in the street by a centaur.

"Mr. Allan," I said, in a half whisper. "Mr. Allan of Richmond."

The hawk eyes flashed. The thatches of brow merged. "I see he has mentioned me, then."

"Only in terms of highest . . . respect and honor. . . ."

He put out his hand then. Turned slightly away and said, with stiff accents, "You're kind to say so, I'm sure. I know full well how the boy speaks of me to other people."

Oddly enough, I warmed to him then. A little. It can't always be nice, I thought, being a fairy-tale figure. And so I opened the door to Poe's quarters and suggested we both wait inside. I took his coat for him and draped it on the mantel. I asked him if he had just come up from New York.

He nodded with some pride. "I managed to catch one of the last steamers of the season. Had to argue down the fare, naturally. If all goes well, I intend to catch the next one back. It was suggested I stay at the hotel, but I see no point in having my pocket picked by some military provisioner when the government does a good enough job already."

There was not a trace of whining in these words, I should say that. Everything he said reeked of principle, fixed in tablets. I suppose, more than anyone else, he reminded me of Thayer, with this difference: Thayer had made himself hard for an idea, not a sum.

"Well, now," I said. "I understand you've recently remarried."

"That is so."

He accepted my congratulations, and then we were quiet, and I was already composing words of farewell when I saw a tremor pass over Allan's face. Found him gauging my *own* face.

"See here," he said. "Mr. Landor, is it?"

"Yes."

"You wouldn't mind a bit of friendly advice?"

"Not at all."

"I believe you mentioned the Academy has enlisted Edgar in some— some *inquiries*, I think you said."

"In a manner of speaking."

"I cannot emphasize too strongly that this boy is *not* to be entrusted with high responsibilities."

"Oh." I stopped. I blinked. "Well, I must say, Mr. Allan, I've found him to be most sincere and—obliging . . ."

I couldn't finish because he was smiling at me now, for the first time, and because this smile could have lanced a boil.

"You must not know him well then, Mr. Landor. I regret to tell you he is one of the least sincere, least truthful fellows I have ever met. Indeed, I make a point of refusing to believe a single thing he says."

I would have guessed that to be his last word on the subject—it had been close enough to my *own* last word. What I didn't count on was the relish with which Allan would warm to this particular theme.

"Do you know," he said, jabbing the air, "before that boy came to the Academy, I gave him a hundred dollars—a hundred dollars!—to pay his Army substitute. I was told it was the only way the Army would release him to come here. Well, two months later, I received the most vile and threatening letter from this same substitute, a Sergeant Bully Graves."

I wish you could have heard him pronounce that name, Reader! As though someone had dragged offal into his parlor.

"This Sergeant Bully Graves informed me that he had never received his payment. He informed me that when pressed, Edgar had said, 'Mr. Allan would not part with the money.' *Mr. Allan would not part with the money*," he repeated, pounding each word into his palm. "Oh, but that is not all. Our Edgar made a point of telling Sergeant Graves that I was 'not very often sober.'"

He came toward me then, as though the words had come straight from *my* mouth. Stood two feet away from me and smiled. "Do I appear sober enough to you, Mr. Landor?"

I replied that he did indeed. Unappeased, he went to have words with the window.

"My late wife was fond of him, and for her sake, I have put up with his profligacy and his snobbery—his *affectations*. Even his rank ingratitude. No longer. The bank is closing, Mr. Landor. He must stand on his own feet or give way altogether."

And in that moment, it was as if Poe and I had joined ranks in some curious way. For hadn't we both, at some time or other, tried to bend ramrod-straight fathers who could never in a million lifetimes be bent?

"Well," I said, "he's awfully *young*, isn't he? And I don't believe he has any other means of support. The Poe family, I'm told, has fallen on hard times."

"He has the United States Army, does he not? Let him finish what he started. If he lives up to the terms of his appointment—an appointment, by the way, that *I* secured for him—if he completes his four years, then his future will be assured. If not, well . . ." He turned his palms up. "It will be one more in a string of failures. And I will shed not one tear."

"But you see, Mr. Allan, your son—"

That was as far as I got. His head snapped round, and his eyes got small as pins. "What did you say?"

"Your son," I repeated, faintly.

"So he's told you that, too?" A new tone now: slow-kindling, all-suffering. "He is *not* my son, Mr. Landor, I wish to make that clear. He is no relation to me whatever. My late wife and I took pity on him and housed him just as one would a stray dog or an injured bird. Never once did I adopt him, nor did I ever give him to understand that I would. Such claims as he has on me are the same as any other Christian soul. No more, no less."

The words poured right off the wheel. He had made this speech before.

"From the time he reached his majority," Allan continued, "he has been a continual irritant to me. Now that I have remarried and taken on the claims of genuine relations—flesh-and-blood relations—I see no point in carrying him any longer. From this day forward, he must go his own way. And that's what I mean to tell him, by God."

Of course he does, I thought. *And this is just the dress rehearsal.*

"What I was trying to say before, Mr. Allan, is that your—your *Edgar* has been under some strain in recent days. I don't know if this would be the best time to—"

"Now's as good a time as any," he said, flatly. "The boy's been molly-coddled long enough. If he wishes to be a man, then let him give up these childish dependencies."

Well, it happens sometimes, Reader. Someone is speaking, and you hear suddenly an overtone, which is not their voice at all but the echo of some-one else's, and you know then that these same words were spoken many years earlier, wielded like a mace against the very man who's wielding them now, and you understand these words are the truest legacy any family can have, and the worst. You know *all* of this, and still you hate these words, and you hate the man who's saying them.

And realizing that was the same as being free. I found I no longer had any need to appease this merchant, this Scotsman, this Christian. I no longer had any need to pretend he was taller. I could stand squarely on my feet and peer straight into his goat eyes and say:

"So, Mr. Allan! You will slap this young man down and wash your hands of him and the past twenty years in, oh, five minutes—*four*, if he doesn't talk back—and then be on the next steamer back. Oh, you *are* a frugal man."

His head tilted an inch to the side.

"See here, Mr. Landor, I don't like your tone."

"And I don't like your eyes."

It surprised us both, I think. That I should grab him by his marseille waistcoat and throw all my weight against him until he was flat against the wall. I could hear the window frame shudder behind me. I could feel the good hard flesh beneath his coat. I could smell my breath on his face.

"You bastard," I said. "He's worth a hundred of you."

And when was the last time, I wonder, that anyone had dared to lay a hand on Jock Allan? Not for a generation, probably. Which may explain why he put up so little fight.

But then I had not much fight left in me, either. I freed his waistcoat and took a step back and said, "If it's any consolation, Mr. Allan, he's worth a *thousand* of me."

By the time I left South Barracks, my eyes were stinging, and it was a relief, honestly, to feel the cold north wind sweep in and set my whole face aflame. I walked quickly, and I didn't look back until I had reached the offi-cers' quarters. And it was then I saw, bearing in a slow, straight line toward his barracks, the tiny figure in torn cloak and leather shako. Head tucked into the wind. Moving toward his latest doom.

TAKE COURAGE

That was the only thing I could think to tell him in the end. I scrawled it on the back of a trade bill and left it the only place I could be sure he'd find it: under our secret rock in Kosciuzko's Garden.

And having accomplished that, I lingered there, I don't know why. Maybe it was just having the place to myself. I sat on that stone bench, gazing out across the Hudson, listening to the bubbling of the spring in its basin—and asking myself what, *what* did I mean by leaving such a message? Why should Poe hearken to *anything* I said? And if I was just trying to clear my conscience, how could I expect a pair of words to perform such heavy labor?

Questions, one upon another, and pricking through the questions, shards of the scene that lay at my feet: a blush of feldspath, a marbling of water, an ear-shaped peak disappearing into a beard-shadow.

"Good morning."

Lea Marquis stood before me. Flushed with walking. Her cape hanging negligently on her, as though someone had hurled it at her as she passed. Nothing on her head but a bonnet of the palest rose, toppled to one side.

My surprise kept me from locating my manners straight off, but I was on my feet before too long, motioning toward the bench.

"Please," I said. "Please sit down."

She took care to leave a yard of space between us and did nothing more at first than rub her slippers against each other.

"Not so very cold today," I said. "Not so cold as yesterday, I think."

I remembered then—too late—how it had gone for poor Poe when he tried to talk about the weather. I braced myself for the rebuke . . . but none came.

"Well," I said after a while, "I'm glad for the company. It doesn't feel right after all, keeping such a sweet spot to myself."

She nodded, briefly, as though to reassure me that she was, in fact, hearing me. Then, frowning into her lap, she said:

"I'm sorry Edgar and I coaxed you into our little *spectacle* at Uncle Gouv's. We were having a bit of sport, and we weren't . . . we didn't properly consider the consequences. For *other* people, I mean."

"There were none on my side, I assure you, Miss Marquis. And even Mr. Poe, I'm told, escaped all—"

"Yes, I know."

"So there's . . . not really . . . but I do thank you. . . ."

"Of course," she said.

And having fulfilled that duty, she looked up once more, and her eyes now actively sought mine, and in those pale irises a peculiar luster had taken hold. It seemed to quicken her whole frame, so that I *felt* her in a way I never had before.

"Mr. Landor, I see no point in coyness or dissembling. I followed you here with a mission in mind."

"Then by all means, carry it out."

She paused to work her mouth around it. "I know . . ." Another pause. "I know that my brother has been, for some time now, the object of your inquiries. I know you suspect him of doing terrible things. I know you would place him in arrest, if you had proof."

"Miss Marquis," I said, blushing like a boy. "You must understand, I—I can't discuss—"

"Then allow *me* to speak plainly enough for both of us. My brother is innocent of anyone's death."

"Spoken like a true sister. I'd have expected no less of you."

"It is the truth."

"Then it will out."

"No," she answered. "I'm not certain that it will."

Abruptly, she stood. Advanced toward the river and stared down the escarpment.

"Mr. Landor," she said, her back still turned to me. "What will it take to call you off?"

"Why, Miss Marquis, I'm surprised at you. Surely we're not well enough acquainted to be bribing each other."

She wheeled round, took a step toward the bench.

"Would you like that?" she cried. "To be better acquainted?"

What a sight she was then, Reader! Cruel in the lips, hard in the eye. A positively indecent flare to her nostrils. All icicles, with a volcano underneath. In every way, magnificent.

"Actually," I said, "I'd prefer to leave you to this view."

And just like that, all the fire, all the ice were consumed. She stood there with her arms hanging limp.

"Ah," she said, in a chastened tone. "I was right, then. You weren't after that." She laughed. "I'm afraid you will have to go down as one more of Mother's failed intrigues. Very well, then, what if I promise you will never have to marry me? Or set eyes on me again?"

"No man in his right mind would demand such a condition, Miss Marquis."

"But you are different from other men," she said. "I mean only that the chance of loving . . . again . . . is not where you find your purpose, I think."

My eyes swerved past her, to the river, where a blue barge was making its way southward in a coat of haze. A mourning dove was skipping like a stone over the water's troughs.

I thought then of Patsy. How she'd recoiled from me the last time I saw her. And how part of me had mourned and part of me . . . had rejoiced. At getting what it had always wanted.

"It's true," I confessed. "I seem to have pulled myself out of that little hunt."

"Only to take up arms in *another* hunt. You mean to chase down my brother and claim my whole family as your spoils."

"I mean to see justice done," I said, levelly.

"*Whose* justice, Mr. Landor?"

I stopped just as I was about to answer. For a change had come over her. Not all at once, no; I saw it first in her eyes, which were simmering in their sockets. I saw her cheeks go white as sugar, saw her mouth open like a bear trap.

"Well, now, that's a very full question," I said, taking care to keep my voice light. "I suggest you take it up sometime with your friend Mr. Poe, he's awfully good at that sort of thing. In the meantime, I have work to do and not much time to—"

"*You can't!*"

The words roared out of her, almost before her mouth was ready to receive them. They shattered the air and sent the fragments spinning.

"*No!*"

It was not the cry she had uttered in Gouverneur Kemble's study. No, that was her own sound, a *human* sound. *This* one came from a place I'd never been.

And I suppose it was almost a relief, Reader. To know that whatever was harrowing her had nothing to do with me.

"Miss Marquis . . ."

But she was beyond hearing me now. And all the same, you might have thought she was embarrassed by her conduct, for she began to totter *away* from me. As if she were being driven by some private sense of failure.

"Miss Marquis!" I called after her.

I can't believe how gingerly I followed her at first. I think I knew even then what her body was trying to accomplish, and still I couldn't make my limbs answer the call.

Her limbs were answering, though, even as they began to stiffen and fail. Somehow, somehow she hauled herself to the overlook . . . stood there on the brink, tottering and quivering . . . and then flung herself over the side.

"No!" I shouted.

I caught her arm just as the rest of her disappeared—and it was already too late, for the *purpose* of her body was carrying everything else before it, carrying *me*, and over we went, the two of us, in a gush of rocks and a burn of wind. And still I held on, even as I felt the earth drop away.

And then, out of nowhere, the earth reappeared. Caught us once more in its grip.

I opened my eyes. Nearly laughed to feel the gouges in my back and knees. Because it was such a small price to pay, after all! We had dropped some eight feet onto a granite outcropping, and we were—we were *saved,* weren't we? Still bound in our human chain but—*saved*.

How wrong I was. We were in even greater danger than before.

Lea hadn't landed at all, she had swung clear of the outcropping, and she was now—how slow I was to understand!—*hanging* in midair, completely suspended. And I—*I* was her sole lifeline, and a poor excuse for one, perched at the rim of that granite shelf and holding on for both of us.

And under us: nothing but air—gallons and gallons of it—and the water-sanded rocks lying hundreds of feet below, waiting to smash us to atoms.

"Lea," I gasped out. "Lea."

Wake up! Those were the words I wanted to scream. But I knew enough of her condition to know how futile that would have been. She had passed into full seizure now—her body was hard as a pulpit, *bucking* in fast brutal spasms that made it nearly impossible to keep my grip on her. Her hand had curled into a fist, her pupils had rolled up into her head, and a fine line of foam was skimming across her teeth. There was no calling her back.

And even now, I could feel her slipping away, in tiny tiny increments.

"Lea!"

I never once called for help; I called only for *her*, because I knew she was the only one, finally, who *could* help. We had chosen too remote a drop to be seen by anyone. Even the dugouts and skiffs that came feathering down the river, even they would pass us by without another thought, bent on their own errands.

Indeed, in that moment, I felt just as helpless as I had in Artemus' closet. Once again I was locked in a private contest, with nothing to call on but my own wits and mettle, and how unequal they seemed to *this*. To the prospect of a life—*two* lives—dangling by a few fingers.

More and more of her was slipping away, and more of *me* was going with her. Inch by inch, I was being dragged from that shelf, drawn closer and closer to the wet black rocks that waited so patiently below. . . .

And then at last my hand succeeded in locking round her wrist. The slippage ceased, and buoyed by the stillness, I began to canvass my surroundings, flailing in the dark, as it were, groping for a fulcrum . . . anything, *anything* to attach to . . . and nothing would come . . .

Until my fingers closed round something hard and dry and calloused.

I read it as Blind Jasper might, with my skin. It was a root. The exposed root of a tree, jutting from the rock face.

Oh, how I grasped it! Oh, how I *squeezed* . . . while with my other hand, I began to haul Lea up.

There were moments, I admit, when I thought I might be torn apart, so fierce were the forces on each side of me. I soon learned, though, that they *weren't* quite equal. The root, under the combined drag of our two bodies, was starting to bend.

Please, I entreated it. *Please hold.* But it paid me no mind, just bent further and further back, began *cracking* like a spine, and before long, my silent plea had been replaced by another, spoken out loud this time: the same words, again and again. It was days before I remembered what they were.

"You can't. You can't."

Something of a divine petition, you might say, Reader. And from me! A man who wouldn't have been caught dead in prayer. I will only say that when the root finally broke, my hand was already climbing—by intuition, by miracle—to the next outcropping of root, and that *this* root held fast, and that the next thing I knew, I was straddling the ledge, and before me lay Lea Marquis, still trembling . . . still alive.

I had the luxury then of some time before I had to contemplate the rest of the journey. It would be no skip and jump, that was clear: we still had eight feet to scale before we reached level ground, and Lea was still unconscious, though no longer shaking so violently as before.

We had one thing in our favor: a line of exposed roots that made a zigzagging trail to the top. How to get us *both* up, that was the trick. After some trial and error, I found that if I kept my back to the cliff face and locked my legs round Lea's waist, I could turn us into a single unit and drag us *both* up the side without throwing her against the rocks.

Oh, but Christ, it was hard work! Slow, sweaty, *mulish*. More than once, I had to claim a spot of rest by bracing myself against one of the roots.

Too old, I recall thinking at one point. *You're too damned old for this.*

It must have taken us a good fifteen minutes to climb half as many feet. But I was measuring the journey in inches, and every inch we seized somehow made it possible to seize another inch: no matter how much the rock face was slashing my flesh, no matter how my legs wobbled under the burden of Lea's body, I could still go one more inch, couldn't I?

And so the inches added up, and at last we reached the plateau, where we collapsed into a jumble of arms and legs. After pausing to catch my breath, I picked her up and carried her to the stone bench. Stood over her for several minutes—panting—aching and bleeding in every corner. Then gathered her into my arms. And as I felt her twitches subside and her arms unlock and her body slowly return to her, the terror in me gave way to a kind of tenderness.

For I understood her better now. I understood, at least, a little of the sadness that clung to her even in her gayest moments. And this, too, I understood: how little I knew of her. Or would ever know.

When next I looked down, her pupils had scrolled back into place, and her eyelids had begun to blink of their own accord. But still her body trembled against mine, and it seemed to me this must be the worst time for her, coming out of the darkness—not into light but into some nether region, where she could be drawn back in either direction.

"You should . . . ," she managed to say.

"Should what?"

A full minute passed before she was able to complete her sentence.

"You should have let me go."

And, yes, it was another minute before I could say anything in reply. The words kept wedging in my throat.

"What would that have solved?" I at last managed to ask her.

I ran my fingers back and forth along her brow, and her features began to shimmer into life. The light came back to her eyes, and she gazed at me with a look of bottomless pity.

"Never fear," she whispered. "He said it will all turn out. Everything will."

Who said? That should have been the next question out of my mouth, but no, I was too struck by her words to think of anything else.

After some minutes, she was able to raise her head, and after another minute, she could sit up. She passed a hand over her brow and said, faintly:

"I wonder if I might trouble you for some water."

My first thought was to go to the spring. But just as I was about to dip my hat in, I heard her voice, a little stronger, coming after me.

"And a morsel of food, if it's not too much trouble."

"I'll be back directly," I said.

Up the steps I climbed, two at a time. Glad to be on my feet again—moving, *doing*—and wondering where I might be able to roust up food at that hour of day. I was almost at the hotel when I reached in my pocket and came up with a small, hard square of pemmican. Brown and hard and wizened as a beggar, but better than nothing, I thought, as I reversed course and headed back down the steps to the garden.

She was gone.

Quite thoroughly gone: I looked for her behind shrubs and trees, I followed the gravel walk past Battery Knox, past the Lantern Battery, all the way to the Chain Battery; I even, yes, peered down the escarpment to see if she had made a second attempt. She wasn't to be found. My only remaining company was her voice, calling to me wherever I turned.

It will all turn out.

The very thing my daughter had said.

Professor Pawpaw doesn't care for surprises—mainly, I think, because it leaves him no time to prepare his own. And without surprises, he is . . . well, all I'll say is I nearly failed to recognize the man who opened his door. After searching in vain for Lea, I'd climbed on Horse and traveled straight to the professor's house, arriving a little before dusk. The jasmine and honeysuckle had died away. Gone were the frog bones; gone were the birdcages hanging from the pear tree; gone was the dead rattler over the doorway.

And gone, too, was Pawpaw. Or so I thought when I saw the man standing in the doorway, with his drab pantaloons and vaguely striped stockings. Nothing round his neck but a bare ivory crucifix.

So this is how he looks, I thought, *when no one's around. Like a retired sexton.*

"Landor," he growled. "I'm not disposed."

We weren't, I knew, such good friends that he would let me in anytime I wished. So it was a measure, I suppose, of the desperation that rose from me like stink that he did, in the end, yield. Took a step back from the door and, by his very stillness, ushered me inside.

"If you'd come yesterday, Landor, I could have offered you some bullock's heart . . . ."

"Thank you, Professor. I won't keep you long."

"Well, then, come to it."

And having traveled all this way, I found myself wondering, not for the first time, if I was wasting time and breath over something of no more substance than a whim.

"Professor," I said. "Last time I was here, you mentioned a witch hunter who went over to the other side. A fellow who was burned at the stake and . . . something about casting his book into the flames. . . ."

"Of course," he answered, waving a vexed hand. "Le Clerc. Henri le Clerc."

"He was a priest, I believe you said?"

"Indeed."

"Well, now, I was wondering if you had a picture of him somewhere. An engraving, maybe."

He eyed me closely. "That's all you want? A picture?"

"For now, yes."

He took me then to his library. Went right to the shelf he wanted and, with no boost from me, scaled the thing like a squirrel. Came back down with a half-crumbling duodecimo.

"Here," he said, holding the book open. "Here's your devil worshipper."

I looked down at a man in a priest's collar and a richly pleated dark robe. Lightly chiseled bones, clement eyes, a full and level mouth: agreeable manly open features—a face made for taking confessions.

Pawpaw, old fox, saw the light go on in my eyes.

"You've seen him before," he declared.

"In another rendering, yes."

We looked at each other then. Not a word passed between us, but after a minute, he reached round the back of his neck and unsnapped the chain with the ivory crucifix. Dropped it into my hand and closed my fingers round it.

"As a rule, Landor, I'm not one for superstitions. But once a month or so, I take them like sweets."

I smiled. Pressed the crucifix back into his palm.

"I'm already beyond the pale, Professor. I do thank you, though."

The envelope was propped against my hotel-room door, waiting for me when I got back that night. Not a moment's doubt as to who had written it, not with that flourish of cursive, not with the very angle of the thing (a crisp forty-five degrees) announcing its author as clearly as any signature.

For a moment, I stood over it, wondering if I could safely ignore it. And decided, with some sadness, I couldn't.

Landor:

I owe you no earthly obligation, but as you once—or so I believed!—took a wholesome interest in my affairs, I supposed that you might be curious to learn of the new course upon which I have resolved. Not five minutes ago, Lea and I plighted our troth. In short order, I shall resign my Academy commission and take my wife—as soon she shall be—far, far from this wilderness.

I desire from you neither congratulation nor commiseration. I desire <u>nothin</u> from you. I wish you only surcease from the hatred and recrimination that have so disfigured your soul. Farewell, Landor. I go to my beloved.

Yrs,

E.A.P.

So! I thought. *Lea has wasted no time.*

And indeed, it was the very suddenness of the news that began to unnerve me. Why *was* it happening so quickly? So soon after Lea's brush with death? Poe, of course, would be ready to act at the first sign from his beloved, but what would Lea gain from eloping? Why would she abandon her brother and family in the hour of their greatest need?

Unless this had nothing to do with matrimony. Unless some greater urgency was screwing everything to a higher pitch.

And then my eyes came to rest on those words—*Farewell, Landor*—and they jumped at me like grapeshot and sent me spinning down the hallway, leaping down the stairs.

Poe was in danger. I *knew* that as I've never known anything. And to save him, I'd have to find the one man who could—or, under the right pressure, *would*—answer my questions.

It was a half hour before midnight by the time I reached the Marquis house. I pounded on the door like a drunken husband back from the tavern, and when Eugénie, bleary-eyed in her nightgown, planted herself in the doorway and opened her mouth to chide me, something in my face made the words lock in her throat. She invited me in without a sound and, when I asked where her master was, pointed with vague alarm to the library.

A single taper was burning. Dr. Marquis was seated in a large velvet armchair, a monograph spread open on his lap. His eyes were shut, and he was lightly snoring, but his arm remained just where he had left it: fully extended, with the fingers curled round a glass of brandy, the brandy itself level as a pond. (Poe used to fall asleep the same way.)

I didn't have to say a word. He shook his eyes open and set down his glass and winced into the dark.

"Mr. Landor! This is a pleasant surprise." He started to rise. "Do you know, I've been reading the most fascinating treatise on the puerperal fever. I was thinking *you*, in particular, might appreciate the—the discussion of sovereign specifics . . . oh, but where is it?" He studied the chair he had just left, whirled round in a heavy daze, then found the treatise, still in his lap. "Ah, here we are!"

He looked up expectantly, but I was already moving to the looking-glass. Examining my whiskers, brushing lint from my chin . . . making sure I was *ready*.

"Where's the rest of your family, Doctor?"

"Oh, the hour is too advanced for the ladies, I'm afraid. They've retired."

"Ah, yes. And your son?"

He blinked at me. "Why, he's in barracks, of course."

"Of course."

I crossed the room in slow segments, brushing him softly each time I passed (for the room was exceedingly narrow) and feeling his eyes tracking me every step of the way.

"Can I offer you anything, Mr. Landor? Brandy?"

"No."

"Some whiskey, perhaps. I know you like your—"

"No, thank you," I said, stopping just a couple of feet away and grinning at his face in the candlelight. "You know, Doctor, I'm a little put out with you."

"Oh?"

"You never told me what an illustrious ancestor you had."

From the crater of his mouth a half grin came flickering up. "Why, I don't think . . . you know, I'm not sure who you—"

"Father Henri le Clerc," I said.

He dropped like a winged partridge, straight into his chair.

"Oh, I grant you, Doctor, it's not a name that would stir up a lot of notice now. But in his day, I'm told, he was the finest of witch hunters. Until he became one of the hunted. May I borrow your light?"

He made no answer. I took the taper and carried it toward the bookcases, toward the niche that housed the antique oil portrait. The portrait to which I'd paid no more than passing notice the first time I saw it. A near-perfect likeness of the engraving in Pawpaw's book.

"This is le Clerc, is it not, Doctor? Oh, he's a fine-looking gentleman, your ancestor. I would have wanted him on my side, too."

I brought the taper lower and watched as the cameo of the young Mrs. Marquis flared into view. Setting the cameo to one side, I rested my hand on the coarsely matted surface that lay beneath, the musty gray cover I had once mistaken for a pillow.

"And this is his book, is it not? I'm ashamed to say I didn't even know it *was* a book. Has such an unusual texture, doesn't it? Wolf skin, if I recall correctly."

After a moment's hesitation, I pried my fingers underneath and lifted. What a weight it had! As though every page had been lined with lead and embossed with gold.

"*Discours du Diable*," I said, opening it to the front leaf. "You know, Doctor, there are people in this world who'd pay a considerable sum for this volume. You could be a rich man before another sun had set."

Closing the cover, I returned it with great care to its place on the shelf and set the portrait of Mrs. Marquis back on top.

"Your family has been quite a puzzle to me, Doctor, I don't mind saying. I could never get a fix on who was—who was in *command*, I suppose, who was setting the cadence. At one time or other, I suspected each of you. It never occurred to me it might be someone else altogether. Someone who wasn't even alive."

I stood in front of him.

"Your daughter suffers from the falling sickness," I said. "No, please don't deny it, I've seen it for myself. In the course of her spells, she imagines herself to be in contact with someone. Someone who tells her things, sends her instructions, maybe." I pointed to the painting on the wall. "It's *him,* isn't it?"

In the end, Dr. Marquis was a poor dissembler. Not from a lack of skill but from a lack of bent. Some people, I think, can build up secrets like layers of shale—pile them higher and higher, I mean, and let nothing crack. Others need only the lightest tap to bring their whole edifice down. And for these folks, you don't even need a face like Father le Clerc's. You just need to be on hand when it happens.

So it was with Dr. Marquis. He was ready to talk, and talk he did, as the taper sputtered down, as the night wore into morning. And whenever the flow of words abated, I would pour him another brandy, and he would look at me as if I were an angel of mercy, and the words would once again flow.

He told me the story of a beautiful girl-child, marked for all the brilliant things a girl can be marked for: marriage, status, children. Marked, in the same stroke, by illness. *Ghastly* illness, seizing her when no one was looking, stopping her brain and shaking her like a gourd.

Her father tried every medical regimen he could think of—nothing worked. He even brought in faith healers, but they, too, failed to stop the terror. And gradually, this terror took over the whole family and changed every one of them. So that they abandoned the comforts of New York in favor of the isolation of West Point. They swore off friendships and kept largely to themselves. The father gave up his ambitions, the mother grew bitter and eccentric, and the children, left to their own devices, developed bonds of unnatural closeness. They were all, in their own way, in thrall to this disease.

"For God's sake," I said, "why didn't you tell anyone? Thayer would have understood."

"We didn't dare. We didn't want to be shunned. You have to understand, Mr. Landor, it was a terrible time for us. When Lea turned twelve, her spells got much worse. On more than one occasion, we despaired of her life. And then one day, it was—it was an afternoon in July, she came to herself, and she said . . ."

He stopped.

"She said what?"

"She said she'd *met* someone. A gentleman."

"And this was Father le Clerc?"

"Yes."

"Her great-great-great-grandfather, or whoever he was."

"Yes."

"And she *spoke* with him?"

"Yes."

"In French?" I asked, rolling my eyes.

"She was fluent, yes."

There was a touch of defiance in his tone, unusual for him.

"Tell me, Doctor. How did she know who this mystery man was? Did he bother with introductions?"

"She'd seen his picture. I kept it in the attic in those days, but she and Artemus, they'd stumbled across it somehow."

"In the attic? Please don't tell me you were ashamed of your forebear."

"No. No." His hands fluttered. "It's not like that. Père le Clerc wasn't . . . he was never the man he was reputed to be. He wasn't evil at all, he was a *healer*."

"Misunderstood."

"Precisely, yes."

"And so this poor misunderstood healer, this creature of your daughter's imagination, begins to instruct her. She, in turn, instructs Artemus. And at some point your own wife, Doctor, becomes a student, too."

It was just a guess, honestly. There was no piece of paper pointing to Mrs. Marquis, only the proof of my own senses—the way sound carried in this closely built house—nothing could be done in private for very long. A hunch, yes, but from the way the doctor's face fell, the way it kept falling, I could see I'd hit the mark.

"Well, it must have made for an interesting curriculum, Doctor. The main subject, as far as I can see, was sacrifice. *Animal* sacrifice—until they reached the point where animals would no longer do."

His head was moving from side to side like a pendulum.

"What would your precious Galen have said, Doctor? What would Hippocrates have said about sacrificing young *men*?"

"No," he said. "No. They swore to me Mr. Fry was already dead. They swore they would never take a human life. Never."

"And you believed them, of course. But then, you also believed a man could rise from the dead and chat up your daughter."

"What choice did I—"

"*What choice?*" I shouted, as my fist found the back of his chair. "You of all people! A physician, a man of science. How could you place your faith in such madness?"

"Because I . . ."

His hands closed over his face. A high girlish moan came trailing through.

"I can't hear you, Doctor," I said.

He raised his head and cried in his own voice:

"Because I couldn't save her myself!"

He smeared the damp from his eyes. Coughed up one final sob and held out his hands in a mute entreaty.

"My own art was useless, Mr. Landor. How could I object to her seeking a cure elsewhere?"

"A cure?"

"That's what he promised her. If she did what he asked her. And she did, and she got *better*, Mr. Landor. No one can deny it. The spells didn't come nearly as often, and when they did, they weren't nearly as severe. She got better!"

I leaned against the bookcase. Tired, suddenly. Tired beyond all measure.

"So if her health was on the mend," I said, "what did she want with a human heart?"

"Oh, she wanted none of it. But he told her it was the only way she could be free. Once and for all."

"Free from what?"

"Her curse. Her gift. She was through with it, don't you see? She wanted to be whole again, she wanted to live as other women do. She wanted to *love*."

"And all she had to do was offer up . . . somebody's *organs?*"

"I don't know! I told Lea and Artemus they weren't to tell me anything of what they are doing. It was the only way I could—I could keep silent."

He wrapped his arms round himself and let his head droop. Oh, it's a hard thing, sometimes, witnessing human weakness. Which is, in my experience, what most venality comes down to. Weakness. Hiding itself as strength.

"Well, Doctor, the problem for you is your children keep roping other people into their little devils' academy."

"They swore they weren't responsible for—"

"I'm not talking about Fry," I said. "I'm not talking about Ballinger or Stoddard. I'm talking about someone who's still with us. Or maybe you aren't aware your daughter is engaged to be married to Mr. Poe?"

"Mr. *Poe*?" he cried.

His astonishment was too piecemeal to be feigned. He couldn't make sense of it, and so he tried to absorb it in stages, and each new stage worked on him like a hiccough, shaking his whole system.

"But Mr. Poe was here," he sputtered. "This evening. No one said a word about an engagement."

"Poe was here?"

"Yes! We had a nice chat, and then he and Artemus went to the parlor to have a little nip of something. Oh, I know it's against the rules," he said, flashing his mighty teeth, "but a drab now and then never hurt anyone, I believe."

"Artemus was here, too?" I asked.

"Yes, it was quite a—quite a party. . . ."

"And when did Poe leave?"

"Well, I don't know. He couldn't have stayed long, he had to get back to his quarters, just as Artemus did."

I often wonder if things would have turned out differently if I'd been on my game from the start. If, say, I'd thought to ask about that family portrait the first time I saw it. Or if I'd understood the importance of Lea Marquis' condition when it was first described to me.

Or if I'd recognized right off what I saw when I entered the Marquis house that night.

No, it took me more than half an hour to realize what it was, and as soon as I did, I leaned into Dr. Marquis and hissed the words right into his face—the reproach that should have been mine alone.

"Tell me, Doctor. If Poe left your house, why is his cloak still in your front hall?"

It was the only article still left on the coat rack. A bundle of black wool, standard government issue, except for the . . .

"Except for the tear," I said, holding the cloak. "Do you see, Doctor? Nearly the full length of the shoulder. Probably came from sneaking through the woodyard so many times."

The doctor stared back at me. His lips bubbled and went slack.

"If there's one thing I've learned, Doctor, it's that cadets never go any-where without their cloaks. Nothing worse, is there, than turning out for reveille on a winter morning without some padding?"

I set the cloak back on the rack. Gave it a couple of brushes. And said, as casually as I could, "So if Mr. Poe didn't leave, where did he go?"

Something flashed in his eye. The tiniest spark.

"What is it, Doctor?"

"They were . . ." He turned round now, trying to get his bearings. "They were taking out a trunk."

"A trunk?"

"Old clothes, they said. They were throwing out old clothes."

"*Who* was?"

"Artemus. And Lea was helping. And they had their hands full, so I opened the door for them. And they . . ." He opened the door. Took a step onto the landing and peered into the darkness, as if he expected to find them still there. "I don't . . ."

He turned back to me, and as his eyes met mine, his face went white, and his hands flew to his ears. It was the very same position I'd seen him assume in Kosciusko's Garden that day with his wife. The position of a man who wants to shut everything out.

I grabbed his hands. I pulled them down to his sides and locked them in place.

"Where have they taken him?" I asked.

He fought me. Fought as though *he* were the stronger one.

"It can't be far," I said, trying to keep my voice steady. "You can't carry a trunk too far. It must be somewhere within walking distance."

"I don't—"

"*Where?*"

I meant to scream it, right into his naked ear, but something snagged my voice at the last moment, strangled it down to a whisper. And yet it might as well have been a scream, for his face blew back under the force of it. He closed his eyes, and the words dribbled from his lips.

"The icehouse."

Narrative of Gus Landor

37

December 13th

A saber wind was driving down from the west as Dr. Marquis and I went hurtling down the Plain. The trees were whistling, and a screech owl was flying, near-somersaulting, over our heads, and a cedar bird was chattering like a mad monk . . . and Dr. Marquis was chattering, too, even as he ran.

"I don't—don't think we need . . . bring in anyone *else*, do you? Family business and all that. I'm sure I can—*talk* to them, Mr. Landor . . . once that's done, no one's harmed . . ."

Well, I suffered him to go on. I knew his biggest fear was that I would call in Hitchcock and a full party of reinforcements, and since I had my own reasons for settling the matter in private, I held my peace. That is, until two young cadets came striding toward us in long bounds.

"Who comes there?" they cried in near unison.

One of Hitchcock's newly ordered double postings. Seething with belts and cartridge boxes and brass and steel.

I felt the doctor's hand on my arm like a prayer.

"It's Mr. Landor," I said, trying to sound as calm as I could between pants. "And Dr. Marquis. Out for some late-night exercise."

"Advance and give the countersign," they said.

I was well enough known at the guard posts by now that on a normal evening, this request would have been a mere formality. Such were the changed times that the older sentinel, far from relaxing, thrust out his chin and repeated the order in a crackling man-boy voice.

"Advance and give the countersign!"

I took a step forward. "Ticonderoga," I said.

He held his stance for some time, and it was only when he heard his companion clear his throat that he pulled his chin back.

"Carry on," he said gruffly.

"Excellent work, gentlemen!" Dr. Marquis called back as we dashed away. "I feel safer, I'm sure, seeing you on the job."

The only other person we saw abroad that night was Cesar, the mess steward, who appeared, improbably enough, on the brow of the hill and waved at us like a boy on an outing. We were too busy running to return his greeting. Two minutes more, and we were standing before the icehouse, staring up at that homely little barn with its stone walls and thatched roof, and I had a sudden memory of Poe atop those very heights, peering down at me as I wedged little rocks in the turf. No way for us to know, then, what we were looking for—Leroy Fry's heart—lay just below us.

"Where are they?" I asked now.

No more than a whisper, but Dr. Marquis shrank back a step.

"You know, I'm not entirely sure," he whispered back.

"Not *sure*?"

"I've never *been* there. They found it many years ago while they were playing. It's some kind of crypt or—or catacomb or something."

"But where *is* it?" I asked in a louder voice.

He shrugged. "Inside, I think."

"Doctor, that icehouse is no more than fifteen feet on each side. Are you suggesting it contains a *crypt*?"

A feeble smile. "I'm sorry, that's—that's all I know."

We had at least brought lanterns, and in my pocket was a box of phosphorous matches. All the same, after opening the sheepskin-covered door, we paused there on the threshold—at the first breath of that cold-fuming darkness—and might have held off longer had there not lain before us the example of Artemus and Lea, who had come here as mere children and found a way to go inside. Couldn't we do the same?

We almost came to grief, though, at the very start. Neither of us was ready for the four-foot drop, and as we recovered our footing and raised our lanterns once more, we were startled to see nothing more than . . . ourselves.

We were standing before a shining tower of ice—hacked last winter from the nearby pond and laid in, block by block, for the long year ahead. And now it stood before us, a warped mirror in which our images eeled and bubbled and our lanterns dimmed into old suns.

It was only ice, of course. The ice that would prevent Mr. Cozzens' butter from running, and grace Sylvanus Thayer's dessert table the next time the Board of Visitors came calling . . . and, yes, keep the occasional body a little fresher until it could be committed to the earth. Frozen water, nothing more. And yet what a fearful place this was! I couldn't have told you what made it so. Maybe it was the odor of damp sawdust everywhere. Or the faint squeaking of the straw that had been stuffed into every cavity. Or the jabbering of mice inside the double wall, or the sweat that breathed off the ice and stuck to you like new skin.

Or did it come down to this? There's something wrong about entering a place set aside for winter.

"They can't be far," murmured the doctor, shining his light on a long shelf of axes and hoisting tongs.

His breathing was heavier now—an effect, maybe, of this air, which was warmer and closer than I'd expected. My own lantern had already picked out the hard metal lines of an ice plow, flashing its shark-teeth, and I felt in that moment as if we were dangling from some giant palate, bobbing on currents of breath.

The vents in the ceiling were breathing, too: soft drafts of night-air, tickled with starlight. I took a step back, the better to admire the view . . . and felt the back of my foot give way. My other foot shifted to compensate, then gave way altogether. I was dropping now, or more properly angling away, on a long slow tangent. I grabbed for a purchase, but the nearest thing was—ice—and my hand came off like paint, and I knew then what was happening: I was literally going down the drain, and in the explosion of my lantern against the wall, I caught the look on Dr. Marquis' face: fear and, yes, concern, I do remember that, and also impotence. For even as he thrust out his hand, he knew, probably, there was nothing he could do. I was *falling*. . . .

*   *   *

The funny thing is, I never lost my footing until I reached the bottom, and even then, it was only the impact of the ground that threw me onto all fours. I raised my head. On either side were stone walls; beneath me, a stone floor. I had dropped into some kind of corridor—bare and musty, a remnant, maybe, of the years when Fort Clinton was being built—some twenty feet below the icehouse interior.

I took a step forward. One step only, and there came an answering sound: thin and crackling.

I drew a match from my pocket and struck it against the box.

I was standing on bones. The whole floor was strewn with them.

Tiny, most of them, not much bigger than Pawpaw's frog bones. The skeletons of squirrels and field mice, a possum or two, a goodly number of birds. Hard to say, really, for the bones had been strewn across the floor with no care or order. Indeed, they seemed to function only as an alarm, for you couldn't set a foot anywhere without crunching them.

And so I dropped once more onto all fours, and I began to *crawl* down that corridor, holding the match with one hand and, with the other, softly sweeping the bones from my path. More than once, a leg or a tiny skull worked its way into the crevices of my fingers. Each time, I shook it free and kept on my course, sweeping and crawling, sweeping and crawling.

When the first match died out, I struck another—raised it toward the ceiling—and saw a colony of bats hanging there like dainty black purses, throbbing with breath. Through the walls I could hear, for the first time, a weave of sounds—impossible to define—murmurs changing to squeals, a hiss broken by a wail. Not loud, by any means; not even real, perhaps; but they had, all the same, an authority, as if they'd been building up like the rock itself, piling themselves in layers.

I began to work faster. And as I swept my way down the corridor, I noticed that the flame of my match was growing less distinct. Something—something was *competing* with it.

I blew out the match and squinted into the boiling darkness. Ten feet ahead, a patch of light cut through a chasm in the wall.

The strangest light I've ever seen, Reader! Cold as cream and stranded like a net. And as I drew nearer, the net began to run into streaks, and the streaks blurred into sheets, and suddenly, I was peering into a room. A room of fire.

Fire on the walls: tapers blazing in rows of sconces. Fire on the floor: a circle of torches, and inscribed in the circle, a triangle of candles. Fire nearly to the ceiling: a charcoal brazier, so savagely stoked that the flames were the height of a parlor, and next to the brazier, a single pine tree, braced in the stone and also streaming with fire. So *much* fire, so much *light* that it was an act of will or despair to see the things that weren't light. The letters, for instance, that someone had etched at the base of the triangle:

$$\text{ƧHꓔ}$$

And the three figures, moving with such quiet purpose among the torches and candles. A tiny monk in a gray homespun robe, and a priest in a cassock and surplice . . . and an officer of the United States Army, wearing, as best I could tell, Joshua Marquis' old uniform.

I had come in the nick of time. The curtain had just gone up on the Marquis family's private theater.

And yet, what sort of theater *was* this? Where were the savage rites I'd seen pictured in Pawpaw's book? The winged demons dragging their babies? The hags on brooms and the bonneted skeletons and the dancing gargoyles? I had expected—had *wanted,* I think—to see Sin writ large. And instead I'd found . . . a costume ball.

And now one of the revelers—the monk—was turning toward me. I drew back behind the wall—but not before the torchlight had revealed, inside the monk's cowl, the bare cold rabbit-features of Mrs. Marquis.

Nothing like the brittle, grinning woman I had known before. She had become the dullest of acolytes, waiting for her next command. It came before another minute had passed. Came, fittingly enough, from the Army officer, who bent his head toward her and spoke, in a gentle voice that carried straight to my ear:

"Soon."

Artemus, of course. Dressed in his late uncle's uniform. It didn't fit him nearly as well as it did Poe, but he still carried himself with all the pride that had made him captain of Table Eight.

And if *that* was Artemus, then the third figure—the slow-treading priest with the bowed head and rolled shoulders, even now moving toward a rough-hewn rock altar—this could only be Lea.

Lea Marquis, yes. Minus the white collar I had torn away from her outside Benny Havens' tavern.

She was speaking now—or maybe she had been speaking all along—in a voice of unusual resonance. Now, I'm no good with foreign tongues, Reader, but I'm willing to bet that what came out of her mouth wasn't Latin or French or German or any language ever uttered by a human. I believe it was a tongue newly minted, on the spot, by Lea Marquis and Henri le Clerc.

Oh, I could try to write it down for you, but it would come out looking something like *skrallikonafaheerenow,* and you'd think it the purest nonsense. Which it was, but with this difference: somehow it had the effect of turning *all* language into nonsense, so that even the words you'd been speaking for nearly half a century could seem as random as dirt clods.

Well, at any rate, this language must have made some sense to Lea's companions, for after some minutes, her voice rose to a higher cadence, and the three of them turned as one and stared at a shrouded object that lay just outside the magic circle. And this is how much they held me in their spell: until now, I hadn't even noticed the thing, though it was there to be seen in the back-glow of a torch. And even in the act of studying it, I could see only what Dr. Marquis had seen: a bundle of clothes. From which a single bare hand protruded.

Artemus knelt down. Peeled away the garments, one by one ... to reveal the prostrate form of Cadet Poe.

His coatee had been stripped away, but the rest of his uniform was still in place, and he lay there like a candidate for a five-gun salute: so pale in the face, so rigid in the fingers that I had about given him up for lost. Until I saw a tremor pass through his frame like a current. And in that moment, I was glad of the cold.

And, oh, it was cold! Colder by far than the icehouse, colder than the polar caps. Cold enough, yes, to keep a heart in good condition for many weeks.

Artemus was rolling up the sleeve of Poe's shirt now ... opening a doctor's bag much like his father might have used . . . extracting first a tourniquet and then a small marble cruet . . . then a narrow-gauge glass tube . . . then a lancet.

I didn't cry out, but Lea comforted me as if she knew I was there. "Sssshhhhh," she said, to no one in particular.

Ah, yes. She was telling me *it would all turn out.* And though I didn't believe it, I didn't protest, either. Not even when Artemus' lancet found the thin blue streak in Poe's forearm. Not even when the blood began to dribble through the tube into the waiting cruet.

It was done in five seconds—Artemus had learned well—but the lancet's prick had stirred something in Poe's body. A buzzing in his legs and shoulders. He murmured, "Lea." The hazel eyes startled open and beheld the spectacle of *himself,* disappearing into a bowl.

"Strange," he muttered.

He made as if to rise but whatever strength he had was already ebbing away. It seemed to me I could even *hear* it ebbing, like rain leaking through a joist: drip . . . drip . . . drip. . . . And whenever the blood flagged, Artemus gave the tourniquet a squeeze.

He'll die, I thought.

Poe raised himself on his elbow. He said:

"Lea."

And said it again. Said it with more purpose, for somehow he had found her. Through the blaze of torches and candles, through the screen of her own vestments.

And she—she was ready for him. Knelt by his side, hair spilling over her shoulders, wearing a smile like a dream. A smile that should have been a blessing but which affected him like the most terrible of afflictions. He tried to drag himself away and, failing that, tried once more to raise himself, but his strength again failed him. And the blood . . . for Artemus had indeed cut true . . . kept up its steady trickle: drip . . . drip. . . .

Lea ran her hand through his matted hair—a gesture of wifely affection—caressed his jaw with long gentle strokes.

"It won't be much longer."

"What?" he stammered. "I don't—what?"

"Ssshhhhhh." She put a finger to his lips. "Just a few minutes more, and it will all be done, and I'll be free, Edgar."

"Free?" he echoed, faintly.

"To be your wife, what else? What better?" Laughing, then, she gave her robes a tug. "I suppose I shall have to give up the priesthood first!"

He stared at her as if she were changing shapes with each word. Then he held up his arm and pointed to the glass tubing and, in a child's voice, said:

"But *this*, Lea. What's this?"

I was so very close to answering him myself. Oh, yes, I wanted my voice to blaze through that ice-cold cloister. I wanted to shout it to the very bats. . . .

Haven't you figured it out yet, Poe? They need a virgin.

Narrative of Gus Landor

38

Truth be told, it had only just hit *me*. I'd been recalling those odd remarks of Artemus' in the darkened stairwell: "*It's my suspicion that you've not yet, oh, given yourself, shall we say? To a woman.*" I'd been going over those words for days, waiting for the glimmer—and the glimmer came—and I knew then that Artemus had put the question not out of vulgar curiosity but in behalf of another party: Henri le Clerc. Who, like any good sorcerer, would demand, for the grander kind of ceremony, only the best kind of blood.

"Listen to me," Lea was saying, tucking her fingers under Poe's chin and tilting his face toward hers. "This *must* happen, do you understand that?"

He nodded. Whether it was his own doing or the action of her fingers, I don't know, but he nodded. And then watched as she cupped her hands round the cruet of his blood.

It was nearly full by now, and she held it like a bowl of hot soup, watchfully, as she carried it to the rock altar. Then, turning, she gazed round the chamber, meeting each pair of eyes in turn. She raised the cruet over her head . . . and calmly overturned it.

The blood fell in a plunging drift. Pooled on the top of her head and charged over the side, sliding down her face in shining bands. It gave her an almost comical look, Reader, as if she had draped a fringed lampshade over her head, and yet the fringe clung to her like sin, and as she gazed through her veil of blood, the words that came out of her were, shockingly, English. And perfectly distinct.

"Great Father. Release me from thy gift. Release me, O Most Merciful Father."

She reached behind the rock altar . . . fumbled in a small niche in the stone wall, and removed a small wooden box. A cigar box, I think it was, probably one of her father's. She opened it and stared at the contents with a pure fixity, and then, good teacher that she was, held it out for her comrades to see.

How slight it seemed, after all, in its little container! Not much larger than a fist, as Dr. Marquis had said. Scarcely worth all the trouble.

But it had been the start of everything, that heart. And it would be the end, too.

From Lea's mouth now came pouring a bright stream of . . . of *oaths*, I'd call them. She was speaking again in her alien tongue, but the smack of consonants against her lips, the cruel savor of each sound, she gave her utterances the feeling of deepest obscenity. Then her voice died away, and the cloister fell silent as she raised the heart toward the ceiling.

I knew then we were on the brink of something. I knew there was no longer anything to gain by waiting. If I was going to save Poe, I'd have to *act*, and act now.

Oddly, it wasn't the danger that made me pause, it was a queer feeling of *pride*. I didn't want to be just another player in the Marquis theatricals. A player who didn't even know his lines, and had only the vaguest idea of the plot. . . .

This much I had come to see, though: there was a weak link in this family chain. And if I exploited it quickly enough and kept my head about me, then maybe I could brazen this thing out, and get Poe to safety . . . and live another day.

Oh, but I never felt so old as in that moment, lingering in the corridor. If I could have found someone else to do it for me, I'd have pushed him through that doorway without a thought or care. But there *was* no one else, and Lea Marquis was angling her face upward as if she were stacking linen on a high shelf, and that single motion—and all it portended—was enough finally to drive me on.

I took three long strides into the chamber. Stood there with the heat from the torches raking my face. Waited for them to see me.

Not a long wait, as it turned out. Within five seconds, Mrs. Marquis' cowled head had swung round. Her two children followed her lead in short order. Even Poe—drugged as he was, the life force draining from him in a slow red stream—even *he* managed to fasten his eyes to mine.

"Landor," he whispered.

The heat of those torches was nothing compared to the heat of those *eyes,* all boring in on me, and behind the eyes, a single shared demand. I would have to account for myself. Nothing could continue until I did.

"Good evening," I said.

And then, after consulting my pocket watch:

"I'm sorry, good *morning.*"

I kept my voice as light as I humanly could. But it was still an *outsider's* voice—the voice of someone who hadn't been invited—and Lea Marquis flinched before it. She set her cigar box on the floor and took a step toward me and extended her arms in a gesture that hinted of welcome before it resolved into defiance.

"You don't belong here," she said.

But I was already ignoring her, turning instead to the woman who stood close by—the woman whose mouth I could see trembling inside her monk's cowl.

"Mrs. Marquis," I said in a balmy voice.

The sound of her name seemed to cause a change of sorts in her. She threw off the cowl, the better to show off her curls. She even—ah, she couldn't help herself, Reader!—she even *smiled* at me! Looked for all the world as if she were back home on Professors' Row, coaxing us to the whist table.

"Mrs. Marquis," I said. "I was wondering if you could tell me. Which of your children would you care to save from the noose?"

Her eyes darkened; her smile swirled with confusion. *No,* she seemed to be thinking. *I must have misheard.*

"Don't, Mother!" called Artemus.

"He's bluffing," said Lea.

And still I ignored them. Bent all my attention, all my *force,* on their mother.

"I'm afraid you have no choice, Mrs. Marquis. The plain truth is *somebody* has to swing for all this. You do see that, don't you?"

Her eyes began to flick back and forth. Her mouth folded down.

"Cadets can't be killed and carved open with impunity, can they, Mrs. Marquis? If nothing else, it would set a bad precedent."

And now the smile was utterly gone, wiped clean, and without it, how bare her face was! Not a trace of joy or hope in any corner.

"You have no business here!" shouted Lea. "This is *our* sanctuary."

"Well," I said, folding my hands out, "I hate to contradict your daughter, Mrs. Marquis, but I believe that little heart of hers—the one she was just holding, yes—I believe that *makes* it my business." I tapped my finger against my lips. "*Academy* business, too."

I began to walk now. Slow easy steps—no clear pattern—no sign of fear. But that sound still followed me: the *drip drip* of Poe's blood on the stone floor.

"It's a sad business," I said. "A very sad business, Mrs. Marquis. Especially for your *son*, who has such a—such a brilliant career ahead of him. But you see, we have here a human heart, which in all likelihood came from a cadet. We have a young man who's been drugged and kidnapped and—and I think it's fair to say, assaulted. Isn't that right, Mr. Poe?"

He met me with a blank face, as if I were talking about somebody else entirely. His breathing—I could hear it—fretful and short. . . .

"Why, what with one thing and another," I said, "I'm left with very little alternative, Mrs. Marquis. I do hope you see that."

"You've forgotten one thing," said Artemus, the muscles flaring along his jaw. "We have you outnumbered."

"Do you now?" I took a step toward him and cocked my head like a sparrow . . . but my eyes never left his mother. "Do you think your son really means to *kill* me, Mrs. Marquis? On top of all the others he's killed? Would you *stand* for such a thing?"

She'd been reduced now to pushing her curls into place, a faint echo of the coquette she must once have been. And when at last she spoke, it was in a mild, propitiating tone, as if she'd forgotten to put someone's name on her dance card.

"Come, now," she said, "nobody's killed anybody. They told me, they *assured* me there was no—"

"Hush," hissed Artemus.

"No, please," I said. "Please, Mrs. Marquis, I insist you speak. Because I still need to know *which* of your children I'm to save."

And this was her first reflex: to look first at one, then the other—to weigh them, as it were, in the balance—before the horror of weighing them at *all* grew too strong for her. Her hand went to her collarbone, her voice tumbled out in fragments:

"I don't—I don't see why . . ."

"Oh, yes, it's a very difficult business, isn't it? Now if you're worried about Artemus' cadet standing, then maybe you're hoping his *sister* was the mastermind of all this, and he was just a *dupe*, as it were. Much like *you*, Mrs. Marquis. Why, if we could make a strong enough case against *Lea*, then Artemus might get by with, oh, a few days in the brig, and still be around to collect his brevet commission next spring. All right, then!" I clapped my hands together. "*The Case Against Lea Marquis*. We begin with the missing hearts. We ask ourselves, *who* would have need of human hearts? Why, your daughter, of course! To please her beloved ancestor— and cure her tragic condition."

"No," said Mrs. Marquis. "Lea wouldn't—"

"She needs *hearts*, yes, and she knows her brother doesn't have the . . . should I say the *stomach* for it? So she recruits his nearest and dearest friend, Mr. Ballinger. And on the night of October twenty-fifth, she sends Mr. Fry a note to lure him out of barracks. How thrilled he must be! A covert tryst with a handsome belle. Why, he must think his wildest dreams have come true! How disappointing, then, to find Ballinger there instead. With a noose. Oh, yes," I said, glancing over at Poe, "I've seen how easily Mr. Ballinger can disable an opponent."

"Lea," said Mrs. Marquis, gouging her fingers into her palm. "Lea, tell him—"

"Ballinger being such a good friend of the family," I went on, "he'll gladly do anything for your daughter. He'll even *hang* a man . . . and, under Lea's guidance, carve the heart out of his chest. The one thing he won't do, I guess, is stay quiet. And so he has to be taken care of."

Keep moving, Landor. That was the command I kept foremost in mind as I wove a path round those torches, as I listened to the dripping of

Poe's blood . . . as I smiled on Mrs. Marquis' crumbling white face. *Move, Landor!*

"I suppose that's where Mr. Stoddard comes in," I said. "Being, I suppose, *another* admirer of your daughter's—so many to choose from, eh?—he takes care of Ballinger. The only difference is, he doesn't wait around for someone to take care of *him*."

For the first time, even Poe found the strength to protest. "No," he murmured. "No, Landor."

But he was already being overridden by Artemus' voice, whistling with cold: "You are vile, sir."

"Well, there you are," I said, smiling like an aged uncle upon Mrs. Marquis. "*The Case Against Lea Marquis*. It's not a bad one, I think you'll have to admit. And until Mr. Stoddard can be found, I'm afraid it will have to stand as the likeliest explanation. Of course"—and here I lifted my voice to a still lighter register—"I stand *ready* to be corrected. So if I'm wrong . . ."

And now, for the first time, I met Artemus' eyes. Met them straight on.

"If I'm *wrong*," I said, "somebody really should tell me. Because, you see, I need just *one* person to hand to the authorities. The rest of you may do as you like. Why, as far as I'm concerned . . ." My eyes took a quick sketch of the torches and the burning tree and the charcoal brazier, with its ceiling-high flames. ". . . as far as I'm concerned, you may all go to Hell."

We had come now to the part of the play that was out of my hands. *Enter Time.*

It was Time, yes, that would have to pile atop young Artemus Marquis, bow him down until all he could see was the choice that fronted him. And as though to dramatize the transaction, his shoulders did indeed begin to bow, and the skin started to sag from those proud cheeks . . . and when he again spoke, even his voice had dipped below its usual frequency.

"It wasn't Lea's idea," he said, faltering. "It was mine."

"No!"

Her eyes steaming, her finger pointed like a rapier, Lea Marquis came charging on us.

"I will *not* allow this!"

With a sweep of her cassock, she bent her arm round Artemus' head and drew him back a space, locked him into a private conference right there among the torches. Much like the one Poe had overheard, probably: a steady drone broken by scalding whispers.

"Stop a minute . . . what he's doing . . . *divide* us . . ."

Oh, I could have let them go on, but Time had made its exit, and the play (I felt this with a kind of tingle) was once more mine.

"Miss Marquis!" I called. "You might be well advised to let your brother speak for himself. He is a first classman, you know."

I don't think they even heard me, to be honest. No, what pried them apart finally was his *silence*. For after the first exchanges, the only voice that could be heard from their huddle was hers, and the more she talked, I think, the clearer it became: he had already started down that road of his. Nothing to do, then, but watch him go.

So it was that in the very moment her arm crooked more tightly round his neck, in the very moment her voice rose to accents of new urgency, he chose to step away from her, to stand in the murdering glare of the brazier fire, his features baked into a mask of resolve.

"I killed Fry," he said.

His mother doubled over, like someone absorbing a knife thrust. Spat out a groan.

"I killed Randy, too," he added.

Lea, though . . . Lea made no sound. Dead in the arms, dead in the face. Except for this: a single tear, traveling down the chalky plains of her face.

"And Stoddard?" I probed. "How was he involved?"

For a second, Artemus looked as helpless as I'd ever seen him. Waved his arms in the air like some inept conjuror and said, "Stoddard was my accomplice, if you like. He might be said to have panicked. You might say he panicked and ran."

How many different notes there were in his voice—how horribly they clanged against one another. I could have spent many days trying to set him in tune. But I didn't have days.

"Well," I said, rubbing my hands together. "That sounds just fine, don't you think?"

For confirmation, I turned to Mrs. Marquis, who was on her knees now.

The monk's cowl had once more fallen over her head. Not a single human extremity could be found among those coarse brown folds; the only thing left was her voice, faintly rasping.

"You can't," she whispered. "You can't."

Don't think I wanted for pity, Reader. But understand: I had, at the same time, the sound of blood in my ear. *Poe's* blood, still dripping on that stone floor. I would have done anything to make it stop.

"Yes, yes," I said. "All that's left to do . . . yes, I think *all* that's left to do is claim the evidence. Miss Marquis, I'd be *most* grateful if you'd hand me that little bundle of yours."

But she'd forgotten where the box was! How frantic she seemed as she cast her eyes round her, sifting through the patches of dark and fireglow— before finding it in the last possible place: right by her feet.

Opening it once more, she gazed at its contents with a frozen wonder. Then switched her gaze to me. It will be a long time before I forget that look of hers. *Cornered*, yes, the hounds baying on every side, but with this distinction: the slightest inkling of hope, as though some path of escape lay just beyond her tether.

"Please," she said. "Leave us alone. It's almost done. It's almost—"

"It *is* done," I said, quietly.

She backed away: one step, two steps. I matched her. And by now, she had given up any idea of putting me off. The only idea she had left was: *Flee*.

Which was what she did. Dashed straight for the rock altar with the box still in her hands.

My first thought was that she would destroy it, that last bit of evidence, hurl it into the brazier or hide it behind a rock or God knows what. But when I went to follow, I found Artemus cutting me off, *Artemus* opposing his weight to mine.

And so we were joined, the two of us, in perfect silence, just as we'd been joined in that closet, battling over Joshua Marquis' saber. And this time, there was no doubt about who had the upper hand.

Youth, yes, was having its way with age, and Artemus was driving me back—and not simply *back*, I soon realized, but in a very particular direction. I can't say when it occurred to him, but as soon as I felt that first stab of heat on my spine, I knew where I was headed: straight into the pyre of that charcoal brazier.

How strange to look into Artemus' eyes and see nothing there—nothing but the reflection of that towering fire. From somewhere nearby, I could hear Mrs. Marquis' low keening, and Lea's litanies, but the sound that weighed most heavily on me was the crackle of that fire—caressing my back—engorging my skin.

A fire in my legs, too: the burning muscles of resistance. *Futile* resistance, for the distance between me and the flames was falling away, and the fire was kissing my shoulder blades, tongueing the very hairs on my neck. I could see it, yes, in Artemus' eyes, I could see *him*, steeling for this last push.

And then, for no apparent reason, his head jerked back. I heard him cough out a cry. And I looked down to find, fastened like a tick to Artemus' trouser leg, the balled-up form of Cadet Fourth Classman Poe.

Drugged though he was, and bleeding freely, he had crawled toward us and closed his teeth on the left calf of Artemus Marquis—a bite of thoroughly respectable breadth and depth. And he was now undertaking the one job he could still manage: *anchor*. Trying to drag Artemus to earth.

Oh, Artemus tried to shake him off, but Poe's will seemed to have grown in ratio to his frailty, and he wouldn't be budged. And Artemus, knowing he couldn't take on both of us, chose to move against the weaker part. He raised his fist and, after a brief calibration, prepared to smash Poe's crown.

He never got that far. In the time it took him to make his strike, I was already making mine. My right fist caught his jaw, and my left seconded it in short order, slamming him under his chin.

Down he went, and down went Poe, still keeping vigil on that leg, so that when Artemus tried once more to rise, Poe's weight kept him pinned to the ground. By then I had grabbed one of the torches and lowered it to Artemus' face, and held it there until it raised a chain of shining sweat along his brow.

"That will be all," I said, between clenched teeth.

Whether he had it in mind to argue the point, I'll never be able to say, because that was when the sound came. The sound of something going terribly wrong.

Lea Marquis stood before the rock altar—her eyes big as moons, her cheeks smeared with something that looked like clay. She stood there, yes, clutching her throat with a red hand.

It was clear in an instant what she'd done. Seized her final gambit, that's what. Mad to win herself new life, she'd followed Henri le Clerc's instructions down to the letter, and it was the last thing I would have expected and maybe the first thing I *should* have expected. Instead of offering up that heart, she had consumed it. Swallowed it whole.

Narrative of Gus Landor

39

In the end, I think, it came down to this: she couldn't see it all the way through for Henri le Clerc. Something in her bridled. And so the heart she was tasked with devouring lodged itself halfway down her throat—and began drawing away her life's breath. Her knees buckled . . . her body curved in on itself . . . she *spilled* onto the ground like a load of kindling.

And Artemus and I, who not twenty seconds before had been wishing each other dead, now rushed to her side, and behind us came Mrs. Marquis, her slippers scuffing the stone, and dragging after her, Poe. All of us gathered round Lea Marquis' sprawled form and stared down at that pale face, rouged with heart tissue, and those *eyes,* jolting from their sockets.

"She can't . . ." Mrs. Marquis gasped. "Can't . . ."

Breathe, that was the word she was searching for. And in fact, no words at all were coming now from Lea Marquis, not even so much as a cough. Just a high forlorn whistle, like the song of a bird trapped in a chimney. She was dying before our eyes.

Poe had both of his hands pressed round Lea's head. "Please! Please, God, tell us what to *do!*"

God being absent, we did our best. I levered up her torso, and Mrs. Marquis pounded her on the back, and Poe cooed in her ear: help was coming, help was on the way. I looked up then and found Artemus standing over us, holding the very lancet he had used to open Poe's vein.

He never proposed, never explained, but I knew at once what he meant to do. He was going to carve a channel of air straight through his sister's throat.

Such a fierce look to him as he straddled Lea's chest . . . such a terrible glint to that blade . . . I could well see why Mrs. Marquis moved to take the lancet from him.

"It's her only chance," he growled.

And who were we to argue? Lea Marquis had ceased even to protest, and blue ponds had formed round her lips, round the very beds of her fingernails, and the only parts of her still moving were her eyelids, flapping up and down like awnings in a stiff wind.

"Hurry," I whispered.

Artemus' hand shook as it measured out the sections of her throat. His voice shook, too, as it called up the words of his father's textbooks. "Thyroid cartilage," he muttered. "Cricoid cartilage . . . cricothyroid membrane. . . ."

At last his finger stopped. And maybe his heart stopped, too, in that moment before the lancet plunged.

"Oh, God," he moaned. "Please, God."

Just the slightest pressure from his hand: that was all it took to drive the blade like a sounding rod into his sister's throat.

"Horizontal incision," he whispered. "One half inch."

An eye of blood welled up round the blade.

"Depth . . . one *half* inch . . ."

Quick as light, Artemus drew out the blade and plunged his index finger into the slit in Lea's throat. A strange gurgle rose up from inside her, like water rustling through pipes. And then, as Artemus began looking round for a tube to insert, the eye of blood slowly broadened into a pool.

No longer subsiding now, it was *widening*. Weeping through the wound and rolling away in a steady tide—*washing* over Lea's marble skin.

"There shouldn't be this much," Artemus hissed.

But the blood kept coming in full defiance of man and medicine, pouring forth in fresh waves, painting Lea's throat. The gurgle grew louder, then louder still. . . .

"The artery," gasped Artemus. "Did I . . . ?"

Blood was everywhere, bubbling, burbling. In a rush of despair, Artemus drew his finger from the opening with an audible pop, and droplets of blood scattered from his hands like tiny pearls. . . .

LOUIS BAYARD

"I need . . ." A sob caught him in midsentence. "I need . . . please . . . something to bind . . ."

Poe was already tearing at his shirt. I was doing the same with my own, Mrs. Marquis was rending her robe . . . and in the midst of all this thrashing lay Lea. Perfectly still, except for her blood, which came boiling up from inside, more and more of it, never ceasing, never slaking.

And then, quite unexpectedly, her mouth opened. Opened to form three words, as audible as speech.

I . . . love . . . you.

It says something about Lea Marquis, I guess, that each of us might have thought himself the beneficiary of those words. She wasn't looking at *us,* though. She had found the way *out*—at last—and she was watching herself go, smiling as the light in her pale eyes flickered away into nothing.

We knelt there in silence, like missionaries on a foreign shore. I could see Poe driving his palms straight into his temples . . . and in that moment, my impulse was not to comfort him but to ask the question that had stuck in my head like a piece of grit. I growled it straight into his ear:

"*Is it still poetry's highest theme?*"

He looked at me with unseeing eyes.

"The death of a beautiful woman," I snarled. "Is it still a poet's noblest subject?"

"Yes," he said.

And then he fell on my shoulder.

"Oh, Landor. I shall have to keep losing her. Again and again."

I didn't even know what he meant. Not then. But I could feel the rhythmic shudder of his rib cage against mine. My hand found the back of his neck and held it . . . a few seconds . . . a few more seconds . . . and still he wept, without tears, without sobs, until everything that lay inside him had been turned out.

Mrs. Marquis, by contrast, seemed more in control of her faculties than any of us. She was filling the air with her cool, easy voice:

"It wasn't supposed to be like this. She was to be a wife. . . . A mother, yes."

That word, I suppose: *mother*. It sent something flying up inside her. She tried to cap it in her mouth, but it burst through her fingers. It was her own cry.

"*A mother! Like me!*"

She listened until the echoes had died away, and then, with a low, guttural moan, she threw herself on her daughter's body. Pounded it again and again with her tiny fists.

"No!" called Artemus, dragging her back.

But she wanted more. She wanted to thump that body into paste. She *would* have, too, if her son hadn't held her off.

"Mother," he whispered. "Mother, stop."

"We did it for *her*!" she screamed, lunging at her daughter's still form. "All for *her*! And then she goes away and dies anyway! That horrible, horrible girl, what was it *for*? If she didn't . . . what was it *for*?"

She went as far as she could go in that direction, and then, in the common way of grief, swung back hard. Pushed Lea's hair from her face and wiped the blood from that white throat and kissed that white hand. And sank into the moat of her tears.

What more arresting sight is there, Reader, than sorrow writ so large? I gave myself over to it. Which is why, I think, it took me so long to hear the sound that was coming from above us, settling like dust on our heads.

"*Mr. Landor!*"

I turned my face toward it.

"*Mr. Landor!*"

Laughter, that was my first impulse. I was sorely tempted to laugh. For my savior had come . . . and lo, his name was Captain Hitchcock.

"Down here!" I called.

It took my voice a few moments to wind its way through the corridor and up the shaft. Then, from above:

"*How do we find you?*"

"You don't!" I called back. "We will find *you*!"

I put my hands round Poe's shoulders and drew him to his feet. "Are you ready?" I asked.

Dazed with pain, scarcely remembering where he was, he peered at the oily sheen on his arm. "Landor," he mumbled. "Might I have a bandage?"

I stared down at my shirt sleeve, dangling by the merest of threads. It was the bandage I had meant for Lea, but it would do quite as well for him. I wrapped it round his wound as tightly as I dared. Then, draping his other arm round my shoulder, I began to walk him toward the door. The only thing that could have stopped us now was this *voice*, soft and beseeching.

"Do you think . . ."

It was Mrs. Marquis. Pointing in abject humility toward the stone altar, where Artemus was now sitting.

Not by himself, no. He had dragged Lea's body there with him, and he was cradling her head in his lap, and he stared back at us with a challenge all the wilder for being unspoken. His mother could only turn her face toward mine with a mute entreaty.

"We'll come back for Lea later," I said. "I must get Mr. Poe to—"

A doctor. The words caught in my throat like the beginning of a joke, and the joke seemed to be taken up at once by Mrs. Marquis. I had never seen that smile of hers quite so brilliant. Which meant only that it was fueled by every human feeling—by such a *blast* of feeling I wouldn't have been surprised to see her teeth melt.

"Come, Artemus," she said as she followed me and Poe into the corridor.

He watched her with hollow eyes.

"Come, darling," she repeated. "You know, we can't—we can't do any more for her now, can we? We *tried*, didn't we?"

Even she must have realized how weakly her words sounded, but no matter how she coaxed and wheedled, he made her no reply.

"Now, listen to me, darling, I don't want you to worry. We're going to speak to Colonel Thayer, do you hear? We're going to explain *everything*. He understands all about—all about misunderstandings, darling . . . why, he's one of our oldest and dearest friends, he's known you since you were . . . he would *never* . . . do you hear me? You'll still be graduated, darling, you will!"

"I'll come directly," he answered.

There was in his voice a curious lightness—a *light* is the better word—and that was, I suppose, the first signal. The second being this: instead of preparing to rise, he settled himself more thoroughly where he was. Drew

Lea's head closer toward his chest. And only then did I see what he'd been hiding from us. The lancet that had so lately been carving open his sister's throat now lay embedded in his side.

Who knows when he did it? I never heard so much as a grunt from him. No speeches, no flourishes, no slash across the neck . . . no fuss of any kind. He wanted simply to be gone, I think. As slowly and quietly as he could effect it.

Our eyes met then, and the knowledge of what was happening passed between us in a current of fellow feeling.

"I'll be there directly," he said in a fainter voice.

Maybe a man, in his final minutes, attends more closely to the world around him. I only suggest it because Artemus, for all his distress, was the first of us to lift his eyes to the ceiling. And even before my eyes had followed suit, I was *smelling* it. Unmistakable: the odor of burning wood.

This was, in a way, the biggest surprise of all, that such a room, carved out of rock, should have something so prosaic as a wooden ceiling. Who knew what it had been in the old days? A holding cell? A root cellar? A tap room? It's safe to say it had never held such a grand and glorious fire as the one the Marquises had fashioned. For its builders would have known that fire can be no friend to wood.

And now that wooden ceiling, tortured by the brazier's flames, was charring and snapping—and giving way. And as the beams cracked open, the strangest weather began to fall from the sky. Not snow but ice. The entire contents of the West Point icehouse came dropping down.

Not the tinkling cubes that went into Colonel Thayer's lemonade, no, these were *slabs*, fifty-pound *blocks*, with the weight and sound of marble, falling slowly at first, but falling with purpose, gouging the stone floor with each collision.

"Artemus . . ." The slightest edge had crept back into Mrs. Marquis' voice as she stood watching from the safety of the corridor. "Artemus, you must come *now!*"

I don't know if she even understood what was happening. She took a step back into the room and was making as if to drag him out by his heels, when a huge chunk of ice landed just a few feet from her. The shattered crystals flew into her face, temporarily blinding her, and then another block landed, even closer, forcing her to take a step back. And as I grabbed her arm and pulled her back out of the room, all she could do at first was utter his name, in a tone that smacked almost of resignation.

"Artemus."

She was thinking, maybe, the ice would stop. Thinking, maybe, her son was safe where he was. The next wave of ice showed her how wrong she was. The first block clipped the side of his head—a brief blunt concussion—and threw him onto his side. The next caught him midsection, and the next crushed his feet. He was still alive enough by then to howl, but the sound lasted only as long as the next installment of ice, which made a bull's-eye of his head. Even from twelve feet away, we could hear the crack of his skull against stone. And then we heard nothing more from him.

His mother, though, chose that moment to find her voice again. And there I was, Reader, thinking she had already spent her grief, when in fact she had many rooms more inside her just waiting to be emptied. The only thing that could have made her pause, I think, was the sight of something so unexpected that no grief was equal to it. Through the falling ice, we saw a figure slowly rise.

Artemus, I remember thinking, hauling himself up for one last stand. But Artemus lay where he'd fallen. And the figure that drew itself up—like a barroom brawler peeling himself from the floor—this figure wore not a uniform but a priest's cassock.

Two feet planted themselves on the stony ground. Two legs tottered toward us. We saw pale arms and chestnut hair, we saw rouged cheeks and blue eyes, startled into light. We saw Lea Marquis rise and walk.

No mere apparition. Flesh and blood—*blood*. One hand was reaching for us, the other was clasped round the slit in her throat. And from her shredded, strangled body came a cry such as no human or animal has ever made.

It found its match, though, in Poe. Together they made a perfect anthem of horror—a rising, rasping wail that woke the bats from their beds and sent them bouncing off the walls and skidding through our legs and scrabbling through our hair.

"*Lea!*"

Weakened as he was, Poe did all he could to go back to her. He tried shoving me to one side, and when that failed, he tried to get round me, and when that failed, he tried to get *over*—yes, he tried to *scale* me! Anything, anything to get to her. Anything to die with her.

Mrs. Marquis, too: she would have done the same, she cared nothing for the danger. It was *me* who held them both back. Without ever asking myself why, I locked my arms round their waists and dragged them away. In their depleted states, they were no match for me, but by dint of struggling, they did succeed in slowing our progress. So that even as we passed down that corridor, away from that cursed chamber, we could see, framed in the doorway, the vision of the woman we had left behind.

"Lea!"

Did she even know what was happening? Did she know what was slamming her against the hard stone—piling on top of her with such grim purpose—grinding her down in the very minute of her rebirth? Nothing in that voiceless cry of hers gave any sign of understanding. She was being *crushed,* that was all. Crushed as surely as the bats that came squealing past her—dozens upon dozens of then, slammed between ice and stone, screaming all the way to Death's door.

And still the ice came dropping like thunderbolts, block after block ... swallowing the torches and candles and tapers ... splitting open Lea's head and hammering her cassock ... striking her again and again, in a hard bleak fury that she met with nothing but a soft bare open body.

So hard did it come, so fast, that before another minute had passed, the doorway was impassable, and the ice had begun to spill into the hall. And all the same, we lingered there, scarcely able to believe in such vengeance. For the ice was still falling. Falling in heavy choirs. Falling in shivers of mist. Falling on the Marquis lineage. Falling like death.

Narrative of Gus Landor

40

December 14th to 19th

Here, I suppose, was the final miracle. The ground above us never so much as shook. Not a single alarm was raised, not a single cadet was jarred from his sleep. Not a kink was thrown into the Academy's daily routine. At the first hint of dawn, as on any other morning, the Army drummer stepped into the assembly area between North and South Barracks and, at the cadet adjutant's cue, brought his sticks down on the drumhead, in a cadence that grew and blossomed until it was echoing across the Plain, pulsing into every ear—cadet, officer, soldier.

Until I saw that sound being made, I don't think I'd ever tied it to a human being. For me, hearing it from my room in Mr. Cozzens' hotel, it had always the air of an inner prompting, a stir of conscience, maybe. But conscience had kept me *here* for the remainder of the night, here in the North Barracks guardroom, briefing Captain Hitchcock and then writing down, as best I could, everything that had happened. *Almost* everything.

It was the last text I would ever give Hitchcock, and he received it with all due ceremony. Folded it in half and tucked it inside a leather pouch, to be forwarded in due time to Colonel Thayer. Then he gave me a slow grave nod, which was the closest he would ever come to saying, *Well done*. And with that, there was nothing left for me to do but go back to my hotel.

Except I had a question. Just *one* question, but it needed answering.

"It was Dr. Marquis, I suppose?"

Hitchcock gave me a look of civil blankness. "I don't follow you."

"The one who told you where we were. I'm guessing it was Dr. Marquis?"

He shook his head softly. "I'm afraid not. The good doctor was still sitting by the icehouse when we got there. Much wailing and gnashing of teeth, very little information."

"Then who . . . ?"

The tiniest of smiles crept over his face then. "Cesar," he answered.

Well, if I hadn't been so distracted at the time, maybe I'd have figured it out myself. I'd have wondered why a mess-hall steward was gadding about on the Plain at such a late hour. But would it have occurred to me that this same Cesar—so kindly, so courteous—was the agent who'd been tasked with following Artemus Marquis? That after tracking his quarry to the icehouse, and then seeing me and the doctor follow close behind, he'd take himself straight to the commandant and sound the alarm?

"Cesar," I said, chuckling and scratching my head. "My, but you're a deep one, Captain."

"Thank you," he replied, in that dry ironical way of his. But all the same, there was something rising in him, something not so ironical—demanding to be heard.

"Mr. Landor," he said at last.

"Yes, Captain."

He must have thought it would be easier to say it if he turned away, but it was still a torment.

"I wish to note that if—if the exigencies of this business have rendered me . . . which is to say, if I ever, out of intemperance, impugned your—your *integrity*, or your competence, then I'm—I'm very . . ."

"Thank you, Captain. I'm sorry, too."

Which was as far as we could go without fatally embarrassing ourselves. We nodded. We shook hands for the last time. We parted.

And I left the guardroom just in time to see that drummer beating the reveille. The first rumbles of life were coming from inside the barracks. Young men were tumbling out on hand and knee, kicking their bedding and seizing their uniforms. Beginning again.

*   *   *

Mrs. Marquis, since leaving the icehouse, had taken the signal step of *not* retiring to her bed. The pressure of grief had forced her upright. She refused every offer of escort and wandered in and out of the assembly yard on missions held close to her bosom. So it was that a pair of third classmen, coming back from sentinel duty, were accosted by a hard-grinning woman in a gray monk's robe, who asked if they might help "raise her children." It would take just a minute, she assured them.

There was, in fact, no thought of recovering the bodies anytime soon. That would be a labor of days. And until then, there was other work to be done. *Work,* that was Dr. Marquis' answer to grief. In his last official act before submitting his resignation, he even bound the wounds of Cadet Fourth Classman Poe. Upon which he took the young man's pulse and declared that he'd lost no more blood than a physician would have drawn in the course of a normal bleeding. "Might have been the best thing for him," announced Dr. Marquis.

The doctor himself looked in excellent health. His face had never glowed so redly. Only once did I see it lose color: when he passed his own wife in the assembly yard. They shrank from each other, yes, but *found* each other, too. Their eyes met; their heads angled together as if they were old neighbors passing in the street. And in that crossing, I thought I could glimpse the future that lay in store for them. Not a brilliant future, no. Dr. Marquis' conduct would bar him from military postings, and though he might (in light of past service) escape court-martial, the taint of his past would trail him even into the civilian world. They would never realize Mrs. Marquis' dream of returning to New York—they'd be lucky to find a practice on the Illinois frontier—but they would survive, and they would seldom if ever talk of their dead children, in public or in private, and they would treat each other with grave courtesy and would wait, with all manner of calm, for the closing of Life's account. So, at any rate, I imagined.

Poe was put to bed in Ward B-3, the same ward that had housed both Leroy Fry and Randolph Ballinger. In his normal cast of mind, he might have thrilled to the chance of communing with dead spirits—might even have been moved to scrawl a poem on the transmigration of souls—but on this occasion, he fell dead asleep and didn't wake, I was later told, until halfway through afternoon recital.

I myself managed some four hours of sleep before one of Thayer's lackeys came pounding on my door.

"Colonel Thayer requests an interview."

We met in the artillery park. Stood there among the mortars and siege guns and field pieces: trophy guns, many of them, seized from the British and inscribed with the names of the battlefields. And what a noise they'd make, I thought, if we fired them all in unison. But they sat in stillness, and the only sound was the flag, halfway down its staff, snapping in the wind.

"You've read my report?" I asked him.

He nodded.

"Do you . . . I don't know if you have any questions. . . ."

His voice came back low and hard. "None, I fear, that you can answer, Mr. Landor. I want to know how I can possibly have dined and fraternized with a man all these years, known his family nearly as well as my own, and never fathomed the depths of their distress."

"That was by design, Colonel."

"Yes," he said. "I know."

We were both looking northward now. To Cold Spring, which rippled like a fable through the furnace vapors of Gouverneur Kemble's foundry. To Cro' Nest and Bull Hill, and further on, the blurred seam of the Shawangunk Mountains. And sewing them all together, the river: flat and puckered with winter light.

"They're gone," said Sylvanus Thayer. "Lea and Artemus."

"Yes."

"We'll never know why they did all they did. Or even *what* they did. Where one crime began and another ended, we'll never know."

"True," I allowed. "Although I have ideas on the subject."

He bowed his head an inch. "I am all ears, Mr. Landor."

I took my time about it. Truth be told, I was just getting a fix on the business myself.

"Artemus did the cutting," I said. "I'm sure of that; I saw his work up close. A born surgeon if I ever saw one, even if he did make a . . . well, it was—it was a difficult business with his sister. . . ."

"Yes."

"I'd wager Artemus was also the one who dressed up as an officer. He's the one, probably, who shooed away Private Cochrane from Leroy Fry's body."

"And what of Lea?"

Lea. The very sound of her name made me hesitate.

"Well," I said, "I'm fairly certain she was at Benny Havens' that night. With Artemus. I assume she was following Poe to see if he was in league with me. And having found he *was* . . ."

She did *what*? That I still didn't know. She might have resolved to be rid of him. Might have sped up her plans for that very purpose. Or she might have decided to love him—love him even more for betraying her.

"It must have been Lea," I added, "who planted the shell outside Artemus' door. To draw suspicion away from her brother. She may even have planted the heart in his trunk just to keep us guessing."

"And the mother and father?"

"Oh, Dr. Marquis wouldn't have been any use to them. They wanted only silence from him. As for Mrs. Marquis, well, she may have held open a door or lit some candles, but I can't imagine her holding down a strapping young cadet or stringing a noose round his neck."

"No," said Thayer, running a finger along his jaw. "That, I presume, was the job of Mr. Ballinger and Mr. Stoddard."

"Things look that way, surely."

"And that being the case, I can only assume that Artemus killed Mr. Ballinger to prevent from alerting the authorities. And that Mr. Stoddard ran away rather than become the next victim."

"You could assume that, yes."

He peered at me as though I were the evening sky. "You're cagey to the last, Mr. Landor."

"Old habit, Colonel. I do apologize." I gave my arms a shake. Kicked my boots together. "In the meantime, we'll just have to wait to hear what Mr. Stoddard has to say on the subject. If we ever find him."

Maybe he heard that as a reproach, for his voice took on an armored tone. "We would be most obliged," he said, "if you would meet with the emissary of the chief of engineers when he arrives."

"Naturally."

"And make a full report to any official court of inquiry."

"Of course."

"Otherwise, Mr. Landor, I declare your contractual duties fulfilled to the letter, and I hereby release you from your contract." He wrinkled his forehead. "I trust that won't displease you."

Or Captain Hitchcock, I thought. But held my tongue.

"At the very least," added Thayer, "I hope you won't object to accepting our thanks."

"Oh, I wish I deserved them, Colonel. There are. . . ." I rubbed the side of my head. "There are *lives* that might have been saved if I'd been a little sharper or faster. *Younger.*"

"You saved at least one life. Mr. Poe's."

"Yes."

"Not that he will necessarily thank you for it."

"No." I shoved my hands in my pockets, rocked on my feet. "Well, never mind. Your superiors should be pleased, Colonel. The jackals in Washington will soon be in retreat, I hope."

He made a close study of me then. Deciding, maybe, if I meant it or not.

"I believe we've won a stay of execution," he said. "A stay only."

"Surely they can't shut down the Academy over—"

"No," he answered. "But they can shut down *me.*"

Not an ounce of protest. Not a drop of sentiment. He was stating it as flatly as if he'd read it in one of his newspapers that morning.

I won't forget what he did then. He leaned his face into the bell-shaped muzzle of a brass eighteen-pounder and . . . *held* it there for a good half minute. Daring it, I thought, to do its worst.

Then he rubbed his hands lightly together.

"I'm embarrassed to confess, Mr. Landor, that in my vanity, I once considered myself indispensable to the Academy's survival."

"And now?"

"Now I believe it can survive only *without* me." He nodded slowly, drew himself a little taller. "And it will, I think."

"Well, Colonel," I said, extending my hand. "I hope you're wrong about the first part."

He took my hand. And, no, he didn't smile, but his mouth twitched into an angle of wryness.

"I've been wrong before," he said. "But not about you, Mr. Landor."

We stood outside the eastern entrance to Benny's tavern. Stood a yard apart, staring clear to the other side of the river.

"I came to tell you it's over, Patsy. The job's all done."

"What of it?"

"Well, we can—we can go *on*, that's what. As before. And nothing else matters, it's *finished*, it's—"

"No, Gus. Stop. I don't care about your job. I don't care about the damned Academy."

"Then what?"

She looked at me for some time in silence.

"Oh, it might as well have been you, too, Gus. They made your heart a stone."

"Stone can—stone can live."

"Then touch me. Just once, as you used to."

As I *used* to. Well, that was an impossible task. She must have known it, too, for there really was regret in her eyes when at last she turned away. She was very sorry to have troubled me.

"Good-bye, Gus."

Before another day had passed, Private Cochrane brought all my clothes and belongings back to the cottage in Buttermilk Falls. I smiled a bit to see him salute me—Lieutenant Landor! He yanked the black bay's reins, and in another minute, the Academy phaeton had disappeared over the brow of the hill.

For the next few days, I was alone. Hagar the cow still hadn't come back, and the house didn't quite know me as before. The Venetian blinds, the string of dried peaches, the ostrich egg—they all stared as though they were trying to place me. I walked warily through the rooms, taking care not to alarm anything, and I stood more than I sat, and I went for walks, only to scurry back at the first suggestion of wind. I was alone.

And then, on the afternoon of Sunday, December the nineteenth, I received a visitor: Cadet Fourth Classman Poe.

He blew in like a rain cloud and stood there darkly on my threshold. And when I look back on it now, I can see it *was* a threshold.

"I know," he said. "I know about Mattie."

Narrative of Gus Landor

41

And now, Reader, a story.

In the Highlands, there dwelt a young maiden, no more than seventeen. Tall and lovely, graceful in line, sweet in repose. She had come to this remote clime to help her father live and had instead watched her mother die. The two of them were left to spend their days in a cottage overlooking the Hudson, where it was no hardship making the time pass. Father and daughter read to each other and played at cyphers and puzzles and went for long walks in the hills—the girl had a strong constitution—and led an altogether quiet life. Not too quiet for the maiden, who had in her pockets of hard silence, not to be penetrated by anyone.

The father loved his daughter. In his heart, he allowed himself to believe she was his consolation from God.

But there were more things to do on earth than console. The maiden began to pine, in her quiet way, for company. And might have pined in vain—her father having become, after his long career in the city, a hermit—except that a wealthy cousin of her late mother, the wife of a banker in nearby Haverstraw, took pity on her. Lacking a daughter of her own, the older woman found in the maiden a pleasing substitute, a creature of inborn graces who could be molded into something still finer—something that would redound to the older woman's glory.

*   *   *

And so, against the father's objections, the older woman took the maiden on carriage rides and introduced her round at dinner parties. And when the time was ripe, she invited the maiden to her very first ball.

A ball! Women in pounds of silk and muslin and merino. Frock-coated men with the hair of Roman emperors. Supper tables teeming with cakes and custards and the glint of port glasses. Fiddle players and cotillions! The rustle of women's dresses, the whir of fans. Copper-buttoned beaux ready to lay down their lives for a single dance.

The maiden had never coveted any of this—maybe because she'd never known it was there?—but with good cheer, she gave herself over to dress fittings and deportment drills and lessons from French dancing masters. And whenever her father looked grim at seeing her in a new ensemble, she laughed at him and made a pretense of tearing up the dress and, before the day was out, promised once again that he was the only man for her.

The day of the ball came. The father had the satisfaction of seeing his daughter step into a landau like the flower of one of New York's finest families. She gave him a curt wave through the window and then was gone, whisked away to her cousin's house in Haverstraw. For the rest of the evening, he imagined her growing giddy and dry-mouthed as she was whirled round the parquet floor. He imagined quizzing her when she got back, demanding a full reckoning of all she'd done and seen, even as he heaped a dry scorn on it. He imagined asking her, in as polite a tone as he could muster, when she thought she would be done with all this foolishness.

The hours passed. She didn't return. Midnight, one o'clock, two. With a sick heart, the father took a lantern and went to search the neighboring byways. Finding no sign of her, he was making ready to mount his horse and ride all the way to Haverstraw—his foot was already in the stirrup—when she appeared, limping down the lane in her slippers. A vision of brokenness.

*   *   *

The hair that had been massed in such dainty ringlets now lay limp and tousled. A long seam of petticoat showed where the lilac taffeta gown had been torn from her. The gigot sleeves she had taken such delight in modeling had been ripped from her shoulder.

And there was blood. Blood on her wrists, blood in her hair. Blood *there* . . . so profuse that she must have taken it as a signal of her shame. She refused to let him wash her. Refused to tell him what had happened. For some days, she gave up speaking altogether.

Stung by her silence, mad with grief, the father went to his wife's cousin (whom he had already sworn off) for an account of the evening. She told him then of the three men.

Young, straight-backed, personable men who had appeared out of nowhere. No one could recall inviting them or even having met them before. Their speech was educated, their manners good, and their dress unexceptionable, though there was a general sense that the clothes were too ill fitting to be truly theirs. One thing was never in doubt: their delight at being surrounded by so many females. They behaved, said one guest, as if someone had set them free from a monastery.

One female in particular attracted their interest: the young maiden from Buttermilk Falls. Lacking the wiles of the more sophisticated girls, she was at first grateful for their attentions. When she began to see where these attentions were tending, she retreated into her accustomed silence. Far from being troubled, the three young men kept their cheer and continued to track her progress through the various rooms. When the maiden stepped outside for air, they bowed their respects and followed right after.

They never came back. Nor did the maiden. Rather than present herself in her torn and bleeding state to her hostess, she took the long road home.

The wounds to her body healed soon enough. Something else didn't heal, or maybe it simply changed into a *deeper* silence. A silence of a singularly watchful kind, as if she were waiting for the sound of wheels on the road.

*   *   *

Her brow was clear and untroubled, she never failed in her devotion to her father, was never less than attentive, and yet beneath her acts, there lay this biding. What was she expecting? He kept catching fragments of it, like a familiar face slipping in and out of a crowd, but he could never put a name to it.

Some days he would come home to find her on her knees in the parlor, her eyes closed, her lips moving soundlessly. She would always deny she was praying—she knew how little use he had for the religion of *his* father—but after each of these times, she would grow still quieter, and he had the uneasy sense that he had caught her in the middle of a conversation.

One afternoon, she surprised him by suggesting a picnic. Just the thing, he thought, for drawing her out of her reveries. And what a day it was! Sunny and cloudless, with an incense-breeze coming over the mountains. They packed ham and oysters and hasty pudding and peaches and some of Farmer Hoesman's raspberries, and they ate in peace, and it seemed to him that the specters began to recede from them a little as they sat there on the bluff overlooking the river.

One by one, she put the plates and silverware back into the picnic basket: she'd always been a tidy child. Then she pulled him to his feet and, after looking into his face, embraced him.

He was too surprised to embrace her back. He watched her walk to the lip of the bluff. She gazed north, east, south. Turned round and, with a face free and smiling, said, *Everything will be all right. It will all turn out.*

And then she raised her arms over her head and arched back, like a diver. And with her eyes still fixed on him, she flung herself over the side. Went blind, never once looking where she was going.

The body was swept away by the river. Afterward he would tell neighbors that his daughter had run off with another man. A lie that hid a truth. She *had* run off. She'd thrown herself right into his arms and done it with a serene heart, as though this had been the true end of her days. She went knowing *he'd* be waiting for her.

There was this much to be said for the maiden's death: it freed her father to pursue the idea that had been forming in his head without his quite knowing it.

One morning, he opened a volume of Byron's poetry—opened it only because *she* had once loved it—and found there a chain. It was the chain she had clutched in her hand the night she came back from the ball. She'd taken it from one of the men who set upon her, and she'd held it so tightly it gouged a circle in her palm. Still, she would part with it only when her father wasn't looking.

Why had she kept such a dark token, tucked away in her most treasured volume? Unless she had meant for him to find it. Use it.

The chain was attached to a lozenge-shaped brass plate, and this plate was embossed with a coat of arms. The arms of the Corps of Engineers.

And after all, why *shouldn't* they have been cadets? Three young men, coming out of nowhere, wearing ill-fitting clothes, hungry for women. And with a perfect alibi if anyone ever came asking questions. They'd been in barracks all night! And no cadet ever left the Academy reservation without permission. . . .

This cadet had carried his undoing with him. A brass plate engraved with the initials L.E.F.

It was easy work finding the owner. The names of West Point cadets were a matter of public record, and only one cadet had those initials: Leroy Everett Fry.

*   *   *

That very week, by chance, the father heard the name mentioned in the precincts of Benny Havens' tavern. This Leroy Fry was one of the barmaid's legion of cadet admirers, though among the least noteworthy. Night after night, the father went back to the tavern, hoping for a glimpse of him. Until he found him.

A smallish fellow. Mild and pale and redheaded and spindle-shanked. No one would have thought him a threat to anyone.

The father stayed the whole evening, watching this cadet as closely as possible without being watched himself. By the time he went home, he knew what he would have to do.

And every time he faltered in his undertaking, every time he fretted for his soul, he realized he had nothing left to fret over. God had taken *her*. God had nothing more to claim from him.

Mathilde was her name—Mattie for short. Her hair was chestnut, and her eyes were of the palest blue, shading sometimes into gray.

Narrative of Gus Landor

42

On his previous visit, Cadet Fourth Classman Poe had come like a man walking into an art gallery. Senses flung open, moving in straight lines from the Venetian blinds to the ostrich egg to the peaches, interpreting each in turn. . . .

This time, he came as a commander. Crossed the floor in long strides and tossed his cloak on the mantel as if he didn't care whether it stayed there and turned his back on the Greek lithograph he'd never much liked and folded his arms . . . and dared me to speak.

I did speak. With a calmness that surprised me.

"Very well," I said. "You know about Mattie. What has that do with anything?"

"Oh," he said. "It has everything to do with everything. As you know full well."

He took a slow turn of the room, letting his eye graze off each object without sticking. He cleared his throat and straightened his spine and said:

"I wonder, Landor, if you'd care to know how I found you out. The complete trajectory of my inferences, would that interest you?"

"Of course. Certainly."

He eyed me closely, as though he didn't quite believe me. Then resumed his tour.

"I began, you see, with a rather startling fact. There was but one heart in that icehouse."

He paused—for dramatic effect, I assume, and to wait for my response. Meeting with none, he pressed on.

"Initially, I found myself unable to recollect anything of what had occurred in that infernal chamber. Everything lay cloaked in a—a beneficent amnesia. But as the days passed, I found more and more of that strange proceeding returning to me in detail of the finest grain. And if I yet shrank from contemplating that—that particular horror, I mean, which . . ."

And here he shrank once more. Stopped to collect himself.

"If I could not look directly into *that*, I could at least travel round its perimeter in the manner of a tourist, with a mind sharply attuned to everything I'd seen. And in the course of these reconnaissances, I found myself drawn time and again to that conundrum, that . . . *single* heart.

"Let us suppose it to have been Leroy Fry's heart. Very well, then, where were the others? The hearts of those farm animals? *Ballinger's* heart? Where was that—that *other* part of Ballinger's anatomy? Those were nowhere to be seen."

"Stored away," I suggested. "For future ceremonies."

A slow dark smile. What a fine professor he would have made.

"Ah, but you see, I don't believe there were meant to *be* future ceremonies," he said. "That was to be the final rite, isn't that obvious? And so the vexing question remained. Where *were* those missing hearts? And then I made a second and apparently unrelated discovery. It happened while I was . . ." He stopped to let a ripple pass through his throat. ". . . while I was looking over Lea's letters. As I had declined the privilege of attending her memorial service, these devotions were the closest I might come to honoring her memory. In the midst of these—these loving offices, I chanced upon the poem she wrote for me. Perhaps the sole surviving remnant of her verse. You may remember it, Landor, I copied it out for you.

"In reading through it once more, I recognized—for the first time, I blush to confess—that the verse was, in addition to its other virtues, an acrostic. Did you notice, Landor?"

From his pocket, he removed a scroll of stationery. The faintest breath of orrisroot blew over us as he spread it across the table. I saw at once that the first letter of each line had been written over, enlarged.

Ever with thee shall my glad heart roam—
Dreading to blanch or repine.
Gather our hearts in a green pleasure-dome,
All wreathed in a rich cypress vine—
Richer still for that you are mine.

"My own name," said Poe. "Staring me in the face, and I never knew it."

He rested his hand on the page, then gently rolled it up again and returned it to the pocket by his heart.

"Perhaps you can guess what I did next. Would you like to guess, Landor? Why, I took out a copy of that *other* poem, the—the *metaphysically* commissioned verse which you were at such pains to damn. And I read it with new eyes, Landor. See for yourself."

Out came that length of foolscap, the one he'd scratched out in my hotel room. It took up nearly twice as much space as Lea's letter had.

"I didn't catch it right off," Poe allowed. "You see, I was trying to incorporate the indented lines into my calculations. But once I had removed those from the picture, the message shone forth plain as the sun. *Look,* won't you, Landor?"

"I don't think I need to."

"I insist," he said.

I lowered my head over the paper. I *breathed* over it. And if I were a more fanciful sort, I might have said it breathed back.

'Mid the groves of Circassian splendor,
In a brook darkly dappled with sky,
In a moon-shattered brook raked with sky,
Athene's lissome maidens did render
Obeisances lisping and shy.
There I found Leonore, lorn and tender
In the clutch of a cloud-rending cry.
Harrowed hard, I could aught but surrender
To the maid with the pale blue eye
To the ghoul with the pale blue eye.

In the shades of that dream-shadowed weir,
  I trembled 'neath Night's loathsome stole.
'Leonore, tell me how cam'st thou here
  To this bleak unaccountable shoal
  To this dank undesirable shoal."
'Dare I speak?" cried she, cracking with fear.
  "Dare I whisper Hell's terrible toll?
'Each new dawn brings the memory drear
  Of the devils who ravished my soul
  Of the demons who ravaged my soul."

Down—down—down came the hot thrashing flurry
  Of wings too obscure to descry.
Ill at heart, I beseeched her to hurry . . .
  "Leonore!"—she forbore to reply.
Endless Night caught her then in its slurry—
  Shrouding all but her pale blue eye.
Darkest Night, black with hell-charneled fury,
  Leaving only that deathly blue eye.

"Mathilde died," murmured Poe.

And after letting the quiet gather, he added, "An unequivocal message. Once again hiding in plain sight."

I felt the ghost of a smile on my lips.

"Mattie always was fond of acrostics," I said.

I could feel his eyes on me now. I could hear his voice struggling to keep its balance.

"You saw it yourself, didn't you, Landor? That's the reason you tried to persuade me to change those lines. The *beginnings* of the lines only. You wished me to rewrite this—this dispatch from the Elysian Fields—before it could be read."

I showed him my palms. Said nothing.

"Of course," he went on, "I had but a name and a predicate. I was soon to discover, however, that I had more than that. Two additional pieces of text, Landor! Allow me to show them to you."

He fished a pair of scraps from his pocket and set them side by side on the table.

"Now *this*—this is the note that was found in Leroy Fry's hand. You were careless enough to leave that with me, Landor. And *this*, well, this is the *other* note you left for me, do you remember?"

There it was, Reader. The message I'd written to ease my conscience, knowing it couldn't be eased.

TAKE COURAGE

"I found it just the other day," said Poe. "In Kosciusko's Garden, right under our secret rock. A noble sentiment, Landor, and one that does you all credit. But I'm afraid I was *most* struck by the shape of your characters. Capital letters, as you know, are every bit as unique—and as damning—as lower-case letters."

His index finger moved back and forth between the two messages.

"Do you see? The A, the R, the G, and the E. Virtually identical to the ones in Leroy Fry's note."

His brows ran together in a crease of surprise, as though he were making the discovery for the first time.

"You may well imagine my astonishment. *Could the same man have written both notes? How could that be? Why would* Landor *have any reason to correspond with Leroy Fry? And how could any of this relate to Landor's daughter?*" He shook his head, made a soft clucking sound. "Well, as luck would have it, I was patronizing Benny Havens' establishment that night. *La divine* Patsy was once again in attendance, and knowing of her innate truthfulness, I deemed it perfectly natural to ask her what she knew about—about Mattie."

He stopped at my chair. Rested his hand next to my shoulder.

"That was all it required, Landor, a question. She told me the whole story, or at least as much of it as she knew. The three nameless ruffians—a 'bad bunch' indeed, just as Leroy Fry had said." He drew his hand away. "You sought her out, didn't you, Landor? The day Mattie died. You swore her to secrecy, and then you blurted out the whole terrible business. And she kept your secret, Landor, you must credit her with that. Until she decided it was killing *you* to keep it."

I knew now what it was like to be on the other end—to be Dr. Marquis, listening to someone peel away your hidden life. Not so terrible as I would have guessed. Something close to sweet about it.

Seating himself on the maple settee, Poe stared at the ends of his boots. "Why did you never tell me?" he asked.

I shrugged. "It's not a story I enjoy telling."

"But I might have—I might have *comforted* you, Landor. I might have helped you as you helped me."

"I don't think I *can* be comforted. On that particular subject. But I do thank you."

Whatever had softened in him was stung back into hardness. He stood. Knotting his hands together behind his back, he took up the recital once again.

"You can see, I'm sure, what a curious affair this had become. A young woman, beloved of *you*, Landor, speaking through the medium of poetry. For what purpose? I asked myself. Why should she have wished to awaken *me* to her existence? Was it to announce a crime? A crime in which her own father was most intimately involved?

"Well, then, I did exactly what *you* would have done. I set about reexamining all my assumptions, beginning with the very first one. I believe it was you who phrased it best, Landor: 'What were the chances,' you asked, 'that two different parties would have had designs on the same cadet in the same evening?'"

He inclined his head toward me, waiting with great patience for my answer. Receiving none, he sighed with the faintest trace of exasperation and answered for me.

"*Small.* Small indeed the chances. Coincidences of that sort can't be admitted into logical analysis. Unless . . ." He wagged a finger at the ceiling. "Unless we see one party as being contingent upon the other."

"You'll have to speak more clearly, Poe. I'm not so educated as you."

He smiled. "Yes, the vein of self-deprecation. You do work that quite ruthlessly, don't you, Landor? Allow me to put it like this, then. What if one party is simply on the lookout for a dead body? Not as yet feeling extreme urgency, perfectly amenable to waiting until an opportunity presents itself. And then, on the night of October twenty-fifth, an opportunity magically does just that.

"To this first party—let us provisionally call them Artemus and Lea— to such a party, the *identity* of the dead man is strictly irrelevant. Leroy Fry per se means nothing to them. He might be a second cousin once removed, for all they care. They would appropriate any body that came along, provided it had a heart. The one thing they won't do is kill for it. No," he said, "it is the *other* party who is willing—and ready—to kill. And to kill *this man* in particular. Why?

"Might it be revenge, Landor? As motives go, that boasts one of the most ancient of pedigrees, and I can reliably report that in the last several weeks alone, *I* have desired the death of at least *two* separate personages."

He began to circle me—just as I had circled him in that hotel room and so many others in the old days—weaving loops round the guilty. Even his voice was beginning to sound like mine: the lilting rise and fall, the soft press of statements. An homage! I thought.

"We come now," said Poe, "to the *other* party with designs on Leroy Fry. Let us provisionally name him, oh, Augustus. This *second* party, having been interrupted in his deathly errand, though not before its successful resolution, steals back to his delightful little cottage in, let us say, Buttermilk Falls. He takes some solace in the fact that despite being surprised during his crime, he has escaped unnoticed. He is all the more shocked, therefore, to be summoned back to West Point the very next day. Indeed, he might reasonably conclude he has been apprehended, eh, Landor?"

Yes, I wanted to say. *Yes.* He *would* believe that. The whole way to West Point, he would be saying his prayers, to a God he doesn't credit.

"We can scarcely conceive his shock," Poe continued, "when the second party, provisionally named Augustus, learns that in the intervening hours, the dead man's body has been most horribly mutilated. Not only has this ancillary crime provided Augustus with an extraordinary cover for his own act, but it has even prompted the West Point authorities to seek his assistance in finding the evildoers. What a turn of events is this! He must think God himself is on his side."

"I don't think he's under that illusion."

"Well, God or the Devil, there is a providence working in his behalf, for it sends him Sylvanus Thayer, does it not? Our Augustus is forthwith placed at the head of the Leroy Fry inquiry. He is given carte blanche to roam the Point at will. He is granted official investiture, passwords, and paroles. He is able to go anywhere and talk to anyone he likes. He may, as it were, close the noose round his *other* victims and strike as soon as he sees his chance.

"And all the while, this second party, this Augustus, may essay the role of the brilliant investigator, whose infallible instincts and purely natural intelligence enable him to solve the *very crimes he himself has committed*."

He stopped circling. His eyes sparkled like fish scales.

"And as a result of his cunning, the members of that unfortunate *first* party, whom we will provisionally call Lea and Artemus Marquis, will forever go down as murderers."

"Oh," I said easily, "there's no 'forever' about it. They'll be forgotten just like the rest of us."

All the pretense, all the indirection vanished in that instant. He came straight at me, his hand clenched by his side. Ready to strike, I'm sure of it, but at the last moment, he grabbed for the weapon he had always been most comfortable with: words. Leaned over and jammed them in my ear.

"*I* shall not forget them," he hissed. "*I* shall not forget that you dragged their names through the gutter."

"They did a fine job all by themselves," I answered.

He took a step away, flexing his fingers as though he really had thrown a punch. "Nor shall I forget how you played the rest of us for fools. *Me* in particular. I was your prize fool, was I not, Landor?"

"No," I said, looking straight at him. "You were the one I was to deliver myself to all along. I knew that from the moment I met you. And here we are."

And because Poe had nothing to say to that, the recital came to a close. He sank back into the settee, and his arms flopped to his side, and he stared into space.

"Oh, my manners!" I cried. "May I fix you up with a whiskey, Poe?"

The slightest tensing in his joints.

"Don't worry," I said. "You can watch me pour the drinks. I'll even take the first sip, how's that?"

"You needn't."

I poured a couple of fingers for him, a couple more for me. I remember watching myself with some interest. Noting, for instance, that my hands never shook as they poured. Never spilled so much as a drop.

I gave him his glass, and I sat down with my glass, and I warmed myself a little in the silence. It was the kind of quiet that used to spill over us in the hotel room sometimes, when all the talk was exhausted, and the bottle was nearly finished, and there was nothing left to say or do.

But I couldn't make it last this time. I had to break it.

"If you want me to say I'm sorry, Poe, I will. Although I don't think 'sorry' would begin to cover it."

"I don't want your apologies," he said stiffly.

He twirled his glass slowly in his hand, watching the light from the window bounce and scatter.

"You might clear up a few questions for me," he said. "If it's no trouble."

"No trouble at all," I said.

Out of the corner of his eye, he examined me. Wondering, maybe, how far he could go.

"The note that was found in Fry's hand," he ventured. "From whom did Fry think he was receiving it?"

"Patsy, of course. He was always rather sweet on her. I was a bit careless not to take the note back from him, but as you say, I was in a hurry."

"The sheep and the cows, they were your doing as well?"

"Of course. I knew that if I was going to kill the other two men, I'd have to take out their hearts—to make it look like the work of satanists."

"And give yourself cover," he added.

"Exactly. And, since I didn't have Artemus' training, I had to practice on some other specimens first." I took a swig, swallowed it in stages. "Although I must say, there's nothing prepares you for carving one of your own species."

The sound, I mean, of a saw cutting open human flesh. The splintering of bone, the sluggardly motion of dead blood. The tininess of that swaddled bundle inside the rib cage. It's not an easy business, no—not a *clean* business.

"And of course, you planted the cow's heart in Artemus' trunk," Poe said.

"Yes," I admitted. "But Lea outfoxed me. She left that bomb, you see, just outside his door. Gave her brother a very nice alibi."

"Ah, but in the end, you were still able to extract a confession from Artemus, weren't you? In return for sparing his sister. That must have been why you went to the icehouse alone instead of calling for Captain Hitchcock. You didn't want truth; you wanted a conviction."

"Well," I said. "If I'd taken the time to go to Hitchcock, I might not have been able to save *you*."

He pondered that for a while. Stared into his glass. Licked his teeth.

"And you would have let Artemus hang for *your* murders?" he asked.

"Oh, I think not. Once Stoddard was taken care of, I'd have figured out something. I like to think so, at least."

He drained the last dregs of his whiskey. And when I offered him more, he surprised me by declining. For once, I think, he wanted to be in full control of his faculties.

"You learned of Ballinger's involvement from Fry's diary?" he asked.

"Of course."

"So all those transcribed pages you were feeding to Captain Hitchcock every morning . . . ?"

"Oh, they were the real article," I said. "They just had a few missing items in them."

"And among those missing items was Ballinger's name. And Stoddard's."

"Yes."

"*Ballinger*," he repeated, his face newly troubled. "Did he . . . when you . . . did he confess to you?"

"Under duress, yes. Fry, too. They both recalled her name. The name of the hostess that night. They even recalled what Mattie was wearing. They told me a good many things, but they drew the line at betraying their comrades. Nothing would make them do that."

"*I won't tell*," they'd said, as though they'd been drilled for the occasion. "*I won't tell.*"

"Well," I said, snorting the memory away. "It would've saved me a great deal of time and effort if they *had* told me, but I guess their—their *gentlemen's* code wouldn't permit it."

The skin hung in light folds now from Poe's ashy face.

"Only Stoddard," he muttered. "Only Stoddard, it seems, has escaped your justice."

And that was my fault, I wanted to say, but I didn't. You may not credit it, Reader, but of all the things I did in the name of love and hate, of all the things I regret and wish undone, there is one thing that *embarrasses* me more than anything. That I tipped my hand. That having found Stoddard's name in Fry's diary, I made the mistake of going straight to the mess hall for the sole purpose of laying eyes on the man I would soon kill. I was marking him, I guess, as I'd marked Fry himself in the tavern that long-ago night. Except that I could no longer dam up my feelings as before. Stoddard raised his eyes to mine and saw what was in them . . . and knew he was done for. And fled.

"You're right," I said. "Stoddard's gone, and I haven't the will or the strength to chase him down. I can only hope he'll spend the rest of his miserable life looking over his shoulder."

He looked at me then. Trying, I think, to find the man he'd once known.

"It was a terrible thing they did," he said, groping his way back, testing each word like a loose floorboard. "An appalling, a savage thing, yes, but you, Landor . . . *you* are a man of Law."

"The hell with Law," I said calmly. "Law didn't save Mattie. It didn't bring her back. Law means nothing to me now, God's or man's."

Poe began to carve the air with his hands. "But from the moment your daughter was injured, you might have gone straight to the West Point authorities. You might have made your case to Thayer, secured confessions. . . ."

"I didn't want them to confess," I said. "I wanted them to die."

He bent his glass to his lips, realized it was empty, set it down again. Sank back in his chair.

"Well," he said in a gentle voice, "I thank you for enlightening me, Landor. If you don't mind, I have but one question remaining for you."

"By all means."

He didn't speak right off. And by this silence, I came to believe we had arrived at the crux of something.

"Why did you turn on *me*?" he asked. "Of all people, why me?"

I frowned into my drink.

"As long as you were partial to me," I said, "you would never see the truth."

He nodded, several times in succession, and each time, his chin sank a little lower.

"And now that I *see*," he said, "what now?"

"Well, that depends on you, Poe. By the fact that you've come alone, I take it you haven't yet told anyone else."

"What if I had?" he asked, gloomy as a church. "You have covered your tracks too well. All I have is a pair of notes that might have been scrawled by anybody, and a ridiculous poem."

It was still lying there on the table, that ridiculous poem. The creases were etched across it, the blackened letters rising from the page. I ran my finger slowly around the border.

"I'm sorry," I said, "if I made you think badly of it. I'm sure Mattie liked it."

He coughed out a bitter laugh.

"She *should* like it," he said. "She wrote it."

I had to smile myself.

"You know, Poe, I often wish she'd run into *you* the night of that ball. She loved Byron, too. She would have been glad to hear you go on. Oh, it's true, you might have *talked* her to death, but otherwise, she'd have been quite safe in your hands. And who knows? We might have become a family indeed."

"Instead of what we are."

"Yes."

Poe pressed his hands against his brow. A sound came through his slackened mouth.

"Oh, Landor," he said. "I think you've broken my heart more—more *comprehensively* than anyone else."

I nodded. Set my drink down and rose to my feet.

"Then you may have your revenge," I said.

I could feel his eyes following me as I went to the hearth and reached into the marble vase and drew out the old flintlock. Ran my hand along the smoothbone barrel.

Poe began to rise. Then fell back.

"It's not loaded," he said warily. "You told me it just makes noise."

"I've since filled it with some balls from the West Point arsenal. Delighted to say it's still in working condition."

I held it out to him like the gift it was.

"If you'd be so kind," I said.

His eyes were scrambling in their sockets.

"Landor."

"Pretend it's a duel."

"No."

"I'll stand very still," I said. "You needn't worry. And when you're done, you may simply drop the pistol and—and close the door on your way out."

"Landor, no."

I lowered the flintlock to my side. I did my best to smile.

"The thing is, Poe, I won't go to the gallows. I've seen too many hangings in my career. The drop is never quick enough, the noose tends to give. The neck never breaks clean. A fellow may swing for hours before he dies. If it's all the same to you, I'd rather . . ."

Once again, I held the pistol out to him.

"It's the last favor I'll ask," I said.

He was standing just a few feet away now, touching the ramrod just beneath the barrel. . . .

Very slowly, as if he were already recollecting the moment, he shook his head.

"Landor," he said. "That's the coward's way, you know that."

"I *am* a coward."

"No. A good many things, but not that."

My voice was weakening now. It could scarcely climb from my throat.

"You'd be doing me a mercy," I whispered.

He looked at me with great tenderness, I will always remember that. He hated to disappoint.

"But you see, I am no angel, Landor, to be dispensing mercy. You must take it up with another authority." He rested his hand on my arm. "I'm very sorry, Landor."

With heavy cadenced steps, he gathered his cloak (still with its torn shoulder) and made his way to the door. He turned and looked one last time at—at *me*, with my useless pistol hanging by my side. He said:

"I shall treasure . . ."

But he couldn't finish his sentence. Stuck for words! the silver-tongued Poe. All he said in the end was:

"Good-bye, Landor."

Narrative of Gus Landor

43

December 1830 to April 1831

The truth is, Reader, I *was* a coward. Otherwise, I would have done it the moment Poe closed the door on me. Followed the lead of all those Greek and Roman ancients, snuffing out their candles at the first hint of scandal. But I couldn't.

I began to wonder then if there might not be a *reason* I'd been spared. And so, by stages, I came to this idea of setting it all down, as best I could, laying out the document of my crimes and letting justice rain down as it will.

Well, once started, there was no stopping me. I worked day and night, like Gouverneur Kemble's foundry, and I no longer minded so much that people stayed away. Visitors would only have been a bother.

Oh, I still ventured out on occasion—to Benny's, more often than not, though in the daytime so as not to encounter cadets. Nothing, though, could keep me from running into Patsy, who greeted me with the same cool courtesy she had always shown me in public. Which was, all things considered, the best I could have hoped for.

It was from Benny's regulars that I got word of Poe, who had become a particular favorite of theirs. Sometime after the Christmas holiday, they told me, Poe had mounted his final campaign against West Point. A very quiet sort of campaign it was, consisting of . . . not showing up. Not showing up for French or mathematics. Not showing up for church parade or class parade. Not showing up for roll call or guard mounting. Missing everything he could miss, ignoring every order he was given . . . a perfect paragon of nonobedience.

Within two weeks, Poe had what he wanted: a court-martial. He offered next to no defense and was, that very day, dismissed from the service of the United States.

He told Benny he was going straight to Paris to petition the Marquis de Lafayette for an appointment in the Polish army. Hard to see how he'd get there—he had no more than twenty-four cents to his name when he left the Point, and he'd given Benny his last blanket and most of his clothing to pay his bar bills. When last seen, he was cadging a ride from a teamster bound for Yonkers.

He made it out, though. And he managed to leave behind a legacy, in the form of a small local legend.

None of Benny's regulars saw it happen, so I can't vouch for it, but the story goes that on one of his final days at the Academy, Poe was ordered to turn out for drill armed and in crossbelts. Well, that's just how he turned out: armed and in crossbelts . . . and nothing else. Stood there on the Plain naked as a frog. Benny says he was just wanting to show off his *South* Point. Me, I think he was probably making an argument against shoddy language. If it really happened, that is, which I doubt. Poe never could abide the cold.

I didn't hear from him again, not in person. At the end of February, though, I got, addressed in his hand, a clipped item from the *New-York American*. Which read as follows:

> *Melancholy Occurrence.*—On the evening of Thursday last, Mr. Julius Stoddard was found hanged in his chambers on Anthony Street. No letter was discovered on his person, and no one was seen to enter or leave the premises. It is reported, however, that Mr. Stoddard was overheard by Mrs. Rachel Gurley, a neighbor, in animated conversation with another gentleman, of unknown identity. The connexions of the unfortunate Mr. Stoddard are considered highly respectable, and certain relics discovered about his person appear to indi-

cate that he was lately a Cadet of the United States Military
Academy.

I've read it countless times since, and with each reading, I find new
questions swarming round me. Was *Poe* the gentleman caller? The one
who was having such an animated conversation with Stoddard in those
final moments? Was it Poe who fastened that rope around his neck and
hauled him to the rafters and slipped out again when no one was looking? Could my Poe begin to *do* such a thing—even in the service of old
alliances?

I'll never know.

Not long after, I got another package addressed in his hand. Again, no
letter, no note. A little volume, that was all, in yellow-gray cloth: *Poems* by
Edgar A. Poe.

It was dedicated to the U.S. Corps of Cadets, which I assumed to be
a joke until Blind Jasper told me that Poe had somehow wangled half the
corps into being his subscribers. That would come to some 131 cadets, each
shelling out upward of a dollar and a quarter for the privilege of seeing
Poe's verses into print.

Well, it's true what they say: no cadet ever missed a chance to spend
his pay. I'll bet they were disappointed, though. Not a single squib about
Lieutenant Locke in the whole damned book. Jack de Windt said he saw
a bunch of cadets hurling their copies from Gee's Point. No doubt those
volumes will be found centuries from now, layered in silt and sailor's bones
at the bottom of the Hudson, still awaiting a Reader.

One thing else I noticed: the epigraph. From somebody named Rochefou-
cault. *Tout le monde a raison*. I had to dig around for Mattie's old French
dictionary, but once I'd found it, the translating was quick work.

Everybody is right.

Which is either the most wonderful or the most terrible thing I've ever
heard, I can't decide. The more I chew on it, the more it gets away from
me. But I can't help thinking of it as a private message from him. Whatever
the hell it means.

* * *

Sometime in March, I received my first visitor in a long while: a fellow named Tommy Corrigan. He was one of a gang of two hundred Irishers who, on a certain night back in '18, invaded the Tammany wigwam. They were plenty tired of being kept off the ticket, and they kept shouting "Down with the Natives!" and "Emmitt for Congress!" and, yes, breaking furniture and tearing down the fixtures and making a grand mess. Tommy, sad to say, was accidentally knifed by one of his own and died before the night was out. I remember, though, how he shivered one of the windows with a chair and then popped the glass away, fragment by fragment, with his pinkie finger. A dainty gesture. Strange I should recall it after all these years, but on that current of memory he came riding in. Stayed at least three weeks, too. Kept badgering me for shandy.

Right after that, it was Naphthali Judah, an old sachem who'd helped himself to tens of thousands of dollars from the Medical Science Lottery and once gave me a cast-off lamb's-wool coat. Wanted it back now, he said. Said his wife needed it, her lining was wearing out.

A day later, it was Alderman Hunt, dead these seven years, and the day after that, my late mother, who marched in as if she owned the place and started cleaning exactly where Patsy had left off. Next day, my old Newfoundland retriever. Next day, my very own wife, too busy arranging tulips to pay me much mind.

I should have been more troubled, I suppose, entertaining such a crowd, but you see, I had come to a new way of thinking about time. It's not the hard and fixed thing we imagine it to be, no, it's something soft and pleated, and under extreme pressure, it folds . . . so that people generations apart are knocked together, forced to stand the same ground and breathe the same air, and it no longer makes sense to speak of "living" or "dead," because no one ever does one thing or the other, not completely. Lea studies at the foot of Henri le Clerc, Poe writes verses with Mattie Landor, and I—I chew the fat with Alderman Hunt and Naphthali Judah and Claudius Foot, who still wants me to know it was the damned *Baltimore* mail he robbed, not the *Rochester* mail.

They don't take up much space, these guests of mine, and mostly they leave me to my work. In truth, I find it heartening to see them still carrying on the business they had in life. No heavenly choirs for them. No flames of hell, either; there's too much to *do*. I wonder if they'll still be here when I'm gone. Maybe I'll even get to join them, in which case we might carry on together for all time.

And maybe Mattie will be there, too. It's possible. It makes it easier, at any rate, to think about the end. Which is now.

Epilogue

The work is done. Everything's been written that can be, and now there's only judgment.

I set down my pen. I leave the manuscript in the back of my desk drawer, behind a row of inkwells. It won't be found by the first comer. No, it will require a more curious eye to look for it. But it will be found.

I wave to my wife, sifting ashes by the hearth. I bid good day to Alderman Hunt and Claudius Foot. I give my Newfoundland a scratch behind the ears.

It's lovely outside. The first warm weather of the year: winter light yellowing with pollen; tulip trees steaming with pink; a gang of robins in the meadow. I think it's always best to leave when the world is at its glory. You can be sure your mind is clear.

I follow the same path that Mattie and I once took. I stand on that same bluff, staring down into the river. Even from this great height, you can see how the Hudson carries itself. The winter crust has been shrugged off, and the water comes charging from the north, froth on its gums.

I'll have to go like this, I think: looking straight down, eyes open the whole way. Because I don't have your faith, Mattie. I can't fly into his arms when I don't know he'll be waiting . . . when I don't know *anyone* will be waiting. Isn't that what I always used to declare? We close up like shops, and nobody comes calling. Nobody even remembers the street.

So here I stand. Tell me now, daughter. In your own voice. Tell me. Tell me you'll be waiting, too. Tell me it will be all right. Tell me.

Acknowledgments

My duty to history requires me to point out that no cadets were ever murdered, or even seriously injured, under Sylvanus Thayer's tenure. Thayer, Hitchcock, Kemble, and other real-life personages do find their way into these pages, but they are conscripted in a purely fictional enterprise, as is Edgar Allan Poe himself, who, to the best of my knowledge, killed only on paper.

Of the many sources I consulted, the most helpful was James Agnew's *Eggnog Riot*, which may be the only other novel set at West Point in the 19th century. (*Salut* to Colonel Agnew's spirit.) I am very grateful for the help of Abby Yochelson at the Library of Congress, USMA historian Steve Grove, and Army historian Walter Bradford. Any historical errors are to be laid at my door, not theirs.

Special thanks go to: Marjorie Braman, a remarkable editor who understood my story better than I did; my publicist, Michael McKenzie, the hardest-working man in show business; and my agent, Christopher Schelling, who makes me spit up with laughter on at least a weekly basis. My brother, Dr. Paul Bayard, provided pro bono consultations on medical details. My mother, Ethel Bayard, offered her editorial eye; my father, retired Lieutenant Colonel Louis Bayard (USMA '49), gave his blessing. Don did the rest.

Also available in paperback

MR. TIMOTHY
LOUIS BAYARD

'A mock-Victorian tour de force . . . that touches the heart and
makes it race' *Wall Street Journal*

'Not so tiny any more, that's a fact'

So begins Louis Bayard's enthralling tale of mischief and murder. The Tiny Tim of
Dickens's *A Christmas Carol* has now grown up, cast his crutches aside, and buried
his father. Determined to shed his ties to his benevolent 'Uncle' Ebenezer, Mr.
Timothy as he is now known lives by day in a house of ill repute and spends his
night dredging the Thames for dead bodies and the treasures in their pockets

Suddenly his life is turned upside down when he discovers the bodies of two girls,
each seared with the letter 'G'. The discovery of a third girl, branded yet still alive,
gives him a purpose once again: to protect her, whatever the cost . . .

Through the teeming markets, shadowy passages and thick brown fog of
London's Victorian underworld, this brilliantly imagined Dickensian thriller
dazzles at every turn.

'Vigorous, well imagined and thoroughly entertaining. Louis Bayard
can write up a storm'
Literary Review

'Fabulous . . . shimmering . . . one truly engaging book'
Entertainment Weekly

£7.99

ISBN-13 978-0-7195-6702-5
ISBN-10 0-7195-6702-5